WINNER TAKES ALL

"You need to ante again, Erin." His soft deep voice enveloped her.

"With what?"

"A kiss."

Their eyes locked. It must be the champagne, Erin told herself, else why did she think it a reasonable request?

He pushed the cards aside and slid closer to her. His arms encircled her, and she melted against him, his lips hot against hers.

Cole's kiss deepened, and Erin felt she was drowning in a bath of fiery desire. Every part of her burned.

His lips moved to her throat, and she felt his fingers work at the buttons of her dress.

"One kiss," she whispered. "You said one kiss."

Bending his head, he brushed soft kisses at her throat, and then, in tortuous slow motion, went down further. Hot desire flowed in her veins.

Everything seemed to be happening much too slowly, and at the same time much too fast. No sooner did he teach her one new delight than he moved on to the next. More, she cried silently, she wanted more of everything he had to give. The room was spinning around her, then fading from view.

Only she and Cole existed. . . .

BESTSELLING HISTORICAL ROMANCE
from Zebra Books

PASSION'S GAMBLE (1477, $3.50)
by Linda Benjamin

Jessica was shocked when she was offered as the stakes in a poker game, but soon she found herself wishing that Luke Garrett, her handsome, muscular opponent, would hold the winning hand. For only his touch could release the rapturous torment trapped within her innocence.

YANKEE'S LADY (1784, $3.95)
by Kay McMahon

Rachel lashed at the Union officer and fought to flee the dangerous fire he ignited in her. But soon Rachel touched him with a bold fiery caress that told him—despite the war—that she yearned to be the YANKEE'S LADY

SEPTEMBER MOON (1838, $3.95)
by Constance O'Banyon

Ever since she was a little girl Cameron had dreamed of getting even with the Kingstons. But the extremely handsome Hunter Kingston caught her off guard and all she could think of was his lips crushing hers in feverish rapture beneath the SEPTEMBER MOON.

MIDNIGHT THUNDER (1873, $3.95)
by Casey Stuart

The last thing Gabrielle remembered before slipping into unconsciousness was a pair of the deepest blue eyes she'd ever seen. Instead of stopping her crime, Alexander wanted to imprison her in his arms and embrace her with the fury of MIDNIGHT THUNDER.

RAPTURE'S GAMBLE

Keller Graves

ZEBRA BOOKS
KENSINGTON PUBLISHING CORP.

ZEBRA BOOKS

are published by

Kensington Publishing Corp.
475 Park Avenue South
New York, NY 10016

First printing: April 1987

Printed in the United States of America

To Emma, Karla, and Martha

Chapter One

At twenty, Erin Donovan was at least a year younger than the half-dozen West Pointers headed her way, but they still seemed like children to her. She was seeking a man.

"My dear, I do believe you've attracted the attention of some of our young officers."

Erin looked up at the stately woman beside her. "I guess I have, Mrs. Smythe-Williams," she said, trying to smile, but her amber eyes were dark with nervous anticipation.

From Mrs. Smythe-Williams's left came a male voice. "The men are honored by your lovely presence, Miss Donovan."

Erin glanced at the speaker, Lieutenant Gerald Nathan, who was an instructor at the Point. Sharp-faced and smooth as oil, he was definitely not the man she had in mind, and, tugging indelicately at the neck of her yellow brocaded gown, she turned back to face the onslaught of younger men.

At the forefront of the young gallants was her hostess's son Gordon, who had received his commission and degree only that afternoon. The party in the crowded, flower-draped mess hall was in celebration of the graduation, and Erin was determined to enjoy the evening.

At the request of her guardian Hud Adams, she'd spent the past three weeks in the Smythe-Williamses' Gramercy Park mansion trying to smooth out her rough edges. Dear Hud. He'd done so much for her, and staying East to widen her experiences in genteel society seemed little enough to do for him. Saints above! It had become plain during Julie's European tour that Hud had been right. Riding recklessly around Texas and frequenting gambling tables had ill prepared her to contribute much to parties and the idle talk that passed for conversation. She'd even come around to regretting the way she'd ignored the well-meaning teachers at her Dallas school.

She had tried to look on her stay as an adventure and had to admit that although frequently made uneasy when confronted with the appraising face of some hefty dowager, she had enjoyed much of it. Mrs. Smythe-Williams had been kind enough to say her natural charm did much to make her a success with men. Not one of them, though, had invited her to leave the stultifying Smythe-Williams mansion in New York to see Coney Island, Delmonico's, or any of the fancy gambling houses that she knew beat anything in northern Texas.

Visits to art galleries and stumbling through charity balls were growing thin as diversions, and before the proposed trip up the Hudson to West Point had been suggested, restlessness had her longing for Texas. But in her grand Paris gown whose long train she'd finally conquered, and with hours of practice in polite social behavior under her belt, she was ready, by damn, to try herself out as a lady in what should prove to be her most sophisticated experience so far in the East. There was just one thing holding her up.

Drat Coleman Barrett anyway, she thought as the jubilant graduates bore down on her position. Only his

8

continued absence was spoiling the occasion she had spent grueling hours preparing for.

She smiled in welcome at the young officers gathered in front of her. It was Gordon Smythe-Williams who reached out to take her hand. "Miss Donovan," he said.

Erin settled her eyes on the young officer standing ramrod straight in front of her. "Good evening," she said, including all of the young men in the greeting, but reserving a special glance for Gordon. The young man's parents, though strict regarding social matters, had been very kind to her.

As she watched Gordon lift her hand to his lips, she was dazzled by the glistening rows of brass buttons on his tunic, and was reminded of the dashing cavalry officer Cole Barrett she had met four years ago at a Dallas horse auction. On the dais set up for officers at the graduation exercises earlier in the day, Captain Barrett had looked a lot less dashing and carefree. His face shaded by a wide-brimmed Kossuth hat, he had sat looking grim and uncompromising as General Sherman enlarged on the Indian problems at the frontier.

But Erin was undaunted by the captain's forbidding looks. If she were to enjoy the rest of the night, she must find him soon. There was something she had owed him since Dallas, and now that she had a little money, she was determined to pay her debt.

The strains of a waltz filled the hall. "Miss Donovan, I believe I have this dance," Gordon said.

Erin thought of the folded card hanging from her wrist. She would take his word that this was his dance, since she wouldn't be able to tell by looking at the card. Her other dances had gone to Superintendent Ruger and his aide, and stiff ones they had been, too, with white-gloved hands resting hotly on her back, and her mind more on what her feet were doing than on the conversation of her partners.

Unconsciously she gripped the skirt of her gown. She was as unsure about her dancing as she was the other social skills Easterners considered so all-fired important, but she was determined to try again. Besides, from the middle of the floor she could more easily locate the elusive man she sought.

She flashed a smile at Gordon. "Why, Lieutenant, of course this dance is yours," she said, gathering up the train of her gown.

Young Smythe-Williams bowed stiffly to Lieutenant Nathan and then to his mother. If Erin hadn't known better, she would think the two had never met. Everything at West Point was so formal, so regimented, so traditional. No matter how hard she tried, she still preferred Texas, where she could ride hellbent across the vast lands in the company of cowboys who didn't know a waltz from a maverick calf.

Gordon turned his admiring gaze to her. "Shall we?" Behind him the other officers were already whirling their partners around in rustling clouds of pastel taffeta.

"Of course, Lieutenant Smythe-Williams."

"Gordon, please."

Erin readily agreed. The young man's full moniker was a mouthful. It was just like a Yankee to use two last names when one would do just fine. On Hud's ranches back home she'd known several cowboys who didn't claim to have even one.

Holding her at a distance, Gordon glided onto the dance floor, and Erin forced her body to relax and respond to the music. The count of *one-two-three* echoed in her head, and she was reminded of the willowy older man Mrs. Smythe-Williams had engaged to instruct her in the intricacies of the ballroom. She and her seedy-looking teacher had turned precisely and solemnly around the ballroom in the mansion while Mrs. Smythe-Williams had sat primly in the corner reading.

The young lieutenant proved an excellent partner, and Erin let her thoughts wander as he whirled her about the room. Civilized society wasn't completely onerous, the way she had feared when Hud and his wife Julie, who was an opera singer, had seconded Mrs. Smythe-Williams's proposal that Erin stay in New York. Erin had certainly been aware that during Julie's triumphant tour of the continent she had had trouble coping with the fripperies of civilization.

Besides, Hud wanted her to learn etiquette, and that was reason enough. He'd generously become her guardian seven years ago when her father had died in a saloon brawl, and after his marriage, his Julie, an Australian, had become her second mother. If at times Erin was thoughtless, she and Hud seemed to understand it wasn't that their loving support wasn't appreciated. That support had even extended to giving Erin financial independence, though it had been in a way they'd never imagined.

Every time Erin remembered visiting the Australian acreage that had been her eighteenth birthday gift, she smiled. So far, visiting it had been the highlight of her life. She could still remember scratching through a rock, "big as a washtub" as she liked to describe it, and finding it solid gold. She was rich. Not that she had figured out what to do with her money just yet, but that would come with time.

While Julie was appearing in New York after her tour through Europe, she had met the Smythe-Williamses through her old friend and teacher Professor Fiorelli, now an assistant director at the Academy of Music. Soon after, Marcia Smythe-Williams had become an almost fanatic champion of Julie's operatic career.

Since Mrs. Smythe-Williams's money and her influence did much to bolster up the always shaky finances of the Academy, she was listened to, especially when it

11

came to arranging other tours for Julie. Erin suspected that with her only child now away at West Point, Mrs. Smythe-Williams needed another outlet for her mother-hen proclivities. Thus the offer to integrate Hud's charge into society.

As Gordon guided her around the flower-decked hall, she could almost feel at ease. Almost. Ever since this afternoon she'd thought of little else but finding Captain Coleman Barrett and clearing up the matter that lay between them. She couldn't relax until she had done so. Scanning the crowd for him while she danced proved fruitless. In their blue uniforms accented in yellow, all of the men looked alike. Besides, Gordon was whirling her around so fast she could see nothing but a blur of muted color passing behind him.

When, finally, he began to guide her into more sedate movements, she was able to consider the problem of getting the information she needed about the where-abouts of Captain Barrett. Flattery seemed the best bet. It sometimes worked with Hud when he had other things on his mind besides thwarting her efforts to organize poker games and help on roundups. In fact, although he never made her feel unwanted, her only activities Hud really approved of were visits to his bank and the interest she took in making money.

Erin smiled brilliantly at Gordon. He hadn't been ungracious when she'd been introduced to him, but he hadn't been particularly welcoming either. Still, she thought she could find out what she needed to know.

"Gordon," she said, raising her voice over the sound of the music, "you must be very proud of your accomplishments."

His face crinkled into the first smile she'd drawn from the solemn young man. "Miss Donovan, I confess I am. Why, the class of 1878 may go down as one of the finest."

"Especially with the instruction you've received."

12

"There's no better faculty anywhere, and their methods work under the most adverse conditions."

"I was especially impressed with one of the speakers today. The one who spoke on"—her voice sharpened—"serving at the frontier."

"You must mean Captain Barrett. He's one of the best. Why, he's only been here one year, but those of us fortunate to study under him feel we could handle a whole tribe of those murdering Indians." He stopped abruptly as Erin stumbled against him. "I beg your pardon, Miss Donovan. I didn't mean to speak of matters so harsh."

Erin's eyes flashed darkly. It was time she stopped reacting so strongly to people's misapprehensions about Indians. After all, the average citizen had few opportunities to learn the truths she knew. But whenever she decided she could tolerate the seemingly universal viciousness toward the red man, something happened to renew her fierce repugnance for it. Something like the speeches of Captain Barrett and General Sherman at the afternoon graduation ceremony.

She swallowed anger and felt her stomach lurch from the effort. "Do you think the good captain will make an appearance this evening?" she asked sweetly.

"The faculty is required to attend, I believe. But Captain Barrett"—Gordon's face again broke into a smile—"is a man to go his own way. I can't say for sure what he'll do. Besides, I think he was assigned to the Point for only this one year. He might not be obliged to be here."

Drat, thought Erin. If he didn't come here, then she would have to seek him out. She didn't like debts hanging over her.

The music ended and Gordon guided her to the side of the dance floor. "Would you like a glass of punch, Erin— I may call you Erin?"

13

"That would be very nice." As she watched Gordon walk away, she decided she hadn't charmed him out of much information. Perhaps the direct approach would be better. She sat down to think about that, and watched Gordon pick his way through the crowd toward the punch bowl. He hadn't gone very far when a pretty girl in a low-cut, turquoise dress reached out to him, laying her hand possessively on his arm. The two conversers looked in Erin's direction.

Even from halfway across the hall, Erin could read animosity in the girl's glance. No wonder Gordon had proved a polite but unenthusiastic suitor. There was someone else occupying his mind. But Erin knew how to play the cards that had been dealt her; Gordon's disinterest might very well prove to be her ace in the hole.

When Gordon at length returned, Erin took the grape punch and downed it gratefully, then delicately patted her damp brow. "Wouldn't you rather be outside awhile where it's cooler?" she asked.

Gordon brought his gaze from the girl in turquoise and held out his arm. "Of course," he said, "whatever you wish, Erin."

"Although," Erin said as she stood, "there's no reason for you to stay with me." She glanced at the girl, who was sitting by a horse-faced matron. "Not if there's someone else you would rather be with."

"Well"—Gordon looked embarrassed—"I had promised Miss Rutledge the next dance."

"I understand. There is, however, one thing I'd like to know before you leave. Does this Captain Barrett live nearby?"

"Over on Professor's Row where the unmarried instructors live. Across the Plain."

Erin found the news that Captain Barrett was still single strangely welcome, but when she smiled Gordon looked at her suspiciously. "Excuse my asking, but why did you want to know?"

Erin didn't want to lie to the young man, but there seemed no getting around it, not if she were to find out the information she sought. "I just wanted to be sure he was close by and could make it to the dance before long. His speech this afternoon made a real impression on me." She gritted her teeth. "Especially the part about handling the savage red man."

Gordon nodded in agreement and gave her more explicit details concerning the whereabouts of the captain's quarters. "It wouldn't take him five minutes to get here," he said.

Erin smiled her thanks and, when he turned away, left abruptly, taking the quickest way to the garden outside. Various couples whispered in oases of darkness under the lantern-strung trees, but she ignored them.

Once clear of the garden, she didn't waste a second. Gathering the ruffled train of her gown in her hand and giving a quick curse to the dressmaker who had dreamed up such ridiculous garb, she headed across the Plain. It was only a matter of minutes before she found herself walking down the street that Smythe-Williams had referred to as Professor's Row. Four stone houses stood like sentinels against the night. If the young officer had given good directions, she would find the man she was seeking in the last building on her right.

Without a thought for the propriety of her actions, she ran up the path and began to pound on the front door. Except for Hud, she had never been in debt to any other man. So the memory of her only meeting with Captain Barrett was galling, and was the sole thought on her mind as she tapped her slippered foot impatiently and waited for him to respond.

Inside, the man she sought listened in disgust to the sound of knocking. No doubt the Superintendent had

15

sent for him to make sure he attended the celebration. Cole was going all right. He always did what was required of him, but that didn't mean he always enjoyed it.

He turned down the wick of the lamp in the hallway and, reaching for his jacket, flung open the door.
"I'm—"

Cole was struck dumb by the sight which greeted him. A woman, for God's sake! And what a woman. Red hair was piled atop her head, and tumbled down in soft ringlets beside her face. High cheekbones. Deep-set eyes the color of golden topaz. The front of her yellow gown was cut low, and lace framed the swell of her breasts. His eye fell to her narrow waist and gently curving hips, then slowly moved back up to study her face.

Erin, too, had been stunned when the door suddenly opened, and she found herself trapped by the thickly lashed gray eyes that studied her so openly. His puzzlement over her presence at his door had given way to what she could describe only as admiration, and, for the moment forgetting her purpose, she returned his look.

Wonderingly, she studied his finely chiseled features and full lips. As memories of a young Dallas cavalry officer came to her, with absolute clarity she realized what had bothered her at their first meeting, as much as the incurring of debt. He'd been handsome and charming, but he'd treated her as he would a mischievous child.

Yet that wasn't the way he was looking at her now, and a small tingle of anticipation quickened her breath. Somewhere between that mocking young man she'd met in Texas and the rigid captain of this afternoon lay the real Cole Barrett. Her eyes inventoried him. The sky-blue trousers fit his hips perfectly, and it didn't take a great deal of imagination to picture the long legs underneath. Up close and covered only by a thin cotton undershirt,

16

his chest was much broader than she remembered, and his strong tanned neck rose from a hastily tied black silk scarf.

She forced her eyes upward. An errant wave of black hair fell across his forehead, softening the lean lines of his face. It was a moment before Erin found her voice. "Captain Barrett, I need to talk to you."

Cole was too wrapped up in the sight and sound of her to answer. Whoever this beauty was, she seemed somehow familiar to him.

"Captain Barrett"—her tone was more insistent—"I've something to give you."

Cole listened carefully to the cadence of her voice, realizing he had heard it before. Back in Texas. His mind raced. He was sure they had met; somehow his memory of her was related to a slightly disreputable event.

He looked out into the moonlit street. "Are you alone?"

She nodded. "Under the circumstances, it seemed better to take care of our business in private."

Cole's eyes burned with interest. Whoever she was, she had no business in his quarters alone, but as he looked down at her, propriety was the last thing on his mind.

He tossed his jacket onto a nearby table and stepped aside. "Then perhaps you should come in."

Erin hesitated for a moment. All her life she had parried successfully the amorous advances of tough cowboys and tougher gamblers, but Coleman Barrett was different. Four years ago in just one hour over a poker table he had attracted her in a way no man had since. She warned herself to be wary. Perhaps she *had* been a child when they'd first met, but she was very much a woman now. Stepping through the doorway, she felt at once vulnerable and exhilarated.

Cautiously she moved into the room and, when she

17

heard the door close, whirled around. "Let's make this quick," she said.

Of course, Cole thought. He knew what this evening visit was all about. Either in gratitude for the past year's instruction or as a prank, his students had dreamed up a special surprise for him—the enchanting visitor standing in front of him. She certainly didn't look like a woman of the evening, but a lady would never have sashayed into an officer's private quarters. And as far as Cole knew, there were only two kinds of women—the kind who were loose with their favors and the kind men married.

He grinned at her. "So you want to get this over quickly, do you? Well, if that's your choice, although it's not my usual style. There are some things it is better not to rush."

Men! Erin shook her head impatiently as if to cast off the effect his provocative teasing had on her. Obviously Coleman Barrett had misunderstood her purpose in coming. Erin's quick mind saw the situation as he must have seen it—their first meeting over a poker table hadn't been very proper eithen—but she soon found her attempts to explain only mired her further from the truth.

"Captain Barrett—"

"Under the circumstances call me Cole. Why stand on formalities when we can lie on a soft bed?"

Erin gasped at his boldness. Glancing around the parlor in case she needed a line of retreat, she saw a small horsehide sofa and an oversized chair. To her right was a closed door, which she assumed led to the bedroom.

She decided to ignore his suggestive remarks and spoke briskly. "Please understand, Captain, this is strictly a business transaction, and I would like to get it over as soon as possible."

Cole stepped closer to her. Still unsure of just how far this young lovely planned to carry the joke, he let his

18

eyes rove at will. At six feet, he stood some seven inches over her. From his vantage point he could study the graceful line of her slender neck and the swell of her breasts. In his mind's eye he pictured the dark tips barely hidden by satin and lace.

His voice became husky. "I don't know who sent you here, but you must tell me so I can thank them."

Coleman Barrett's eyes seemed to see into Erin's very soul, and if not that far, at least through the fabric of her dress. Seared by his frank stare, she felt naked standing in front of him yet powerless to move away.

She took a deep, steadying breath. "Coming here was entirely my own idea," she said. "When I saw you at the ceremony this afternoon, I knew I had to talk to you in private."

"Talk?" he asked softly. "Is that what you had in mind?"

Erin pulled herself away from him. She had to clear up his obvious misconception, and fast. If she didn't, the odds favored her doing something decidedly more foolish than she'd done the last time they met. He had been in Army uniform then, too, and her hatred of frontier soldiers had tricked her into trying to get the better of him—that and the provocative way he had grinned at her. But, she reminded herself as she'd done a hundred times since, a debt is a debt. It was time to pay up.

"You don't remember me, do you?"

He shook his head in puzzlement. "Not quite, but there's something about you that seems to be playing at the edges of my mind. I've felt it ever since I opened the door."

"Dallas," she said. "Four years ago."

Cole's mind went back to 1874. He had just graduated from West Point. At twenty-six, he had been older than most recent graduates, but that wasn't the only distinguishing thing about him. He was also a Virginian

19

who had enlisted as a youngster in the army of the North. His duty had been on the frontier. He'd never fired a bullet against his fellow Southerners.

But that didn't mean there were no bitter memories lurking in wait for him if he let his mind wander back too far. He concentrated on Dallas.

Where might he have seen this delectable miss? He'd only been near Dallas once, when he was surveying the county for the Army. One evening he had gone into town for a horse auction, and had wandered into a back room behind the stables.

Of course! The scene flashed through his mind. This was the impudent young girl who had gambled with him so daringly. He'd teased her about being a child playing at a man's game, but then she'd removed her hat and sent gleaming red hair tumbling almost to her waist. He'd struggled to remember she was no more than a girl.

What had been her name? Something curious.

"Dawn Flower!" he exclaimed.

Erin winced at the use of the name she had signed to the paper acknowledging her debt. The last thing she wanted was to explain it to an Indian fighter for the United States Army.

"You have the right occasion, but my name is really Erin Donovan."

"And Dawn Flower?"

"It was a name my mother called me." She hurried on without providing further explanation. "I didn't want you to know who I really was and show the paper to my guardian—not because I didn't want to pay what I owed. But it was my debt, not his. I recognized you right away when I saw you at the ceremony this afternoon. I've come to settle my loss."

Cole grinned broadly at her. This evening was becoming more delightful by the minute. She must lead

at unnamed guardian a merry chase. Well, he would
ot question her about it. How she planned to pay her
ebt was much more interesting to consider.

"Let's see, Miss Donovan, I believe the sum you owed
e was in the neighborhood of four hundred dollars."

"Four hundred and three, to be exact." Erin's face
urned. She had never before lost such an amount to
nyone, and for the first time since her sudden windfall
ix months ago she was delighted to be rich.

"You know, you really don't have to be concerned
bout paying me," Cole said gallantly, giving her a
hance to leave with honor. "I've thrown away that piece
" paper long ago."

"I don't work that way. A debt is a debt. I certainly
ould have taken your funds if you had lost. Plus
terest."

They still stood less than two feet apart. Cole felt his
ale response to her nearness. She was clothed in
xpensive satin and lace that hugged her curves in
elightful ways, and he knew enough about women's
shions to know her gown had not been cheap. It
ppeared that she could afford far more than the four
undred she owed him.

"Then I wouldn't want to rob you of the chance of
estoring your honor."

There was an edge to his voice that had not been
ere before, as though he were disappointed in her, but
rin didn't stop to question it. The air was becoming too
ose in the small room. "I don't have it on me, of
urse," she began.

"I can see as much."

She ignored the interruption. "You'll have to collect it
New York."

"You want me to visit you in New York?"

"I want you to visit my banker."

"If you insist," Cole said, having no intention of doing so, "although I'll be heading out for Richmond early in the morning. It will take awhile for me to get there." His gray eyes darkened to obsidian. "That will take care of the capital. What about the interest you mentioned."

Erin tossed her head angrily. "If you want more than the four hundred and three dollars, you figure out the total."

"It's not money I had in mind." He reached out and his fingers played at her throat. To Erin the movement was stunningly sensual, and she felt the façade she'd erected to confront him wash away in the waves of pleasure brought on by his touch.

"I haven't offered anything else," she managed to get out, wondering if he could hear the soft words over the pounding of her heart.

"Funny," he said, "I thought you had." Stepping closer, he trailed his fingers up to her ear and then to the soft red curls around her face. "Do you know there are more riches in your eyes than in any New York bank. Dark flecks of gold I'd like to count someday."

There was magic in his touch and in his voice, black magic that pulled her toward him. Feebly her hand pressed against his shirt, and as his lips neared hers, she realized her hands were pressing harder, not to push him away, but to feel his tight, hard muscles and the beating of his heart.

Their lips touched and parted, and in that moment of contact, everything changed. Something deep within Erin stirred, and for the first time in her life she took pleasure from a man. Unthinking, she placed her arms around his neck and entwined her fingers in his thick dark curls. His light kiss held promises of a sweet delight she was ready to claim.

It was Cole who pulled back, and for a moment Erin

22

elt abandoned. "Is something wrong?" she whispered, her eyes warmly narrowed.

"Nothing," he said huskily, "if you know the danger in what you're doing."

Danger. He was trying to warn her of something, and Erin was just barely enough in control to take heed. "Perhaps," she said softly, "you should explain it to me." Her hands dropped to her sides, and with his fingers resting lightly on her shoulders, she looked expectantly up at him for an answer.

The only sound she heard was a knock at the door to his quarters. "Damn," he muttered. Then, letting go of her, he moved the few steps to the window that looked out onto the stoop. "Damn!" This time the curse was more forceful. "What in hell does the superintendent want?"

Erin recognized the urgency in the captain's voice. "Why don't you ask him in and find out?"

His gray eyes turned on her. "I'm afraid you have no concept of the impropriety of your presence here," he said. "If you're found, you are in for no little embarrassment." Not that this young beauty let such matters dictate her actions. He'd thought that when he'd first opened the door, and nothing she had done since had changed his mind.

As she studied his face, the banked fires of need grew cold within her. "You don't want to be found with me, do you?" She was shaking now as she had been moments before, but this time it was from fury.

Cole recognized her anger and knew he wasn't being fair with her. True, she had sought him out, but he had invited her into his quarters against regulations. He was the one who was supposed to live by the book, not she.

"Look," he said gently, "we still need to talk. But I'd rather you weren't seen here, for your sake whether you believe me or not." He gestured toward the door that Erin had spied earlier. "Wait in the bedroom until he leaves. Please."

Somewhat placated by his manner, Erin allowed herself to be shuffled out of sight. The room was small and stuffy. Officers certainly didn't live in grand surroundings. At first she tried settling herself on the bed, and then, her curiosity growing, she tiptoed across the room and pressed her ear against the heavy door. The sound of men's voices penetrated through the paneling, but little more. She could make out only a word or two.

She grew restless to hear what the two were discussing. In her ignorance of the military pecking order, she wondered if the superintendent had been sent to find her. Again she pressed her ear to the door but could hear only disjointed words.

The door at the back of the room looked more promising. Glancing through the window beside it, she saw that it led outside. Perhaps at the rear of Captain Barrett's quarters she could find a better spot from which to eavesdrop. After all, the men could very easily be talking about her.

That plan was a better one than she had realized, for once out in the narrow alleyway, she found another window that looked directly onto the parlor. True, the window was high and the ground beneath it muddy from a recent rain, but an empty wooden box which had been tossed into the alley solved both problems.

With some effort she positioned it under the window and, lifting her skirts indelicately, stepped up onto it. The box moved a little under her but held her weight, and to her delight she found she now had an excellent vantage point from which to see and hear what was happening.

". . . but Superintendent Ruger," the captain was saying, "I told you my answer already."

24

"I thought, Cole, that you might have reconsidered after hearing General Sherman's speech today. I'll admit the Point has been stagnating lately, but it's in for some real improvements."

"Excuse my saying so, but William Tecumseh Sherman is not the man to sway me." Erin was surprised at the disdain in Coleman Barrett's voice. Even she knew that General Sherman was head of the United States Army; everything she had observed about the spit-and-polish captain indicated he would honor such a post above all others.

To her amazement, the superintendent chuckled. "I forgot. You're a son of Virginia, aren't you?"

"Yes, sir. I still have . . . ties there."

"Virginia is a lovely state. Just where is your home?"

"I consider my *home* wherever the Army chooses to send me, but my mother and brother live in Richmond, in a home my father named Graypoint."

"Confederate gray, no doubt."

"My father was a graduate of the Academy and a true follower of General Lee."

"Cole, you have a strong bond with the Academy. Why won't you take on a permanent teaching position here?"

"Because I'm just not comfortable with it. You know, sir, Congress gives us no money and the textbooks are forty years old."

"And you're a forward-looking man?"

"There is more room for advancement out West, but it's a little more than that. The savages aren't subdued, and I'd rather be in Texas fighting Indians than here fighting politicians and antiquated Army personnel. Begging your pardon, sir. Besides, I have a personal score to settle out there."

"Relax, Cole. I understand. If I were twenty years younger, I'd go with you and fight the red devils."

Erin drew away from the window in anger. She was not going to listen to such a conversation, not when she was unable to express her own ideas about what the Army ought to do. She would slip back into the bedroom, and when the superintendent left, she would arrange to repay Coleman Barrett what she owed him—without touching him again. She placed most of the blame for that hot little scene earlier on him; if it happened again, she could only blame herself.

As she shifted to step down from the box, a movement close to the ground caught her eye. She gasped, then relaxed when she realized it was only a dog. And a small one, at that. In the pale moonlight, she could see its tail wag. Thank goodness the pup was friendly.

Unfortunately, he proved *too* friendly. The train of her gown trailed on the ground, and gripping a teasing ruffle between his teeth, the dog began to tug at it. A low, playful growl issued from his throat, as he tossed his head back and forth.

"Shhh." Erin pulled at her gown, but the puppy was only encouraged by her actions. The human wanted to play.

Forgetting her precarious position, Erin pulled harder, but the puppy's sharp teeth held tight. In her anger and frustration, she reached down for him. When the box began to teeter dangerously, Erin tried to right herself, but she was too late. In a flurry of yellow brocaded satin she crashed face forward to the ground.

The puppy thought her fall great fun, and began to run in circles around her, sending his high yip into the night air. Erin pushed herself up. She felt mud clinging to her face and to the exposed skin of her breast. She couldn't bring herself to look at her satin and lace gown.

Slowly she turned over and sat upright on the muddy ground. With delicate care she brushed her hands against

26

her sleeves and began to wipe the filth from around her eyes.

"What in the hell is going on out there?"

The gruff sound of a man's voice penetrated her shocked senses, and she looked up. Staring at her from the window directly above her head was Superintendent Ruger. Behind him she could make out the sharp, angry features of Captain Coleman Barrett.

Chapter Two

With the full moon bathing the alley in light, there was no place for Erin to hide, and she shifted nervously. Through yards of brocaded satin she felt the mud squish beneath her. Under the combined glares of Ruger and Cole Barrett, even the puppy was intimidated, and, his tail tucked between his stubby legs, he disappeared down the narrow passage, leaving his playmate to devise her own plan of action.

The visages of the two men were framed by the window, like a painting from one of the galleries Erin had visited in New York, and as she stared, speechless, she saw the anger on the superintendent's face settle into astonishment. "Why, it's a young lady." He turned to Cole. "Do you know anything about this, Captain?" His voice crackled with authority.

Much as she wanted to hear Barrett's reply, Erin couldn't let him take the blame for her foolish impetuosity so she set up a tearless wail that would have drowned out cannon fire.

She paused for breath and heard the superintendent mutter, "My God in heaven." Deciding she had blasted them enough with sound, she subsided into a fit of sniffles and hoped that the filth clinging to her face didn't hide the pitiful expression she tried to assume.

She needn't have worried, for within seconds Ruger was standing beside her prone body in the alley. She looked up at him with eyes encircled by rings of black mud. The dratted stuff even clung to her lashes, and she found blinking a dangerous undertaking. At his elbow she spied an immaculate Cole Barrett.

Her amber eyes darted back to Ruger. "Oh, Superintendent," she wailed, "how could I have been so clumsy? I'm so embarrassed!"

"Miss Donovan?" he asked incredulously.

"Yes," she admitted in a mournful voice. "A very foolish Miss Donovan."

"Let me help you up," he said, bending his knees, but Cole stepped in front of him.

"I'll do it, sir," Cole said. "No need for you to dirty your hands."

Even in her pitiable state, Erin managed to glare indignantly at the captain. Touching her was dirty work, was it? She was sure he spoke with a forked tongue. As he knelt beside her, his broad shoulders cast a shadow over her, and she reached down to scoop up a handful of the gelatinous mud that coated her dress and skin. With unerring precision she deposited it in his extended hand and squeezed hard, at the same time purring her appreciation for his kindness.

She wasn't through. Ignoring the warning look in his eyes, she rubbed her hand across the broad expanse of his chest. The movement was a mistake, however, for even in her ridiculous state she was affected by his muscled hardness, and she pulled away. Allowing herself only a quick glance at him, she thought she saw a hint of amusement in his gray eyes. But that was impossible. The set of his mouth told her that.

She struggled to rise unassisted, but to her surprise Cole scooped her up in his arms and held her against him,

29

completing the job of soiling his uniform that she had begun. With his back to Ruger, he winked solemnly at her, and Erin's eyes drifted down to the full lips that had touched hers a short while ago.

Suddenly she got a clear picture of what she must look like to him. Wink at her, indeed! There was no way he could find her appealing, and she knew the rascal must be laughing at her, much the same way he had mocked her at a Dallas poker table. Once more he was beating her at her own game. Unwilling to suffer his arms' holding her any longer, she flashed him an unmistakably angry glare, and without ceremony he stood her on her feet.

Summoning the soiled fragments of her dignity, she faced Superintendent Ruger. "It was the dog's fault, sir." She allowed herself a sidelong glance at the rather dirty Captain Barrett.

"What dog?" the superintendent asked.

"The puppy. Didn't you see him running around me when you looked out the window?"

"Ah, yes, I do seem to recall a small dog, but I'm afraid the sight of you erased him from my mind."

Erin gushed out her lies. "Well, sir, when I went outside for a breath of fresh air, I started to walk around a little. Then the puppy appeared, and he seemed to be lost. I started following him and the first thing I knew we were in this alley and I didn't have the faintest idea where I was. Somebody had put a box in the path and, well, you know the rest."

At the end of her speech, Ruger let out a long sigh. She heard nothing from Cole and, refusing to look his way again, began to sniffle about how stupidly clumsy she was.

"Not at all, Miss Donovan," Ruger assured her. "It could have happened to anyone."

She glanced suspiciously at the superintendent. Could he possibly be making fun of her? His look was so serious

30

and concerned that she decided he was not, and, weary of solving her own problem, she gave herself up to his wisdom. "What on earth am I to do? I can't go back to the ball like this."

Ruger took command. "My aide is out front. I'll send him for my carriage, and also give him a message to take to Mr. and Mrs. Smythe-Williams to notify them that you're returning to the hotel." He bowed graciously to her. "I'll escort you, if you have no objections."

"None." She sighed in relief. She needed all the help she could get. The sooner she got away from Cole Barrett, the better off she would be. The man meant nothing but trouble for her.

"Good. Cole, if you will kindly stay with the young lady . . . oh, pardon my manners. I don't believe you two have met. Miss Donovan, may I present Captain Coleman Barrett, one of our finest instructors at the point. Cole, this is Miss Erin Donovan, a visitor who has been staying with the parents of young Smythe-Williams in New York." Despite the friendly formality of his words, Erin thought she detected a twinkle in his eyes and again she wondered if he were making fun of her.

She found a clean spot on the bodice of her gown and, wiping the back of her hand, extended it daintily. Without blinking an eye, Cole lifted it to his lips. "Charmed," he murmured. "Now, Miss Donovan, if you will excuse me for a moment . . ."

He saw the superintendent into his quarters and returned in a few minutes, a damp towel in his hand. "I thought perhaps you could use this, Miss Donovan."

Ungraciously she jerked the damp towel from him and began to clean her arms and throat as best she could.

"Allow me." He pulled her to him and with deliberate slowness used the towel to wipe the mud from her forehead, the fingers of one hand playing all the while in her red locks. His eyes warmly followed the movement of

31

his hands, and Erin wondered why she had ever thought gray a cold color. Unable to move, she held her breath and gave herself up to his ministrations.

Slowly he stroked around her eyes and lips, and at last down her throat to the rising swell of her breasts. The intimacy of his actions hypnotized Erin, and just as she had done earlier in his room, she fell under his spell.

He bent his head to hers. "You have a rather unusual approach," he said. He rested one hand on her cheek and his thumb stroked her brow. "Unusual, and very effective. I'm not liable to forget you again."

His words shattered the spell, and she pulled herself free of him. Approach? Why, he was treating her like some wanton woman determined to trap a man.

"You've made a mistake, Captain Barrett. I told you why I came to your quarters tonight. I assumed, and wrongly, it seems, that you have the good sense to believe the truth when you hear it."

"I do. Whenever I hear it."

Now he was implying that she lied! Erin didn't give too much time to thinking that through. Besides, she had done only what was necessary to save his precious reputation. He should have been grateful that she could think so quickly.

They were eyeing one another with varying degrees of indignation and amusement when the superintendent returned. "The carriage is on its way, Miss Donovan. Are you ready to leave?"

"I most certainly am, sir," she said. "In fact, I'm ready to leave New York and head back to Texas."

"I'm sorry to hear that," the superintendent said. "Your departure will leave our state a much duller place. I hope you'll reconsider."

Erin shook her head and, gathering her soiled skirt about her, let him guide her through the captain's

32

quarters. She took great pleasure in knowing the long train of her gown was leaving a heavy trail of mud across the floor.

Without looking back, she climbed unassisted into the waiting vehicle and rode in silence beside the superintendent. There was little conversation on the short ride, and it wasn't until he was walking with her toward a back entrance to the hotel that Ruger's composure broke.

He chuckled. "You realize, young lady, that unbelievable as it may seem to you, I was once young and almost as smart as you are."

"And as clumsy?" Erin asked.

"No, and neither are you clumsy, young lady." He turned a twinkling eye on her muddy dress. "You can come clean with me. With the Army in its present shape, I'd never ruin the career of one of its finest engineers by besmirching Captain Barrett's reputation, and I'm glad to see that you won't either. When he returns from leave at his home in Richmond in a couple of weeks, I hope to persuade him to remain at West Point."

Erin looked sidelong at him. Why, she hadn't fooled him for a minute with that ridiculous story of hers. And Cole, no doubt realizing it, had let her rattle on. The rat. Thank heavens he was leaving tomorrow for his home in Richmond, and their paths wouldn't cross again. She would just have to find another way to give him the money she owed before heading back to Texas.

The thanks she gave to Superintendent Ruger were from her heart, and as she scurried up the back stairs, she realized during the past hour she had come very close to disaster. On several fronts.

Locked in the privacy of her room, she removed the ruined gown and began to bathe away the last evidence of her debacle. Why is it, she thought, that every time I am

33

around Cole Barrett, I do something foolish? Normally, she was very much in control of herself, and of those around her as well. It must be that dratted Army uniform.

She remembered the first time she had met him. Erin had managed to sneak away from the Presbyterian school where her guardian Hud Adams had placed her, and was busy doing what she did best—dealing twenty-one. She knew most of the gamblers. At the ripe old age of sixteen she'd already been playing against them for over a year. At first she had been an oddity; after only a short while she was treated with respect.

But Cole Barrett had been different from the start. She was already dealing when he entered, and the scattered coins and bills before her were evidence that she was holding her own. In her boy's pants and shirt, her red hair tucked up under a hat, she looked like a child, but her card-handling was that of an expert.

In spite of her distaste for the United States Army, its uniform was undoubtedly dashing thanks to brass buttons and yellow braid. When the officer introduced himself and asked to be dealt in, Erin caught her breath. Everyone else in the room she had played before, but not the young lieutenant, and he threw her off her game. One by one, the others dropped out, until there were just the two of them.

After an hour, her supply of cash was depleted, but when he asked if she were ready to quit, she answered by tossing her hat aside, shaking her red curls loose so they hung thickly about her shoulders, and saying, "If you'll let me play light. I'm good for it."

The expression in his gray eyes became admiring and he played recklessly, looking more at her than at his cards as though he cared little whether he won or lost. Of course, he won. Erin got in deeper and deeper until at last he insisted on ending their encounter.

Angrily she demanded he write an IOU, and grabbed at the paper he handed her a minute later. No Army rake was going to say she didn't pay her debts. She signed it hastily, glancing only at the figure. Over four hundred dollars she owed this Cole Barrett. Hud would give it to her, of course; he had drilled into her that gambling debts were not to be taken lightly. Unfortunately, money from him would come with strings such as unreasonable requests that she learn to read and write and stay out of gambling halls.

Sometimes her guardian could be a veritable tyrant.

The answer to her problems lay, of course, at the poker table. Finding someone to stake her had been easy, but days later, when she at last won the money to repay him, Cole was gone from the area, and her efforts to find him had been unsuccessful. Until today.

As she donned a clean gown and slipped beneath the covers of her bed, she decided she would have been better off never having seen him again, and for a much more serious reason than her tumble in the mucky alleyway. Since that little session in his room, when he had held her in his arms and kissed her, she had felt a vague disquiet deep within her, a longing to complete something that had been started. What that something was, she wasn't sure. But it most definitely involved Captain Coleman Barrett. Somehow, she knew, she would see him again.

But that was absurd. She and the man were natural enemies. He may have been attracted to her momentarily, but if he knew everything about her, he most likely would have been repelled. He was a soldier, an Indian fighter. And in her veins flowed the blood of her Comanche grandmother.

She was three-fourths Irish, but it was her Indian heritage that fascinated her, perhaps because she could not remember her grandparents. Her father had told her they were most likely dead, either from some soldier's

35

bullet or from starvation.

Her grandfather, a white hunter, had turned his back on his own world when he'd married a squaw, but Erin's mother Prairie Dew had told her they were happy. That was before her mother had been killed in a dastardly white man's raid on a peaceful Comanche camp. Erin had been only four years old, but she was still haunted by vague images of the assault, of blood and women's screams. Her father had come for her, and rather than return to the Indians she so little resembled, Erin had begun accompanying him on his travels to the gambling halls and saloons of the west.

Drink had done him in, along with a quick-drawing card shark who didn't take kindly to accusations of cheating. Hud Adams had witnessed Shaun Donovan's death and taken her in as his ward. Erin knew she owed him everything. Certainly his decision to leave her in New York under the tutelage of Tyburn and Marcia Smythe-Williams to learn a few things the Presbyterian school in Dallas hadn't been able to teach her had seemed like a simple enough request. But look where it had got her.

A knock at the door startled her from her thoughts, and in dismay she heard the soft voice of her hostess. Only it wasn't quite as soft as it usually was, and she geared herself to tell the same story she had tried on Superintendent Ruger.

"Now, Erin," Marcia Smythe-Williams said in no uncertain terms as she entered the room, "just what is going on?"

"I'm all right," Erin assured her. "Nothing happened, really, except my dress was ruined. And you said it was cut too low anyway."

Mrs. Smythe-Williams stood tall beside the bed. "I told you a great number of things, Erin. I didn't know you took notice."

36

Erin grimaced. Mr. and Mrs. Smythe-Williams had been kind to her and generous with their time and efforts. She owed her an explanation.

"I really have noticed, Mrs. Smythe-Williams, although I'm sure it doesn't show. And I'm sure you've noticed how clumsy I am. And impetuous."

"Your unique characteristics have been noted, although I never considered you particularly clumsy. Except perhaps a time or two at dancing lessons."

Erin sat up straight and smoothed the covers of her bed. "Please sit down and let me explain what happened."

"Thank you, my dear, but no," Mrs. Smythe-Williams said, but there was no cordiality in her voice. "I'd rather stand to hear what you have to say."

Erin shuddered. This was not going well at all, and she wished she could simply relate the truth. But how could she ever tell the grand lady pacing beside her bed that she had gone to an officer's quarters at night to repay a four-year-old gambling debt? That she and the officer had been alone for some time, and that when the superintendent had made an unexpected appearance, she had hidden in Cole's bedroom, leaving only to find a more suitable place to eavesdrop?

The answer, of course, was that she couldn't. Society easterners might understand concerts and art and the correct placement of forks, but concerning some of the more rudimentary facts of life, they were woefully shortsighted. Marcia Smythe-Williams, and of course her husband who must most definitely be told, would be shocked, hurt, and disappointed. From such feelings, Erin was determined to protect them. Her motives were pure, she told herself as she prepared to lie.

"Well, you see, Mrs. Smythe-Williams, there was this little puppy. . . ."

"Yes?"

"He seemed to be lost." Under Mrs. Smythe-Williams's stony glare, Erin felt a little lost herself.

"And are you going to tell me you followed him to Professor's Row?"

Erin looked at her in amazement. "How did you know what happened?"

"I don't. I only know what I expected you to tell me." Mrs. Smythe-Williams harrumphed. "A pile of nonsense. I've expected it since you and Gordon disappeared at the ball."

"Gordon disappeared, too?"

"Yes, and we were all quite worried, although I assured my husband when we found out you weren't together that you were capable of taking care of yourself, no matter what you had gotten into. Perhaps not in a way that would meet with my approval, but one that would prove efficacious. And then in came the superintendent's aide with that preposterous dog story. I figured out, of course, that the whole thing was a fabrication."

"How?" Erin asked in wonder.

"Because you were found in the alley behind Captain Coleman Barrett's quarters. When Gordon finally showed up, he admitted, most reluctantly, mind you, that you had been asking some very specific questions about one of his instructors only minutes before your disappearance." Her frown softened. "That naughty boy wouldn't tell where he had been so long, only that he hadn't been with you. But he was sticking quite close to Bethany Rutledge, and she was looking quite flushed."

Mrs. Smythe-Williams's tone was indulgent and Erin found hope in it. She actually looked pleased about her son's conquest, but then Erin had to admit the Rutledges, whoever they were, most certainly could be considered a better catch for the Smythe-Williams progeny than a half-wild Donovan of doubtful parentage. Considerate her hostess might be, but also watchful of her own.

"That seems to be good news about Gordon," Erin said. "I guess you like this Miss Rutledge?"

"Oh, yes, but Gordon hadn't said a word about inviting her to his graduation." Mrs. Smythe-Williams had the grace to look embarrassed. "I guess he knew we'd—I'd—make too much of it and not give him a minute's peace." She paused and her eye fell on a pile of stained and rumpled yellow brocade in the corner of the room.

"But enough of Gordon's whereabouts during the ball, Erin. I've yet to hear your explanation."

Erin took a deep breath. In going to Professor's Row she had been seeking the honorable end of a situation that had bothered her for a long time, but she realized the truth would be no more palatable than her ridiculous tale about the dog. She had to find a story that Mrs. Smythe-Williams could at least pretend to believe. It was so confounding that one lie always seemed to lead to others. But Erin didn't want to hurt anyone so, in consideration as much for her hostess as for herself, she set out on another tangled trail of lies, uncertain where it would lead.

"Mrs. Smythe-Williams, I guess the truth is that despite all you've done for me, you just can't make a silk purse out of a sow's ear. I wasn't entirely truthful with you."

"And how was that?"

"I've known Coleman for a long time."

"Coleman, is it? You never mentioned him when I suggested your going to West Point for Gordon's graduation."

"Well, when I agreed to stay in New York, it wasn't entirely to please Hud and Julie."

"Captain Barrett, I suppose, was part of the reason. Gordon wrote months ago about him, calling him the best instructor at the Point. One all the young men hoped to emulate. I'm surprised you two are acquainted."

"We met in Texas." She avoided the woman's eyes. "I planned to tell you the whole story when I got back to the dance, but as I was leaving his quarters, I fell in the mud and had to come here."

"I heard you had been sullied somewhat. I trust it was only your gown."

Erin looked up angrily. Her hostess had never spoken to her in such tones before, and she was tempted to tell her that the honorable Captain Barrett had taken advantage of her presence and held her in his arms. What's more, he had placed a sweetly lustful kiss upon her lips.

But Mrs. Smythe-Williams spoke first. "I'm sorry, Erin. That remark was uncalled for. I'm afraid you've taken me by surprise. Please go on with what you were saying."

Erin felt worse than ever about the lie she was about to tell, but there was no retreating now.

"Well," she said, "Cole and I met in Dallas while I was in school and living part time with a friend of the family. Hud and Julie never met him." She paused and, remembering the soft touch of the captain's lips on hers and the muscled hardness of his chest under her probing fingers, went on with what was fast becoming more closely akin to fantasy than fabrication. "We fell in love."

Mrs. Smythe-Williams sat on the bed beside Erin. "You surprise me more and more, my dear. Although, after learning about Gordon's attachment for Bethany Rutledge, I shouldn't wonder at anything young people do."

Erin tried to smile. The more she talked, the more she seemed to be at the mercy of her own words. They issued from her lips unbidden. Desperation, she told herself, was spurring her on.

"I was very young when we decided how we felt about

40

each other. Cole wanted to wait to see if we felt the same later. It was my idea to surprise him in his rooms. He didn't even know I was at the Point." At least that last part was the truth.

"And do you feel the same about each other?"

"Yes, ma'am. He wants me to meet his mother in Richmond. He's going down there to prepare her for my arrival. If, of course, you agree."

Mrs. Smythe-Williams ignored the implied request. "He wants you to meet his mother?"

Erin nodded, and from somewhere in the recesses of her mind, she pulled out the big lie she had been unknowingly and inexorably headed for. The idea was at once preposterous and provocative. Even as she spoke it she had the good grace to blush. "As soon as Mrs. Barrett agrees, the Captain and I plan to be wed."

Chapter Three

By the time the train from New York entered the outskirts of Richmond, Erin's spirits were as low as the sun nestling on the edges of the western horizon. If only she hadn't come up with *quite* so involved a scheme to extricate herself from a scandal that could have spread from New York to Texas . . .

Her lies, each told to prop up the others, had simply gotten out of hand, a fact she had been aware of even as she'd told them, but she had been powerless to stop her prattling. Too bad her scruples about paying gambling debts were not matched by a need to tell the truth, she thought.

Leaning her forehead against the cool panes of the window, she stared into darkening space. There was no one within a thousand miles who knew the real Erin Donovan. Not that she cared much for anyone's opinion, except perhaps for that of the tall, dark-haired captain. At first he had thought her a wanton, and then later, no doubt, a ninny as she wallowed in the mud behind his quarters. Each view was wrong, as well as hurtful.

And to make bad matters worse, she knew he would probably misinterpret her unselfish actions in coming all the way to Richmond. The man was impossible and would never recognize her pure motive.

A small sigh escaped her lips and she sat up straighter, the better to forget her morbid thoughts. With any luck her little fibs were at an end and could be forgotten, along with any embarrassments she had suffered. Soon she would be safely out of Virginia, all debts paid. A pair of gray eyes floated before her, Coleman Barrett's gray eyes, mocking her as they'd done in the privacy of his parlor and later as he'd held her muddied body to his chest. She would never again see that silvered look directed solely at herself. No doubt, his family would be gathered around and nothing was likely to happen now to keep her from heading west.

"Anybody meeting you at the station, my dear?"

Erin turned to the middle-aged woman who was acting as her chaperon. "Of course, Mrs. Jones. Why, Cole says he can't wait to take me to meet his family."

Cole. She'd never even called him by name to his face, but away from him she spoke in the most endearing of terms. Darling Cole. Dearest Cole. *Damned* Cole was closer to the truth. If he hadn't distracted her so, she might have been gone from his quarters before the superintendent had arrived, and she wouldn't have to face him now masquerading as his fiancée.

Mrs. Jones's approving voice cut into her thoughts. "Well, he couldn't have a prettier young miss to be bringing home."

Erin smiled her thanks for the compliment. Knowing she looked the part she was about to play helped lift her spirits. She wouldn't even mind the exorbitant sum she had paid for her blue cotton day dress, picked out by Marcia Smythe-Williams and expertly altered by Mrs. Jones, if it got her in and out of Richmond. Printed in blue lines that gave it a watered-silk effect, the sheath dress gently followed the lines of her body. A tie-back skirt was draped from hip to mid calf, giving way to white pleated gingham that swept the tops of her slippers.

Smoothing the mass of red hair twisted in a topknot, she carefully placed a Tuscan straw poke bonnet on her head. Around the hat's brim and trailing loosely down her back was a row of dainty artificial cornflowers that picked up the blue of her dress. Her skin might be a little too tawny for her to look entirely fashionable and her amber eyes a little too direct, but otherwise even the redoubtable Mrs. Smythe-Williams had not been able to find fault with her when she sent her on her way.

Erin shuddered when she remembered the night of the West Point debacle. In the end it had been Coleman Barrett's unsullied reputation, and not Erin's pleas, that had won the day. Gordon Smythe-Williams, home on leave, had convinced his mother that the instructor who had so inspired him could not be guilty of encouraging young women to visit his rooms.

Erin's lips curved into a wry smile as she remembered the way that circumspect instructor had looked at her that night and had kissed her. He may not have invited her to his quarters, but he had certainly welcomed her in. No doubt there was a side to the good captain unknown to the mothers of West Point cadets, if not to the students themselves. What Gordon really believed, she didn't know. It was enough that he had stood up for her.

It had taken great persuasion on Erin's part to keep her benefactress from summoning Barrett and offering him congratulations on his engagement. It was so late, she pointed out, and everybody was scheduled to leave early the next morning. Even the captain would be on his way to Richmond; they had said good-bye before he left to prepare his mother for the meeting with his fiancée.

Looking beset with unanswered questions, Mrs. Smythe-Williams finally left to go to bed. In the four days since they had arrived back in New York, she had been a whirlwind, preparing to send Erin off as befitted a young girl of impeccable reputation. It would not do, she said, for a Southern lady such as Barrett's mother to get any wrong impressions.

Happily Marcia had bustled around town, Erin reluctantly in tow and agreeing that, yes, it was lucky the Widow Jones, a seamstress, was planning to visit a sister in the Virginia capital and would accompany Erin. As the train moved steadily into the city, all that remained for Erin was to, somehow, send Mrs. Jones on her way, and, once she had located the Barrett house, to pay the captain his money and then get away to the freedom awaiting her in Texas.

Erin's initial problems were solved more simply than she dared hope. As the train pulled into the depot, she spied a line of carriages for hire. Descending in front of the slow-moving Mrs. Jones, she hurried through the crowds to scan the faces of the drivers. At last she found what she was looking for—a kindly-looking black man with smile lines around his mouth and eyes, and hair streaked with gray.

Pulling a handful of coins from her purse, she thrust them into his hand.

"Please don't ask any questions. Just follow me and agree with everything I say."

"But, miss—"

"You won't get in any trouble, I promise." She smiled at him. "I'm not asking you to break the law."

White folks—she could read his mind—*not much telling what they'd be asking a body to do*. He jingled the coins for a second, then to her vast relief said, "I'll be right behind you, miss."

Quickly she led him to her very angry chaperon. "Miss Donovan, that was most improper of you to run away like that."

"Oh, I do apologize. But I thought I saw Cole waiting for me and"—she cast her eyes downward—"I did want

45

to greet him in private."

Mrs. Jones clucked disapprovingly. "Even worse. And where is your young man?"

"I must have made a mistake. He was nowhere in sight. But I did find an old family servant, uh, George." She glanced back at the carriage driver, who had his eyes firmly trained on the ground. "From the way Cole described him, why I would have known him anywhere. George practically raised him. I knew if Cole couldn't be here, he would trust only his old friend to take me to him."

"Most irregular for a servant we don't know to be sent."

Mrs. Jones was not a decisive woman, Erin thought, and would most likely not pose a problem.

"George is practically a member of the family."

Erin stepped aside and let the woman get a good look at George, who stood tall, broad, and dependable, with just the right touch of humility in his rounded shoulders to befit his station in life. Silently she congratulated herself on her choice. "Isn't that right, George?" Erin asked, opening her reticule so he could see the leather purse containing money.

George snatched a worn felt hat from his fleecy head and bowed slightly in Mrs. Jones's direction. "Yes'm. I been with Mr. Cole's family always. They trusts me to do the right thing."

Before her chaperon could bring up other objections, Erin took her by the arm, pulling her gently toward the telegraph office window. "You can rest assured, Mrs. Jones, that you've done all that Mrs. Smythe-Williams expected of you. We promised her a wire that we arrived safely. Shall we send it now? I know you're anxious to get to your sister."

Erin tore off a form and, keeping one eye on her newly

46

acquired old family retainer, handed it to the widow. "Here. Just write in ten words that we have arrived safely."

"If you think . . . Well, I guess it's all right. We are here and my sister's employer does have such a servitor." She cast a dubious look at George, then dutifully began to write.

"Now," said Erin when the missive had been delivered to the man in the window, "we'll drop you off all safe and sound. I can wait that long to see Cole. In fact, I'm getting cold feet about meeting his family." What an understatement that was!

She continued to chat guilelessly, all the while helping George stow luggage, get them settled in his carriage, and extract the address of the dressmaker's sister.

When at last they had delivered Mrs. Jones safely to a small, neat house, after a reassuring and voluble farewell, they continued on down the tree-lined street, and Erin leaned back in the carriage and heaved a sigh of relief. After a quick stop to drop off her payment, she would be well on her way to Texas, as reported in the telegram Mrs. Smythe-Williams had insisted she send Hud and Julie. According to their schedule, the pair were in Chicago, soon to go to St. Louis, then back to Fort Worth for a well-deserved rest. Erin had been able to dictate the telegram out of the hearing of her hostess, and there was not a word in the message about either Virginia or Coleman Barrett.

Erin was congratulating herself on covering all bases—a phrase she'd learned at the ball game she'd attended in New York with Gordon, behind his mother's patrician back—when a chuckle from the driver's box in front of her reminded Erin she wasn't completely clear of problems yet. She still needed the cooperation of this stranger to get her out of Richmond.

Ignoring the chuckle, she leaned forward in the seat to tap him on the back. "Thanks, George, for your cooperation."

"Miss, you sure were powerful eager to get rid of that lady—not that it's any of my business."

Erin smiled brightly. "I'm afraid I need another favor."

The driver pulled the carriage to a halt.

"I'll pay, George."

He turned and cast his dark eyes down at her. "The name's Homer, miss. You know, like the Greek poet."

Erin looked at him blankly.

"The man what owned me," Homer explained, "taught me. You know, to read and things."

He sounds almost embarrassed, Erin thought. How foolish. He was certainly better off than someone who had never bothered to learn her letters, and she ought to know. In her head Erin could calculate complicated sums, but the only words she could read or write were the names "Dawn Flower" and "Erin Donovan."

"Well, Homer," Erin said bluntly, "you're one up on me. I can't read and I need help. You know where the family of Captain Coleman Barrett lives? His father was a colonel, I believe."

"Lots o' colonels around here, miss."

"Well, this one graduated from West Point. Captain Barrett has been an instructor there for the past year. I imagine his place in Richmond is quite grand." She searched her memory for the words Cole had used to describe his home to Superintendent Ruger, the place to which she had told the Smythe-Williamses she had sent a wire accepting Cole's invitation to visit. Of course the message had never been sent. "Think the place is called Graypoint."

Homer snorted. "So happens I knows the place, all right. It's over on East Clay Street but grand it ain't."

Probably just a summer home, then, Erin thought. She could imagine Captain Coleman Barrett only in very elegant surroundings. He might be willing to perform his duty on the field of battle, but he would want to balance that life with a luxurious home.

She had put off the inevitable too long. "Will you take me there?"

"Sure will, miss. Is the captain your young man? Pardon my asking. It's none of my business."

"I'll bet you find out a lot that way," Erin said.

"What way, miss?"

"Asking a question and then humbly saying it's none of your business. You've done it to me twice."

The driver grinned, then turned to cluck the cart horse once more into a slow forward gait. "Whatever you say, miss," he said.

"Well, for your information, I don't have a young man," Erin said in protest to his broad back. "I just have some business to take care of and then I'll be on my way. To a hotel and then back to the station for the first train heading west."

West. The word had a comforting sound to it, and as Erin rode through the broad Richmond streets she compared them to the wide expanses of uncivilized land she called home. She even conjured up the perfect horse she meant to buy as soon as she returned. No, not a horse but a steed like the one carrying St. George to slay the dragon. In the Louvre she'd had eyes only for pictures with horses in them. Now she rather fancied St. George had gray eyes.

The carriage jolted to a stop before a house that unceremoniously erased all her images of gallant men and horses. Behind an unpainted wooden fence the two-story frame house loomed dark and uninviting. Gray-point. It seemed uncommonly well named. Untamed shrubs and grass, looking colorless in the waning evening light, lay between her and the front door; she shuddered to think that Cole's family might match their exterior surroundings. A mother and brother, he had told Superintendent Ruger. What were they like to live in such a place?

Hoping some mistake had been made, she turned to Homer. "Are you sure this is the Barrett residence?"

"Used to be fine once," Homer said. "Not no more."

"What happened?"

"Lots o' things happened, miss, to lots o' folks. Leastways they's still got a roof over their heads. You sure you won't be stayin'? I can help you with that bag."

Erin was not to be dismissed so lightly. If Homer knew anything about the family living behind those gloomy walls, she needed to extract the information from him. At this stage in her circuitous route back to Texas any information she might glean about this place could be to her advantage.

"Have you ever met any member of the family, Homer?"

"Richmond's a big city, miss, but still lots o' folks knows lots o' thing about each other," he said.

"Is there anything I should know before approaching them about my business?"

"Not my place to carry tales, miss," he said, staring over the head of the cart horse.

"Well, I just thought I'd ask," Erin said, adding softly, "not that it's any of my business."

A white smile broke the dark expanse of the driver's face. "It's my feeling, miss, you'll be all right. I'm thinking maybe I best warn Miz Barrett you're coming."

It was evident that as far as Homer was concerned, the subject of the Barrett family was closed, and as she looked at the shabby home waiting ominously in the dark, she resigned herself to forge ahead in ignorance. Thrusting several bills into his hand, she asked him to wait in the carriage. Her goal was simple, really. She would quickly make certain the good captain would allow her to honor the gambling debt, then let Homer see her safely ensconced in a hotel.

Breathing deeply of the sweet Southern night air, she made her way through the weeds of the yard and knocked gently on the door. There was no response, and she pounded harder. Suddenly the door was flung open, and a large black woman greeted her with a surly "We don't want none."

"None what?" Erin asked, her self-confidence shaken by the reception.

The woman eyed her suspiciously. "Beggin' your pardon, ma'am. Thought you was a salesman."

"I've come to see Captain Barrett."

"Who?"

Erin's worry gave way to irritation. "Captain Coleman Barrett. This is the Barrett residence, isn't it?"

"Yes'm. But the cap'n ain't here."

A minor setback, Erin thought, no more. "When do you expect him?"

"You'd have to ask Miz Barrett about that."

"And may I speak with her?" she asked patiently. To her amazement, the door closed and she was forced to wait on the stoop. Feeling alone and foolish, Erin fought the urge to run back to the safety of the waiting carriage.

The woman was a long time in returning. "Come with me," she said curtly. "You're to wait in the parlor until Miz Barrett gets some clothes on, and gets down a cup of coffee. Not exactly used to strangers droppin' by."

Erin followed the servant down a narrow hallway and into a large room of good proportions but made shabby by scarred wood and patched draperies. Without a word, the woman left Erin perched on the edge of a once-elegant Chippendale settee; the air was hot and stale, as though it had been trapped inside for years. Try as she might, the

51

young woman could not connect the faded grandeur of the parlor with the dignified Captain Barrett.

Where were the photographs, the mementos she had expected? Erin had never had a home to call her own, but she knew what Cole's ought to look like. In her mind's eye she had pictured a close family unit gathered together at the end of the day. She couldn't imagine such a meeting ever taking place in the room where she now sat.

As she reassessed the Barrett household, she wondered nervously what Cole's mother would be like. Tall and self-assured like her son? If Erin were forced to tell her lie, would the woman believe her, or would she be tossed out on her ear like the impostor she was?

Whatever Erin had been expecting, it certainly wasn't the woman who paused in the doorway a long fifteen minutes later. In the shadows she appeared to be still handsome, but as Mrs. Barrett moved into the room, the dim light revealed the deep lines carved into her face. They gave her a harsh, forbidding look. And where Cole's gray eyes were clear and penetrating, hers were dull like unpolished pewter. Strings of dark hair escaped the loose bun at the nape of her neck and straggled to her rounded shoulders. Her once-white dress, now faded to the dingy color of curdled cream, dragged behind her.

Erin realized she had been staring. Smoothing the soft folds of her fine gown, she tardily stood up when the older woman began to speak.

"Please excuse my taking so long. I wasn't expecting guests. I'm Fiona Barrett. To whom am I speaking?"

She spoke slowly, as though she must consider every word, and the idea that she might have been drinking something stronger than coffee flitted through Erin's mind, followed closely by the thought that this visit might be another social error. Probably she should have presented Mrs. Barrett with one of those calling cards which Mrs. Smythe-Williams carried. Well, Erin had never ordered any, and it was too late now to present one anyway. Becoming more nervous by the second, she blundered ahead.

"I'm Erin Donovan. Actually, Mrs. Barrett, I didn't come to see you. I came to see your son."

The woman's eyes narrowed. "I'm afraid I don't understand. I didn't realize Justin had a lady friend."

Justin? That must be Cole's brother. "No, Mrs. Barrett, I've come to see Cole."

As Fiona Barrett stared at her, the air in the room grew closer, and perspiration popped out on Erin's forehead. "Why are you seeking him here?" the woman asked.

"I thought Graypoint was his home."

Under Mrs. Barrett's sharp scrutiny, Erin had to work to retain her poker face. She knew it was improper for a young lady to call on a gentleman unannounced, but doing so shouldn't arouse actual animosity. For long seconds the two faced each other with the measuring looks of adversaries.

Suddenly the woman relaxed as though she liked what she saw, and Erin was certain that it was the expensive cut of her dress rather than her innocent look that caused the change. She wasn't used to considering the effect of her wealth on others. Ashamed of her suspicious thought, she nevertheless grew more wary.

Fiona smiled. "Well, it most certainly is Cole's home, although I'm not expecting him until tomorrow. He was called unexpectedly to Washington." The slur was gone from her voice, replaced by a soft purr of graciousness that was at odds with the sharpness in her eyes.

Forgetting to disguise her tenseness over the whole situation, Erin said, "How terrible! I've got to see him!"

"Could I help you, Miss Donovan? Has my son done something to you?"

Erin cast about desperately for a reply, but all she could think of was the big lie that had brought her to

53

Richmond in the first place. She had never intended to use it again, but then she hadn't planned on the private, intense scrutiny of Fiona Barrett.

A vision of Homer waiting outside to carry her away passed through her mind. Should she make her departure now? Then Erin remembered Cole lifting her out of the mud. Without questioning whether a debt of honor or some more elusive reason was behind her decision, she knew she couldn't leave just yet.

As easily as she had faced Marcia Smythe-Williams, she looked at Fiona Barrett and the words came unbidden. "Well, Mrs. Barrett, I didn't want you to find out this way, but—"

"Child, are you in trouble because of him?"

There was no time now to stop and consider the wisdom of her reply. Spurred to irritation because Fiona Barrett could so quickly doubt her son, all Erin could think of was her need to scotch the misconception the woman was obviously entertaining.

"No, of course Cole has done nothing dishonorable," she said. Catching the disappointment that flashed through Fiona's eyes, Erin added with the fervor of the righteous, "It's just that, well, Cole and I are *betrothed!*" She was proud of the last word. It sounded so genteel and so Southern.

Fiona Barrett looked positively stunned, and Erin wasn't sure she felt complimented. "Mrs. Barrett, we wanted to be together when you found out. I've been traveling the last few days and was unaware Cole's plans had been changed. I'm sure my news is quite a shock to you."

As Erin spoke, the older woman seemed to regain her composure. "Not at all. I long ago gave up trying to anticipate my son's actions. I can only say you have brought me welcome news, but you will understand if I need a little time to digest the matter. I've not been well,

54

I'm afraid."

"Oh, Mrs. Barrett, I'm so sorry. If you'll tell me when to expect Cole, I'll go now and wait in a hotel until I hear from him."

"Nonsense, my dear. Cole would never forgive me. I'll have Lizette show you to an upstairs room and we can talk in the morning."

Without waiting for a word of acquiescence, Mrs. Barrett tugged on a frayed bellpull, and the time for Erin to present the cash she had tucked in her reticule seemed past. The inspired ability to improvise she'd displayed up to now deserted her when she needed it most.

To avoid the uncomfortable silence that settled between them, Erin went outside to fetch her portmanteau from the carriage and to dismiss Homer, who looked at her with surprise when she announced she would be staying after all. He'd struck her as an intelligent man. What must he be thinking? Nothing, she was sure, nearly as preposterous as the truth.

With dragging steps she reentered Graypoint and followed the servant Lizette upstairs. The room she was taken to was dark and musty, and it took both of them to open the window to the night air. Still questioning her own actions but unable to change anything until morning, Erin unpacked her belongings, glancing occasionally at the servant, who showed little inclination to depart. Finding the maid's attitude almost insolent, Erin shrugged. There were mysteries shrouding Cole Barrett's Virginia home, and she might as well explore them as long as she was stuck. Lizette might prove much more voluble than Homer.

"Have you worked here long, Lizette?"

"As long as I can remember. I was bought over to Norfolk when I was just a girl."

"Does Captain Barrett have a large family?"

"Used to. Before the war. That was when the old

55

colonel was still alive. And the twins. Now there's just Miz Barrett and Justin."

Well, at least she wouldn't have to be subtle about pulling out information. "The twins?"

"Master Seth and Master Simon." Erin was sure the woman shuddered. "Captain Barrett's older brothers. Mean 'uns, they were. Colonel Barrett was killed at Cold Harbor. I don't rightly recall where the twins got theirs."

So much for the myth of loving family servants, Erin thought. This woman's voice was filled with scorn.

"You mentioned a Justin."

Her voice softened. "He's the captain's younger brother. Got injured when some soldiers were marchin' through and ain't been completely right since. That was when we was still living in the country."

With only one more question, she discovered the plantation had gone to pay for taxes, along with their summer home in Newport. Whenever Fiona Barrett's name was mentioned, the servant's voice tightened, as though there were something disgraceful about the hard times that beset the widow.

"Graypoint should be gone, too," Lizette said. "The only reason she's still got a roof over her head is 'cause of the captain. Not that I ever heard her thank him. She don't generally care for much the captain does."

The captain. Lizette admired Coleman Barrett as much as Marcia Smythe-Williams did, but for reasons that seemed far different. The more Erin learned about the man, the more he became a mystery.

A question concerning the relationship between Cole and his mother hovered on her lips, but something in the way Lizette spoke of the woman made the usually incautious Erin back off.

"Why didn't Captain Barrett fight alongside his father and brothers?"

"He went to live with his uncle in Washington before

56

the war and ended up fightin' on the other side." Her eyes glittered in her dark face. "Master Cole never was much like his mama or them twins." She studied Erin for a moment before giving her one parting bit of disquieting advice. "Jes don't be expectin' Miz Barrett to welcome the captain's bride."

The captain's bride. What an absolutely preposterous masquerade this was turning out to be. Feeling trapped in the smothering, soft down mattress, Erin spent a restless night, and when she descended early the next morning for breakfast, she felt guilty of a crime far worse than holding back on a debt.

Fiona Barrett was already seated at the head of a long table, looking far more presentable in her simple cotton dress than she had the night before. Her hair was carefully twisted into a bun at the nape of her neck, and there was even a hint of artificial color on her cheeks. Obviously she had taken great care at her toilette this morning.

To Fiona Barrett's right was a pale, thin man. His watery eyes looked up at Erin incuriously, then dropped to the empty plate in front of him.

It was the woman who spoke first. "Good morning, Erin. You don't mind if I call you by your given name, do you?"

"Not at all, Mrs. Barrett," Erin murmured.

"Oh, please call me Fiona. We mustn't stand on ceremony. Not as long as we're to be family."

Erin winced. Drat that ridiculous lie. If only she could take it back.

Fiona picked up a crystal bell and rang it gently. When no one appeared, she rang again and gave a shrill little laugh that blended with the tinkling sound of the clapper.

In a moment the servant Lizette thrust her head through the door. "Yes, Miz Barrett?"

"Please bring Miss Donovan her breakfast." She

57

dismissed the servant with a wave and turned her eyes again on her houseguest. "Do sit down and tell me all about your engagement to my son. I had no idea he had any intention of settling down."

Erin felt like a lamb at slaughtering time as she sat in the chair to Fiona's left. Across from her, his eyes trained on his plate, sat the man her hostess had not yet introduced. Some manners, Erin thought. Even *she* knew enough to make simple introductions.

Fiona seemed to read her mind. "Do forgive me. This is my son Justin. Justin, this young lady is Erin Donovan. She's about to become your sister."

Erin choked on the coffee that had been placed in front of her. Justin Barrett glanced up, an admiring look flashing in the depths of his pale eyes. The hint of a smile almost broke the downward turn of his mouth, and Erin wondered if perhaps he weren't more like Cole than she'd thought at first glance.

Fiona's voice broke the slender thread of communication that for an instant bound Erin to the silent man. "Now, dear, about your engagement to my son."

Erin forced her impostor's eyes to look directly at the woman. "Well, Fiona, we met in Texas when Cole was stationed there. I'm afraid I was a little young, but our love was as strong then as it is now." At least, she thought, there was nothing untrue in that statement.

"And why was I not told of your plans?" Fiona's soft drawl failed to conceal the sharp edge of anger.

Forgetting for a moment the engagement was a ruse, Erin felt her own anger flare because Fiona obviously did not approve of the situation. The servant Lizette's story burned in her mind, and she felt a compulsion to defend Coleman Barrett to his mother.

"I'm sure Cole had a good reason for not telling you, but you'll have to ask him what it was," she said, then shrugged. "I only did what he wanted me to do. I never even mentioned him to anyone."

The sharpness that Erin had noticed last night returned to Fiona's pewter eyes. "He does manage to get his way, doesn't he? I assume after you're wed, he'll take you out west." The woman seemed to be assessing Erin as she spoke. Justin continued to study his plate.

With nervous verbosity, Erin proceeded to describe the travels they had planned, until her food was placed in front of her and she studied the array of silver lined up on either side of her plate. Why hadn't she paid more attention to the lessons of Mrs. Smythe-Williams? In her own faded way, Fiona Barrett seemed to know as much about such civilities as the New Yorker.

Erin grabbed a spoon at random and scooped up an orange slice. The smile on Fiona's face was proof she had selected the wrong utensil.

"You know, my son deserted his family once before. Before the war. Even after the death of his father and brothers, he didn't return."

Erin was shocked at the bitter words.

"And poor Justin here languishing in a Yankee hospital with his leg cut off."

Suddenly no longer hungry, Erin put down her spoon. She glanced up at the man across from her. "I'm so sorry."

At least he had the good sense to be embarrassed by his mother's diatribe. "If you will pardon me, I'll leave you ladies to talk. I've heard Mother's stories before." He rose and, taking a cane from a nearby chair, limped slowly from the room, his crude peg leg thumping on the floor.

Erin turned to attack, but Fiona Barrett, obviously an old hand at conversational combat, was too much for her. For the next few minutes she heard more of her fiancé's vicious exploitation of family and friends, including accounts of several of his scandalous affairs with young

Virginia ladies. No wonder Cole would rather face an Indian war party than remain in the East with his bitter mother.

As soon as she was able, Erin excused herself and in the privacy of her room sifted through the nightmare that had been breakfast. She had had glimpses into the dark closets of Coleman Barrett's life. If his mother could be believed, how different it was from the picture he presented to the world.

The more Erin thought about Graypoint's somber residents, the more upset she became. She was used to cowboys and gamblers, whose actions, while not always admirable, were at least direct. Such wasn't the case here.

Fiona Barrett was devious, but she obviously didn't approve of her son's engagement. Indeed, if what Lizette said was true, she didn't like anything about her son. Judging by her vicious stories, she was trying to destroy her son's upcoming marriage. Erin's ancestry, Irish and Indian, contributed to her sudden fury.

Fiona would not succeed in her purpose. Having taken an intense dislike to the woman, Erin forgot that no such marriage was planned.

Chapter Four

Finding no relief from the summer heat of Washington in the stale, smoky air of the crowded bar, Cole Barrett inserted a forefinger inside his jacket collar and unobtrusively opened the two top buttons; then, dropping his hat beside an empty glass, he signaled to the bartender for another drink. Maybe the liquor would settle the restlessness he'd been unable to shake during his days in the capital. It was worth a try.

Polished boot on the brass rail, he picked up the double shot of rye, downed it in one swallow, and set the glass down by his hat. Briefly he looked at the blue enamel and gold engineering emblem pinned to its looped brim. Engineers were the aristocracy of the Army, and Cole had been proud to follow the likes of Robert E. Lee out of West Point. Hell, he was still proud, but the longer he stayed in the East, the less he saw of the elite fighting men spawned during the war. The place had been given over to politicians who seemed to have less honor and more slyness than the red-skinned savages he had fought on the frontier.

When Superintendent Ruger had accepted Cole's final decision to seek reassignment, he had asked that Cole use what influence he had in the capital to intercede for the

Point as well as for himself.

"Get down there and tell them once more the problems we're facing here at the Point," he had instructed. "There ought to be at least one senator who will listen."

Skeptical of his chances for success, but eager to help his alma mater, Cole agreed to detour by Washington on his way home. All he had met with thus far was frustration. Not even Uncle Thaddeus had been able to find any political trade-offs that could help the Point. War was not imminent and the Army had been relegated to the bottom of the priority list. Washington was more interested in stopping strikes and unemployment in the North, expanding business, creating railroads, and hiding corruption from the fanatic reform movements.

There were, of course, the parties and balls that seemed to go on no matter how hard the times. The people frequenting them were usually effervescently cheerful, the conversations were sparkling, and always before he had managed to find a gracious beauty to provide stimulating diversion, enough to make him forget any past entanglements, no matter how intense they had been. But not this time.

Rachel Cox had been dead for a long while, but her image had seldom been erased from his mind. As he twirled his empty glass, he tried to summon a vision of the yellow-haired young girl who had been his first and only love, but for the first time her features were an indistinct memory. Must be the rye making her pale hair darken to rich red, and her pale skin to sun-drenched ivory.

In the noisy saloon bar, images of Erin Donovan intruded on his thoughts, just as they had the past sleepless nights in his unfamiliar bed at the Willard Hotel. Erin in pants and shirt, hair pushed under a disreputable-looking man's hat; Erin, with hair piled intricately atop her head, sitting in a mud puddle; Erin in his arms, her breath hot on his cheek, her strangely amber eyes glowing.

Although he didn't understand it, he accepted that for the first time another woman's face had supplanted his memory of Rachel as he had last seen her alive. She had stood waving good-bye from under the drooping limbs of the mulberry tree at the edge of her father's property, and her ethereal blondness had gradually grown smaller and had finally disappeared. Except in his memory.

Again Cole tugged at his collar, then raised a finger to the bartender who brought the bottle and refilled his glass. He raised it gingerly and sipped at the liquor, then turned to lean once more on the bar while he surveyed the crowd around him. A dozen conversations issued from the throats of congressmen, newsmen, political hangers-on, and lobbyists of all descriptions. His was the only uniform.

In his mind's eye, however, Cole saw men in uniform, his comrades in Texas, the men who had joined him in tracking down the Indians who'd killed Rachel. 1868. Ten long years ago. How young he had been, and very much in love. That love had become so mixed with hate that at times he had been unable to separate the two.

Having served on the frontier since before the end of the War Between the States, Cole was very much aware that Indian behavior could seldom be explained in white man's terms. Bands of savages roamed over vast areas and frequently appeared with no sign to foretell their coming. It was the lot of Cole and other young soldiers to serve as escort to parties, both civilian and governmental, venturing into such territories.

Cole and eight other troopers, among them a sergeant, had just escorted rancher John Cox and his hands back to their Young County homestead following delivery of forty head of cattle to Fort Belknap. Cole was well known in the area and was a welcome suitor for the hand of the beautiful young Rachel Cox.

It was a perfect spring day, a day for living, not dying. He and Rachel spent the afternoon riding and picnicking by a nearby creek. Finally, summoned by Sergeant Duncan, he reluctantly left her, turning at the last moment to wave to his blond bride-to-be.

He and the other troopers had not ridden far when they heard prolonged gunfire behind them, followed by ominous silence. Without discussion the nine turned and thundered on laboring horses back to the Cox homestead. Halfway there they heard the high-pitched ululations of Indians. A victory war cry. The sound had haunted Cole's sleep for years thereafter.

Heedless of danger, the men pushed on. The scene which greeted them was one they had all seen before, a gruesome spectacle all the more horrible because of its familiarity. The house was burning, and the bodies of Cox, his wife, and ranch hands lay scattered about like broken toys. Cole found Rachel's mutilated body under the flaming roof of the barn to which she had apparently run seeking safety.

But he had no time for mourning. On Sergeant Duncan's orders, he mounted with the rest and urged his tired horse to gallop after the Indians, who only minutes ago had whooped away through the tangled trees, taking their dead with them. The wood seemed to have swallowed them, and it was almost two hours later when Cole spotted a band of six Comanches in the distance.

"After them, men!" shouted Duncan.

They spurred recklessly into a dense thicket of scrub oak. From its depth, as if by magic, at least fifty Indians sprang up around them, and Duncan's horse went down in a hail of arrows. Cole dismounted and, covered by the Winchester rifles of his comrades, dragged Duncan behind some taller trees growing in front of a large boulder.

Quickly he assessed the sergeant's injuries. His leg was broken, but that wasn't the worst damage. An arrow had pierced his chest, and from Duncan's labored breathing, Cole knew it had punctured a lung. Duncan ordered Cole and the others to retreat and leave him. That rasping command robbed him of his last breath, and he slumped lifeless against Cole's arms.

The carnage was not yet ended. Troopers Harmison and Hunter were killed outright, and Proffitt, Johnson, and Carlton fled back the way they had come. Carlton's horse went down and the soldier's body was impaled on a small tree stump. Proffitt and Johnson didn't stop until they were safely back inside Fort Belknap, and Cole never blamed them.

Their departure left Cole and two surviving companions at the scene of the ambush. Cole pointed to the left and they crawled cautiously toward their horses, dragging rifles along with them. Suddenly from the dense woods behind them six mounted Indians dashed, heading toward the cavalry horses.

Instinctively, Cole took command. "Rise and fire, men," he shouted; then he knelt and coolly took aim at the Indian in front of the pack. He was a battle chief and rode easily, his bow ready to loose the arrow he already held.

Cole fired. The Indian toppled backward to lie across the trail. Behind his still body five warriors halted and sat looking irresolutely at the small band of soldiers. One uttered a shrill yell and from all around, other shrill cries answered.

"They won't cross the body of their chief," said Cole. "They'll retreat. And I'll go after them."

"You crazy? You can't follow them," said Dalton Laster, a grizzled old soldier who had served for years on the frontier. "We'll bury our dead. There are only three of us and thousands of them red devils."

Of course he was right, and Cole turned to the crushing duty that awaited him. Far into the night they labored to bury, first, their fellow soldiers, and then, in ceremonial solemnity, the mutilated bodies of the Cox family, Rachel last of all.

"We'll go now and leave you," Dalton said to Cole, "if you promise to come to the fort by sunup. Remember, there are millions of them damned redskins out there, so don't go after them alone."

As he sat by her grave, Cole had struggled to keep that promise. He wouldn't go after the war party that had killed his dreams. But neither would he forget them, nor forgive. Comanches they had been, renowned as skillful horsemen and hunters. And just as skillful at human slaughter.

They had killed his beautiful Rachel. Sweet, delicate Rachel who even in the harsh, wild land she called home had always maintained her ladylike demeanor. Why, she had never even allowed him to kiss her on the lips. In his mind she would be forever young and pure.

Sometimes Cole dreamed of Dalton, the rough-talking soldier who had labored willingly to dig Rachel's grave extra deep, a hard task in the rocky Texas soil. None of the multitudes of Indians Dalton had railed against had killed him. He had died on his feet in a saloon brawl in Fort Griffin, but not until he had once again saved Cole's life in a running battle with Horse Back, the venerable Comanche battle chief who led a band that included his adopted son, the half-white Quanah Parker.

Cole sighed. So many good men dead, so many young girls slaughtered and kidnapped. The area around Fort Belknap was now relatively peaceful and the soldiers had moved farther west to set up other forts. He would not be sent back there, would not see Rachel's grave again.

His attention turned to the impressive bulk of Thaddeus Lymond as it glided ponderously toward him, the crowd parting like the sea before Moses. Without Uncle Thad he would have been unable to support Fiona and Justin. He owed a great deal to the man.

Although he'd gone North long before the war, Thaddeus Lymond believed in taking care of his family. His ties to the Barretts were slender, his late wife having been Fiona Barrett's sister, but he had nevertheless begged Cole's father to sell his slaves and join him in Washington. The South could not long survive, he had said as long ago as 1850. He had been right then and, as Cole had observed, was usually right about most things.

Rebelling against his mother and his spoiled, older twin brothers as much as against slavery, Cole had run away to his uncle when war had seemed imminent. Thad had secured him a position in the frontier Army where he would be unlikely to fire on his fellow Virginians. And it was to Thad that Cole owed thanks for his appointment to West Point.

Thaddeus had great physical presence and Cole knew his influence behind the scenes in Washington was awesome, due in part to his shrewd backing of Rutherford Hayes and the Republican party. Cole might not be able to stomach politicians, but such was not the case with his uncle. Thad had grown rich during the war manufacturing shoes for the Army of the Potomac. There were other business dealings his uncle had hinted at, but Cole preferred not to think about them.

Not that he hadn't picked up a few useful traits from the old man. On his return to Texas as a young lieutenant fresh out of the Point, Cole had carefully invested his meager salary—and an occasional windfall at the poker table—in hides and cattle. There was money to be made out west. If Uncle Thad wouldn't accept revenge against the Indians as a motive for Cole's returning, he would certainly understand the lure of profit. Hell, the old rake would even appreciate that a saucy, red-headed beauty might just possibly be beckoning.

"Captain Barrett!" Thaddeus Lymond's voice boomed over the noise of the saloon.

Cole grinned at him. "Uncle Thad. It's good to see you, sir."

Thad leaned his significant weight against the bar, signaled to the waiter for drinks, and turned his broad, bearded face to his nephew. "Good to see me, is it? Must be since you've seen me every day you've been in town."

"Well, I wanted to thank you for the help you've given me in trying to stir up support for the Point."

"Don't try to outslicker me, Cole. We agreed last night the Academy is a lost cause, at least for right now. You've got something else on your mind."

Cole's lean face was solemn, but his gray eyes softened with amused affection. "That I do, Uncle Thad. But I did talk to several of the congressmen you sent me to today."

"Did they even bother to listen?"

"Of course. A letter from you will open just about any door in town, even one at the White House."

"You want to talk to the President? That what this is all about?"

"No."

"Good. It's Congress that would vote the appropriations for the Academy, and right now there's damn little Hayes could do to influence them one way or the other."

Cole nodded in agreement. "You're right, Uncle Thad. It's not about the Academy that I wanted to see you."

Thaddeus eyed him carefully. "You've been restless ever since you got to town, Cole. Never seen you turn your back on a beautiful young lady before this week, but the other night there were several who were fluttering around you like moths at a wool coat. Not that it did them much good." He shook his head in disgust. "All those heaving bosoms thrust your way. Not like you to ignore such feminine charms."

"They weren't completely wasted, Uncle Thad. You seem to have noticed them. As I recall, several of the ladies favored you with their attention."

"Power, Cole. That's my attraction. More than one woman has been known to trade her favors for what it can bring. Seems to stimulate 'em. As for you, it's something entirely different they're after."

"Don't sell yourself short. There's more than one widow in the capital who is laying traps for you. And a few you ought to be looking at."

"You suggesting I take a wife?"

"Marriage seems to bring some men comfort."

"And why not take your own advice?"

"I will . . . when I find the right woman."

Thad snorted in disgust. "Still trying to match that girl you lost, are you? Can't be done."

Cole downed his drink. The conversation was one the two men had had before, and he could see it headed for its usual impasse. Suddenly the muddied face of Erin Donovan flashed into his mind. No pale, untouchable beauty there. She had managed to extricate herself from a rather delicate situation by using her wits. Uncle Thad would definitely approve.

"Actually," he said slowly, "I have met someone who interests me."

"Anyone I know?"

"I doubt it. She's not from Washington."

"Tell me about her." It sounded like an order.

Cole grinned at his uncle. "She's beautiful, red-headed, and spirited. More so than any dozen women I've met around here. Her name is Erin Donovan."

"Irish, eh? That could spell trouble."

"It already has," Cole said but hurried on without further explanation. "She can spin a yarn that would fool an old hand like you. And she deals a mean hand of poker."

69

"Sounds like the perfect woman, Cole. You plan on marrying her?"

Cole looked away. Marry her? That was hardly his intention. The woman who had come to his quarters on Professor's Row hardly had marriage in mind. But she was provocative, more so than anyone he had met since . . . well, since a long time ago. He wouldn't mind taking her to bed.

He turned back to his uncle. "I have to find her again first. And therein lies the problem."

"Which is?"

"She's on her way home to Texas."

Thad let out a long breath. "So that's what this evening is all about. You want to leave the Point and head out west again."

Cole thought about the old pains haunting him, hurts that were lessened when he sought revenge on the savages that had caused them, but he realized that was no longer the sole reason he wanted to return to Texas.

His gray eyes darkened as he met Thad's eyes in the back bar mirror. "I gave the Academy a year. It's just not for me. I feel my destiny lies in that sprawling, untamed land in Texas." The words surprised even Cole. He'd never thought in terms such as destiny.

Thad cleared his throat but said nothing, and Cole hurried on. "I know, Uncle, you never expected me to say anything so un-Army."

Thad found his voice. "So poetic, don't you mean? That girl . . ." He trailed off without specifying which girl.

The two men stood silent and thoughtful. Thad spoke first. "All right, son. If it's Texas you want, it's Texas you'll get. I'll see that your orders are changed. After all, I do have business interests there that could be profitable for both of us one day. But I'm still damned if I know why I give in to you so fast. This Erin Donovan better treat

70

you right."

Cole remembered her hands stroking his neck as he kissed her and didn't bother to deny her influence. "She will, Uncle Thad, she will. I need to see a few more people about the Point before I go looking for her, though. I owe Superintendent Ruger that much. Then I'll ride on down to Richmond for a few days and as soon as I receive my new orders, head out."

"How is your mother getting along, Cole?"

"Fiona always manages." A thin edge of scorn underlined his words.

Thad shook his head sadly. "Even with your brother there, the time must hang heavy on her hands. Life has not treated her kindly."

Cole started to speak, then held up. Fiona Barrett was the one person his uncle couldn't see through. She was, after all, the sister of his long-dead wife. Cole was not hampered by illusions about her. He would take care of her and pay the calls of a dutiful son, but there was little else he could manage. He knew her too well to do more than the little family obligations demanded.

The visit in Richmond would be brief and probably grim. More than likely if he and Justin only had time to themselves, they could become friends, but Fiona never left them alone, as though she were fearful Cole would turn her other son against her. She didn't even know him well enough to realize he would never be so cruel.

Fiona Barrett stood in the dim parlor of her Richmond home and stared at the telegram in her hand. The message was clear; Cole would soon be home for a few days before leaving for a post in the West. It was what the message *didn't* include that puzzled her. He made no mention of the loving bride he would be taking with him.

How unlike Cole to make such an omission—unless, of

course, he had no intention of marrying the rather forward young woman who had intruded herself into the Barrett home last night. Fiona smiled. Could the obviously wealthy Erin Donovan have mistakenly interpreted a romantic dalliance as something more permanent? The thought was intriguing. Certainly Cole was not above indulging in a romantic tryst. It was the one thing she and her son had in common. Fiona knew Cole had foolish dreams about finding a perfect woman, but he wasn't saving his manly charms until such a woman came along.

The more she thought about it, the more Fiona became convinced she was right. There was no engagement. And thank heavens for that, for if Cole did marry the wealthy young woman, he would just take the money away and dole out to his poor mother what *he* thought she needed. She knew her son well, even if she had no motherly feelings toward him.

The twins had been different. Despite their wildness, they had needed her more than Cole ever had. Even as a child he'd been strong. Kept to himself more than her other boys. She'd not been surprised when he'd moved to Washington before the war. She'd not even been sorry.

Cole thought her incapable of handling her own affairs, but she'd handled them fairly well already. Wouldn't he be shocked if he knew now.

If Erin proved to be wrong about the engagement, then she might hurry off broken-hearted and take her money with her. Fiona simply couldn't allow that to happen, and she rang for Lizette. "Ask Miss Donovan to come inside. I believe she's walking in the garden."

The servant grinned, then silently nodded and left. Well, thought Fiona, perhaps garden *was* an inappropriate word to describe the rutted, weed-choked stretch of land behind Graypoint. Once the area had been carefully sculptured with shrubs and flower beds, like an English garden. That had been when the colonel was alive. A generous man, the colonel. She should have appreciated him more.

But Seth and Simon had occupied her time. Wild boys they were, a little like her. If only . . . The sound of approaching footsteps pulled her to the present. No use wandering around in the past, not if she hoped to survive in these perilous times.

"You wanted to see me, Fiona?"

She smiled brightly at the young woman who entered the room with such effortless grace. Red hair isn't at all the thing now, Fiona thought, and neither is that dreadful skin. Why, the girl looks as though she actually stays out in the sun without a parasol. And she isn't at all genteel, not with her direct stare and her insistence on walking about the neighboring streets without escort her first day in Richmond. And her manners! After observing her at only two meals, Fiona had given up entirely on hoping the young woman would select the proper fork.

Still, Erin Donovan did have an air about her that would catch a man's eye. There were those that might even call her beautiful. Not Fiona, of course. The only thing she appreciated about the girl was the expensive cut of her clothes.

Thoughtfully Fiona fingered the telegram thrust into the folds of her skirt. "My dear," she purred, "do come in out of that dreadful weather."

Erin's eyes widened. "But the sky is a beautiful clear blue, and the sun—"

"Precisely. The sun. You really must avoid exposing yourself to its harmful rays." Before the young visitor could respond, she hurried on. "I have a little surprise for you." The girl looked nervous. One would think she didn't like surprises.

"What is it?" Erin's voice bordered on the ungracious.

73

"Nothing you haven't been waiting for. A telegram from your fiancé." There it was again, a look of panic flashing in those curiously amber eyes. Fiona began to study Erin more carefully. She pulled out the crumpled piece of paper. "Would you care to read it?"

"I can't . . . what I mean is, I shouldn't read it. He sent it to you."

"And how do you know that?"

Erin smiled. "Because it's already opened. I'm sure you wouldn't have read it if it had been addressed to me."

Damn. The girl looked almost smug. Still, she had been decidedly upset, even if only for a moment, upon hearing the telegram had arrived. A strange reaction for a young girl awaiting the arrival of her beloved. Was she perhaps having doubts about the promises a dashing Army captain might have made in the heat of passion?

"Then I'll tell you what it says. Cole has been held up in Washington for a few days, but he'll be leaving shortly. He should be arriving by the end of the week. Then he'll leave for a new posting." Fiona spoke slowly, unable to keep the sarcasm from her voice. "I assume the latter is referring to you, my dear. There's no other mention of your upcoming nuptials."

"I . . . I must have arrived sooner than he expected. You know how Cole is. Never listens to what you're saying."

Fiona knew exactly how Cole was. He listened to *everything*. Like a hunter stalking a fox, she bore in.

"You know, Erin, that I was glad to welcome you into my home, even if your coming was a surprise." She fixed her pale gray eyes on the girl. "The biggest surprise of all, of course, was *you*."

Erin looked wide-eyed at her. "What do you mean?" she asked.

"Just that you weren't at all the sort I would have thought Cole would choose."

Gone was Erin's timid look, and a hint of fire flashed through her amber eyes. "And why not?"

"The few young women I've seen him with have all been somewhat more subdued in their appearance. Fair, rather than so . . . colorful."

"Perhaps that was their problem. They were too pale to hold his attention for long."

"Perhaps," Fiona murmured, at the same time silently cursing the girl's sharp tongue. Abruptly she changed the subject. "What about your family, Erin? I've asked few questions—not wanting to pry, you understand—but surely someone is worried about where you are." Fiona was pleased to see the girl's unease return.

"There's only my guardian and his wife, and they're on a tour of the country. Hud and Julie trust me to take care of myself. Besides, they know I'll be on the way home shortly."

"And of course they know and trust my son."

"Of course."

So Erin didn't have a family other than a wandering guardian. What she needed was a home and someone to care for. Fiona fought to keep a smile off her face.

"It's just curious that Coleman didn't send a message to you," she said, the solution to all her problems beginning to form in her mind. "I thought I had raised him better than that. Why, Justin wouldn't forget to send love to his fiancée." A little heavy-handed, maybe, but Cole would be arriving soon and Fiona had to work fast. She had seen definitely sympathetic looks pass between the girl and her younger son. Many a marriage had been started on less than that.

"You say he'll be arriving by the end of the week?"

"That's right. But you don't sound happy to get the news, my dear. Is something wrong?"

"Of course not. It's just that, well, I guess I'm a little nervous. Cole can be so . . . overwhelming."

75

Now that was one thing Fiona could agree with, but it was a curious sentiment to come from a young girl supposedly in love. Perhaps it wouldn't be so difficult to persuade Erin to cast her eyes in the direction of the younger Barrett son.

Long after Erin excused herself, Fiona sat in the parlor thinking of how to approach her problem. She must make Erin feel completely at home in Richmond. Perhaps Hilmer could come up with an idea. Through the years she'd called on her neighbor for several favors. Not that she didn't pay him back. Colonel Hilmer Turpin was well paid; Fiona saw to that, at the same time relieving her own lonely nights.

In the meantime, she would talk to Justin and try to plant the seed of an idea in his mind, that he should woo and wed Erin Donovan. Unfortunately, her youngest son could be rather stupid at times. At least he always seemed so when she was trying to involve him in a scheme to alleviate their circumstances.

As she left the room to seek him out, Fiona set her lips into a grim smile. Despite her rough manners, Erin Donovan was possibly the best thing to come along since the end of that dreadful war, and Fiona was damned if she would let her get away with her obvious riches intact.

Chapter Five

When Erin awoke the next morning, she vowed to leave Richmond as soon as possible. That very day wouldn't be too soon. The arrival of Cole's telegram had brought a clear, cold picture of her presence in his home, and it was worse than she had imagined on the train. At least then she had planned to shed the dust of Richmond in a hurry. Instead, she'd stupidly stayed on.

And Fiona Barrett wasn't helping to make her feel at ease. Every time Erin was in her presence, she found herself being judged, and more often than not found wanting. So Cole usually was attracted to fairer women, was he? She'd seen the type in New York—blond hair, pale eyes, milk-white skin. Delicate creatures who would never find themselves in a mud puddle behind a West Point officer's quarters.

If they were what the captain wanted, he was welcome to them; his preferences in women were none of her concern. With extra vigor she began to brush the tangled mass of red curls that had resulted from her restless night, and her cheeks became flushed with the effort. Erin studied her reflection in the bedroom mirror. The deepened rose color heightened her already prominent cheekbones, and her eyes were round and darkened almost to topaz. There was nothing pale or delicate in the reflection staring back at her, and why should there be, when her ancestors were Irish and Indian? In the circles she'd frequented lately, both were considered uncivilized.

Determined more than ever to leave this place that made her feel so inadequate, she tamed her hair into a tight bun and slipped into the demure blue gown she had worn on her journey from New York. It wouldn't take her long to complete her preparations to leave.

But she hadn't counted on the unbending graciousness of her hostess.

"My dear," Fiona announced at breakfast after Justin had excused himself, "I've invited our neighbors Colonel Hilmer Turpin and his wife to tea this afternoon. If you're to be a part of this family, you must meet them."

Another colonel, was Erin's first thought. The driver Homer had said there were many of them in the city. "I'm not sure I'll be here this afternoon," she began.

"Nonsense. Where on earth would you go? Not out in the hot sun, I hope."

"I was thinking of a little farther than a stroll around the neighborhood. You've been kind in putting up with me, but I really think I need to be going back to New York. My stay has already been much longer than I intended. Cole can find me there after his business in Washington is settled."

"Again, nonsense."

Despite Fiona's words, Erin thought the woman was fighting back a smile. She seemed pleased that Erin was unwilling to wait any longer for the arrival of her fiancé.

Before Erin could reply, Fiona hurried on. "I guess you're just miffed that my thoughtless son sent no word to you. Men can be hopelessly unromantic."

Unromantic? Erin's mind went back to her last meeting with Cole. She might have had few experiences with men, but it seemed to her everything he had done that night, from kissing her to lifting her gently from the mud, had been decidedly romantic.

But if Fiona insisted on misinterpreting her departure, let her. "As a matter of fact," Erin said, "I am beginning to feel a little forward for invading your home and intruding on your hospitality."

"That's not at all the way I feel about it, my dear," Fiona purred, "and I can assure you, neither does Justin. Just put such ideas from your mind. Besides, I was so looking forward to this afternoon. Don't deny an old woman her few pleasures. At least wait until tomorrow."

Erin hesitated a moment, weighing the pros and cons of remaining. "All right," she finally agreed, "I'll stay. But just until tomorrow." According to his telegram, Cole wouldn't be arriving for several days. She could still be long gone to Texas before he appeared.

When Fiona greeted her guests in the late afternoon, Erin thought she looked better than on previous occasions, whether that was because of her lace-trimmed linen dress or her welcoming smile, she couldn't decide. Obviously Fiona was making an effort to be gracious. Was it to impress her houseguest or Colonel Hilmer Turpin?

The colonel was short and broad and sharp-eyed, the kind of man who would hold his cards tight against his chest in a poker game. He would also be good at bluffing. His wife Louise was a contrast in fluttering hands and eyes, her softly ruffled dress covering a rounded body.

"Miss Donovan," she said in a sweet, slow voice, "I'm so pleased to meet Cole's fiancée. What a surprise your visit has brought us all."

Erin shifted nervously under Mrs. Turpin's frank inspection. Meeting Cole's friends and neighbors somehow made her fraud seem more serious. Perhaps she had misread Colonel Turpin's sharp-eyed look. It seemed ages since she had faced anyone over a poker table. Maybe the knack of doing a quick reading of someone's character was a skill easily lost.

"Please call me Erin," she said, her usually incisive mind a jumble.

Louise's response was close to a giggle. "I just can't get used to this informality we live with now. You know, since the war."

"Nonsense, my dear," her husband responded. "The war's been over for more than a decade. Time we forgot about it."

"Hilmer's right," Fiona chimed in. "Why, Erin's called me Fiona since we first met."

"Well, then," her guest responded, surprising Erin with her curtness, "she can just call me Louise."

The sharp look that passed between the two women didn't go undetected. What is going on between them? Erin wondered. She hadn't been in polite society enough to judge; perhaps the coolness she sensed between them was perfectly ordinary, and she chalked up one more reason why she preferred Texas. Everyone seemed less complicated there.

She felt Colonel Turpin's eyes on her, and when she turned to look at him, he smiled. "Fiona tells us you're from Texas," he said. "Since your state was part of the Confederacy, I'm sure you'll recognize and respect the residues left by that terrible conflict. My dear wife, along with the rest of us, has had a difficult time adjusting to a different way of life. In that unfortunate conflict, we all lost much of what we had."

Erin recognized the look in his eyes. He was assessing her the way Fiona had, and she felt a curious shame at her finery. "Actually," she said defensively, "I wasn't in Texas during the war or for a long time afterward."

"Where is your home?" he asked.

"I don't have one . . . that is to say, I didn't at that

time. My father's business kept him on the road a great deal. Right up until his death."

Now why did I say that? Erin wondered. As though my father had been a respectable businessman. Perhaps she should go on to describe the shootout in the New Mexico saloon which had resulted in her falling under the care of Hud Adams. Then again, she thought, remembering Marcia Smythe-Williams's lessons on acceptable teatime conversations, perhaps she had better not. Anything bordering on the truth about her past life would hardly make her more acceptable, but murmured solicitations of sympathy would surely make her more ill at ease.

"Tell us about Texas," said Louise Turpin. "We hear such terrible things about the savages running wild about the countryside and"—her voice trembled—"raping the women."

"Louise!" her husband said sharply. "Miss Donovan is a guest in Richmond. I'm sure Texas is a wonderful place. We also hear about a lot of fortunes being made out there. That state has pulled out of the war faster than we have." He turned to Erin and smiled. "Isn't that so?"

Erin sipped from the thin porcelain cup, then set it on the table. She didn't know which of the Turpins to respond to first.

"Actually," she said, thinking of the bustling area around Fort Worth and Dallas, "railroads and banks are moving in to add to the cattle fortunes that are being made. A lot of the growth has been the result of forcing Indians to live on reservations."

"But we hear of such unspeakable atrocities," Louise said. "Like the killing of that handsome General Custer and all his men."

"That wasn't in Texas," Erin said flatly. "Besides, that battle was two years ago. Those Indians have paid for their victory many times over."

Hilmer Turpin spoke up. "You seem to care a great

deal about the Indians, Erin. I'm sure we don't understand all their problems, although I did hear a speaker from the Indian agency in Washington not long ago. He said that until more people came, not much will be done to help them. I remember thinking that the Indian probably looks on the white man the way we viewed Yankees after the war."

He smiled grimly, but before Erin could add her agreement to his words, Fiona spoke up.

"Erin, I was telling the colonel that you were recently at West Point for the graduation ceremonies."

"Ah," Turpin said, his face lighting up, "perhaps you met my nephew there."

"Was he one of the cadets?"

"Oh, no. He's an instructor. Lieutenant Gerald Nathan."

Erin remembered the sharp-faced man she had last seen standing beside Marcia Smythe-Williams at the graduation ball. "Yes," she said, "I saw him briefly." What a damnably small world this was turning out to be. Could the lieutenant have heard of her near disgrace and passed the information on?

Hilmer Turpin continued to smile at her. "I'm sure he will remember you, then. Such a pretty thing you are."

"Now, Hilmer," Fiona spoke up, "don't embarrass my daughter-to-be with your flattering words."

His wife echoed the sentiment. "Hilmer always did admire an attractive woman."

"That's why I married you, my dear," Turpin said graciously.

Since leaving Texas, Erin had grown used to hearing the gallant flattery of men who had practiced pretty speeches all their lives. Still, she found it difficult to separate socially acceptable insincerity from downright lies. Somehow she felt the colonel's speeches didn't match the glances he directed toward his fluttery wife.

"Miss Donovan," he continued, "you must let me introduce you to some of Cole's friends here in Richmond, men and women he's known since he was a boy. The lad has always been very popular hereabouts, even if he didn't see fit to fight for our cause."

Louise Turpin spoke up. "Cole's true friends understood his going west." Her eyes flicked over to Fiona before settling on Erin.

Again Erin felt the friction between the two women, and she spoke up quickly. "I'm afraid I won't be here for much longer."

Turpin frowned. "That's too bad. But surely you're not going today?"

"I thought tomorrow."

"Good. Then you can come to a small soirée at our place tomorrow afternoon. There's no train until evening. I've been traveling lately to see about some small business affairs—and dull work it is, too—so I've become familiar with the schedules in and out of town. You'll have plenty of time."

"If you're sure," Erin said, unable to think of a reason to decline. And after all, Colonel Turpin had shown some sympathy toward a problem that seemed of little importance to most people. If he wanted to have a gathering in his home for her, the least she could do was attend.

"I'm sure," the colonel said; then he turned to his wife. "Right, Louise? We'll have a dozen or so of Cole's closest friends for Erin to meet."

Erin wondered briefly how many pale women would be included in the assembly. Later in the evening, safely ensconced in her room with Lizette, she attempted to find out.

"Mister Cole don't have no special women friends around here," the servant said. "At least not that Miz Barrett has ever talked about."

83

Erin shuffled a deck of cards and prepared for Lizette's second poker lesson in as many nights. "Would she necessarily know?"

"Miz Barrett would know. She makes it a point of knowing everything that's going on about Mister Cole. It's as I told you before. She don't rightly like him."

Erin was still puzzled. Even her father had seen that she was fed and clothed, and what was more important, loved. And so had Hud Adams, even though there was no blood tie between them.

"Was it only because the captain fought with the Northern troops?"

"Trouble between those two started long before the war. Miz Barrett just plumb preferred those twins."

Erin gave up. She would never understand a mother who would deny her own son. Even the Comanches, whom Fiona would be quick to call savages, valued their offspring. The more Erin was around the woman, the more her heart softened toward the formidable captain. If it were true that he supported his indolent and unloving mother without receiving a single word of gratitude in return, he was a man of singular honor.

But that didn't mean Erin would hang around to tell him so. Right after the promised visit to the Turpins, she would head for the train station. Cole might be surprised to learn he had just missed his fiancée, but he was a smart man and could come up with a story for his mother, one that wouldn't involve marriage. He'd been smooth enough with Superintendent Ruger.

Throughout the next morning Erin found Fiona pushing her into the company of Justin, and when she wasn't extolling the virtues of her younger son, the woman was praising Colonel Turpin. According to Fiona, the man was generous, kind, and benevolent, an evaluation Erin was reserving judgment on. A tight-fisted poker player, she'd thought at first. Only his sympathy toward the Indians had made her soften that view.

Despite his mother's cajoling, Justin declined an invitation to attend the party, pleading ill health, so, under the afternoon sun peeking through the thick magnolia trees that grew along the path, the two women strolled next door. The colonel's home was certainly more gracious than Graypoint. He claimed that, along with his fellow Southerners, he'd lost almost everything, yet his furnishings showed none of the faded gentility of the Barrett household. The large parlor easily accommodated the dozen guests, among whom, Erin noted, was not one pale, unattached young woman. Couples mostly, Cole's age or older, greeted her warmly, and Erin's sense of self-righteousness gave way to a smothering awareness of the foolishness of her charade. Why hadn't she imagined what these scenes would turn out to be?

For a while, as she listened to the stories of Cole's childhood, she wondered if she shouldn't behave outrageously, so that after her sudden departure that evening, his friends could rest easy knowing Cole was freed from a most unfortunate liaison. Surely she would have no trouble thinking up something. Why not tell them the truth, that she was part Indian and illiterate? That ought to ruin her in their esteem.

But an overheard conversation squelched that idea. She had been sent by Louise to fetch additional cups for the punch bowl—a curious errand, she thought—when she noticed the back door leading to a veranda had been left ajar. Along with the acrid smell of cigar smoke, the voice of Hilmer Turpin drifted in. The colonel was talking to several of the men about what he called "the plight of the unfortunate savage," and Erin found herself unable to move away. Dissident voices protested, but Turpin would not be swayed.

"We've spent too long feeling sorry for ourselves," he said. "It's time we thought about others who are less fortunate."

"First time I ever heard you talk like that, Hilmer," a skeptical voice drawled. "Didn't know you could be so charitable."

"Didn't know I could be either, but that little lady who got herself affianced to Cole helped me see the error of my ways."

"Thought there might be a woman behind this," another said.

"I'll have no talk like that," Turpin said angrily. "The rest of you men might do well to listen to what I'm saying. I just wish there were some way I could help those poor people. I've got lots of connections with influential people, but a man with little cash is not seriously listened to. It was that way before the war, and I guess it always will be."

Erin's mind raced. Hilmer Turpin had connections but no money; her situation was reversed. The one thing they had in common was a desire to help the Indians. At last Erin saw a purpose to her newly acquired riches, something far more important than new clothes and proper manners. It might not be the kind of goal Hud had in mind for her, but she knew he would agree to something that mattered so much, something that would help others.

She had to talk to the colonel immediately, and without thinking of the propriety of her actions, she slipped through the open door.

"Colonel Turpin," she said, ignoring the curious eyes that turned to her, "I'd like to talk to you. As soon as possible."

"Why, Miss Donovan," he said, "is there somethin' wrong?"

"Not at all." For the first time in days Erin found

herself smiling naturally. Perhaps something beneficial would come out of this disastrous trip after all.

"Well, you have certainly piqued my curiosity." He turned to his companions. "Gentlemen, surely you will understand if I leave you to the night air? The pleasant duties of the host call."

He led Erin through the kitchen in the direction of the parlor.

"Could we talk in private, Colonel?" Erin was barely able to contain her growing excitement.

"Of course." In a moment Erin found herself sitting in a small room the colonel referred to as his library, even though there were no books in sight. Sitting upright in a straight-backed chair, she looked across the colonel's large, cluttered desk. The colonel stared back at her expectantly. Gone were the traces of a controlled card player she had noticed earlier.

"Colonel Hilmer, I have a confession to make."

"It can't be anything so terribly serious, Miss Donovan. You seem too happy to make it."

"For the first time since gold was found on my land, I am. You see, Colonel, I have money."

"That's nothing to be ashamed of."

"And nothing to be proud of, either. At least until now." Erin kept her eyes trained on his. "I was listening to your conversation a few minutes ago. When you were talking about helping out the Indians. You said the only thing that was holding you back was money."

"That is true, Miss Donovan, but you should hardly worry yourself about such matters."

"But I must. I have what you need. Please, Colonel Turpin, help me see that it does some good."

"Now, now, Miss Donovan, please think about what you're saying. Do you really want to invest in a cause that has so little chance of success? Few people care about the Indian the way you do. You won me over, but others may not be such an easy conquest."

"I'm not easily discouraged. Just tell me what you think we should do. You mentioned connections."

"Yes, in New York. There are very few powerful people left in Virginia right now. The money lies farther north. My thought was to enlist the aid of these people, give them a charity, a cause. Most of them are through trying to reform the South. Let them turn their eyes to the West."

Erin thought of the charity balls she had been forced to attend with Mr. and Mrs. Smythe-Williams. Deadly dull, she had thought them, but Colonel Turpin was right. New Yorkers were great people for causes, and she could tell them tales of hardship and even starvation among the Indians, stories that were familiar to every Texan whether sympathetic to the red man's cause or not. The tales would break their hearts.

Her wealth was not so great that single-handedly she could bring about a reversal in the fortunes of her people, but spread around in the right places, it could influence others to help. She looked at the colonel's proposal as a high-stakes poker game. You had to gamble a lot to win anything.

For the next half-hour she and Turpin went over plans for balls he would schedule; he would leave the persuading to her. In fact, once he set everything up, he wouldn't even remain in New York.

"How much money will you need to get things started?" Erin asked.

He avoided her direct gaze, and Erin decided the man was too much of a gentleman to enjoy asking a woman for money. "You're a generous young woman, Miss Donovan, and I wish I didn't have to take advantage of that fact. But we fight for a cause greater than our pride. I'll need four thousand dollars."

Erin didn't blink an eye. The sum was larger than she had imagined; it would, indeed, take most of the funds that Hud had helped her deposit in her New York bank to use during her stay, but she was too fired up to reconsider the colonel's proposal.

"I'll have the money shortly after we arrive in New York."

"Miss Donovan, do you mind if I give you some advice? It's the men who control the finances. They'll be more disposed to listen to me than to a young woman from Texas. At the parties you can charm them, but first you must let me set everything up." He paused. "If you're sure you want to do this, that is."

"You don't want me to accompany you to New York?"

The colonel gave her an avuncular smile. "It would be unseemly, my dear, for a beautiful young woman such as yourself to travel with a man without a chaperon. Neither my wife nor Fiona is up to the journey. Of course, if you have doubts—"

Doubts? Once she had made up her mind to something, Erin tried not to let them clutter her mind. She studied Turpin carefully and again saw the face of a fellow poker player. Well, that was all right. She would rather deal with a cautious man than one who gambled recklessly without considering the hand he held, or the hand of his opponents.

"What do you propose, Colonel?"

"Turn over the money to me, and I'll take care of all the arrangements. I'll leave tonight, but please give me a day to set everything up. I'll have a great deal of running around to do." Again the smile. "You don't know much about New York, do you?"

"Not much. Of course you're right," Erin said. Well, one more day in Richmond probably wouldn't be incautious. Besides, with the glow she was feeling from her prospective endeavors, she felt she could handle anyone who crossed her—even Coleman Barrett, and she proceeded to tell Turpin of the arrangements regarding her bank account.

Turpin carefully sharpened the point on his pen. "Would you like to write out authorization for the money to be turned over to me?"

"Oh, no," Erin said hastily. "You'll know what to put down. I'll just sign."

She watched as the colonel made what looked to her as meaningless marks on a thin piece of parchment, then thrust it in her direction.

"Please read this over carefully and sign at the bottom." He watched her hesitation. "Have you changed your mind? Please speak up now."

Erin stared at the paper. "Oh, no. Where do I sign?"

"There at the bottom. The paper indicates the place."

"Of course." Erin picked a blank spot directly under the markings and, dipping the pen into the pot of ink, carefully wrote out her name. At least she could do that.

A knock at the door startled her, and she turned as Fiona Barrett entered the room. The woman looked past her to stare at the colonel. There was suspicion in her eyes, as if she didn't trust the man. Well, she probably didn't. Erin knew she certainly wouldn't approve of his planning to give money away to charity.

The colonel smiled blandly at her. "Well, Fiona, your son's fiancée and I were just getting to know each other a little better. Won't you join us?"

Fiona ignored him. "I was looking all over for you, Erin," she said sharply.

"Oh, I'm sorry. I was sent for more cups for the punch, and I forgot all about them."

Fiona's laugh was without humor. "Erin, we'd have long ago expired of thirst if we'd waited for you to bring

90

cups. The guests are beginning to leave, and I thought you would want to tell them good-bye."

"Sounds like a good idea. I need to do the same," the colonel said. "Tell them we'll be right along."

Fiona stared at him for a moment. She didn't care for his curt dismissal, that much was obvious. Erin was convinced there was more to the relationship of this pair than just neighborliness. She'd felt it yesterday afternoon, and it seemed even more apparent today. What was more, the colonel's wife Louise knew it, too.

"Don't be too long," Fiona said sharply. "Your guests are waiting." She slammed the door behind her.

"She's right," the colonel said in the silence that followed her departure.

Erin nodded. The social amenities. Of course they must be seen to, but she wondered at the hypocrisy of a society in which husbands were unfaithful yet courteous. Well, the colonel's private life was none of her concern, and neither was Fiona Barrett's. Erin would return to Mrs. Smythe-Williams's New York home tomorrow evening to begin her work for the Indians, and she wasn't about to question the morals of the man who had made it possible. With the lies she had been telling lately, she didn't feel like judging anyone.

She was about to excuse herself when she noticed a look of hesitation on the colonel's face. "Are you having second thoughts, Colonel Turpin?"

"Certainly not. It's just that, well, I'd rather that news of what we're up to not get around just yet. There are those who think the only just cause can be found at home. You do understand, don't you?"

Erin certainly did. The conversation that had floated into the kitchen was sharp in her mind. Turpin's sympathetic words concerning the Indians of the West had raised ire in several of his fellow Southerners.

91

"Of course I won't say anything until you tell me it's all right." She looked him directly in the eye. "But what about Fiona? Should I tell her of our plans?"

Turpin rose from his chair. "Not just yet," he said hurriedly. "Let's make it a pleasant little surprise for her, after we are assured of success. I'm afraid Fiona just doesn't put much faith in Yankees, and she'll only try to discourage you."

Erin doubted that Fiona would ever consider giving money away "a pleasant little surprise," but as they joined the other guests, she agreed to his request.

No longer in a rush to leave, Erin let the good-byes drag out until early evening, and as she strolled back to Graypoint with her hostess, she let her mind wander down the paths of possibilities concerning the charity balls. Fiona interrupted her reverie with questions about her impressions of the people she had met. The only time she smiled was when Erin said she would stay for one more day.

Gradually Fiona turned the conversation to Hilmer Turpin. "You and the colonel seemed to become friends rather quickly," she said as they passed through the front gate leading to the house. Justin, who was waiting for them on the front porch, saved Erin from having to reply.

"Erin," he said, "would you mind stepping into the parlor for a minute?"

Erin was too grateful for his rescue to question his request or to notice the curious smile on his face; slipping past him, she walked down the hall and into the dimly lit room. She didn't even miss the sound of his peg leg against the hardwood floor behind her, a sound that should have echoed her footsteps but didn't.

It was the door closing behind her that caught her attention, and she whirled around in time to see a tall, dark figure moving toward her. Strong arms swept around her, and she felt herself pulled against the hard body of a man.

"Darling," she heard him say. "What a wonderful surprise."

And then all talking ceased as his lips came down against hers. Before she could protest, Erin felt herself slipping once again under the magical touch of Captain Coleman Barrett.

Chapter Six

Cole. Sweet memories sang in Erin's mind as she felt lips soft and warm move expertly against hers. But this was a more thorough kiss than she'd felt before, not so gentle, more demanding and passionate than delicately enticing.

Closer. She wanted him closer. It was all she could think about, and the fists she had planted against him opened. Under her exploring fingertips she felt, even through the thickness of his uniform, the tight, broad chest, the wide shoulders, and at last the strong neck and thick hair at the edge of his collar.

He moaned, the deep, vibrating sound more felt than heard, and slowly lifted his mouth from hers. Powerful hands framed her face and silvery eyes studied her lips. Erin gave herself up to the moment. Remembering Cole and the effects of his nearness was one thing; standing with his body pressed to hers, the warmth of their flesh intermingling, was something entirely different.

His lean face with its hint of black bristles was roughly chiseled and smooth at the same time, like hotly hewn granite, and a shock of untamed hair the color of night fell across his forehead. His gray eyes were hooded, so she dropped her gaze to his full lips. Her hands slipped down to press against his chest, and she felt a trembling beneath her fingertips. He was as moved as she, Erin thought, and yet when he spoke, his voice, though little more than a whisper, was mocking. The spell was shattered.

"A warm welcome indeed, Miss Donovan, for a weary traveler. All men should have such pleasant surprises."

Miss Donovan indeed! His arms were still around her, his lips scant inches away, yet he spoke as though they were mere acquaintances.

Erin replied in kind. "The surprise is mine, Captain Barrett. Do you greet all women like this?" His face moved closer to hers, his breath warm against her cheek, and Erin's voice quavered as she spoke. "How about a simple hello? Or a handshake? If the lady offers her hand."

His lips bent into a smile. "I take whatever I'm offered, Miss Donovan. That is, if I'm interested."

Erin shoved against his chest, freeing herself from his embrace. "Your interest, sir," she said tightly, "is hardly difficult to come by."

"As a matter of fact, it usually is. Except, of course, when I'm greeting my brides. I always offer them the best I have to give." He looked once again into her eyes, and she detected no trace of mockery or humor, only warm appreciation. Captain Barrett liked what he saw.

Far from being embarrassed, Erin realized that she liked the admiration in his eyes. In another time, another place she would have enjoyed trying out her fledgling skills at flirtation. Unfortunately, as his words reminded her all too clearly, she had gone beyond the early stages of courtship and leapt impetuously into betrothal. Before she could think about furthering her acquaintanceship with the man, they must first become disengaged.

She cleared her throat. "Captain Barrett, obviously your brother told you what he thinks is the reason for my being at Graypoint."

"Obviously."

"And you told him—"

"Nothing. Your secret, as well as your sweet body, is safe with me. For the time being."

Again the mockery was in his voice, and Erin spoke out angrily. "Captain Barrett, please don't tease me. This is difficult enough without your insults."

He bowed slightly. "My apologies. But under the circumstances, don't you think you ought to call me Cole?"

"Under the circumstances—" she began, but a knock at the parlor door stopped her.

Without waiting for an answer, Fiona Barrett entered the room. "Cole," she said, "I grew weary standing in the hall. Surely you have greeted your . . . fiancée sufficiently by now."

Erin's eyes were on Cole, and she saw an expresion akin to dislike flash across his face.

"Mother." He made no movement to embrace her, to kiss her cheek. "How are you?"

"You well know how I am. Justin tells me you visited our lawyer this evening before coming home."

"Just putting things in order. And it seems you've been managing very well."

"With the restrictions put upon me, it's a wonder I can get by." She glanced at Erin. "But enough of private chatter. After all, Erin is not part of the family yet. I must say, Cole, that her coming here was somewhat of a surprise."

"For both of us," Cole said. "I'm afraid the last time we spoke, we didn't sufficiently clarify our plans." He stepped beside Erin and, placing an arm around her shoulder, pulled her to him. "Did we, darling?"

Erin's eyes darkened as she looked up at Cole. "You must learn to listen to me, dearest," she said sweetly, then looked back at Fiona. "You know how men are."

Her words seemed to anger Fiona for a minute, but the woman's voice was controlled. "Only the colonel. My late husband. And you're right. Often he didn't pay attention to what I had to say."

Erin felt Cole stiffen. "How difficult it must have been, Mother, to find yourself surrounded only by men."

"And what do you mean by that?"

"Father and four sons, of course."

"The difficulty came," she answered sharply, "when I lost some of them."

The wrong ones, Erin could almost hear her say, remembering the way Lizette had described Fiona's love for the twins who had died in the war. The close, stale air of the parlor was now charged with the almost visible tension between mother and son. She glanced up at the tight-faced man who held her. Here was a Cole that Erin didn't care for, an angry man whose light, teasing sarcasm had turned to scorn, and she pulled away.

"Cap—er, Cole, perhaps I should leave you and your mother alone."

He looked down at her, and his eyes softened. "No need. I'm afraid Mother and I always talk this way. It's a tradition with the Barretts."

"Telling family secrets?" It was Justin, standing in the doorway.

Cole grinned at his brother. "And scare my bride away? Give me credit for more sense than that."

With every reference Cole made to their engagement, Erin felt his mother's eyes on her. Never had she felt more like an interloper. She simply had no business intruding into the domestic scene unfolding in the parlor, but before she could excuse herself, Justin spoke again.

"You'd be a fool, Cole, to frighten her off," he said, smiling. "And so would Mother. I've come to make sure you two can be alone."

No longer the meek, watery-eyed man Erin had met two days ago, Justin seemed to draw strength from Cole. The glimpses of humor and quiet sympathy she'd seen in him when Fiona wasn't looking were now easily visible, and in comparison to that first morning at Graypoint, he was being boldly outspoken.

"Thank you, brother," Cole said. "She and I have much to talk about." He turned to Erin. "Would you like to stroll in the garden? The moon is full this evening and there's an old apple tree out there I'd like to see."

By day Erin had seen the weed-choked beds and almost invisible paths that stretched behind the house. Not a very romantic setting, but then it wasn't romance they were seeking. He'd said they had much to say to one another, but Erin knew he meant it was she who must do the talking.

Well, she had dealt herself a losing hand. It was time to fold her cards and slip away. She wished she could go quietly but Cole wasn't going to allow it, and indeed she could hardly blame him. She had invaded his home, taken advantage of the hospitality of his mother, lied to his friends and family. And truly all for the sake of honor as she saw it. She plummeted into new embarrassment at all the misunderstandings. Outside she would simply have to summon her self-confidence and explain what was really a very simple situation. At the same time perhaps she could find out why he hadn't immediately denounced her.

With a brave smile she excused herself to Fiona and Justin and led the way outside. Behind her she heard the pitiless footsteps of her inquisitor. All too soon she drew to a halt in the shadowed path some dozen yards from the porch that stretched across the back of Graypoint, well beyond where their low murmurings could be heard. Out of sight and sound from any who might help her, she turned to face the formidable captain.

Cockleburs pulled at the skirts of Erin's dress and she reached down to pull them free. "I suppose," she said softly, her eyes directed to her task, "that you would like an explanation."

"Unless you would like me to draw my own conclusions."

Erin stood upright. "And what could those be?"

Moonlight drifted through the thick-leafed tree beside the path, bathing them both in mottled silver. Cole's eyes rested on the rounded softness of her breasts above the neckline of her gown. "You said you were going back to Texas. There can be few reasons why you are here instead."

"Among them being?"

"That perhaps you weren't satisfied the last time we met."

She inhaled sharply. "That's not true!"

"Then you were satisfied?"

"I most certainly was not!"

"Make up your mind, love. There's a vast difference between the two."

"Captain Barrett, I don't know what you're talking about. I'm here for two reasons. First, to save a number of people from embarrassment. A betrothal seemed the one acceptable reason I might have sought you out in your quarters, and that's the story I told Mrs. Smythe-Williams. Second, I still wanted to pay my debt to you. There was no time at West Point, and it's important to any gambler to pay a loss."

Cole ignored her explanations and took up the first part of her speech.

"I'm sure you know exactly what I'm talking about. I warned you I take whatever I'm offered from a woman— if I'm interested." He moved closer to her and his hands stroked her silk-covered arms. "And have no doubt about it. I'm definitely interested."

"Interested, yes, but just in taking my presence as some kind of offer. You're not listening to what I have to say." She tried to be angry at his insolence, but as his hands trailed lightly up and down her arms she slipped toward another, more compelling emotion. She said weakly, "I thought you'd want to know the real reason I came to be here."

His voice was low and thick. "Later. I'm not much for conversation with women."

"Are we too quick for you?" she managed to ask.

"Not usually." His eyes locked with hers. "Although you might be the exception." Warm words enveloped her. "I think I'd like very much the company of a woman who is both quick and fast."

Saints above, as her father was wont to say when the cards had deserted him. Where was the ire of her ancestors when she needed it? Cole Barrett thought she had come to crawl into his Richmond bed, that much was clear, as though she would ever do such a thing. Intractable, that's what he was. And brash and insulting and any other number of things she couldn't call to mind just now, for what he was most of all was irresistible.

"Captain Barrett." Her voice was barely a whisper.

"Cole." His fingers encircled her arms. "Let me hear you say it."

"Cole."

His hands moved up to her shoulders and his thumbs lightly massaged her throat. "A sweet sound it is to a man, Erin, to hear a beautiful woman whisper his name in such a voice."

"Cole," she whispered again just as his lips brushed softly against hers. A feathery touch, but it carried with it all the power of nature. The light tremblings she had felt ever since he first held her in the parlor sent her heart pounding, then receded, curling within her to become

100

desire, a sweet, aching warmth she had never known before.

Without rational thought, Erin did what seemed right and good. Her lips opened to him and as his mouth captured hers, she felt the thrust of his tongue inside her, tasting, exploring, demanding everything she had to give.

And still this joining was not enough. Her breasts ached for his touch. For the moment she was without shame as she pressed herself against him, wanting only to slip through the rough-textured cloth of his uniform to the hard body underneath. His lips still claiming hers, she felt one hand stroke the exposed softness of her breasts. For one tantalizing second, fingers slipped inside her silken gown to capture full roundness. Deftly he unfastened the tiny buttons of her gown, pulled down the thin chemise, and, moving his hands to her shoulders, dropped his head to trail soft kisses across her breasts, to take first one and then the other into his mouth.

Her back arched as she thrust herself closer to him. Incredible sensations. As much as she wanted to explore his body, she gave herself up to whatever he wanted to do with her. She knew so little about a man, or, she was discovering, about herself.

Slowly his hands moved down her back, to her waist, and then farther down to her hips, pulling her against him. Even through the layers of silk and wool that separated them she could feel his manhood. Hot, tight desire gripped her. How natural it would be to open her thighs, to let him press against that part of her that throbbed for him.

Natural and terrifying. Erin felt herself slip almost out of control. For most of her life she had taken care of herself; now just as she was on the edge of complete surrender to someone else, she pulled back.

Her body stiffened, resisted the natural pull of promised sweetness that was beyond her ken, and Cole responded to her withdrawal, just as he had to her willing supplications moments before. Slowly his head lifted, and she felt the pressure of his hands against her buttocks lessen.

"Cole."

"Somehow, love," he whispered, his breath warm against her cheek, "that doesn't have the same sweet sound it did." For a moment he seemed to lean against her, then she felt him pull back until their bodies no longer touched.

She looked down at her open gown, saw her breasts exposed to his eyes and his lips, and felt the shame she had not felt earlier. Quickly she fastened the buttons.

How to tell him of her feelings? "I'm sorry—" she began.

"For what?" The soft regret of a moment ago had vanished; the anger now in his voice had the sting of a whip. "For leading me on too far, or for stopping too soon before I was completely trapped?"

In her innocence Erin had supposed he would want to know what had made her pull away. She should have known better. The upright captain was always judging her and finding fault.

She studied his face, let her eyes trail insolently down his body and then back up again. Much as he had studied her. "I'm certainly not sorry for anything I have done. The problem is your lack of honor," she snapped. "Would you really have taken me here in the weeds of your mother's garden?" She saw his jaws tighten, his gray eyes darken almost to black. Her words had hit their mark.

"That's a question, Miss Donovan, that neither of us can answer to any satisfaction. Of course I would say no, and of course you would not believe me."

"Right, Captain Barrett. Now if you will excuse me, I'll be going in. Tomorrow I'll leave. Urgent business calls me to New York. With any luck we'll not be bothered with each other's presence again."

As she hurried past him, tears welled in her eyes. She couldn't remember the last time she had cried. Why in the world was she behaving so foolishly now? She had never minded being a woman before, as long as she didn't have to act like one. Well, tonight she felt very womanly indeed and was none the happier for it. In fact, she couldn't remember when she'd been more miserable in her life.

Coleman Barrett might be an officer, but he was no gentleman, his reputation to the contrary. For a few fiery minutes she had let herself forget her distrust of soldiers, had thought only of the man beneath the uniform. As she hurried inside the house, she vowed not to make that mistake again.

Cole leaned against the rough trunk of Graypoint's lone apple tree and stared at the darkened house, wondering what the hell kind of game Erin Donovan was playing and why he was letting her play it with him. Never had he allowed any woman to manipulate him, not since he'd lost Rachel, but Erin had been hard to forget even after their one brief kiss in his quarters at the Point.

He thought of the soft red curls that framed her finely sculptured face, of the golden eyes that looked at him so provocatively, of smooth, warm skin the shade of ivory. No, not quite that pale, more sun kissed. A shaft of moonlight bathed a low apple branch before him and he halted as new and confusing thoughts arose.

Erin was right about one thing. He had behaved dishonorably, at least in terms of the time and place for their lovemaking. He had professed innocence in planning to take her here in the garden, but to himself he admitted that had she been willing, he would have stripped them both and found the satisfaction they craved. He tortured himself with memories of her body, her perfect breasts, her tremulous responses to his touch.

As much as she excited and intrigued him, she also was a puzzle. What was her game? No lady would have behaved as she had done, twice seeking him out. Was she really after a husband? Something so simple as that? Cole smiled. If so, she had a direct way of going about acquiring one. Perhaps she wasn't as wealthy as she appeared in her fine clothing. If that were the case, she would be sorely disappointed in him. He was ambitious— he intended to make his fortune in the West, but for the present much of his meager pay and his income from investments went to support his mother and brother in Richmond.

The thought that Erin might be seeking security by way of his bed depressed him, and he decided it was best he leave in the morning. He had already taken care of the few business details that must be seen to for his mother, and there was nothing else to keep him here. Besides, he needed to report to Superintendent Ruger about the seeds, probably infertile, that he had sown in Washington for the Point; he could await his orders there.

He would make his good-byes by way of a note of apology. When he thought about Erin Donovan's sweet lips and soft body—and the way she had, for just a moment in the garden, let him hold her against him—he knew he could never expose her little charade.

He could see no harm in letting his family think they were engaged; then she could make an honorable exit as soon as they were away from his home. Business in New York, she had said. He didn't want to think what kind. With Erin, there was no telling what it might be.

* * *

Erin descended the next morning long after the usual breakfast hour at Graypoint. There was no way she could have brought herself to sit across the table from Captain Barrett. After last night, she couldn't even think of him as Cole. Just as she had hoped, the dining room was empty and the table bare. Perhaps later, when she had a little appetite, she could prepare herself a cup of coffee. But not just yet.

The sound of voices drifted in from the kitchen. Women's voices, Fiona's and Lizette's. The men were nowhere to be seen. Quietly she slipped out the front door and headed for the Turpin home next door. She needed to reassure herself that the colonel hadn't changed his mind.

It was a frustrated Erin who returned shortly to Graypoint. The colonel was gone, his wife had said firmly, and she didn't know when he would return. Erin had told her she would be staying at the Smythe-Williams's New York home in Gramercy Park. He could talk with her there about their plans.

Louise Turpin had looked at her without expression, as though she didn't know what Erin was talking about, but she didn't ask what plans her husband might be making with a single young lady. It seemed peculiar that the Turpins hadn't discussed the colonel's plans for Indian charities, but, as she let herself in the front door of the Barrett home, Erin shrugged and let it pass.

Ever since she had returned last night from making wonderful plans with Colonel Turpin, things had not gone right. For a while Cole Barrett's insistent love-making had made her forget about those plans; when she thought about the two of them in the garden, she blushed. If all women were such fools over men, she had never been told of it. She needed a long talk with Julie about what other trials might await her, she decided, but she sighed when she realized it was too late for that.

As she walked into the parlor, Fiona looked up from a piece of needlepoint.

"Another stroll in the sun, Erin?" she asked.

Erin shrugged. "Do you want to talk to me?"

"Yes. I have something for you. From your fiancé."

Erin tried to smile. Before last night, her charade had been absurd and potentially embarrassing, but it was not hurtful to her. This morning that was no longer the case.

"Is he not here to give it to me himself?" she asked softly, not knowing what she wanted the answer to be.

"I'm afraid not. He departed early this morning for West Point. He left this for you."

Erin looked down at the envelope in Fiona's extended hand. Damn! A note. How in hell did he expect her to read it?

Well, of course he would expect her to. Hardly anyone in the East knew she couldn't read. She took the envelope and studied its broken seal. Probably Fiona had already read the message, and she felt the woman's eyes on her as she looked at the orderly markings on the paper inside. Should she smile? Blush? Grow angry?

Fiona's eyes narrowed. "I trust it's not bad news."

"Of course not. It's very personal, you understand. You know how men are."

"I remember you said that to me last night, Erin. About understanding men. I certainly do understand my own son, but perhaps not in the way you do."

Oops. Erin was forever saying the wrong thing to the woman. Thank goodness Fiona would never be her mother-in-law.

Erin needed to learn more before she could even pretend to know what was in the note. "Did Cole say anything to you about his plans?" she asked.

"Very little." Fiona's eyes rested carefully on Erin. "Just that he was sorry he was called away. And that he would return as soon as he could. I'm sure he wrote you the same thing."

Erin started to reply in the affirmative, but something in the woman's quiet stare gave her pause. Was Fiona trying to trap her? Suddenly very tired of pretending to be something she was not, she settled for a noncommittal shrug. Nothing seemed to be going right. It was time to leave, no matter what excuses she had to give.

She carefully folded away the note. "I have appointments in New York, Fiona. I'll be leaving on the evening train. Could someone be kind enough to arrange for a carriage? I'm sorry it was too late to tell you last night."

"Justin has gone to take care of some business for Cole," Fiona said. "I hope he gets back in time for you to tell him good-bye. I thought you two were becoming friends."

It came to Erin that the woman had wanted her to cast her eye at the younger Barrett son. Erin felt foolish that she hadn't realized it sooner. That was why Fiona had thrown them together so often, had sung Justin's praises. No wonder she had been so unhappy about Erin's spurious engagement to Cole. Fiona had gone beyond not caring about Cole's happiness; she had wanted Graypoint's unexpected visitor for her other son.

But Erin wasn't so naive as to think she had charmed the woman into wanting to keep her around. Money, that was Fiona's motive. She figured Erin had it, and with Justin married to her, Erin's riches would stay in Virginia. More than ever, Erin knew it was time to bind off all the frayed ends of her journey to Richmond and then leave.

"Fiona, I can see why you are very proud of Justin. He's had a great deal to endure." The woman's eyebrows raised. "I mean with the loss of his leg," Erin added hastily. "He's handled his injury very well. I'm sure he'll find a nice young woman to fall in love with, and once he does, you'll have grandchildren filling your home before long, I'll wager."

Fiona's eyes narrowed. "That's not exactly what I had in mind for Graypoint. As a matter of fact, in the past few days I had allowed myself to hope you might be staying here."

"I can't, Fiona, even for a little while. But before I go, there's a piece of business I must tend to. I owe Cole money, but he got away this morning before I could pay it."

"I don't know what your plans are, of course," Fiona said, her soft Southern voice heavy with sarcasm, "but couldn't you just pay him at your wedding?"

Erin's eyes flashed with pride. "It's an old family tradition that Donovans don't owe money." Shaun Donovan must be spinning in his grave at the lie. It was a tradition, all right, but one that had begun with her.

"Is the debt a large one?"

"Four hundred and three dollars."

Fiona smiled as though she had just been dealt a winning hand. "You could leave the money with me, dear. I'll see that it goes where it should."

Erin readily agreed. Clearing the gambling debt would leave her just enough cash to get to New York, but she couldn't let that worry her now. Her only concern was breaking free of the less than honorable Coleman Barrett. When he couldn't have his way with her, he had written her off by way of a note left with his mother.

That was fine with her. Paying the debt would eliminate her only reason for seeing him again. As she went slowly upstairs to pack, she wished she could feel more relieved.

Chapter Seven

On the long ride back to New York, Erin found no relief in her escape from Richmond. Questions about her mixed feelings chased themselves through her mind, and the only answers she came up with were decidedly unacceptable.

By the time she arrived at the Gramercy Park mansion, her look was grim, but that didn't stop the inevitable questions from Marcia Smythe-Williams. Erin was inspired anew to swear silently that if she ever got out of the East, she would never tell another lie, no matter how expeditious it seemed.

But that was the problem. She was still not safely on her way to Texas. Patiently, she allowed the New Yorker to draw a few more fibs from her. No, she said, the trip had not been successful. At least that part of her tale was not a lie. And yes, she said, the engagement was off; the breaking of it had been so painful that she had left without tracking down the redoubtable Mrs. Jones.

Finally, the charade behind her, Erin heaved a sigh of relief and turned her thoughts to the charity balls that Colonel Hilmer Turpin was arranging. After unsuccessful attempts to dissuade Erin from her determination to help the poverty-stricken Indians, Mrs. Smythe-

Williams reluctantly agreed to help her and the two set out the next day for Erin's bank. Since no letter had arrived at Gramercy Park, perhaps the colonel had left a message for her there.

Erin missed him by less than an hour, but the money she had signed over to him had been withdrawn, leaving her account almost depleted. There was no reason to inform her host and hostess of her financial situation. After all, the ball gowns she had bought in Paris—minus, of course, the yellow brocaded satin—would be sufficient for her plans with the colonel, and there was still plenty of money awaiting her in Texas. Watching her expenditures until she arrived back there was really no problem. If necessary, she could sneak out and find a game of twenty-one.

The next few days were long ones. No word came from the colonel, and at last she asked the Smythe-Williamses for help. They were often involved in charity affairs and would know who to ask about what the colonel was arranging. Ask, they did; no one knew what they were talking about. The colonel's plan was apparently a hoax.

Poor little thing. Erin could read the pity in her hostess's eyes. First she had lost her handsome fiancé; next she'd been duped by a Southern sharper. An anger unlike any Erin had ever experienced consumed her. Reasonably or not, she laid the blame for her problems before the polished boots of Captain Coleman Barrett. He had mishandled her visit to Professor's Row; he had mauled her in the garden; it was his old family friend, introduced to her in his home, who had stolen her funds and, what was worse, betrayed her dreams for helping the Indians. By damn, he could put all that integrity of his to work and see that justice was done. The colonel must be forced to return the money.

West Point was only a boat ride up the Hudson River. According to Fiona Barrett, that was where Cole had

110

scurried the morning after his assault. The rat. Well, he hadn't gone far enough to hide from her.

Another lie was necessary to extricate herself from the watchful eye of Marcia Smythe-Williams. A telegram had arrived, she said, in response to a letter she had sent to the Point. Captain Barrett could help her out, but he needed to see her there. Arrangements had been made for her to stay at a nearby hotel. There was no time to arrange for a chaperon, but Mrs. Smythe-Williams was not to worry. All was entirely proper because the captain's mother was visiting him from Richmond and, yes, Erin would pass on greetings to Superintendent Ruger.

Not that she planned to see him. A brief confrontation with Cole, this time in his office, and then she would leave. He could send whatever cash he managed to recover to Texas. Somewhere amongst all those cadets and officers, she could find a card game to finance her journey home.

But not with Cole. Never again anything with him. The thought went round and round her head as she waved good-bye to Mrs. Smythe-Williams at the Hudson River pier. Erin might be impetuous and naïve, but she wasn't stupid. Around Cole, she knew from bittersweet experience, she lost control of herself, and what was worse, he knew it, too.

During the fifty-mile journey up the wide, tree-lined river, Erin had a long time to drill into her mind the necessity of cool detachment when she faced him. In her high-necked, blue cotton gown and with her flaming hair tamed as much as possible into a chignon, only a few wisps of red curls escaping to frame her face, she looked as demure as she could manage. All she needed to do now was address him in a businesslike manner and he would soon realize how much he had misjudged her intentions toward him.

111

Unfortunately, she hadn't let herself remember the way he could look at her. When she had made her way onto the Point and was at last announced to him by a crisply efficient young cadet, the sight of the tall, dark-haired officer, his coat casually unbuttoned at the throat, his gray eyes gazing across the narrow confines of his office in warm surprise, was enough to make her lose all resolve.

She waited until the door closed behind her to speak. "Don't say it," she warned.

"All right." He paused a moment, his face solemn, his eyes disturbingly light. "But would you mind telling me what I'm not supposed to say? I wouldn't want to offend you."

"Anything that in any way refers to my offering myself to you."

"I'll fight the urge."

"That's not the only urge you'll have to fight. I've come about a more serious matter."

"What could be more serious than making love to a beautiful woman?"

Erin's fingernails dug into her hands as she vainly sought a pain that would help her forget the pleasure his words provoked. "Captain Barrett," she said sternly, "remember where we are."

"Do you mean in my office? Behind a closed door guarded only by a young pup of a cadet who will probably tell wild tales anyway about what is going on in here?" He moved from behind his desk and stood facing her from an infinitesimal foot away.

Erin had to catch herself to keep from swaying into his arms. He looked good, and what was more, he smelled good, too. What on earth did he put on himself that attracted her so? Or was it just the natural, earthy aura emitted by a man? Strange that she had never noticed it before on anyone else, she thought, letting her eyes drift

112

down to the dark hair curling over the loosened scarf at his throat.

His voice lowered to almost a whisper. "I know only too well where we are. It's where you found me when you came looking."

Erin found the strength to step back. Not only did he look as good as ever, but he was also as arrogant.

"That's right. I came looking for you. But not for the reason you so quickly assume. *Captain* Barrett."

Cole leaned back against his desk. "I'll go by the facts, then, the main one being that you seem troubled by something. I hope nothing I've done. Didn't you get my note?"

Damn. The indecipherable message was crammed inside the pocket of her gown, carefully hidden until she could find someone she trusted to translate it for her. She would probably be back in Texas before that happened.

"Of course I received your message."

"And do you accept my apology?"

She gave him her best poker face. "I accept it in the spirit in which it was written." Let him interpret that anyway he wanted to.

Cole looked at her in puzzlement for a moment. Good. She had thrown him off stride.

"I had hoped my meaning was clear," he said. "I'm sorry if I offended you in the garden. That was the furthest thing from my mind."

"Sometimes what we intend and what we accomplish are far apart, Captain." At last Erin felt in control. "I came here today for one thing, to demand justice from you. In your capacity as an officer of the Army and as a member of the Barrett family."

He smiled. "And I foolishly hoped you wanted to investigate my capacity as a man."

Erin's newly won self-assurance nearly dissolved in the heat of his words and the lustful look in his eyes.

113

"Wrong again, Captain," she murmured, dropping her gaze to the floor in an attempt to hide the lie he might read in her eyes.

His words took on a sharp edge. "And it's justice you've come for, is it? Don't you know there isn't any such thing?"

She looked up quickly. "There had better be, or I'll skin me a Virginia colonel and use his toughened hide as fish bait."

The surprised look that flashed across Cole's face settled into professional interest; at last, Erin told herself, he took her seriously.

He cleared a chair of its half-packed box of books and moved it closer. "Please sit down, Erin, and tell me what's wrong."

As he settled once more behind his desk, Erin thought about where to begin. Cole Barrett was an Indian fighter and would have little sympathy for do-gooders trying to help what he considered murdering savages. Especially if at least one of the charitable-minded souls confessed she was part Indian herself. Perhaps she had better go easy on some of the facts.

Quickly she launched into a brief recounting of her sudden wealth and the burden it sometimes put on her, especially when she was forced to conform to propriety.

"I can see how bothersome that would be," Cole murmured.

"No you don't. Please don't condescend to me, Captain."

"I'm sorry." His smile was genuine and just as effective as his leer. "Please go on."

Erin cleared her throat. "Your mother introduced me to Colonel Turpin. He in turn convinced me I could put my wealth to work through charity balls in New York— to help out some poor and homeless people. All I had to do was turn some money over to him, and he would set everything up."

As she spoke, the atmosphere in the room changed. Cole was listening to every word, and the set of his lips was firm and uncompromising. She had noticed the change in him as soon as she'd mentioned the colonel's name.

"How much?" was all he said.

"Four thousand dollars."

"Damn!" Cole thought for a moment. "When did you last see Turpin?"

"In Richmond. The night you came home." For a moment the harsh look in his eyes softened, and Erin hurried on, fearful they both would lose their sharp edge of concentration if they thought much about that night. "I went back to his home the next morning but his wife said he was gone. She didn't know where he was or when he would return. I'm sure she was lying."

Cole sat quietly for a moment, and Erin wished she could read his mind. As she sat in the sterile office, with its stacks of sealed boxes against one wall and the file-strewn desk in front of her, she could see the foolishness of her quest. Cole was preparing to leave West Point and would have no time for her. Besides, even if he were staying, the problem which was uppermost in her mind had, after all, nothing to do with the Point or even with the Army.

He looked at her solemnly. "Let's go see the colonel's nephew. He's an instructor of artillery here. Perhaps he can give us a clue to the rascal's whereabouts."

For the first time in days Erin let herself smile as he guided her out of the room. A curious euphoria washed over her, and she no longer questioned her decision to approach him for help. Without question or protest Cole had accepted her problem as his own. She had come to him in righteous indignation and had found consideration. Cole's response had endeared him to her as nothing else had.

Lieutenant Gerald Nathan's office was in a nearby building. An even smaller cubicle than Cole's, it was at the same time less cluttered. No books and few papers were visible, leaving the impression that the room's occupant was merely passing through.

The man who stood to greet her was the same sharp-faced officer she remembered from the fateful graduation ball of early June. Tall, thin, and pale, he seemed all edges, like a two-sided sword. Could it have been only a few weeks ago that she had last seen him? It seemed like an eternity.

"Miss Donovan," he said, "what a pleasure to see you again. An unexpected pleasure, to be sure."

"Hello, Lieutenant." Erin reluctantly held out her hand. What was there about the man that reminded her of a snake-oil salesman? In fairness to him, she admitted his main crime could be his relationship to Turpin.

Cole went right to the matter at hand. "Nathan, we're looking for your uncle, Hilmer Turpin. Do you have any idea where he might be?"

Nathan's pale eyes widened in surprise. "Why on earth would you want to see him?"

Erin started to answer but was cut off by Cole.

"Unfinished business."

The lieutenant paused, his gaze drifting for a moment to Erin. She could read the speculation in the look.

"With Miss Donovan?" he asked. "For heaven's sake, what could it be?"

Erin could be silent no longer. "He owes me money." She ignored the warning glance from Cole. "It would appear, Lieutenant, that your uncle is a thief."

Nathan looked not the least surprised. It seemed the colonel had a reputation among his family members for being somewhat less than honorable.

"Perhaps we should all sit down," he said and, before

116

either Cole or Erin could protest, went to the outer office for chairs.

Erin was grateful for Nathan's quick return. No matter how solicitous Cole was being, she was not ready for the lecture on discretion she could see was on his lips.

Without a glance at her companion, she immediately launched into an abbreviated version of her predicament. "So you see, Lieutenant Nathan," she concluded, "I simply have to find him. He can't be allowed to get away with what he has done."

"Of course not," the lieutenant responded; then he continued smoothly, "If I could just see the receipt signed by my uncle."

The silence that fell went on and on while Erin stared at the smug look on Nathan's face. At last Cole said, "Well, Erin?"

Erin looked down and squirmed in the hard chair Nathan had brought. When she lifted her head, her eyes were fired from within.

"I have no receipt," she said. "You'll have to trust me, Captain Barrett. I met that scoundrel in your home," she continued without drawing a breath. "Hilmer Turpin I was told is the last of an old Richmond family with an honorable history. He'd be an idiot to risk the fuss I'd raise."

"That's just it, Erin," said Cole. "If Turpin could trick you out of four thousand dollars leaving no proof he'd ever got it, the town and the sheriff would believe him. Not," he said, smiling, "some newcomer from the wilds of Texas, no matter how charmingly indignant she might be."

Erin shot from her chair and started pacing. "He won't get away with it," she said.

"I'm afraid he has, Miss Donovan," said Nathan, not without some satisfaction Erin thought. "What on earth must Mrs. Smythe-Williams think of the situation? She

117

is no doubt accompanying you."

Cole interrupted. "The arrangements for Miss Donovan's journey to the Point are of no concern. The location of your uncle is."

"I see." He looked at the two visitors in silence, then let his eyes settle on Erin.

She shifted nervously and sank once more onto the chair. "Can you help us?" she asked.

"I'm afraid not. Since returning to the East I've seen little of my uncle. Although"—his smile was knowing—"I'm not surprised he would defraud a lovely young thing like you. Someone so innocent."

His voice dripped with sarcasm, and Erin seethed. A gentleman would not have asked about a chaperon; beneath the lieutenant's slick words he was inpugning her virtue because she had traveled alone. Erin would have liked to smack him in the jaw, but of course hand-to-hand combat between her and Nathan would have been ridiculous, as well as ineffectual. If only she could catch him in a game of twenty-one.

Cole launched a more civilized attack. "Nathan, our families go back a long way in Richmond. Furthermore we're both officers in the United States Army. Miss Donovan and I came to you seeking help." His voice was commanding. "Try a little harder to see that we get it."

Erin could read not only resentment in the lieutenant's eyes, but also compliance. Coleman Barrett was obviously not a man to be treated with disrespect, particularly in the Army where rank was everything.

"Perhaps I can help after all," Nathan said. "I seem to recall a cabin on Uncle's former plantation. When he lost the place, he was allowed to retain use of it. He just might be waiting there until Miss Donovan is gone."

Cole nodded. "I remember the place. I'm just sorry you didn't recall it a little sooner."

Nathan murmured an apology, then added, "Have you

received your orders to leave yet?"

"They came this morning. I'll be heading for Texas shortly." He glanced briefly at Erin, and she caught her breath. So Cole would soon be in her own part of the country. The thought had tantalizing possibilities.

Nathan's eyes were directed out the room's lone window so he missed the quick exchange that passed between his two visitors. "I envy you leaving this place. No future here for a man with ambition."

"A man makes his own future," Cole said. "Don't you know that by now?" He rose before the lieutenant could respond. "Thank you for your assistance. I would appreciate it if the information Miss Donovan gave you went no farther than this room."

"It most certainly will not. Like you, Captain, I am a man of honor."

Now that was something Erin doubted, but for a change she kept her mouth closed. Besides, she was irritated by the implication in Cole's admonition. Obviously he thought her revelations to Nathan had been unwise.

As they walked back to Cole's office, she wanted to ask him about his orders—when he would be leaving and where exactly he was to be posted, what his duties were to be and if he anticipated having much free time. But there was no telling how he might interpret her questions. Arrogant as he was, he might figure out that, despite the antagonism he often aroused in her, she was beginning to care.

The stares of passing cadets and officers unnerved her as much as the silence hovering between her and Cole, so she settled for questions about Lieutenant Nathan.

"Gerald Nathan is from the New York branch of Turpin's family," Cole explained. "He didn't graduate from the Point. At the start of the war, he was a cadet, but he was allowed to resign and reenlist in the regular Army.

119

Served for a while in the West. Like me, he wants to go back."

"Somehow the two of you don't seem anything alike."

Cole smiled at her. "I take that as a compliment. Nathan's not one of my favorite people."

Nor was he one of Erin's, although she really didn't understand why. Thus far she was operating on intuition picked up in a thousand poker games. Perhaps Cole could justify her feeling.

"Why don't you like him?" she asked as they returned to his cluttered office.

"I don't trust him. Nothing he's ever said or done, just a feeling. He's too busy trying very hard to take care of himself without getting any positive results. I'm never quite sure how far he would be willing to go to get what he wants."

He closed the door behind Erin. "But enough of him. We have more important business to consider."

Erin could feel his breath on the back of her neck. Business was the last thing on her mind. She could feel his body inches away from hers, and the sweet, aching desire that was now familiar swept through her, erasing all thoughts except of his touch. As soon as he made the first move, she would fall into his arms. How foolish she had been to think she could ever do anything else.

But the coaxing pressure of his hands on her body never came. "Erin," he said, "I promise I'll do whatever I can to get your money back."

Hang the money, she almost said, but caught herself. After all, Cole was only doing what she had asked of him. At the wrong time, he had decided to listen.

She turned to face him and, stepping back to think more clearly, said, "Even if you have only my word the theft took place?"

"You say Turpin is guilty. I have no reason to doubt you."

Erin flushed with guilt that she had ever lied where Cole was concerned. "I appreciate your help, but I don't really need it. I may be a little short of cash, but I'm hardly destitute. It's just that I don't like to be taken for a fool."

"I'll admit I don't always know how to take you," he said, smiling, "but I've never considered 'fool' to be one of my options."

Saints above. She wasn't sure she could wait for him to make the first move. "What are your plans now?" she asked and held her breath until he answered.

"To take you home with me."

Well, he was honest enough. "I think—"

"To Richmond."

"Oh."

"You sound disappointed."

Erin kept her eyes trained on the scarf at his neck. Cole Barrett was unlike any man she had ever met before, and she no longer found his remarks insulting. In the recesses of her mind she admitted she enjoyed them, but she couldn't bring herself to answer in kind. Besides, what did he expect her to say? That she wanted to return to Professor's Row and try out that bed he had offered her once before? That scandalous thought occurred to her, but she couldn't let him know it. It was long past time for her poker face.

"I just don't see the purpose in such a journey."

"Eventually the colonel will return hoping you'll be too embarrassed to face him down. And if you're not, he can just explain it all as a misunderstanding. Nathan was right. The colonel will be able to weasel out of this."

Of course. Erin should have figured they were returning to Richmond only to see the colonel. After all, she was the one who had pursued Coleman Barrett, and not the other way around. Although she had always been met with an interest that, to put it mildly, went beyond

121

the merely polite. How great was the captain's attraction in her? Maybe in Richmond she would find out.

She smiled up at him. "Well," she said, shrugging lightly, "I suppose I can just wire Marcia Smythe-Williams that the engagement is back on. If, of course, you don't mind another betrothal."

A smile played at his lips. "Not at all. But this time, please allow me to do the honors and send the wire. There are some things, after all, a man likes to do for himself."

Their journey to Richmond the next day was as circumspect as Erin could have asked for and, with Cole sitting so close beside her, his thigh brushing against hers, his presence fragmenting her thoughts, a great deal tamer than she wanted it to be. He wouldn't even allow her to pull out a deck of cards and challenge him to a few hands of poker.

She ventured a few questions about his earlier service in the West and found to her surprise he had been there twice—once as a young recruit during the war and later, after his graduation from West Point, as the officer who had beaten her in a game of cards behind a Dallas stable. When she tried to ask him about the former service, he shut off her questions before she could finish asking them. As she watched the miles creep by, she realized there was much about the formidable captain that remained enigmatic.

When the train finally jerked to a halt in Richmond, Erin was pleased to see Homer, the well-read driver from her first visit, step up to them on the platform. She drew a handkerchief from her sleeve and, indelicately wiping the soot and grime from her face and hands, gratefully listened as he offered to convey them to Graypoint. Somehow the sight of him alleviated a bit her dread of facing Fiona.

"Miss," he said politely, "welcome again to Richmond. Captain Barrett, sir."

"I see you know my fiancée," Cole said, and Erin was sure a look of surprise flashed across the driver's face.

"I carried the miss along this same street when she first came to Richmond, sir," he said. "Didn't know the importance of her visit. Not that it was any of my business." He carefully avoided Erin's eyes.

How good it was to hear his deep, slow tones. He seemed like one of the few friends she had outside of Texas. As the carriage wended its way through the gathering twilight, she listened to the two men discuss the changes taking place in the Virginia capital. New buildings were going up, and old ones being restored. At last Richmond seemed to be pulling herself away from the devastations of war.

In the fading light, Erin saw a different kind of city from the one the men discussed. She was conscious only of the charm which lay in tree-lined streets and sweetly blooming flowers, not in construction. This was a place that someone could easily call home.

Now what made her think a thing like that? She had left Richmond days ago determined never to return; the only reason she was back was that a crime had been perpetrated against her here. During the trip with Cole, a constant background to her enjoyment of his company had been her dread of once again sharing a roof with his mother, who had easily seen through the engagement charade and had calmly schemed to arrange a marriage with her other son.

Even with Cole at her side supporting her story, she knew that once she entered Graypoint, she would feel more than ever like an interloper. As they pulled up in front of the gloomy structure, she had to fight to keep from clinging to the side of the carriage.

In the parlor, Fiona did little to alleviate her discomfort.

"Erin," she said, "what a pleasant surprise to see you so soon. I'm sorry Justin is visiting in the country, and I'm not sure when he plans to return. He'll be so sorry to have missed you."

Despite her words of welcome, the older woman looked decidedly ill at ease, her eyes darting back and forth between her son and his fiancée. Surely she can have no doubt now about our engagement, Erin told herself. The thought must be making her angry indeed—unless there were other problems connected with their return that she didn't know about.

The last thing she had talked to Fiona about was the old gambling debt to Cole. Erin had assumed the money had long since been returned to him. Was Fiona foolish enough to have kept it for herself without ever mentioning it to her son? Probably. And she'd gotten no receipt for the four hundred and three dollars either. Better not to mention the transaction at all.

Cole got right to the matter that had brought them there. "Mother, have you seen Colonel Turpin in the past few days?"

Fiona's hand went to her throat. "Why do you ask that?"

"Because he has apparently stolen money from Erin."

The woman paled and Erin thought she would sink in a swoon to the parlor floor before Cole could get her to the small settee. Placing her in Erin's care, he left the room and returned in a moment with a glass of amber liquid.

"Here, Mother," he said, replacing Erin at her side. "Have a sip of brandy." When she seemed to have recovered somewhat, he continued. "I didn't realize you would be so upset at Erin's bad news."

Fiona avoided her son's careful scrutiny. "It's just

that I didn't think the colonel would do such a thing." In her voice were the beginnings of anger.

"He told you nothing of his plan for charity balls in New York? Paid for, of course, with cash he withdrew from Erin's account."

Erin watched the woman carefully. She looked as unkempt as the night Erin had first seen her, but there was something even more pitiful about her now—the despair that settled in her pale gray eyes as she listened to Cole. It would have taken a consummate actress to feign such a reaction, and Erin was convinced the woman viewed the colonel's behavior as nothing less than betrayal. Fiona had no doubt told her close friend about the obviously wealthy young woman under her roof, and the colonel had done the rest on his own, without sharing either his nefarious plans or the stolen money.

Cole must have sensed much the same thing and he immediately set about caring for his mother, who didn't protest when he ordered Lizette to prepare her bed.

When the servant was gone, he turned to Fiona. "Get some rest tonight, Mother. We'll see what we can do in the morning."

For a moment Erin thought the two were behaving toward one another the way she had expected they should, with warmth and solicitude. But when Cole attempted to help his mother from the room, Fiona pulled away.

"I'm not so feeble I can't help myself," she said, and without assistance slowly exited.

The events of the past few days had left Erin far too exhausted to remain in the parlor alone with Cole. Around him she needed all the energy she could summon, so assuring him that she could take care of herself, she guided herself to the room she had used on her earlier visit. The soft bed welcomed her and she fell into a deep sleep, not awakening until long after the sun had risen, when she hurriedly went through her morning ablutions and descended to the dining room.

Fiona was just completing her breakfast. "Sit down, Erin, and I'll get you a cup of coffee." No ringing for Lizette, no careful scrutiny of dress and manners. There weren't even very many forks and spoons set at her place. Erin nodded gratefully at the woman's suggestion.

"Where is Cole?" she asked. "Is he not down yet?"

"I'm afraid you missed him," Fiona said. "He visited Louise early and got her to confess that Hilmer was supposed to be somewhere on the road to New York. Cole said something about visiting a cabin on the old Turpin plantation. It's not far out of the city, and he should return by evening. You're supposed to understand."

Erin understood only too well. Cole was checking out the place Gerald Nathan had mentioned, and he was doing it without her. There was nothing she could do but wait impatiently. In the afternoon she attempted to teach Fiona the rudiments of twenty-one but soon abandoned the project. Lizette was a better student and when Justin returned unexpectedly he joined the two women in the kitchen for a game of cards. It all seemed so domestic to Erin. The only thing missing was Cole, and as supper came and went, she began to worry because he hadn't returned.

Excusing herself, she took advantage of the cool evening breeze and strolled in the garden behind Graypoint. In the shadows Cole seemed to be standing, and in the rustling wind in the apple tree, she heard his voice. She stood in the spot where she had let him caress her and realized she wished very much she could relive those few moments of his kiss.

Around Cole she couldn't seem to think straight; in his absence, surely she could see things as they really were. The answer she came to was simple. Ever since she first visited Cole at West Point, she had alternately blamed him and then herself for the turmoil he had let loose in her, but the time was past for blame. The truth was she wanted to get to know him better and let the future take care of itself. Throughout her early nomadic life she had never been able to plan on anything. Why should she start now?

So deep in thought was she that she failed to hear Justin's irregular walk on the garden pathway.

"Erin, are you all right?" he asked softly.

His voice startled her from her reverie, and momentarily mistaking him for his brother, she felt a rush of warmth that was soon replaced by disappointment.

"I'm fine," she said. "Just a little worried that Cole hasn't returned."

"Mother feels the same way. Why don't you join us in the parlor for a glass of sherry while we wait? He's probably run into some old friends he hasn't seen in a long time. I'm sure he'll be here soon."

Of course Justin was right. Cole hadn't been able to see anyone on his last trip home; he was probably in some tavern discussing old times. She readily complied and led the way inside to join Fiona. As the three were about to sit down, a knock sounded at the front door; Lizette responded, and they heard deep voices, some commotion, and then heavy footsteps coming down the hall.

Cole entered first and even before she saw the grim-faced man behind him, Erin knew from the worried look in his eyes that something was very wrong.

She went quickly to his side and, taking his hand in hers, brushed his cheek with her lips. It was, after all, the natural thing for a bride-to-be to do. "I'm glad you're back," she said softly.

"Don't be too sure, love." He stepped inside and gestured to the red-faced, burly man behind him. "Erin, let me introduce Sheriff Walters." He glanced swiftly at his mother and Justin before looking down at her once

127

more. "I'm afraid I bring bad news. I found Turpin, all right, but my timing was a little off. Someone had been to the cabin before me and relieved the late colonel of both the money and his life."

He squeezed her hand. "The sheriff, I'm afraid, thinks that someone might be me."

Chapter Eight

Justin's voice exploded into the stillness of the parlor.
"That must be the dumbest damn thing you've ever
done, Sheriff. Accusing my brother of murder. Cole?
There's not a more honorable man in the state of
Virginia."

Sheriff Walters stepped past Cole to face Justin.
"Now, now, uh, Mr. Barrett, is it?" He twisted a derby
hat between his hairy hands. "I haven't accused anyone
of anything. I'm just gatherin' the facts the way I'm paid
to do."

"You're also paid to analyze them before drawing any
conclusions. Don't forget that part of your job."

Cole looked at his younger brother in pleased surprise.
Not very long ago Justin would never have spoken up
that way, especially to someone as boorishly officious as
the sheriff. Justin was definitely ready to proceed with
the plan the two brothers had already discussed.

It was his mother, frozen in silence, who concerned
him. He had long known—and hated—that she and
Hilmer Turpin were much more than just friends. He had
allowed that knowledge to drive him further from her. As
he looked now at the vulnerable, aging figure sitting
alone, he let her past indiscretions fade from his mind

and he hoped the colonel's death would not hit her too hard.

But with Sheriff Walters looking on, now was not the time for mending breaches in the family. The less Walters knew about Fiona Barrett and the colonel, the better.

"Are you all right, Mother?" he asked.

"Of course," she said, her voice lined with bitterness. Her eyes warned him to say no more.

The momentary warmth he'd felt toward her died, and he turned his attention to the woman still holding tightly to his hand. Erin looked up at him, and her sweet red lips weakly attempted a smile. Fine wisps of hair formed a soft, golden red frame for her face. His breath caught. With her amber eyes deep and dark with worry, Erin was more beautiful than he had ever seen her. As soon as he had her alone, he would cover those eyes and lips with kisses that would banish all her cares.

Reluctantly, he pulled his eyes away. He would have liked to keep her out of the mess he found himself in, but unfortunately she was very much involved. He introduced her and his family to Walters, then added, "Sheriff, please come in and sit down."

"Yes, Sheriff, do join us." Fiona gestured toward a nearby chair. "We were about to have some sherry. May I pour you a glass?"

Cole looked sharply at her. Fiona had made a remarkable recovery from her grief, managing to haul out her aristocratic manners and address the sheriff in her most gracious, antebellum voice. The only thing lacking in her was sincerity.

Cole knew what the crafty old woman was up to; she wanted to make the sheriff feel as out of place as possible. At best Sheriff Walters was an unwelcome intruder in her home, an old-time Southern boy who had managed to better himself in the dark days of Reconstruction, yet

130

Fiona Barrett, who had lately played the role of faded aristocrat, could easily put him in his place.

The strategy worked, for Walters muttered an uncomfortable no.

"At least sit down, Sheriff," Cole said.

"Prefer to stand, if you don't mind, Cap'n. Don't plan to stay long. Just need to ask the little lady a few questions about the money you say is missin'."

Erin's eyes flashed golden fire. "Are you referring to me, Sheriff? The name is Miss Donovan, if you will recall. And I agree with Justin. You'll never solve this case if you think Cole could in any way be part of a murder."

Sheriff Walters looked around at the hostile assembly. "Now folks," he said, lifting one hand, "I never said that. I'm just here to find out where Captain Barrett has been during the past few days. Hard to tell when the colonel was killed, but from the smell—pardon my language, ladies—it wasn't today."

"I'll have that glass of sherry now," Fiona said. "Anyone else?" When the rest declined, she poured herself a drink and downed it quickly. Her hand had barely shaken, but Cole knew from the whiteness around his mother's lips that she was not nearly as calm as she had appeared earlier.

Erin must have sensed it too, for she took a small step toward the settee. Cole held her back, and when she looked up at him, a question in her eyes, he shook his head almost imperceptibly.

She smiled in understanding. No matter what had been Fiona's relationship with the late colonel, the sheriff was not to know. Resting a hand on Cole's arm, she directed her attention to him. "What makes you think the money was stolen, Cole? Couldn't he have hidden it somewhere?"

"I thought of that, but there were signs of a struggle,

131

and under his body was an empty money bag. From your bank in New York."

"I see." She turned to the sheriff. "I suppose you would like to know my part in all of this."

Under her direct gaze, Walters shuffled nervously. "Yes, Miss Donovan, I would."

"I have nothing to hide," she said firmly, then proceeded to tell him her story, making only vague references to "the poor" that she and Turpin had planned to help.

"And, Sheriff," she concluded, "if you want to know where Cole has been for the past few days, he's been with me." She cut off the sheriff's question before he could ask it. "Riding down from New York on a train."

"Beggin' your pardon, Miss Donovan, but ain't you and the cap'n engaged to be wed? Seems to me he said something about that when we were riding in."

Cole interrupted. "And what has that got to do with this matter, Walters?"

The sheriff rubbed his bristled face. "Those trains make a lot of stops, Cap'n. You could 'a hired a horse at one of 'em after you entered Virginny, gone cross country out to the colonel's place, and caught up with the little lady farther on down the line."

Erin gave an exasperated yelp. "The *little lady* was with him all the time, Sheriff."

"So you say, Miss Donovan. But then you're smitten with the captain. It's likely you'd say most anything to clear his name. Especially since it was your money he was trying to get back."

"And just why would I have gone back today?" Cole asked.

"To be sure you didn't leave nothing incriminatin' behind."

For the first time since he had discovered the body, Cole lost control of his anger. "Prove it," he snapped.

"What's that you say?" the sheriff asked.

"Prove it." He put his arm around Erin's shoulders. "I have a witness who says I was nowhere near the colonel's cabin when he was killed. You find someone who says I was."

"Well, I just might do that," Walters blustered. "In the meantime, don't leave town. Now if you folks will excuse me, I have an unpleasant task to perform. The colonel's widow has to be told." With a quick nod to Fiona Barrett, he crammed his hat back on his balding head. "I'll find my own way out."

In the stillness following his departure, Cole tightened his hold on Erin. "He can't do it, of course," he said. "I'm sorry he feels compelled to try. In the meantime he's letting the real culprit get away."

He looked at his mother. "You handled the sheriff very well. Now tell me the truth. Are you really all right?"

"Of course I'm all right," she snapped. "I wasn't about to let that old fool"—she gestured in the direction of the departing Walters—"think any different."

"Colonel Turpin—" he began.

"Is dead." Fiona stared out the window in the direction of the Turpin home. "Now that spineless wife of his has joined me in widowhood. May she find it a loveless state as I have done."

Cole looked helplessly at her. He had been about to suggest she go next door to console Mrs. Turpin, but Fiona had wrapped herself too tightly in a blanket of selfish and bitter recrimination to be of help to anyone else. When had it ever been any different? Years of rancor and misunderstanding stretched between them, and he knew there was nothing he could do to wash them away. As long as he could remember, she had held him away from her; she would do so until she drew her final breath.

It was Justin who deserved his sympathy and help, Justin who must remain in Virginia and mend the tattered remains of the family name. But his younger brother had grown strong, and Cole knew he could stand up to Fiona now. The plans Cole had made for his family's care would be put into Justin's capable hands tomorrow.

"Brother," Cole said, "how about a drink? But none of Mother's sherry. We both need something stronger. Any whiskey in the house?"

Justin nodded. "I'll get it."

He returned shortly with two half-filled tumblers. "Corn whiskey," he explained. "Picked it up when I was out in the country. Some of Virginia's finest, I was promised." He grinned at his older brother. "Unless, of course, you have some objection to imbibing from a bottle that never wore a government stamp."

"Not in the least. After dealing with the good sheriff, I'm not too particular about following the letter of the law." He took a swallow, then expelled a hearty breath. "Prime stuff here, Justin. Must have been aged at least a month."

Erin sat down next to Fiona and looked at the two men in disgust. "One would think neither of you had a care in the world."

Cole turned his gray eyes to rest on her face. "Oh, but I do, love. We need to talk."

"That's our signal, Mother," Justin said. "It's time we left Cole and his fiancée alone. He can tell us more in the morning about what happened." He gave Fiona no time to protest. Taking her arm, he helped her to her feet and maneuvered her out the door.

When they were gone, Cole stood wearily for a moment, running his fingers through an unruly shock of dark hair that fell across his forehead. He had proven a damned poor detective. Maybe he shouldn't have put on civilian clothes and gone racing across the county like some fool knight to the rescue; maybe he should have pinned every medal he'd ever worn to the coat of his uniform and gone to the authorities for their help. But that wasn't what Erin had asked him to do. Standing brave and beautiful in his office, she had made helping her seem like a matter of honor; there was no way he could have refused.

"Cole." Her voice drifted softly across the parlor. "Are you all right?"

All right? He'd spent the morning seeking out a cabin in the midst of a tangled woods only to find the decaying corpse of a man he'd known since childhood. Then he'd been accused of murder by a thick-headed country sheriff who'd had the blind luck to be riding by. At least it had seemed blind luck. The sheriff had been evasive about that.

And yet, as he looked down at Erin, her amber eyes dark and round, her woman's curves beckoning him, he knew that nothing was really wrong, nothing that a sweet while spent with her couldn't wash away. It had been a long time since he had found consolation in a woman's arms—even longer since any woman had stirred more than just his need for physical release.

Briefly, the image of Rachel Cox flashed before his inner vision. He would never forget his helplessness when he'd stood over her body, nor his rage at the heathen devils who had killed her. He'd made a lot of them pay for Rachel's death, but the Comanche blood he'd spilled had not yet washed away the pain.

Until Erin. Beautiful, impetuous redhead that she was, could she help smooth the raw edges of the memories that haunted him? Rachel faded from his mind, replaced by the picture of Erin standing in his office and asking for his help. Just as he had wanted to rid the West of marauding Indians, she wanted to use her money to help the poor and homeless. That's what she'd told him. Her

135

aim was the same as his—to make the world a better place in which to live. They were just going about it differently.

With a sudden urge to comfort her as well as be comforted, Cole moved to the settee and took Erin's hands in his. "I'm sorry I couldn't help you more. If Walters spends too much time on his foolish pursuit of witnesses, I'm afraid your money is lost to you."

"Hang the money. Is there any chance he might find someone who would lie and say he saw you riding about the countryside?"

Cole lifted one hand and lightly traced Erin's lips. "I made a few enemies when I didn't come back to fight for the South, but I've made my peace with most of them." He felt her tremble beneath his fingers. Bending his head closer to hers, he placed light kisses on the closed lids of her eyes.

"What are you doing?" she whispered.

"What I wanted to do when I first came in." His lips touched at the corners of her mouth. "To kiss away your look of worry."

"I . . . I thought you wanted to talk."

His lips hovered over hers, their breath intermingling. "We have. Enough, I think, for now." He cupped her face in his hands. How sweetly she looked up at him, the warm beginnings of desire in her eyes. He'd like to kiss that tender gaze into a consuming fire. Calling up a tortuous control that surprised him, he kept himself from ravaging her and settled for a light touch of his lips, more air than substance. The tip of his tongue outlined her parted lips, then slipped inside to touch the tip of her tongue. She shuddered beneath his hands.

Sweet surrender. He could feel it as his arms embraced her and she seemed to melt against his chest. With simple gestures she drove him wild. Erin. The name rang in his head. She was all he could think about and everything he desired.

His kiss deepened, probing and savoring her, demanding a response she willingly gave. Her hands moved seductively across his shoulders and down his back as far as she could reach.

Cole lightened his hold on her and moved one hand to play with the high collar of her gown, knowing he mustn't give in to his instincts to tear the garment from her body, to stroke the soft, smooth skin and the rounded breasts held captive beneath its folds. God, how he wanted to explore her body, to feel her dark, velvet sweetness enfold him. His palm moved down from her throat in gently massaging motions, and he felt her fullness swell and harden beneath his touch. She wanted him as much as he wanted her.

He forced his lips from hers. "Come to my room," he whispered into her ear. "Now."

He felt her grow still beneath his touch.

"Erin." He held her gently, waiting for her answer.

"I can't," she said at last.

Slowly he turned her face up to his, and saw a myriad of emotions play across her features. Conflicting thoughts were mirrored in her eyes—desire and doubt and the dark hint of something closely resembling fear. Erin afraid? It seemed impossible. Not the bold, impetuous redhead who had sought him out time and time again. No innocent, shy violet had pressed herself into his arms, but a vibrant, passionate flower of a woman.

And she was not playing some kind of coy game. That wasn't her way either. He pulled her to him and let her rest her head against his chest. She had suffered several shocks tonight—his near arrest and the probable loss of her money. For all he knew, that was all the money she had in the world, despite her prosperous appearance, and he was nothing less than a boor to expect her to forget her problems so quickly in his embrace.

His mind raced on, willing his body to settle for the time they had already spent together. He wasn't a saint. If he held her much longer this way, he wouldn't ask her to come to his room. The rug beneath their feet would serve just as well as a mattress for their lovemaking.

He pulled away from her. "Later, then," he said, "if not tonight. We've got some good times ahead of us, Erin. I may not have recovered your money for you, but there are other things I can do. And I promise, you won't be disappointed."

Two days later, her body exhausted from the hastily arranged train ride up from Richmond, Erin sat with Cole in a noisy Washington restaurant and remembered his words. He had told her she would not be disappointed in his lovemaking. If his kisses were any indication, she couldn't imagine that she would be; if something ever did happen between them, it would be nothing less than wonderful.

Whatever that something might be . . . Certainly Erin knew what went on between a man and a woman, but she was woefully ignorant on the finer points. She couldn't have gone to his room in Richmond, not with his family in the house—she and Cole weren't, after all, engaged— but it had been silly to let his seductive plea frighten her so. And it had been unlike her. Why the fright?

Yet, even as she asked the question, she knew the answer. The strong emotions he'd aroused in her had terrified her. Under the throes of such feelings, there was no telling what she might do.

She felt Cole's eyes on her, and her cheeks reddened. Thank goodness he couldn't read her mind.

"What time is your Uncle Thaddeus supposed to meet us?" she asked.

"It shouldn't be very long." He reached over to touch

her hand resting on the table. "I hope the train ride didn't tire you too much."

She smiled at him. "Not at all."

"Good. And don't worry about your belongings. I sent them ahead to the hotel where I usually stay when I'm in Washington. They'll be perfectly safe."

Erin nodded gratefully. Except for the clothes on her back, all the earthly possessions she had with her were in those bags. But she had known Cole would take care of them for her. Cole was taking care of everything. Erin was filled with pride at being escorted by him. She glanced around the room. Cole was clearly the best-looking man in sight, and his uniform enhanced his lean, masculine strength. Weren't several women trying to catch his eye? As far as she could tell, he had thus far failed to return their interest. If they had any idea what his kisses were like, she would have to beat them off with a whip.

How strange it was that the formidable Captain Barrett had made her forget to hate the uniform he wore and the injustices it represented to her. Yet it was easy to look past the garments Cole wore and think only of the man underneath. He was a good man, but to her he was a great deal more than that. When she was around him, she waged a constant inner battle against her urges to caress him and kiss away the worries that lined his face. When they were apart, he filled her mind and her heart with longing.

Of course Sheriff Walters had been unable to turn up any evidence of Cole's involvement in murder and theft. It would be simpler if Cole were content to let the matter rest. But to him settling it was a matter of honor and pride. He wanted no shadows hanging over his head, and he was determined to find out what had happened to her money.

That was where Thaddeus Lymond came in. Cole suspected the federal authorities might be interested in the murder. After all, Turpin had brought stolen money from New York to Virginia. Maybe wiser heads could help the bumbling sheriff.

Unfortunately the trip had raised a serious problem for Erin. Her money was almost gone. She didn't know exactly how long it would take to transfer funds from her Dallas bank, and she hadn't had an opportunity to find out. Besides, wiring for more money would necessitate explaining her predicament. Hud would find out, and he'd never let her forget how foolish she'd been.

Cole had been paying their train fares and food bills, with Erin standing by and keeping a mental account, promising herself all the while to pay him back with her recovered funds. But now it was becoming obvious the entire sum of four thousand dollars was lost, and her hotel bill was looming, as was the cost of the trip back to Texas. It was for just such emergencies, Erin thought, that poker had been invented. Somehow she had to get into a game.

"Would you like to go ahead and order?" Cole asked. "The waiter has already brought us the bill of fare."

"I'll let you select something for me," she replied. "When your uncle gets here."

The wait was short. Erin knew Thaddeus Lymond even before he reached their table and was introduced. Broad, bearded, and powerful, Cole had said. He wasn't a handsome man, but he managed to turn heads as he walked confidently through the restaurant, nodding to the other patrons. Power. She could feel it across the room. Automatically he commanded attention; in that respect, he reminded her of Hud.

She soon found out how outspoken he was.

"Cole," he said, settling into a chair across from his nephew and giving Erin an appraising look, "at last you are introducing me to a real woman. She's everything you said she was."

Cole smiled wryly. "Thanks, Uncle Thad. Keep up that kind of talk and I'll have a lot of explaining to do."

Thad ignored him and directed his attention toward Erin. "Miss Donovan, Cole tells me you're from Texas."

Erin nodded. "Don't you have any comment about how dangerous it must be to live out there?"

"No, I don't. It's a big place and destined to be a great one. Lots of opportunities there for fortunes to be made. Cole is already working on his."

The captain is full of surprises, Erin thought.

"I made some investments when I was in Texas," Cole explained as the waiter came up to take their orders.

While they waited for their food to arrive, Thad brought up the subject of Fiona.

"Think Justin will be able to handle everything down there?"

Cole nodded. "Thanks to your help. The deal went through without any problems." He turned to Erin. "Uncle Thad discovered the old family plantation a few miles out of Richmond was going on the auction block for back taxes."

"And you bought it?" Erin asked.

"Not exactly. I haven't made my fortune yet. But with Uncle Thad's help I came up with enough for a payment. Justin will complete the deal with income from the crops he hopes to grow." He paused. "And believe me, Justin's physical condition won't hinder him in the least. I've watched him walk those furrows with less trouble than he'd have on a Richmond street. He always was more at home in the country."

"And your mother?"

A look of determination settled on Cole's face. "She needs to be out of the city as much as Justin does. She'll be too busy restoring the old homestead to indulge in self-pity. It won't be easy, but there are plenty of men around, both white and black, looking for jobs. Already Justin has come up with several ideas for sharing profits in return for their labor."

Erin smiled in admiration. "You seem to have taken care of everything with great efficiency."

"I'd like to take the credit, Erin, but Uncle Thad had the idea and Justin will do the work. Besides," he said, his voice tinged with regret, "not everything was settled. There is still the small matter of fraud and murder to consider."

Briefly he explained to Thad the events of the past few days, and Erin was pleased to see his uncle listen carefully, ask a few questions, and then write notes on a piece of paper he pulled from his pocket.

"This sheriff sounds like a fool," he said when Cole was done. "I'll see about getting an investigation started. Just put it out of your mind."

He turned to Erin. "You asked if I thought Texas was dangerous. Well, you've got your Indians on the warpath and stage holdups, but that kind of thievery and death dealing seems somehow more honest than the colonel's machinations." He smiled warmly. "All you wanted to do was help the poor. He did much more than rob you of your money. He robbed you of your dreams."

The surging anger brought on by Lymond's mention of Indians was blunted by the rest of his words. Erin knew if she explained to him the red man's true plight, he would understand. And, surely, so would Cole.

But just then a waiter arrived, and the opportunity for serious talk was lost.

"Erin," Thad said, "I think you're a little overdue for a party." He requested champagne for the three of them and throughout the meal their glasses were seldom empty. By the time they were headed for the door after the festive dinner, Erin was lightheaded and without care. Everything had worked out for the best, she decided. She could probably find a game of twenty-one going on somewhere in the hotel where their bags had been sent.

As they stood on the walkway in front of the restaurant, Thad pulled a packet of papers from his coat.

"Cole, here is some information on investments you might want to look into when you're in Texas. As long as you insist on going." He smiled at Erin. "Not that I don't understand your eagerness now. You've got stronger reasons for moving out West than I can come up with for keeping you here."

Erin patted his hand flirtatiously. "Are you sure you don't have a touch of Irish in you?"

"I speak nothing more than what any fool can see, Erin. You make me sorry I'm no longer young."

"You're not old either." She brushed a kiss against his cheek. "Just mature."

Thad's eyes softened. "You remind me of a young woman I knew a long time ago. I haven't thought of those days in quite a while." He turned to Cole. "Take care of her, my boy. You've got a treasure here."

Cole's arm went around her shoulders. "I intend to take very good care of her, Uncle Thad. You have my word on that." Then, with a quick promise to get in touch with his uncle the next day, he helped Erin into the carriage he had summoned to take them to the Willard Hotel.

As they moved into the flow of evening traffic, Erin settled restlessly into the seat. The combination of cool night air and champagne was definitely having an effect on her. If she managed to find a game at the hotel, she wasn't sure the spots on the cards would be clear.

But she wasn't so inebriated that she couldn't worry about that last exchange between Cole and his uncle. What had they meant about seeing that she was taken care of? And what must Thaddeus Lymond think of her for riding off into the night, unescorted, with his nephew, their destination a downtown Washington hotel?

When she tried to ask Cole, he put an arm around her and pulled her close, nestling his face close to hers. "Don't worry, love, about what my uncle thinks. You made a friend of him." His lips brushed against her ear. "And he's not easy to please."

Erin took a deep breath. Saints above, Cole's presence caused more dizziness than the wine. With great force of will, she pulled away. Not so far that she couldn't touch him, but far enough so that she couldn't feel his warm breath on her neck. There was only so much, after all, that she could stand.

She cleared her throat. "Cole, we need to talk about my room at the hotel."

Under the passing street lights she could see the smile on his face—a warm, seductive smile that made Erin's heart quicken.

"All right," he said. "What did you have in mind?"

She forced the answer out. "A room of my own, of course." His smile died, but Erin bravely kept on. "But I can't keep borrowing money from you to pay for it. I was hoping you could find a poker game for me."

"That's the dumbest thing I have ever heard of."

Stung by his words, Erin responded angrily. "And what is so dumb about it?"

"Several things. I'm sure you could find a game, all right, but with the way you look, even in that traveling dress, there's no telling what I would have to do to protect you." He stroked her silk-covered arm. "And I don't feel like shooting anyone. Not tonight."

She jerked away. "I'm not asking you to. I can take care of myself. A lot of tough men in Texas have tried to, well, get my interest, and they lived to regret it. The only thing I want to do is find out where the cards are being dealt. I'll take care of the rest."

"It's been my experience that you don't always win."

The rat! And she had thought him a gentleman.

"If you insist on bringing up the distant past, I used to lose sometimes. But not anymore."

Again he was smiling. "Then let's play again. Just the two of us. For the cost of your room. If you're good enough, you might even earn your way to Texas." His fingers played in the curls above her ear. "And I have no doubt you'll be good enough."

What was he talking about? Of course she was good enough. She pushed away his hand. His touch was definitely distracting, and tonight she would have to concentrate on the cards.

"I accept," she said, assuring herself that she would make certain Thaddeus Lymond found out she and Cole had not shared a bed. "Where do we play?"

"We'll take one room to begin with. After the, uh, game, if you want a room of your own, you can have it."

"I'm not sure that's such a good idea."

"You can trust me. I'll only do what you want me to do. I promise."

He sounded sincere enough—and just a little smug. Nothing would please her more than beating him, but as she accepted his terms, she hoped that Uncle Thad's champagne hadn't muddled her judgment. Cards. That was all she had agreed to. In the privacy of a hotel room, she would have to remember that she just wanted Cole to lose money to her.

Chapter Nine

When they arrived at the hotel, Erin waited in the shadows of a large potted palm while Cole registered at the desk. Their entrance into the crowded lobby had attracted far too much attention to suit her. She had pictured slipping upstairs unobtrusively; she had pictured wrong. Walking in on Cole's arm had had the effect of a brass band. Like his Uncle Thad, he attracted attention wherever he went.

She thought of Marcia Smythe-Williams's instructions on comportment for young ladies. They had been wasted lessons. Once again Erin felt herself slipping into a difficult situation. It had seemed the logical thing to do when she'd left Richmond to come to Washington instead of heading directly home, but in the crowded lobby she couldn't remember what her reasoning had been.

Cole returned before she could decide whether or not to call the whole thing off.

"That was awfully fast," she said.

"Well, I already had made arrangements for a room where our bags could be stored," he said, guiding her to a winding staircase behind her. "I just needed to pick up the key."

"Only one room?" she asked as they made their way to the second floor.

"We can take care of other arrangements later." They came to a halt at a room halfway down the corridor.

They certainly would take care of other arrangements, Erin thought as she let him escort her into the room. She had never given him any reason to suppose otherwise. Surely Cole realized a few ardent kisses were no proof she would spend the night with him.

As soon as he turned up one of the lamps, Erin knew she was wrong. On a dresser to her left was a large bouquet of fresh flowers; beside it was a bucket containing a bottle of champagne. Directly in her path was the bed; the covers had already been turned down.

"Were you expecting company?" She wondered how honest his answer would be.

He shook his head. "Not exactly. Would you care for a glass of champagne before we begin?"

So he was using evasive tactics, was he? She'd have to be on her guard.

"No champagne, thank you. That's the last thing I need." Erin put more distance between them. "I'll get the cards. Have you any idea where they put my bags?"

He gestured toward a large wardrobe in the corner. "This is a very efficient hotel. I assume the help has already unpacked our clothes."

Erin drummed her fingers against her skirt. No matter how entranced she was by Cole, he had not rendered her completely stupid. Not yet, at least. He had no doubt sent very specific instructions to the hotel, covering everything right down to the last petal in the flower vase. Not that he hadn't made overtures to her before, sweet teasing touches that she had been hard put to resist. But those times had come upon them both unexpectedly. It was one thing to be carried away by the passion of the moment and quite another to have her seduction plotted out. She could hardly wait to begin dealing.

He opened a drawer in the dresser. "Here are the cards. I'm afraid there is no table available. Would you mind playing on the bed?"

She took a deep breath to fortify herself. "Not at all. I can beat you there as well as anywhere."

"If that's what you want, although it's not anything I've ever tried before."

Erin got the distinct impression he wasn't talking about cards. Sex, no doubt, was lurking somewhere in his words. But she had his promise to do only what she wanted, and foolish though it might seem, she trusted him to keep his word.

She sat down on the edge of the bed, careful to keep her feet on the floor. "Shall we begin?"

"Certainly." He untied the scarf at his neck. "Would you mind if I take off my coat?"

"Of course not," she lied and concentrated on shuffling the cards until he was seated beside her. She looked up into a pair of warm gray eyes, and her gaze dropped instantly to his lips, then down to the white undershirt that stretched across his shoulders and chest. For a moment her eyes settled on the corded muscles of his arms. Strong arms that had enfolded her. Damn. There was no place safe to look.

"What game do you want to play?" he asked in a low voice.

She cleared her throat. "Twenty-one."

"All right." He reached into his pocket and pulled out a gold coin. "Here's my ante. Where's yours?"

"Well, I certainly can't match that, although I do have a little cash with me. You have to promise to play fair to yourself, too, and not throw away good money."

"You have my word. May I suggest something I would value very much?" She nodded. "The pins in your hair."

She stared at him incredulously. "And you called me

148

dumb. You could buy a thousand pins with that gold piece."

"But you wouldn't have worn them. Believe me, I'm being fair."

He was smooth—she had to give him credit for that. He was willing to risk a gold piece just to see her hair down. Well, she would have to win and use the coin as her next ante. That way, he couldn't make any more personal demands.

"All right," Erin agreed. "Let's cut for deal."

"Put your ante on the bed first."

Erin attempted a casual shrug of agreement, but her hands were shaking as she lifted them to undo her hair. His eyes never left her as she worked. Her hair was thick and long; it had taken her a long while to work it into the complicated knot atop her head. The undoing was much faster, and within seconds a mass of red curls tumbled onto her shoulders and down her back. She shook her head; it felt good to have her hair hang loose once more.

She tossed the pins onto the bed, but Cole, ignoring them, reached out and wound a curl around his finger. "I've never seen anything quite so beautiful. Like sunrise."

Erin reached up to brush him away, and their fingers touched, igniting unbidden, fiery thoughts of what his hands might do if she allowed them to roam. Confused that she could think such things, she pulled away.

The game—that was the important thing to remember. She reached for the stack of cards and cut the queen of hearts. When Cole turned over the ace of spades, she forced herself to look him boldly in the eye. "I hope my ante was worth what it's going to cost you. You cut high. Deal."

Two cards, a ten showing and underneath a five. Cole had dealt himself a jack. Instinct told her to hold, and she did.

"What's your bet, Erin?"

She smiled sweetly. "How about a shoe?" She could be just as silly as he.

"Make it two shoes," he said, tossing out another coin. "What are you holding?" She flipped over her card. "Too bad," he said, displaying a nine to go with his jack. "I beat you by four."

So much for instinct. No doubt it was the champagne. Erin would have to play the odds.

The odds were against her. In the succeeding hands she lost her stockings—discreetly removed while Cole's back was turned—and a velvet ribbon she'd worn around her neck. In a short while the room seemed hot and stuffy.

"I'll have that champagne after all," she said.

"Of course."

The wine seemed to help at first, and she quickly won back her shoes and one stocking. Then the cards turned on her, and she lost them again. She looked at Cole's face, his full lips and wide, warm eyes, and the shock of black hair that fell across his forehead. It was very difficult for her to regret that he had won.

With trembling hands, she tried to straighten the cards, but they scattered about the bed. She couldn't seem to perform the simple task. When she reached out to gather them, Cole's hands covered hers.

"You need to ante again, Erin." His soft deep voice enveloped her.

"With what?" she whispered.

"A kiss."

Their eyes locked. It must be the champagne, Erin told herself, else why did she think it a reasonable request? Slowly she nodded. He pushed the cards aside and slid closer beside her on the bed. Closing her eyes, she raised her lips and waited for the sweet touch she remembered so well.

At first she felt only his fingers tracing the edges of her face, and then the outline of her mouth. She started trembling. She couldn't help it. Her entire body seemed to be responding to his light touch, just as it had in the parlor at Richmond. The night he'd asked her to his room; the night she'd almost said yes.

And here she was sitting on his hotel bed. She opened her eyes just in time to see his slightly parted lips descending on hers, and any protest she might have made was lost and forgotten. His arms encircled her, and she melted against him; when his tongue touched her lips and slipped inside, she savored the invasion in wondrous surprise.

Her hands pressed against his chest, not to push him away, but to feel the hard wall of muscle underneath his shirt. She felt his body tighten, but ignorant as to what he might like, she could only go on instinct. And instinct told her to work her fingers across his chest and around the flat nipples she could feel through the thin cotton weave. Under her touch she felt them harden.

Cole's kiss deepened, and Erin felt she was drowning in a bath of fiery desire. Every part of her burned. Especially the strangely moist valley between her thighs.

His lips moved to her throat, and she felt his fingers work at the buttons of her dress.

"One kiss," she whispered. "You said one kiss."

His breath warmed the side of her neck. "Do you want me to stop?"

Stop? How could she say yes? Erin had been looking for him ever since she'd met him in Dallas. And not to repay a debt. Without realizing it, she had fallen in love with him; every time she had sought him out, it had been for that same reason. Why hadn't she realized it sooner? He was the one man she had been unable to handle, the only man she had ever wanted to please.

She couldn't think too clearly about how he might feel

about her. With his mouth pressed to her pulsating throat, she couldn't think at all. Her emotions were too powerful.

Her hands touched his face, and when he looked up, she touched her lips to his. He had tasted of her, and she wanted to do the same to him. Tentatively she rested the tip of her tongue against his mouth and gained entrance. He was darkly warm and moist. The tip of his tongue grazed hers. She felt his sharp intake of breath. Their lips parted, and with a low moan, he pressed her tightly to him, then back down against the bed. His body was taut over hers.

Erin's heart was beating wildly. "Oh, my sweet love," Cole whispered, and her whole being sang with happiness. Love. He had used the word. When he began to work at the buttons of her gown, she reveled in the sweet abandon of letting him do what he would. He wouldn't hurt her; he could never hurt her.

As his searching hands trailed down to her breasts, to caress what no man had ever touched before, she arched her back to urge him on. "Beautiful," he murmured. His eyes moved slowly up from her bared breasts to her eyes. "You're more beautiful than I ever imagined."

Bending his head, he brushed soft kisses against her throat, and then, in tortuous slow motion, his lips slid down to the hard, dark tips of her breasts. He teased her there with his tongue, making hot desire flow in her veins.

Everything seemed to be happening much too slowly, and at the same time much too fast. No sooner did he teach her one new delight than he moved on to the next. More, she cried silently, she wanted more of everything he had to give. The room was spinning around her, then fading from view. Only she and Cole existed.

With deft, sure hands he slipped the rest of her clothes from her body. Suddenly shy, she pulled at the covers of the bed to hide her nakedness. She wanted very much to please him, but what if, when he looked at her closely, he didn't like what he saw? What if he laughed at the pale hair that formed a golden triangle between her thighs?

"Something wrong, love?" His voice was low and husky.

"I . . ." She paused, not knowing what to say.

"Trust me." His hands began a gentle massage of her bare shoulders and his thumbs trailed across the pulse point of her throat.

How easy it was to do as he asked, and she didn't protest when he slowly began to pull the covers away from her body and let his eyes roam over her at will. Helpless, she closed her eyes, then opened them, fearful of seeing ridicule on his face but afraid not to know the truth. No laughter, just wild, raw hunger was in his eyes.

Under the searing heat of that look, Erin slipped over the bounds of rational thought. Guided by an instinct old as the earth and sky, she tugged his undershirt upward and ran her hands across his bare chest. He shuddered, then helped her slip the shirt from his body.

Erin's hands trailed down to his waist, and she began to work at the buckle of his trousers. When her fingers brushed against his hard fullness, she looked up at him in surprise.

Her body was soft and warm, waiting to join with his. She had not been prepared for the unyielding firmness awaiting her. What a wonder was a man's body, and touching him once again, she looked up with eyes that told him how she felt.

He caught his breath. "What did you expect, love?" Again that beautiful word. His voice was barely above a whisper. "I want you now, Erin. I can't wait much longer."

He lifted her hands and kissed each finger. "Let me." In fluid motions that hypnotized her, he stood beside the bed and undressed. Liquid pleasure poured through Erin's body as she looked at him. Her eyes moved down his chest, past the thickening black hair across his abdomen. The fullness that she had felt beneath his trousers had not prepared her for the unleashed man who slowly lay his body on top of her. She felt so small and inadequate to hold such a man.

He was incredibly light. She should have known he would be, and when he separated her thighs with his knee, she buried the fear that sprang from ignorance. Her legs parted; against her moist, waiting body, he was hard and hot.

He rose slightly and trailed one hand down her body until his fingers found within her secret folds of skin the tender-sweet bud of her desire. Slowly, gently, he massaged her, and Erin felt the first faint tremors of ecstasy.

The tremors grew, splintering her thoughts. Consumed by desire, she gave herself up to the glory of love. Pleasure and passion were hers; Cole was hers. She shuddered, in complete surrender, against him.

As she clung to him, she felt his body shift. "My turn, love," he whispered. Then his lips claimed hers, and she felt his hands slip down the sides of her body and under her buttocks to lift her closer to him. His breathing grew heavy and fast, and she felt a hard probing between her thighs.

Her virgin body resisted him, and when he pushed inside, she felt the shock of a new sensation—pain. She cried out.

"My God," he said, and raised his head. "What have I done to you?"

Anguish, not pleasure, was in his eyes. She was not pleasing him. But she must, she must. Pulling his head back down to hers, she kissed him, then ran her tongue around his lips. He had liked it before; surely he would like it now.

His hard body trembled beneath her touch. "Forgive me, Erin. I can't stop now."

Stop? Was that what he thought she wanted? In slow, undulating motions she moved her hips against him, and with a deep sigh, he picked up her movements, his becoming faster and faster. Gone was the pain, and in its place the same electric thrills as before. Only this time Cole was sharing them with her. How deliriously sweet was shared passion!

Her energy was as boundless as her desire, her ecstasy as great as his. With a frenzy unknown to her, she lifted her hips to match his probing thrusts. Cole filled her heart and soul as completely as he filled her body, and she clung to him in rapturous surrender as he took her with him over the edge of sanity.

Lost in the wonder of his lovemaking, she held him tightly in her embrace. She prayed the moment of fulfillment would last forever. Cole was the only thing that mattered in the universe. Love was all.

Gradually their breathing slowed, and they lay with legs and arms entwined. Sweet contentment was hers. If the world permitted, she could lie in his arms until the end of time.

Cole stirred and, lifting his head, looked down at her. She trailed her fingers through the tight, damp curls of black hair that pressed against his forehead. How wondrous are those curls, she thought, how perfect.

He started to speak but she stopped him with a kiss. Something was bothering him; she could see it in his eyes. Her heart tightened. For her it had been a night of wonder, and she couldn't let him mar that. If she had displeased him in some way, morning was soon enough to find it out.

"Tomorrow," she whispered. "We'll talk tomorrow."

He looked down at her for a long moment, then gently

turning her to her side, nestled her body in the curve of his. They slept.

Erin awakened to the harsh light of day. She was alone. Slowly she sat up and looked around. A half-filled bottle of champagne sat on the dresser beside a drooping bouquet of flowers. Cards and clothes lay scattered on the floor. Her clothes. Cole's were nowhere to be seen.

Panic seized her. Had she been deserted? The thought was painful, unbearable, as memories of shared rapture flashed through her mind. She was now a woman. Completely. She had better be prepared to take the pain as well as the pleasure that such a change must inevitably bring.

She could still feel Cole's lovemaking on her body. A small basin of water was on the dresser. Well, an inadequate bath was better than none. As she performed her ablutions, her eye fell on a folded piece of paper. Her name was on it; at least she could read that much. Well, he hadn't run out without leaving any word at all. A thank you, perhaps?

Stop it, she told herself. Bitter thoughts would do her no good. Twisting her hair into a simple knot, she quickly dressed. The doorknob turned just as she finished.

Cole walked into the room and smiled warmly at her. "Good morning, love."

Happiness flooded through her. After their night of love, she hadn't been deserted after all. Their night of love. The memory of the intimacies they had shared left her suddenly shy, and she couldn't look at him directly, couldn't even answer. He walked across the room and pulled her into his arms. "Haven't you forgiven me?" he asked.

She looked up into his eyes. "For what?"

"For hurting you. I'm sorry, Erin. If I had known, I would have been more gentle."

The meaning of his words was suddenly clear, and she

jerked out of his arms. "You thought that I—" She couldn't go on. Cole thought that she had let other men do what he had done. He had not realized what he was asking of her last night, nor what she had gladly given.

With a low cry he pulled her back to him. "I was wrong, Erin. Please forgive me. I've spent too long finding release with women I could walk away from. I was a fool to think you were that kind." He lifted her chin and smiled. "But you always responded so passionately that you drove me out of my mind. Around you, I've never been able to think clearly."

"Is there"—she had to know—"is there anything wrong with the way you made me feel?"

His smile warmed. "Can you ask me that after last night? Didn't you read my note?"

In confusion, she dropped her eyes. "I only wanted to know that I didn't disappoint you."

He shuddered against her. "No, love. You didn't disappoint me." He paused a moment. "I have a confession to make. I've never made love to a virgin before."

Erin put her arms around him. "Then last night was a first time for both of us." Compulsion drove her on. "I hope you have no regrets."

He tightened his hold. "Erin, you made me feel more like a man than any woman ever has. You made me see how empty my life has been." With one hand he lifted her chin and looked deep into her eyes. "That's why I left the note. I trust, love, that the answer to the question I wrote is yes."

She was afraid to answer him. Had he asked for more of what they had shared last night? Erin hadn't considered what the effects of giving herself to him might be; the sweet urgency of the moment had filled her thoughts.

Cole persisted. "You're not telling me no, are you?"

She was trapped by the look in his eyes. "I could never

do that."

He smiled in relief. "Good. I've already made all the arrangements."

She pulled away from him. "What kind of arrangements?"

He held out a packet of papers. "The train for Texas leaves tomorrow morning. Here are our tickets. And a special license as well." His fingers traced her face. "I can hardly wait to take you there as my wife."

Chapter Ten

The day was a whirlwind of activity for Erin, and she saw little of her husband-to-be. At Thaddeus Lymond's suggestion, she was put into the hands of a dowager friend of his, Mrs. Carlson Craven-Hix. Another double-named Easterner, Mrs. Craven-Hix was even more majestic than Marcia Smythe-Williams and she possessed a buxom figure that Erin found awe-inspiring.

The shopkeepers they visited were just as intimidated as Erin. Milliners, dressmakers, and cobblers were called upon to perform a miracle: to outfit in one day a bride who was on her way to the wilderness, a young woman who would not see civilization again for no one knew how long. Thaddeus Lymond was taking care of the bills. His name worked wonders.

Once she tried to tell Mrs. Craven-Hix about Sanger Brothers in Dallas, but the woman tut-tutted her remarks. No store that prospered by selling to barbarians could possibly be adequate for the wife of Captain Coleman Barrett. Erin's lone sartorial victory came when she adamantly refused to purchase a jacketed blue velvet riding habit complete with feathered hat. The cowhands on Hud's ranch would laugh her right off the range.

Her favorite purchase—a white bridal gown—came

late in the day. Made of fine Swiss muslin, it featured a square neck trimmed with Valenciennes lace, a narrow waist, and a soft-flowing skirt that moved easily with her as she walked. When she tried it on and twirled about the shop, she truly felt like a bride.

Even Mrs. Craven-Hix, looking down at her through a lorgnette, was given pause. "You'll make a lovely bride," she pronounced. "And after the wedding, you can use your needle to add some color to the neckline and waist. It will make a charming ballgown." Never having held a needle in her life, Erin could only nod.

After the purchase of that gown Erin began to think about what was to happen early the next day. She and Cole were to be married. She had lied so much about being engaged to him, it hardly seemed possible her story had come true, especially when the only formal proposal he had made had come in the form of a written note she couldn't read.

Earlier when Cole had made his startling pronouncement, she'd gone into a kind of shock. Thank goodness he had been too busy outlining the wedding and travel arrangements to notice. Only when the minister declared them man and wife would she believe that what she wanted more than anything else in the world was really hers. A lifetime of nights like last night.

Cole hadn't actually told her he loved her, but she was sure it was in the note. The much-folded piece of paper was tucked inside her pocket, and when they were miles away from Washington, she would ask him to read it to her. How sweet it would sound on his lips.

The wedding was scheduled for nine the next morning in a small chapel at Thaddeus Lymond's church. He had wanted to have the ceremony in the larger sanctuary, where presidents and senators worshipped; thank goodness Cole had listened to her pleas for something less grand. After all, except for Erin and Cole, only Uncle

Thad and Mrs. Craven-Hix would be present to stand up for them.

Because of their scheduled departure, there would not be time for a reception, a fact that relieved Erin greatly. Any formal occasion that Mrs. Craven-Hix had anything to do with would feature more forks and spoons than Erin could use in a lifetime. And she'd be the only one there unsure of which ones to use.

Once she almost asked her autocratic guide to let her send a few telegrams to Texas, but then she decided against it. She wanted personally to tell those dear to her that she was wed. The carefree girl they had teased for giving no man the time of day had fallen in love, and when they met Coleman Barrett, they would understand why she had changed.

Except for the bridal gown and a traveling suit, most of her purchases would be delivered directly to the train. Other than the cost of her trousseau, Cole was paying the bills, and Erin had insisted he get her a separate room for her last night in the capital. Propriety, she figured, was very important for the wife of an Army officer; besides, she had secretly vowed to change her bank account to his name and share with him all her wealth.

She didn't see him until the final meal of the day, but he seemed to have so much talking to do with his uncle that she didn't intrude. Sitting quietly and playing with her food, she kept stealing looks at him—at the boyishly dear way his dark hair fell across his forehead, at the sensuous lips and strong hands that could work such gentle miracles on her body. Occasionally he glanced her way; with only a soft look and a half-smile he could start her heart pounding. She would have him alone tomorrow. She could hardly wait.

He left her at the door to her room with a kiss and a whispered promise of what more he would do to her when next they were alone.

161

"Count yourself lucky to get off so lightly tonight," he said. "It's the last time I'll settle for just a taste of you."

Lucky? Didn't he know what his lovemaking did to her? If he didn't, she would have to be sure he found out posthaste.

Rain fell on Washington the day of the wedding, but Erin refused to let it worry her. She was going from carriage to church to railroad car anyway; it wasn't as if she were going to gallop about the countryside at the mercy of the elements. Nothing, absolutely nothing, was going to spoil this day for her.

When Uncle Thad—he insisted she call him that— escorted her down the aisle and she stood beside Cole, she could look at no one but him. He was dressed in the uniform that she had hated for so long, the uniform that symbolized for her the white man's treatment of the Indian. Sometime soon she would have to tell him of her heritage. Without a doubt, she and Cole could compromise on whatever differences lay between them, if for no other reason than that they loved each other.

She had spent much of the night arriving at that belief. Certainly she could understand his side. The Indians, with their nomadic way of life and their harsh codes of behavior, could never exist side by side as equals with the white man. But they were human beings and deserved to be treated as no less, certainly not like cattle herded around the range. That was something Cole must accept.

He might even encourage her to look among the surviving Comanche tribes for her grandparents. Her father had told her they were dead, but she knew he had only been guessing. Only half-listening to the preacher's intonations of love, honor, and obedience, Erin smiled happily. At last her life was beginning to have form and substance. The restlessness which had been a part of her past for so long was no more, and with great hope for the future, she said, "I do."

Cole's kiss was long, deep, and most ungentlemanly. Shaken by it, in a small room beside the chapel, Erin changed into her traveling suit and joined her husband in a closed carriage for the short ride to the station. Uncle Thad had insisted he and Mrs. Craven-Hix follow them in a separate vehicle. That was all right with Erin. She wanted to return her husband's kiss.

They arrived breathless and more disheveled than when they'd left the church, but no one seemed to notice. Uncle Thad greeted them with his wedding surprise.

"Throw away those first-class tickets, Cole. You and your bride are not spending your honeymoon in a coach." He gestured toward the back of the train and his broad face broke into a smile. "While you were taking care of your business yesterday, I did a little arranging of my own."

The station platform was crowded—Erin decided the entire city of Washington must be either arriving or leaving on this particular train—and following Uncle Thad they wended their way past a half-dozen passenger cars before coming to a stop.

Thaddeus indicated the car which would carry them on their journey. White trimmed in gold. A little gaudy, perhaps, Erin thought, but then what did she know. A black man in a crisp white jacket bowed.

"This is Randolph," Thaddeus said. "He'll travel with you to Mobile. If there's anything you want, just ask him."

Cole grinned. "A private car? When did you get one of these, you old rake?"

"It's not mine, actually. I just called in a few old debts. Around Washington, Cole, people live and prosper by the favors owed them. The car is yours as far as Alabama, but there you'll have to change trains for the journey into Texas. I tried to route you through New Orleans, but unfortunately there's a yellow fever epidemic down there

163

right now. It was brought up from Havana, I'm told, and the whole city's quarantined."

"Is the yellow fever in Texas?" Erin asked.

"It doesn't seem to be heading that way." Uncle Thad squeezed her hand. "So don't be worried about it. Don't let anything or anyone spoil your honeymoon, Erin."

His admonition left Erin suddenly shy. "I won't," she managed. "And Uncle Thad, thanks for the gift—and for everything." She kissed him on the cheek.

"Better get your bride on board, Cole, or I'll be keeping her for myself." Thaddeus paused a moment. "I'd like a word with you, son, before you leave."

A private word. Erin understood, and with a good-bye to Mrs. Craven-Hix, she allowed Randolph to help her up the steps. She stepped into a world of velvet cushions and paneled walls with carved inlays of leaves and vines. Like the outside of the car, the interior was white and gold. It looked like one of the Fort Worth houses where fancy women plied their trade—or at least the way she supposed such a place looked.

The plate glass windows were open to the morning air, and the voices of Cole and his uncle drifted in.

"Now, Cole, when you get out to Texas, don't be doing anything foolish. You have a wife to take care of now, and if I'm any judge, in about a year you'll have a son or a daughter."

"You don't have to remind me of my responsibilities, Uncle Thad. I won't let anything happen to Erin."

A responsibility? Was that how he viewed her? It wasn't exactly an insult, but neither was it very loving. Hud might say something like that, but it wasn't what she wanted to hear from her husband.

Uncle Thad's voice sharpened. "I'm not talking about Erin, Cole. I know you'll do right by her. I was referring to you. Don't let your hatred of the Indians lead you into

164

anything reckless just so you can kill a few more of them. Surely with that beautiful young bride of yours waiting for you, revenge should be the last thing on your mind. Bury the dead, Cole. Rejoice in the living."

Cole's answer was lost in the whistle of the train, but Erin had heard more than enough to kill the joy in her heart. Her legs trembled beneath her and she dropped into the nearest chair. Her eyes focused on the gold band around her finger. Who was this man she had married? Thaddeus talked of hatred and revenge, of killing and burying the dead. His words throbbed in her head, recalling unbidden images of a massacre long ago, blurred scenes in which bloodied bodies lay in the dust outside the cave into which a four-year-old girl named Dawn Flower had been thrust by a mother who had never returned. It had been a long time since that horror had assaulted her, but the pain was no less severe. Whose death did Cole want to avenge? Could his loss match her own?

Deep in thought, she made a lovely picture to her husband, who had entered the car quietly. Her head was bent, hiding her eyes, but he remembered the look she had given him in the chapel when she had said the words that made her his. Misreading her quiet pose as the shyness of a new bride, he imagined that look was in her wondrous amber eyes.

Her long slender arms rested against the sides of the chair. Her breasts were seductively full, and her waist narrow. With a rush of hunger, he remembered what she had looked like as she lay beneath him—the smooth tawny skin, the curves and valleys, the beckoning triangle of pale, golden-red hair between her thighs.

He'd been the first—what a fool he'd been not even to anticipate that possibility—and his shock at that had given way to a wild, ungovernable desire. She had urged

165

him on, in ways sweeter than those of any other woman, and the loneliness of his life had faded under her embrace.

The decision to take her to Texas as his bride had come easily to him, even though his thoughts of her weren't like the memories of his lost Rachel—he'd decided long ago a man could expect only one true love in life. But Erin was alive and warm and willing to share herself with him. She'd turned his life inside out; the thought of her with some other man had filled him with a jealous rage. He'd had to make her his.

As he looked at her sitting amidst the splendor of the private car, he caught his breath. He wanted to tear her clothes off and claim her sweet body before they'd even left the station.

Just then she sighed, and Cole was gripped with a fear he'd never felt before. "Having second thoughts, love?" he asked softly.

Erin started. Tormented by her thoughts, she hadn't heard him enter the car. "Second thoughts? About what?" she asked defensively.

He knelt beside her and took her hands in his. "About me." His thumb stroked the wedding ring that encircled her finger. "About the marriage."

His face was level with hers and she studied the man who was now her husband. Fine lines etched the outer edges of his eyes, which were a warm, velvety kind of gray. Thick black brows and lashes, and a hint of bristles along the ridges of his cheeks reminded her of the wiry curls of hair across his chest. His mouth curved in a slight, inviting smile. She moistened her lips with the tip of her tongue. Second thoughts? No, not now. Only Cole filled her mind and heart. Whatever doubts she had been harboring were washed away in a flood of longing.

Only dimly aware that the train was pulling out of the station, she freed her hands to stroke the lean lines of his face. A finger traced his mouth, and then lightly she brushed her lips against his. "No second thoughts," she whispered.

He shuddered under her touch and, pulling her into his arms, spoke softly into her ear. "Let's get rid of Randolph. I have something I want to give you."

She'd forgotten all about the servant, and she suddenly pulled away from Cole's embrace. The sharing of physical affection was new and wonderful for Erin, but it was also a private affair, not meant for the curious eyes of anyone, even a servant who stood with apparently unseeing eyes at the entrance to the car.

Cole stood. "Randolph, we won't be needing you until later today."

"Yes, Captain Barrett. There's food laid out for you and Mrs. Barrett, sir." He promptly disappeared through the door, closing it after him.

"A good man, that Randolph," Cole said, his eyes caressing his beautiful bride. "Now for your gift."

A kiss. What could be more wonderful than that, Erin thought. Anticipating the feel of his lips once more on hers, she closed her eyes, then opened them again when she felt a small package being placed in her lap.

"A wedding gift from your husband," Cole said.

"But I don't have anything for you," Erin said in dismay. Perhaps she should have thought of it, but then she knew little about the finer points of being wed.

Cole grinned. So she thought she had nothing to offer him, did she? Silly woman. He told her as much and watched in delight as she blushed.

Erin concentrated on unwrapping her gift. When her nervous fingers had slowly opened the narrow black box, she stared at its contents—a thin gold chain from which hung a square-cut emerald. Encircling the stone was a row of tiny, sparkling diamonds. Erin touched the necklace lovingly. The only jewelry she had ever worn was a strand of pearls Julie had given her for her sixteenth birthday four years ago. It was all she'd wanted to wear—until today.

"It's not much, love," he said. "Someday I intend to cover you in diamonds."

She smiled up at him. "It's beautiful. Thank you, Cole," she said. "Do you want me to wear it now?"

"No, I don't." He pulled her to her feet. "I don't want you to wear anything right now."

She rested her hands on the sleeves of his uniform. "But it's morning, Cole. Daylight."

"I can see you've got a lot to learn about making love, my innocent bride. The time of day doesn't matter."

She glanced through the open window at the fields and trees slipping past. So quickly they had passed out of the city, but still there might be passers-by who could peer into the interior of the train. Cole sensed the reason for her hesitation and lowered the shades on each of the portals, blocking the view of the Virginia countryside. Only the dim light from one hurricane lamp flickered in the car. Except for the steady rocking motion of the train, they might have been suspended in space.

Fascinated by the movements of his body, she watched as he performed another miracle. At the back of the car he pulled aside a pair of heavy gold curtains to reveal a satin-covered bed—not as wide as the one they had shared in the hotel.

He turned to face her. His eyes seemed to see through the linen and lace of her dress, to the skin that was burning for his touch. This was her husband beckoning to her with the searing look of raw desire, her husband whose parted lips tantalized and hypnotized with the promise of remembered delights. His hands reached out for her, summoning her into his embrace. The distance between them became unbearable, and with a low cry of longing Erin hurried into his arms.

His lips crushed hers, probing, savoring, demanding a response that she willingly gave. Even through the heavy folds of their clothing, she could feel the hard, taut body she loved. Desire licked at her like flames, consuming her reason, and she slipped her arms around him and ran her hands across his back and down to the swell of his buttocks.

Erin. Wild, wonderfully innocent Erin gave herself so trustingly to him that he was caught up in a desire to protect and possess her at the same time—a new feeling, this being a husband, powerful and eternal. His hard fullness nestled into her, and he moved dangerously near the silver-thin edge of control. Breaking their deep kiss, he pressed his lips into the tendrils of hair above her ear.

"Slowly, love, slowly," he breathed. "A man can't last long with such temptations."

Unwillingly Erin lessened her hold on his body, but only because Cole wanted her to. What did he expect of her? To hold him close or back away? She felt confused and glorious and ignorant all at the same time. Her eyes heavy with wanting him, she slipped from his embrace to pull the pins from the thick knot of hair atop her head. He had liked her hair down before. She wanted to do everything he had liked. Long curls tumbled about her shoulders, hair the color of a finely spun rosy dawn.

Erin! Her name sang in his head, a name filled with bewitching promises of mindless joy. Pulling her once more into his arms, Cole kissed her eyes, her cheeks, and again her lips. Oh those sweet lips, so soft and gentle as they moved against his, robbing him of rational thought.

One last long plundering of her mouth, then Cole lifted her into his arms. His eyes burning into hers, he laid her gently on the bed and began to undress her. In this second time of lovemaking, Erin knew what ecstasy lay in store for her, and impatient for his magic to be unleashed, she tried to help him with the myriad buttons

169

of her dress.

He kissed her hands away. "No, love. There are some things a man prefers to do. You must let me teach you." Slowly, deliberately, he stripped her of her dress and silken underthings; his uniform was more quickly shed. The satin covers of the bed were a cool contrast to her hot skin and with Cole's smooth guidance, she lay back in wanton abandon and let his hands roam at will. At each tender touch, she became more his. Meanwhile his caresses grew bolder, exploring, caressing, stroking until she writhed in mindless longing.

Then Cole took her hands in his and showed her how a man should be loved—a sweet lesson quickly learned. With long, sure strokes, Erin explored the length of his body, lingering for tantalizing moments on the flat nipples of his chest, his firm buttocks, and the taut muscles of his inner thigh, a gesture that sent visible tremors shooting through his body.

Taking her hand in his, Cole showed her the ultimate pleasure her soft massage could give him. He felt huge beneath her fingers, but Erin knew that in the wondrous way of the world her husband had taught her, their bodies would join as one, naturally and without pain, each giving and receiving a mind-bending ecstasy that would bind them together forever.

Cole could stand the wait no longer. "I want you now, Erin," he said huskily, positioning his body over hers. In wordless response she enfolded him in her arms and legs and held on tightly, returning the slow, even movements of his hips and thighs. His mind was filled with splintered images of her soft flesh pressed against his. Wrapped in her fiery embrace, he was possessed by her, heart and soul.

Bound by their desire, they drove each other to the precipice of fulfillment, lingering for one tantalizing moment as each savored the pleasure of the other before they hurtled together across passion's threshold. Thrills spiraled through them as Cole slipped his hands underneath her hips and lifted her higher, higher, until he was drowning in the tight moist sheath that was his alone; their hearts pounded as one. No more teaching of love's sweet ways now; instinct, need, the body's own desperate urgings guided them until they slipped their earthly bonds and were transported into glory.

Tightly they clung to one another, stretching out the high, thin edge of ecstasy. No words were spoken; there were only low moans and heavy sighs breathed sweetly into each other's mouth. Then came the inevitable unwinding to the here and now, a gentle journey made together, the completion of life's deepest, most enthralling measure.

Erin's lips touched his neck and the pulse point at his throat. His heart was beating as wildly as hers, then gradually its tempo slowed. After one last heartfelt shudder, Cole moved his body off hers to lie at her side. Beneath them the bed moved in undulating ripples, and Erin was reminded of where they were, not on some celestial plain but in a railroad car hurrying through a Virginia morning.

Relaxed by the gentle rocking of the car, they fell into a love-drugged sleep, only to waken and reach out for each other. This time their joining was slow, almost languorous, though no less sweet because it was not frantic. Once they got out of bed and dined on the fresh fruit and cold meats that had been laid out by the considerately absent Randolph. With his fingers Cole fed her bites of a ripe plum, then kissed the juice from her lips. Their hunger sated, they fell onto the covers and again fed the age-old need whose appetite could not be appeased.

"Is this the way with every man and wife?" Erin asked when much of the day had gone by.

Cole grinned at her. "No, love, I think not. Not every

man is blessed with such a tempestuous lover."

"Blessed? I take it you have no complaints."

"Only one. I wish I had the strength of ten. You know. Like Sir Galahad in the poem."

Erin merely nodded. She had no idea what he was talking about—a man with ten times her husband's strength—but she vowed that as soon as she learned to read she'd put Sir Galahad at the top of her list.

The miles were quickly covered as they traveled southward toward Alabama. The first stop of any length was at Raleigh, the capital city of North Carolina. Erin was asleep in bed when they arrived, and Cole made a quick trip into the city to a street-side flower shop so his wife might awake to a fresh bouquet of roses. The crystal vase Randolph had pulled from his storehouse of essentials.

Then came a long journey down to Wilmington and along the South Carolina coast to the old city of Charleston. They whiled away their waking hours playing cards and letting their redoubtable servant see to their needs; at night they lay in each other's arms. This was an indolent time, a passionate period that they knew could not last.

They arrived in Charleston in the early afternoon. "We'll be here overnight. How would you like to sleep in a bed that doesn't rock under you?" Cole asked as the train chugged into the station.

"Do you mean we're to sleep apart?" Erin batted her long lashes in playful innocence. "I thought you were the cause of all the movement."

"I wish I could say you're right. Unfortunately, I'm afraid once I get you in a Carolina bed, you'll find that much of my charm is really due to an uneven railroad track."

"And I'm willing to gamble you're wrong."

Dispatching Randolph toward a nearby hotel with a valise and orders to get them the finest suite for one night, Erin and Cole headed out for a stroll along the Battery. To their right was a row of large wooden mansions; to the left the wharfs along Charleston Bay. Seeming to rise out of the harbor was Fort Sumter.

"That's where it started, Erin," Cole said, gesturing toward the fort. "The stupid war that almost destroyed our country. Even after all these years, the South has still not recovered."

Erin had never heard of Fort Sumter; indeed she knew very little of the War Between the States. She'd heard more about it in Richmond than she had in Texas. The war had affected Cole's life and thus hers. She wanted to know more, but when she asked him questions, he looked at her in surprise.

"Didn't you study Fort Sumter in school?"

"No." She hesitated. "The schools I went to were, uh, a little backward, I'm afraid." Unless one wanted to learn gambling, she almost added. She'd learned that very well in the saloons her father had dragged her through.

Was the displeasure really in his eyes, or was she just imagining it? If he didn't like her ignorance about a Southern fort, what would he think when he found out she couldn't read? As soon as the right moment arrived, she would tell him. He would understand.

As they made their way back to the hotel, Erin noticed the eyes of several passing women rested longer than necessary on her husband. Why had he chosen to wear the uniform? Surely he knew how handsome it made him appear. And of course he had to nod to them, these Southern women in their ruffled dresses with matching parasols held overhead to protect them from the sun. It seemed to Erin most of them were pale and blond.

Cole sensed Erin's unease. Something he had said or

done had upset her. He had been very busy the past few days learning what she liked. Now he had best spend some time learning what to avoid.

When they arrived at the hotel, he escorted her to their suite. Perhaps they had been too much together. He would give her a little time alone, he decided, and once he had seen her inside, he started to excuse himself. He'd get a drink in the hotel saloon bar while she rested and prepared for dinner.

Erin balked at his decision. "I really feel fine. Can't I join you downstairs?"

"I'm afraid not, love. The hotel proprietors have rather rigid ideas about who should and shouldn't be served in their saloon. I promise not to be long."

He could read the dissatisfaction in her eyes, but he also saw in their amber depths an endearing desire to please him. She saw his hesitation and insisted he go alone. After all, they had a lifetime together; she could certainly part from him while he had one drink.

A wonderful woman, my wife, Cole thought and left her with a promise to return shortly. But downstairs he ran into one of the men he had served with in Texas and they fell to reminiscing about old times. Their talk was punctuated by drinks of whiskey, and before Cole realized it, two hours had slipped by. Discovering the time, he hastily bid his friend good-bye and started to rise. As he did so, a commotion in the doorway caught his eye and he looked up to see his wife arguing volubly with a florid-faced, portly man. The man, his back to the wall, was obviously getting the worst of the verbal sparring.

His reason blurred by alcohol, he hurried to her side. "Erin, what's the matter?"

Her amber eyes flashed angrily at him. "This gentleman"—she gestured in the general direction of her red-faced opponent—"assumed I was looking for something besides my husband. Ladies, I was informed, do not come into Charleston bars."

"They don't. I already told you that." He attempted to pull her aside, out of the sight and hearing of the crowd around them.

"You also told me you would return shortly." She pulled her arm free. "I hadn't planned to come inside. I only wanted to make sure you were all right." The men around them laughed.

Anger masked the apology he tried to make. "I'm sorry I let the time slip away from me, but we can discuss the matter more privately at dinner. In the restaurant."

His words sounded more like a command than a request, and Erin rebelled. "I'm no longer hungry. You can, of course, do as you wish. I'll be in our room."

Her amber eyes were darkened with unshed tears as she hurried upstairs. Vainly she listened for the sound of following footsteps, but there were none. She wanted to apologize for the foolish panic that had overcome her when he hadn't returned and to give him the chance to apologize to her. What had kept him so long mattered little to her now. He had simply been drinking and talking in the saloon. Saints above, she'd seen her father do that often enough, and she knew the hours could fly by. She hadn't thought Cole was the kind of man who'd do that, but perhaps all men did. It was certain that in some ways she simply didn't know her husband very well.

When he didn't come right away, she undressed and slipped beneath the covers. Why, when she loved him so much, did she feel a gap widening between them? The first sign had come when she'd overheard Thaddeus Lymond admonishing Cole about killing Indians for revenge; for a while she'd let her husband's kisses smooth away her fears. But the differences that separated them were becoming harder to overlook, and the love she had thought bound them was more fragile than she could let herself contemplate.

Cole entered sometime after midnight. He undressed in the dark, and when he fell into bed she waited tremulously for him to pull her into his arms. It didn't occur to her that he was waiting for some sign his presence was welcome. As the long hours stretched toward the cruel light of morning, her hopes gave way to despair and at last to resolution. This night of misunderstanding must not be allowed to inflict its devisive hurt onto the days ahead.

As the first rays of dawn penetrated the room, Erin gave up on sleep. Beside her Cole lay in deep slumber and she couldn't bring herself to awaken him to talk. Hunger, that was her problem. She'd missed dinner the evening before. Slipping quietly from the bed, she dressed and went downstairs.

When Cole awoke an hour later, he reached for his wife, but the bed was empty. Sunlight streamed through the open window. Damn! What time was it? Had she left him, showing no concern that he might miss the train?

As he pulled on his trousers, he found his watch still in his pocket. There was still enough time to get to the station. Just barely. Surely Erin had written him a note—he always did for her—but there was no missive in sight. Just then the door opened. His wife entered with a tray on which rested a steaming cup of coffee.

She avoided his eye. "I thought you might be needing this."

The pounding in his heart stilled. She was back. "Thanks," he murmured. He lifted the tray from her hands and set it aside, then pulled her into his arms. Her hands rested on his bare chest, but she didn't try to push him away.

"I'm sorry, Erin."

Her eyes met his. "There's no need to apologize. I shouldn't have come looking for you, but I got so lonely and then worried, and that man at the door was so rude."

They consoled one another with a kiss and were shortly heading for the train. Randolph was waiting for them on the platform, and he hurried them on board just as the whistle sounded.

As the miles sped beneath the wheels of the train, Erin found herself unable to shake off the unease of Charleston. Cole had still not told her he loved her, and she needed his reassurance more than ever. Tucked away in her pocket was the note he'd left her in Washington, the note in which he'd proposed. She was certain it also contained words of love.

But first she had a confession to make. She looked at her husband, who was sitting in one of the overstuffed chairs, a book in his hand.

"Cole . . ."

He looked up, and she was glad to see warmth in his eyes.

"Cole, would you do me a favor?" She held out the wrinkled piece of paper. "Would you read this to me?"

Puzzled, he took it from her and unfolded it. "I don't understand, Erin. You want me to read this out loud?"

"Well, you did propose to me in it. And I never heard you say the words. I'd like to hear it from your lips."

He set his book aside. "All right. 'Dear Erin, please excuse my hasty departure this morning. Know I'll be returning to you soon. If you agree, we will, of course, be married right away. Always trust me to take care of you.'"

Erin was sitting quietly, her eyes trained on the open window. Except for a tightening around her lips, he could read no expression on her face. "Is something wrong?" he asked.

She dropped her gaze to her lap. "It just sounds so . . . so cold."

"I guess it does, but I wrote it days ago. Besides, you knew what it said."

177

Now was the time. She knew it. "No, I didn't." She looked at him defiantly. "Cole, I don't know how to read." The surprise she had dreaded was there in his eyes. Well, another kind of surprise was in her heart. He hadn't told her he loved her. As he had read the damnable words, she'd realized what he was really saying. Her virginity had been an unexpected and complicated surprise; he'd do the honorable thing and make an honest woman of her. And now he was saddled with someone who couldn't even read. He not only didn't love her, he was ashamed of her.

Tiredness overcame her. "I think I'll lie down for a while."

Hurt and disappointment were evident in her rounded eyes and in the listless movement of her body as she turned toward the bed. Somehow, Cole thought, he had let her down. But why had she kept such a thing secret from him? Didn't she trust him to make things right? He had known Erin was not the fantasy woman he'd kept in his heart through the years, but she was warm and passionately loving—and she was his to care for. He had to let her know that.

"It's all right, Erin. I'll teach you to read."

Not bothering to look back, she merely shrugged her shoulders. "If that's what you want. I had already been planning to learn."

During the next two days Erin made excuses to hold at bay the reading lessons Cole had offered. To submit herself to them would have been a humiliation. She was Cole's wife and lover, not his child.

As they neared Mobile, she felt the wedge between them grow. Only when he pulled her into his arms each night did she feel a glimmer of the old magic that had been between them. She had disappointed him—but then

178

he had disappointed her. He should have noticed the distress brought on by her confession and come to her side. He should have told her it didn't matter instead of offering to teach her to read.

But of course it did matter. As an officer's wife, she would be expected to entertain, to send out invitations, to take care of correspondence—in short to read and write.

A letter was delivered the evening of their arrival in Mobile. In one of the coach cars a fellow officer of Cole's was a passenger. He had heard they were on board and was inviting them to dine with him in the Alabama city.

"An old Indian fighter friend," Cole explained as he read the letter. "Do you have any objections to accepting?"

The pressures that had been building seemed close to exploding, but Erin managed to look calmly at her husband. "An old Indian fighter, you say? How many of them would you say he has killed?"

Cole missed the signals of anger. "As many as he could." He kissed his wife on the forehead. "If you don't object, I'll walk up and find him. I'd like to accept in person."

"Of course I don't object." She looked at Cole, a humorless smile on her lips. "Has he killed as many as you?"

"I suppose. Erin, is something bothering you?"

"Of course not. My husband kills Indians. That's what a soldier is supposed to do."

"It's what he has to do. They're savages, Erin. Surely you know that."

Savages—and nothing else. That was what he thought about redskins. Erin's heart pounded. She might sometimes feel awkward about her lack of manners and even ashamed that she couldn't read, but damnation, she was proud of her Comanche blood.

She'd waited far too long to tell her husband the complete truth about her heritage. An idea formed in the back of her mind. She didn't pause to weigh the wisdom of it.

"Go find your friend, Cole. I'll be ready when you return."

He paused a moment, kissed her, and then was gone. Erin set to work. She was an officer's wife and an Indian. Two worlds pulled at her. If Cole was ever to know and love her as she really was, he must see the forces that warred within her.

Brushing her hair out of its chignon, she fashioned it into two braids as she had seen Indian squaws do. The rouge Mrs. Craven-Hix had bought for her to color her lips she streaked in broad curves beneath her eyes. Warpaint. Well, she was at war.

So much for the Indian part of her. The dress she selected was a low-cut green silk with an impossible number of ruffles and bows. As civilized as she could get, she figured. For a final touch she fastened around her neck the emerald necklace that had been Cole's wedding gift. Just as she finished, she heard his knock at the door.

"Erin," he called. "Are you ready? Captain Manning is waiting for us on the platform."

"I'm ready, dear." Erin's heart pounded. Captains Manning and Barrett were her escorts, were they? Two soldiers and an Indian. They'd make an interesting trio at dinner.

Cole entered and came to a sudden stop. "Erin, I thought you said you were ready."

Erin's heart pounded so loudly that she thought surely he could hear it, but it was too late now to change her plans. Head held high, she stepped farther into the lamplight to let Cole get a good look at the red paint streaked on her face and the Indian braids that fell across her bare shoulders.

"I am ready. Aren't we going out with your friend?"

Cole's eyes darkened to obsidian. "Erin, what in hell is going on? Do you think we're going to a masquerade?"

"What's wrong with the way I'm dressed?"

"You're made up like some kind of half-savage. That's what is wrong."

Erin's pride flared, obliterating all thought save her purpose. "I'm dressed like what I am. You'll take me this way, or not at all."

"You're not going out like that."

Erin rebelled at the order—a soldier's order, not a husband's request—and she headed for the door. He jerked her back into the car.

"Wash your face, Erin, and undo those ridiculous braids."

Her eyes glittered dangerously. "Why? Do I remind you of something unpleasant?"

"Of an Indian? Is that what you want me to say? Of course you do. It's what you meant to do. For some reason you've taken offense at my hatred of the red man. Erin, if I had my way, they'd all be rounded up and guarded like the animals they are."

His words chilled her heart. "You'd shoot them, would you?"

"To protect the lives of women and children, yes, I would. Sometimes I think General Sheridan is right. The only good Indian is a dead Indian."

Reason left her, and she lashed out at him with angry words she could never call back. "Then get your gun and shoot me. I have been called by another name, Cole. Dawn Flower. Comanche blood flows through my veins. You've taken as your bride an Indian squaw."

He stepped back, stunned. "What in hell are you talking about?"

"You heard me." Painful outrage consumed her. Cole didn't understand. And he never would. She could see it

181

in his eyes.

Erin turned to put some distance between her and the man she loved, then hesitated in the doorway. "On second thought, you don't have to bother shooting me. The white man has never honored his treaties with the Indian. Why should you start now? I relieve you of your vows, Captain Barrett. Beginning this moment, our marriage contract is no more."

For one shattering final moment she stared into his eyes, then broke away. Unable to cast even a brief glance at the splendid room that had been her paradise, she rushed onto the platform outside the car and slammed the door behind her. As she stared at the cluster of strangers milling about the depot, her only thought was to separate herself from the man who could inflict such unbearable pain on her. Bundling her awkward skirt off the ground, she descended to the crowded walk and with hurried movements slipped past the unseen crowd and hurtled into the night.

Chapter Eleven

Erin set spurs to her fast roan stallion and surged ahead—through shallow arroyos, over a hillock, past sparse groves of scrub oak and bois d'arc.

In the three months since her return to Texas she had spent long hours outside and her body had grown supple and strong. Always a good rider, she now moved as one with the horse into the still-hot October wind. It whipped around her sun-browned face, bringing tears to her eyes, but she noticed only the thrumming of hooves that sang of freedom from the conventions of the white civilization that had threatened to hem her in forever.

She had come to Hud's Rocking J in Wichita County almost a month ago and often rode out alone, going in different directions over the vast acreage, sometimes arriving at camps used by the 'pokes who would stay out all winter gathering and branding strays. Mostly the camps were too far away from the main bunkhouse, though, and she rode alone for hours, slipping away from the watchful eyes of Cur and Pops to do it. She had grown adept at evading them, she thought.

None of her friends and benefactors in Texas had pressed her to reveal the reasons for her uncharacteristically solemn behavior since her return. She had wanted to tell them about Cole and the short, bittersweet time she'd had with him, but she'd found she could not talk about her unhappiness, not even after she'd overheard Julie and Hud blame themselves for leaving her alone in the foreign East without their guidance. She simply hadn't been ready for such an environment, they had decided. Well, that was one thing she couldn't disagree with.

In moments of honesty she knew she couldn't blame Cole for what had happened. *She* had been the one to hide her illiteracy. *She* had been the one to cover up her past. And all because she'd been afraid of losing him. If her thoughts hadn't hurt so much, they would have made her laugh.

Someday soon she would have to tell Hud and Julie the truth about her seeming withdrawal from the world. She owed them that, and she loved them dearly. Sometimes she worried that they'd had some kind of report from Marcia Smythe-Williams, but they never mentioned it if they had.

Not even once had Hud referred to her inability to read little more than numbers. The most he had said was that he welcomed her back to the Victorian mansion he'd built on the Fort Worth Circle B, out on the road to the Jacksborough Salt Mine, and she'd always have a home wherever he was. He had not objected when she'd elected to leave the security of Fort Worth for the questionable safety on the Rocking J, which was not too far south of wild and woolly Fort Sill.

Reminding herself once more to be grateful for his and Julie's unsmothering kind of loving concern, she held the reins lightly over the pommel of the lightweight California saddle she preferred and tried to relax into the rocking rhythm of the horse, now sauntering at a gait calculated to cool him off. If only the restlessness of old had not returned. If only she could forget.

She took off her battered Stetson, feeling the coolness where the sweat-soaked band had circled her head. Then she pulled her shirt from her damp body and, lifting the heavy copper braids hanging down her back, fanned her neck. With her hair in braids, she thought of herself as Dawn Flower, granddaughter of a full-blooded Indian, and it was only through riding out across the arid and lonely acres as her ancestors had done that she could still the pain in her heart.

She turned her mind to the hard-driving strength of the horse under her minutes ago, savoring the smell of the leather in her hands, of sweat mixed with the sweet air. Riding had always come easily to her and for years she had practiced diligently to enhance her ability. She wanted to be as good as the Comanches she could barely remember. Often she saw them in her dreams, bronzed and invincible as they floated over the prairie.

Instinctively she touched the leather amulet that hung suspended around her neck by a narrow strip of buffalo hide. The small square, with its crude Indian painting of the sun, was the only legacy from her slain mother. As a child she had played with it, then set it aside. After her return to Texas, she was never without it.

It was her only adornment. The golden band she'd worn around her finger for such a short while was tucked away back in her room, in a bottom drawer where she wouldn't come across it accidentally. Beside it was the emerald necklace.

Gently she dug a spur into the side of the roan, urging him to keep walking. A champion racer, he was a descendant of the famous Denton Mare raced by the outlaw Sam Bass all over northern Texas years ago. The roan was all the horse she could ask for—big, strong, fearless, and trained to obey by the Comanche who worked in the same stable where she had first gambled and lost to Cole.

So why couldn't she settle on a name for the horse? It could be, she thought, that with a name he might lose the will to be free that she felt in him, a will that matched her own no matter who or what invaded her thoughts and told her otherwise.

It was, of course, possible that the horse obeyed only because he wanted to befriend her and carry her into some unnamable Indian camp, to stop before a venerable old brave and his squaw—her grandparents. Unquestioningly, they would accept her as their own and she would cease to feel the unrest she'd known since she had fled Mobile—first to Dallas to stay at Angel Looney's boardinghouse, then on to the Circle B mansion, and then, discontent spurring her on, even deeper into Texas to Hud's Rocking J Ranch.

Partly, she knew, her vision rose from desperation. She couldn't hide forever, yet she tried not to think about anything but returning to the Indian life of her early childhood. It was a dream of course—most of the Indians were now forced to live on the reservation at Fort Sill—but at least it sometimes kept her from thinking of her ruined marriage. The whole misadventure with Cole and his world had been another gamble she'd lost.

Turning into a dry wash, she straightened in the saddle and cantered more purposefully toward the creek which meandered through this part of the ranch before riding on to within two hundred yards of the bunkhouse. As she jogged along, she practiced the Indian words and gestures she'd been learning from Cur, the big Aussie who had spent the last several years overseeing Hud's interests in the cow business. He had often gone into Indian territory, to deal with the tribes and the Army, supplying them with beef. A trusted friend of the Indians, he had gone with them on buffalo hunts and had easily learned their simple language and the universal hand talk. They had even given the seven-foot white man a name—Tall

Tree. Under his guidance, Erin was fast emulating his achievement in learning the Indian methods of communication.

As they rode or worked around the ranch, Cur drilled her; she struggled now to remember his voice as he intoned the sonorous sounds signifying separate words which were indistinguishable to the ears of most whites. She said them aloud. At the same time her hands moved gracefully to her eyes, chest, heart—rippling through the air, pointing out the natural objects around her in the signs that all Indians recognized. Thus far she had used her skills only with Cur, but she hoped before long to head out on her quest to find her grandparents.

She was pleased that this spoken language came easier to her than the written English word. Her last act before leaving Mobile had been to buy a set of McGuffey readers, the textbooks teachers at the Presbyterian school in Dallas had tried unsuccessfully to force on her years ago. But for days her eyes had been too blurred with tears for the books to do her any good. The farther she separated herself from the man she loved, the less she saw the need for reading. The books were now gathering dust on a forgotten shelf back at the cabin.

After she'd gone through all the words and signs she could remember, Cur's voice continued in her thoughts, repeating their breakfast conversation that morning.

"The soldiers will be riding in sometime soon, maybe even today, to pick up the cattle the Army wants to buy," he had said over a plate of biscuits and steak.

Picking disinterestedly at her food, she'd glanced at Cur. "Isn't it a little unusual for the Army to come after the cattle? I thought you had to deliver."

Cur had nodded in agreement. "Still don't understand it. Kind of late to be buying stock, what with most of it having already gone to Montana. But that's what Hud's man Charlie Horst reported from Dallas. Whatever we

187

could spare. Soldiers are coming all the way from Fort Concho to get 'em."

"Well, I don't plan to be around when they arrive. I'll be riding out."

"Nice of you to tell me this time," he had said dryly.

Erin had ignored his barb. "I'll be all right," she'd said. "No need to warn me about raiding parties sneaking away from Fort Sill. I won't go far. And I'll be back as soon as the Army has gone or at least bedded down for the night—somewhere far off, I hope."

She'd felt Cur's unspoken question hanging in the air. Twice lately men seeking jobs had ridden onto the ranch and she had made herself scarce. Cur had noticed and looked curious but had never said a word. By now, she didn't know why she did it. No one was coming to look for her—not after three months. Not that she wanted anyone to. Still, she knew it was best not to expose herself to the danger of cracking the thin shell of her composure. Smiling brightly at the big man, she had gotten up without a word and had departed to saddle up.

Not five miles away a small contingent of soldiers rode from the southwest toward the Flying J. In the lead was the group's lone officer, Captain Coleman Barrett; behind him straggled the men he'd brought with him to get the cattle back to Fort Concho, a corporal and three privates.

Cole's gray eyes were directed unswervingly ahead, but the monotony of the Texas landscape allowed his mind to wander—to the letter tucked inside his coat pocket, and then to the woman who had drawn him like an arrow across the middle of Texas, along the edge of Apache country, across flat lands and now rolling plains. What kind of reception would he get when he arrived at the ranch? What kind of a reception did he want?

The past three months had been a living hell for Cole, beginning with the arrival of the train in Mobile. How often he had relived those wondrous days and nights before that stop, seemingly never-ending hours when he'd held the passionate body of his wife in his arms; just as often had come his memories of her leaving him. The idea for marrying her had come out of some misbegotten sense of honor, or so he told himself. She'd given him her virginal body without protest or demands; in payment he would give her his name.

Damn, but he had been a fool. The lonely days and nights had convinced him of that. He wanted Erin Donovan Barrett in his bed for as long as he could keep her. And honor had damned little to do with why he wanted her there.

But his wife was not an easy woman to capture, or to keep. There had been magic to their journey south from Washington. Indeed, he had come to regard the private railroad car as a kind of white and gold chrysalis; when Erin had emerged in that ridiculous getup, hurt and anger playing across her face, she was like a broken-winged butterfly. Fragile and frightened she was, and yet she had possessed an inner strength that had helped her elude his grasp.

There was no doubt he had behaved stupidly. Still stunned by her announcement that she couldn't read, he had overreacted to her foolish claim about being a squaw. For some reason she had developed a sensitivity to the problems of the Indians. A perversity to cross him? A sincere desire to help the downtrodden? Or did her wild words contain an element of truth? Whatever their cause, it seemed inconsequential to him now.

He should have handled her differently, asking instead of ordering her to wash her face and undo those ridiculous braids. It was a folly he had paid for many times over since he had run from the train and searched the crowd in vain. Oh, everybody remembered seeing her dart past all right—one would have had to be blind to miss her—but then the stories got confused. She went through the depot; no, she darted down the length of the train; she got on a railroad car. She must have flitted about until no one was quite sure where she was headed.

The nightmare had really begun when he'd found out the yellow fever which they'd hoped to avoid by skipping New Orleans had already spread to Mobile. Much of the city was already closed down, and he'd spent days searching the hospitals, terrified that he would find her fever-racked body, and hopelessly frustrated when there had been no sign of her. She had simply disappeared.

Cole's problem was that he knew too little about his wife. A guardian, she had told him, was her only family. Stupidly, he hadn't even gotten the man's name. The only place he could seek her out was the Dallas stable where he'd met her years ago across a poker table. Erin was a memorable woman; perhaps someone there could help him out.

Well, he had been half right. Some of the oldtimers hanging around the back room certainly did remember her. "Quite a gal," one of them said. "Haven't seen her around here lately, though."

"Do you have any idea where I might find her?"

"Nope. That little thing was like a butterfly flitting in and out of here. Never seemed to land."

Cole grimaced at the comparison. "Well, if you think of anything that might help me, I'll be staying at the St. Nicholas Hotel."

"Hold up." A grizzled old fellow stepped out of the shadows. "Seems to me she was the ward of one of our local bankers. Hud Adams. His place is over to Main Street."

Cole nodded his thanks and hurried the three blocks to

the Adams Bank. There it started out to be the same story.

"Sorry," the manager said. "Erin hasn't been around since she left with Mr. Adams months ago for a trip to Australia. Mr. Adams returned for a while but he's gone traveling with his wife Julie—uh, Mrs. Adams—again, and I suppose the girl—well, I suppose she's more of a woman now—anyway, I guess she'd still be with them. Mr. Adams didn't say where he was going, just whizzed through here, set things straight, and then took off."

Cole listened in exasperation to the long-winded banker. A trip to Australia? Erin never mentioned she had been there. But then there was a great deal his wife hadn't told him before their marriage.

Desperate for the tiniest scrap of information, Cole said, "Mr. Adams has lived in Dallas for a long time then?"

"Why, I've worked for him almost seven years now and he's one of the nicest men you'd ever hope to meet—strict, mind you, but fair. Done a lot for this town and this state since he came here a few years ago. Why, in addition to this bank, he owns a couple of ranches and has businesses all over this part of Texas. His wife Julie is a pretty little songbird. Even entertains potentates in Europe, I'm told. Two lovely children, too. You'll not find a nicer family around."

It seemed to Cole that Erin hadn't been quite so homeless as he had imagined. And this Hud Adams, who had obviously been the source of Erin's fine clothes and money, sounded like a man anyone could admire.

"Mr.—"

"Horst, Charlie Horst."

"Mr. Horst, Hud Adams sounds like a fine guardian for Erin, but I'm afraid she may be in a bit of trouble and I'd like to help. I'm sure your employer would be grateful for any help you could give me."

Horst studied the Army officer for a minute, then, apparently deciding he liked what he saw, proceeded to tell Cole that he wasn't sure where Mr. Adams could be located. "He's in Europe now, I'm afraid. I'll try to send a wire; that's all I could promise."

"What about his other places? Where does he live?"

"Nobody home at his Fort Worth house, or his lodgings here. It's too far to go anywhere else."

Damn. Nothing but dead ends.

Then Horst spoke up. "You might try Mrs. Looney's place north of town. Angelique Looney. A widow that runs a boardinghouse. She's a friend of the family, I believe. Maybe she can tell you about Miss Erin."

If Angel Looney could help him, she didn't say so right away, but when Cole first set eyes on her, he thought he was nearing the end of his quest. A middle-aged woman, she had open smile and soft brown eyes with a gentle intelligence about them. She would know if Erin was around; she would also recognize that he meant his wife no harm.

But as soon as he mentioned Erin's name, Cole knew he was in trouble. The woman's eyes seemed to shutter down, and her smile took on a distant, formal look.

"She doesn't live here." Her words were clipped and final.

Cole refused to give up. "Have you seen her in the past few months?"

She answered his question with one of her own. "Why are you looking for Miss Donovan?"

Miss Donovan. Like everyone else in town, Angel Looney still thought of Erin as a single woman. If, as Cole suspected, she had talked to Erin, she hadn't been told about the marriage. Whether from shame or anger, God only knew, his wife was keeping their wedding a secret. Cole couldn't betray her.

"I . . . I need to talk to her. It's very important."

192

He stood on the porch, his hat in his hand, and watched the woman study him. At one point he thought she was about to change her story, but something made her hold back. A promise, he guessed, to keep Erin's whereabouts a secret. Angel Looney looked like the kind of person who would not betray a trust.

Cole scribbled for a moment on a piece of paper and held it out. "Look, Mrs. Looney, here's where I can be reached at Fort Concho. If you do hear anything, write me there." He touched her hand for a moment. "We both have Erin's best interest at heart."

There hadn't been any reason to hang around. Eventually Angel Looney might change her mind, but if she didn't, he would have to find Erin's guardian Hud and tell him the truth about the marriage.

The ride to Fort Concho was long, hot, and dry; when he arrived, instead of being assigned to Indian patrol as he had wished, he was immediately dispatched to San Antonio to oversee the expansion of the new fort there that was to replace the ancient Alamo as supply center for the frontier armies still engaged in Indian warfare. The fort had been opened in February on Government Hill north of the town.

As much as he admired the beautiful new fort, he grew restless during the weeks he spent in South Texas. Had anyone tried to reach him back at Fort Concho? He had no guarantee that any letters he received would be forwarded to him in San Antonio. The more he thought about it, the more certain he was that news awaited him. At last the fort commander consented to his request to return to the frontier.

Cole's intuition had proven accurate, but not all the news was good. Gerald Nathan, the shifty-eyed lieutenant he'd left behind at West Point, had been reassigned to Fort Concho. Surprisingly he was now a major, one rank step above Cole. Somebody in his family must have bought him his double promotion. It certainly wasn't the first time such a thing had been done in postings to the country's ragtag forces in the West, but that didn't make the news any less galling. When he had less important things on his mind, Cole would think about just how Nathan had come up with the necessary cash.

But he didn't let his anger fester; other news rendered Nathan's status unimportant. Two letters had arrived for him—one from Richmond and the other, the long-awaited message from Dallas. He opened the letter from his brother first, fearful that the second held bad news.

Enclosed he found a check for four hundred and three dollars and a note that the money had been in Fiona's possession. Fiona had, she said, "forgotten" to pass it on. Cole flushed. Erin, it seemed, was endowed with more honor than the matriarch of the Barrett clan.

Unable to wait any longer, he tore into the letter from Dallas. It was from Angel Looney. He had been right on target with his guesses. Erin had, indeed, arrived safely in Dallas—he breathed a deep sigh of relief—but she was also "a mighty unhappy young woman. I suppose you might have something to do with that."

Cole couldn't help smiling. He hoped, by God, he had a great deal to do with his wife's state of mind. A man certainly didn't want to hear that his bride was deliriously happy to be away from him. Satisfaction began to penetrate his relief. After all, Erin had run away from him, not the other way around. A little misery might teach her a lesson.

As far as Angel Looney knew, Erin was staying on one of Hud's ranches, the Rocking J in Wichita County up near the border of Indian Territory. Hiding out is more like it, Cole thought. Well, she would have to run a lot farther than that to get away from him.

Fort Concho was no different from any other post in

which he had served—rations were always needed, especially with the winter months coming on and game getting more scarce. Luckily the records showed cattle had been bought at times from Hud Adams's Rocking J. Gerald Nathan, who was in command in the absence of Colonel Grierson, wasn't hard to sell on his plan, and Cole quickly dispatched a personal telegram to Charlie Horst in Dallas, instructing the manager to arrange for the sale of any cattle the Adams ranch could spare. The Army would send a delegation to get them as soon as possible.

Wondering if he might not have picked up a bad habit or two from his wife, Cole played a little loose with the truth. He had no idea if there were any cattle left on the ranch, and in his current state of mind, he really didn't care. Nathan hadn't asked for proof or confirmation from Dallas. Certain there wouldn't be more cattle than five men could handle, he kept his contingent small and left Fort Concho, heading north. A few men traveled lighter and faster, and Cole wanted to arrive at the ranch before his bride flew to some other place.

They made good time. In less than a week Cole topped the rise that overlooked the Rocking J. Conflicting thoughts beset him. As eager as he was to hold his beautiful wife again, he was filled with anger because she had run away. He frankly didn't give a damn whether she wanted to see him. She didn't have any choice.

Not that he was anything much to welcome, he thought as he looked down at his dust-covered uniform. The braid of his coat was barely visible, and his normally shiny brass buttons looked like little more than pebbles thrown up from a Texas creekbed. Underneath the coat a cotton shirt stuck to his body. Only someone who had never been to Texas would design a wool jacket as requisite wear. About the only things that made sense were his black boots and the broad-brimmed hat which

195

protected his neck and face from the relentless sun.

At first the few buildings of the Rocking J looked deserted. No one stirred in the yard surrounding a porched cabin, a bunkhouse, and a small pen made of zigzag logs, but then an old fellow emerged onto the narrow porch of the bunkhouse, emptied a pail of water onto the cracked dirt at his feet, and disappeared once more inside.

Instructing his men to hold back, Cole rode down. His sharp knock on the door was soon answered.

The old man didn't wait for him to speak. "Why, you must be the Army fellow what come for the cows. People around here call me Pop. You need to see Mr. Adams's man Cur. He has what little is left of the roundup down on the creek. It's a couple miles, but you can't miss the herd. Just follow the creek." He gestured vaguely off to his left.

"Is this Mr. Cur down there by himself?"

"Just call him Cur. Never heard no other name. Now, that's a funny thing for you to ask, young man. 'Course he's got a few of the boys with him."

"Of course." Cole fought his rising impatience. "I meant is there a young woman staying at the ranch. Mr. Adams's ward."

"Oh, Miss Erin. Yep, been here 'bout a month, I reckon."

Again the damnable word *miss.* Erin Donovan Barrett would have a great deal to answer for.

"Well," Pop continued, "I saw Miss Erin go t'other way from the herd. Said at breakfast she didn't want to see no Army fellers."

Oh she didn't, did she? Too bad she would have to be disappointed. Ordering his men to report to a man named Cur at the herd site, Cole ignored their frankly inquisitive stares, as well as the old man's, and hurried off in the other direction, riding in the open on a ridge about fifty yards from the creek. He rode doggedly, determined to find Erin no matter how far she'd gone. An hour later, there was still no sign of her. As Cole was about to descend to the creek for water, the sun in his eyes, he saw the rays glint on something deposited on a large rock—a saddle with an edging of silver on the skirt.

And then he saw her, Erin, riding away from him astride a magnificent strawberry roan, her long, slender legs covered splendidly in tight-fitting buckskin trousers. Relief flooded him—and then the hot, familiar desire she always aroused killed any anger over her desertion in Mobile. The smartest thing he'd ever done was take her to wife, and as soon as he kissed her long and hard, he would tell her so. She would believe him, he was sure.

He started to ride after her but held back. What the hell was she doing riding without a saddle? And instead of sitting upright, she was slipping to the side of the horse. He could see surcingles strapped around the horse's belly, holding on a red and yellow blanket. He watched as she gripped the horse's mane and hooked her knee in the front strap that held the blanket.

Her head dangled perilously near the ground. Cole's heart stopped. She was riding like the Comanche she claimed to be. Only red men had been able to master such dangerous feats of skill. Cole knew. He had tried to master them a few times. He'd come close, but then he was an experienced horseman. Erin was his slender, feminine bride.

Before he could call out, she rose effortlessly, clutching a stick she'd plucked from entirely too near the pounding hoofs of her mount. The horse ran smoothly on in a straight line. She tucked the stick into the hand gripping the mane, then slipped to the other side of the roan. In a second she was upright again—and this time empty-handed, it seemed.

As the horse turned to come back toward where he still

197

sat beside the abandoned saddle, he saw that she was guiding it by knee pressure only. She held a second stick—her hard-won trophy—high overhead. Her face was alight with a smile of victory.

Nothing could have infuriated her husband more. That she had risked her neck in such a foolish pursuit, and then had had the gall to look so absolutely happy, was more than he could take. Without thinking, he urged his horse down the long incline toward her.

Erin's head jerked in his direction, and the light in her eyes died. In his fury, he could see no evidence that she was glad to see him, only amazement and then an anger that almost matched his own.

She pulled her horse up short, gave a small cry, and turning in place, began what looked to him like a desperate retreat. Well, this was no crowded train station where she could easily lose herself; this time she didn't have the element of surprise. With a firm determination that would brook no defeat, Cole dug his heels into the flanks of his mount and headed after his wife.

Chapter Twelve

Erin didn't know where she was riding, except away from the blue-clad man who had suddenly appeared before her, his mounted figure blocking out the paler blue of the afternoon sky.

Her first impulse had been to head toward him as quickly as she could, to throw her arms around him and cover his face with kisses. But the eyes glaring out at her from under a broad-brimmed Army hat and the lips compressed with anger reminded her too quickly of why she had run away. Even if she could have overlooked his rage, the cursed soldier's uniform that covered his body would have driven her to run.

Cole didn't really want her, not the real Erin. He had come to the Rocking J, up the long trail from Fort Concho, but her heavy heart feared it wasn't for a reason that would make her world right.

The roan responded to her urgings as though he sensed her desperation, stretching his long, powerful legs in ever-lengthening strides, his head extended, nostrils flaring. Leaning over the horse's neck, Erin guided him expertly along the path which ran down to the creek. Beside the meandering waterway they galloped, across the hilly ranchland, dipping and rising, heading away from the shallow stream and then back again to follow close along its bank, always winding farther to the east. Clusters of cottonwood and cedar grew along the water's edge, and Erin concentrated on dodging the low-hanging branches obscuring her way.

Closing in behind her was the steady, inexorable pounding of another horse's hoofs. Louder and louder the sounds came to her until she could hear the slap of a crop against flanks and then, God help her, the sharp, deep call of her husband.

"Erin! Watch out!"

A warning cry. Trusting him instinctively, she looked down the way past the trail immediately in front of her. Blocking the path was the huge trunk of a felled cedar tree. To the right of the obstruction grew thick, impenetrable shrubs; to the left the widening creek dipped down into a murky, deep pool. Cole's cry had come too late for her to pull up short. Her decision was quickly made. She headed for the water.

The stream was deeper here, and she cursed herself for not seeing the obstruction sooner. Halfway to the opposite bank, the roan slowed, and Cole was beside her, reaching for the reins, grabbing her arms. She jerked free and suddenly felt his body land heavily against hers. Her moccasined feet slipped from the stirrups. Gripped in a pair of iron-strong arms, she felt herself falling, falling. Husband and wife, their bodies entangled, landed with a splash in the shadowed pool.

At first she tried to fight him, but as they sank beneath the surface of the water, her struggles to pull free proved pitifully inadequate. Cole tightened his hold on her and pulled them both upward.

Then Erin made another mistake—she tried to speak before she had cleared the water and could breathe the warm air. Her words of protest came out an unintelligible splutter.

For one terrifying moment Cole thought she was drowning and he held her even tighter, as if to force out any water which had found its way to her lungs. It was the epithet she yelled in his ear, rather than her continued struggles, which told him she was safe.

He loosened his hold enough to look down into her flashing eyes. "I see by your sweet greeting that you're all right, love."

"No thanks to you!" She tossed her head back and two wet braids flopped against her shoulders. Floating away from her on the current was her old Stetson; not far from it in slow pursuit was a water-stained Army hat, its engineer's insignia glinting in the dappled sunlight.

Cole's eyes narrowed. "You shouldn't have run from me." He hesitated a minute. "Either time."

Beads of moisture clung to his thick lashes, and damp black hair curled thickly around his lean face. Erin lowered her gaze to the water lapping about their waists. "Let me go, Cole."

"Not just yet, Mrs. Barrett."

The words should have been a caress, but they hit her like the slap of an open hand.

"I told you that was over," she said angrily as she tried once more to push away from him.

"The wedding was legal, Erin. And consummated." His eyes glittered darkly. "Or don't you remember?"

Erin threw her head back proudly. Remember? She'd been able to think of little else, but she would be damned if she'd let him know it.

"A fraud, that's what it was, Cole. Admit it. We barely knew each other."

Cole's hands played against her back. "I thought we got rather well acquainted on the train"—his hold on her tightened—"until you pulled that foolish little stunt of running away. Apparently you didn't know me well enough if you thought I would let you get away

201

from me."

When he pulled her against his chest, she tried to cry out in protest, but her words were muffled as his mouth crashed down on hers. A rough kiss without love, a claim that her lips were his to take whenever he chose. Struggling against him, she tightened her mouth against the probing demands of his tongue.

Gradually the kiss softened, and so did Erin's protestations, as though the months of bitter thought and strong resolve were washed away in the flowing waters of the creek surrounding them. For one sweet tender moment she let herself take pleasure in his touch. In a hotel bed, a private railroad car, or a murky, deserted pool, her reactions to him were the same—absolute surrender, consuming desire.

This time when she pushed away from him, he didn't tighten his hold. He'd won. She could almost read his mind. Out of the corner of her eye she saw the roan cropping grass at the water's edge. Cole's mount was not within her range of vision. Probably he was much farther away. If Erin could just reach her horse, she could be back at the Rocking J and under the protection of her friends before Cole caught up with her again.

With small, imperceptible steps she began to move through the water, gradually narrowing the distance between her and the roan.

"If you think you're going to reach that horse before I can stop you, Erin, think again."

She cried out and, forgetting all subtlety, began to splash her way to the sandy shallows. Cole grabbed her wrist and jerked her back to his side. His eyes looked angrily at her, trailed down her neck to the open throat of her shirt, studied for one long moment the leather amulet, and then moved to the thin, wet material that clung provocatively to her breasts. Suddenly the anger in his eyes changed to hot appraisal and then to desire. She could read it in their gray-black depths.

He began to pull her to the farther shore, away from the roan. His fingers held her in a viselike grip she couldn't break. Tremors shot through her when she realized his purpose. He planned to take her, here in the open air—to strip her and, ignoring whatever protests she was able to make, fill her with his unquenchable desire.

The man dragging her through the water was not the gentle teacher who had revealed to her the wonderful secrets of love, not the ardent husband who had played such sweet songs of passion on her body with his hands and his lips. This man was a stranger, an avenging fiend who had swooped down on her in a fury of passion. She trembled, but not in fright. Dark desire whipped at her, a mindless urging to meld her body with his.

It was her own wild need that struck fear in her heart, and with her free hand she tried to pry his fingers from their hold on her.

"Cole, no." Her voice was little more than a whisper.

He looked down at her with eyes like burning coals. "Don't you know, love, that I can't wait for you to say yes?"

She twisted her arm, a futile gesture. Cole's response was to lift her into his arms and wade toward the grassy bank. Holding her tightly, he pressed his lips briefly once more against hers, then whispered soft words into her mouth. "I won't do anything you don't want me to do."

Erin fought in vain against the sweet trap of love. "You always say that," she managed to get out, her eyes on his firm lips, "and we end up the same way."

"I know." Cole grinned. It was the first real smile he had given her since his careening ride after her, and Erin's heart lurched.

Without another word he carried her out of the water; laying her at his feet, he quickly shed his coat and shirt and tossed them aside. Water-darkened blue trousers clung wetly down the length of his muscular legs until they disappeared into calf-tight black boots. His spurs clinked once as he unbuckled his holster and sent his heavy revolver thumping to the ground after his shirt.

Mesmerized, Erin heard every sound, watched every movement. She was powerless to try to run away; it seemed as though some unseen bonds were chaining her to the ground. She looked up at the fine black hairs that covered his chest. They were wet and tightly curled. Against her will, her eyes moved back to the trousers which clung to his narrow hips and long, hard legs. The desire in the depths of his eyes and in his voice had been no illusion. The bulge of his manhood beneath the confines of his tight pants told her he was ready to claim her body once more.

She was dangerously close to complete surrender. The nearer his half-naked body got to her, the harder it was to remember why she had eluded him. Waiting until he sat beside her to remove his boots, she made one last try for escape, a desperate lunge toward the water. With ridiculous ease he grabbed her by the waist and pulled her against him.

Her hands pushed against his bare chest. Wonderfully taut muscles moved beneath her fingers, and instantly she formed her hands into fists to pound against him. Mustn't touch him too much, mustn't let him know what touching him did to her. As though he didn't already know. Harder and harder she struck at him. His only response was to pull her tighter against him, pressing the full length of her legs against his, thrusting his hard waiting manhood against her opening bud of desire.

A low growl came from deep within Cole. "I'll tear your clothes off you if that's what you want, Erin. You turn me into an animal."

His words stoked the growing flames of passion that melted her body to his. An animal, he'd said. And so was she, in his arms; in answer she gave a soft cry and, moving her hands to his broad shoulders, writhed against his naked chest. Sure fingers gripped the opening of her shirt and ripped apart the thin material and she helped by lifting the leather thong from around her neck and tossing it aside.

As Cole's mouth and tongue played at her hard-tipped breasts, Erin stroked his face, his hair. Dear Cole. How could she have imagined she could live without the touch of his lips and hands? Thick-leafed trees blocked out the afternoon sun from their rustic bed of love; Cole's magic blocked out the world.

He raised his head and burned his lips against hers. Their breathing came sharp and shallow, their caresses were frantic. Need replaced thought; savage desire consumed them both. His plundering tongue probed the dark recesses of her mouth; his strong hands stroked, massaged, enflamed her body.

Mindlessly driven, Erin pulled helplessly at the waist of his trousers, then moved her fingers down to rub against the taut bulge between his thighs. He shuddered under her touch, pulled away, and in short, quick movements finished the undressing that had been so explosively interrupted when their bodies had pressed together on the grassy bank.

Naked, they clung to one another, hands and lips trailing fiery paths. Each spot that Cole touched became the center of her widening, pulsating desire. His fingers circled at last the triangle of fine hair that led to the source of her raging demand.

Husband and wife existed only in the ardor that they shared; no longer was Cole the teacher and Erin his willing subject. She answered his arousing strokes with sure, firm touches of her own—across his chest, down his flat abdomen covered in thickening hair, to muscled legs and inner thighs, then upward to hold his precious manhood in her supple fingers.

A long, heartfelt sigh, a violent tremor, and then Cole moved her hand away from his body. "Not that way, love. I want to be inside you. I want your body to hold me as it was meant to do."

He parted her thighs and settled himself against her. How right he felt between her legs, a glorious extension of her own self, more vital to her existence than air and light. Cole nourished her heart and soul.

His entry was quick and smooth. Erin wrapped her legs around him, arching her breasts to rub against the broad expanse of his chest. From every point where flesh pressed against flesh, tiny arcs of delight shot forth; enticing thrills they were for Cole and Erin, promising and demanding always more, driving them onward, binding them tightly.

Molten desire flowed between them as harder and faster their bodies came together. With frenzied thrusts they gave in to the wild tremors that rent all rational thought, all desire, save the savage pleasure they took from one another.

Higher and higher they spiraled until together they slipped across the satin-smooth boundaries that marked the outer edge of ecstasy, into the love-rich, heady heights of sensual fulfillment. For one sweet tenuous moment they held on to that peak of glory, their lips together, bodies irrevocably and forever linked—two minds with but a single thought, to extend to the outer reaches of time the oneness that made them complete.

They asked the impossible. Gradually the world around them began to intrude, at first with gentle sounds of moving water, of birds overhead, the rustle of wind in the leaves of the cottonwood trees that served as a bower around their grassy bed. Still they clung to one another until their embrace became a kind of desperate denial of everything they had to face. Their lips parted and Cole whispered into her ear that he had missed her.

Of course he didn't lie. Not Cole. She had no doubt that he had felt as lonely in the long nights as she. If they could stay isolated and wrapped in each other's arms like this forever, it mattered little that there were deep differences which could threaten their happiness. Away from a censorious world, she knew she could make Cole happy.

She slipped her arms from around his body, trailed her fingers around his lips, then gently began to push him away.

His arms still loosely holding her, Cole watched as the light of love in his wife's eyes darkened to sadness. "What's wrong, Erin?"

She looked past him and up into the thick-leafed trees overhead. "Why did you come after me?"

Cole's body stiffened. "Why did you run away?" When Erin didn't answer, he said more sharply, "It seems all we do is ask each other questions. It's time we had a few answers."

He made no protest when she pulled free of his embrace and sat beside him, her long red braids falling forward across each breast, her legs tucked under her. How smooth and silky was her flesh. Cole had to look away, or else he would have claimed her once again, and this time it would have made damned little difference what she wanted.

But Erin knew only too well what he was thinking. His eyes had lingered a moment too long for her to misread his thoughts. The hooded desire in their gray depths stroked her as it always did, and she knew there was no way she could sit naked in front of her husband's lean, hard body and talk about the differences between them— at least any differences other than the physical ones.

She looked ruefully at the shirt Cole had torn from her body, and at her sodden buckskin trousers which lay rumpled at her side.

"Here," Cole said, holding out his long cotton shirt. "This will cover you while we talk."

And what's going to cover you? she almost asked as she put on the shirt, then watched in fascination as he stood with his back to her and, shaking out the excess water from his trousers, slipped them up his long, powerful legs, covering his narrow hips and tight buttocks. He picked up her buckskins and hung them from a branch to dry, the muscles across his back playing in hypnotic ripples. No matter what happened between them, Erin knew she would never regret the hours spent in exploring her husband's magnificent body.

He turned and looked down at her. Light streaming through the leaves fell across his face; his still-damp hair was darkly curled, giving him a boyish look. She knew by the determined set of his eyes and firm mouth that the look was deceiving—her husband was a man who would brook no lies or foolish denials. She had left him, and she had to tell him why.

Cole spoke first. "You wanted to know why I came after you, Erin. You know damned little about me, if you have to ask. You're my wife and I want you at my side."

"Even if I don't belong there?"

"I don't know what in hell you're talking about. As I pointed out earlier, our marriage was legal. You took the same vows I did."

Erin stood and pulled the damp material of Cole's shirt around her body. "You vowed to take as your wife a homeless girl you had deflowered in a Washington hotel room. Tell the truth, Cole. Honor was what made you write that note of proposal."

Remembering the way her body had responded to him, he laughed sharply. "Was it my honor that made you give in to me?"

"You know full well what made me give in to you. I

don't think very clearly when I'm in your arms. And you haven't denied your reasons for marrying me."

"You haven't given me much of a chance to deny anything."

"Then deny this. You took as your bride an illiterate Comanche who is more at home at a poker table than a dining table. Captain Coleman Barrett. Indian fighter. Of course with the way I was dressed up in all that fancy eastern garb, you didn't know what you were getting. I should have told you right away."

"I took as my bride a beautiful, loving woman who made me realize what a lonely existence I had been leading." His eyes trailed down her slender bare legs, then slowly back again to her face. "You don't look like any squaw I've ever seen."

Erin steeled herself against his look. "Indian blood flows in my veins, Cole. I told you that in Mobile. My mother called me Dawn Flower, after her mother Dawn Breeze. My grandmother was a full-blooded Comanche who fell in love with a wild Irishman. A man who loved the freedom of the West, one who was willing to spend his life in an Indian camp so he could be by his wife."

Cole's unblinking eyes bore steadily into her. Images of blood and broken bodies flashed through his mind. "And where did you get the name Erin Donovan?"

"My mother Prairie Dew also loved an Irishman. A soldier, as a matter of fact, named Shaun Donovan. After the white men killed her, he quit the Army and took to the saloons. I received my education across a poker table, not at a finishing school. And don't think I regret the way I was raised."

"You're the one who seems to be apologizing for the facts of your life. Three-fourths of your heritage is Irish. Have you forgotten that?"

"It's most of the Irishmen and the rest of the whites who won't forget the Comanche blood. I just wish I had told you everything before you made such a terrible mistake."

"Are you telling me it was a mistake, or is that my conclusion?"

"It's a fact. And I could see you realized it in Mobile."

"You didn't hang around long enough to see anything, Erin. That was a damned cruel thing you did, running out into the night in the middle of a yellow fever epidemic."

Erin was very close to tears. "Cruel? You don't know what the word means. Cruel is being honorable and marrying the wrong woman. Cruel is teaching her passion's glory and watching her fall in love without returning the deep affection that would make the union complete. Cruel is wanting to change me into your idea of what I ought to be, rather than accepting me for what I am."

Erin's breast heaved and she breathed in a great gulp of air. "Cruel is never saying 'I love you,'" she whispered, her anger spent.

Cole didn't touch her. "I never meant to hurt you, Erin. Never." His voice softened. "Look up at me. Please."

Slowly she raised her eyes. Her heart stopped at the raw emotion written on his face.

"I love you, Erin Donovan. Dawn Flower. Or whatever else you call yourself. I promise to spend the rest of my life making up for not realizing it sooner. I could have saved us both a lot of pain."

Erin stood, her eyes locked with his. No matter that she knew his hatred of Indians was not gone, that she didn't even know why he had the thirst for revenge his Uncle Thad had mentioned back in Washington; no matter now that she was unpolished in society and couldn't read. Cole had said he loved her, only her. The vision of his ring tucked into its box rose before her, and she went into his arms.

Minutes later after he had kissed away all her tears, she spoke.

"Please understand how things are, Cole. I can't read, I'm never sure which fork to use, and worst of all, I'm part Comanche. Maybe I can take care of the first two, but the last will never change. There may come a time when you can't accept it any longer."

She waited breathlessly for him to answer, to tell her of the reason he hated the red man.

"I won't lie to you, Erin, and say your Indian blood means nothing," Cole said, "but these last weeks without you have been a hell I never want to go through again. I'd be a poor excuse for a man if I couldn't put aside old hatreds for a future with you." He stroked her arms. "You're just going to have to trust me, love."

Their eyes caught and held. Erin wanted very much for him to relieve her worry by saying his hatred sprang from Army training. But he didn't, and she felt she couldn't ask about its source.

Time. That was what he needed to be sure of his love, and perhaps while he was on assignment for the Army, she could still undertake the search for her grandparents as she'd planned. She tried to explain how she felt, but Cole protested with a long, searing kiss.

"Don't talk about leaving me. Ever again." He held her tight. "You feel so good. I was so afraid you were off in some European capital where I couldn't reach you."

She pulled away, her amber eyes glistening with unshed tears. He was so easy to trust. Smiling irrepressibly, she motioned to the untamed land around them. "It's a good thing I came back to civilization."

A chill breeze blew across the water. "It's getting late," he said, reaching for Erin's buckskin trousers on the nearby branch. "I'd hate for you to survive exposure to yellow fever and catch cold because of me. Get dressed and I'll go see if I can round up the horses."

Erin watched as he tugged on his coat and, walking along the bank to a shallow part of the creek, crossed over to disappear through the trees. In the wider pool of water to her left she saw two hats caught in a piece of driftwood at the edge of the water. She rescued them. Her Stetson would never be the same, but Cole's Army hat had somehow managed to catch higher up on the log and was little the worse for its dousing.

When he returned, astride his mount with the roan in tow, Erin was clad in her still-damp buckskins and his long-sleeved shirt; around her neck was the leather amulet. She had unbraided her hair to let it dry. Cole caught his breath. Somehow he had to make her realize her only choice was to leave with him. No more foolish talk of time and separation.

"You're a beautiful woman, Erin. How did you manage to get away from me in Mobile?"

Erin grinned. "I wish I could say I found an all-night poker game and worked my way west. But I wouldn't want to lie."

"Of course not."

She ignored the sarcastic edge to his voice. "The truth is I spent a rather uncomfortable night in an unlocked office at the train station. The next day I sent a telegram to Dallas for money."

No doubt her guardian had provided the funds, Cole decided. The thought irritated him. Erin was the responsibility of her husband, not her guardian.

On the ride back he asked her questions about Hud and his wife Julie, and about the way Hud had taken Erin in when her father was killed. Erin's eyes warmed when she spoke of them, especially of their two young children Glen and Elizabeth.

"And what about the man running this spread? Cur, I think his name is." Cole grinned. "An unusual name."

"He's an unusual man," Erin said, and described Cur's

burly, seven-foot frame and flaming red beard. "Hud got him out of some trouble in Melbourne a few years ago and they've been together ever since. No one knows his real name. Cur is short for currency. Hud said it was what ex-convicts in Australia were called."

"He was sent to the penal colony there?"

"A mistake, Hud said. He's really a very gentle man. He's been a good friend to me."

Cole remembered the anger he'd felt when he'd first seen Erin riding wildly across the countryside. "Like letting you ride Indian fashion so you can risk breaking your neck?"

"He knows a lot about Comanche ways, Cole. He's accepted what I am. Comanches are born riders and I've been practicing since I got this roan. I knew what I was doing."

Her red hair shone in the light and rippled around her shoulders. Her amber eyes with their curious golden flecks flashed proudly at him. High cheekbones. Smooth, tawny skin. How much more beautiful she was than the pale women he'd thought he admired.

"Does Cur know you're my wife?"

"No one does." Her voice softened. "In the past months I've been unsure myself—as though the whole episode was a dream."

His voice caressed her. "Our marriage doesn't seem real?"

"Sometimes it didn't. You changed all that today."

"I did my best. You'll have to tell Cur the truth."

Cole spoke with a sweet firmness that warmed her heart. Even in her darkest moments she'd wanted to tell Cur or Angel or *anyone* about her marriage, to describe the man who had taken her as his, if only for a short while. But of course she hadn't. She'd been so sure the marriage was at an end.

"Of course I'll tell him," she said.

"And Hud?"

Erin smiled. "Everyone. As soon as I see them. I'd like to tell them in person."

Lights from the Rocking J's bunkhouse flickered in the gathering dusk as they rode in. "Go talk to Cur while I see to my men. There are four of them. I suppose there's a place where they can bed down for the night."

Erin pointed in the direction of the bunkhouse behind the small cabin where she slept. "Most of the hands are scattered in line shacks. You'll be able to find plenty of room in there." She turned to enter the cabin and heard the sound of an approaching horse and an unfamiliar voice calling out.

"Captain Barrett!" A soldier rode into view. He was riding hard, and as he approached them, he tugged on the reins, causing the horse to rear briefly. "We've got trouble, sir," he said in a low voice. "Indians."

"Nonsense!" Erin said. "There aren't Indians around here anymore, at least not any that could cause trouble. Most of them have been forced onto the reservation at Fort Sill."

The soldier ignored her. "Around the cattle, sir. I'd swear there's a band of them savages trying to steal the herd."

Cole's eyes were trained on the soldier. "Where's the boss man? Cur."

"Gone to check a pen but we didn't want to say anything to him until we were sure, although he looks big enough to take on the whole five tribes of Oklahoma. 'Course they're right skinny Indians now."

Cole didn't smile. He motioned toward the cabin. "Go inside, Erin."

"No! Your man is mistaken."

"I doubt it. The corporal is an old Indian fighter. That's why I brought him. The other man—Pop, I think he's called—is here and Cur will be back. I'll leave them here with you. Now I can carry you in over my shoulder and tie you up, or you can walk in and stay. The choice is yours."

Erin grew frantic for his safety. She wanted to rail against his needless gesture to protect her, but the unyielding look in his eye told her this one time to retreat. She would have to let him spend the night searching for what were, after all, phantom Comanches or Kiowas or whatever Indians the corporal imagined were marauding the countryside.

Inside, with the sound of departing horses echoing in her ears, she wasn't quite so sure she had made the right choice. What if something happened to Cole? She hadn't even kissed him good-bye. When Cur returned, she asked him to assure her the corporal had been wrong.

"Can't say for sure, Erin. I've told you before, lots of Indians go renegade for short periods of time. Life on reservations is unnatural for them. They're bored and hungry." He looked through the open door. "I'm going to look. Be right back."

Twenty minutes later Cur returned. "It's true, Erin. Herman is in the bunkhouse with an arrow through his hip. Jimbo and Curry have taken off—or been carried off. More than likely ran. Never trusted those two. That's why they weren't sent out on their own to brand strays."

Erin fought rising panic. "What way did the soldiers ride out?"

"West. But forget about following. They're paid to fight Indians and know the risks."

She dug into the bottom drawer of a chest and, emerging with a small box, opened it to reveal a gleaming gold band. She slipped the ring onto her finger.

"Cur, did you get a look at the captain leading them? He's my husband," she said simply. "I can't let anything hurt him. I'm the reason he's here, not the cattle."

Nothing ruffled Cur. "Has he got a name?" he asked.

"Cole Barrett. I met him in Virginia. I know it sounds foolish, but Hud doesn't even know. I don't think."

"Never know about Hud," Cur agreed. "But Erin, if you married this fellow, he must be all right. We'll look for them in the morning if they're not back yet. No use blundering out in the dark."

Erin nodded and, wrapping her husband's shirt tightly around her, blew out the lamp and then sat by a window to wait for Cole's return. In the stillness her thoughts wandered down unpleasant paths. If Cole went very far, he'd be riding through Texas brush country, low hills and scraggly shrubs tall enough to hide a crouching Indian.

Night fell without a sign of anyone's return. Cur was out somewhere keeping watch. He came in occasionally for coffee. Erin fretted so much about the injured Herman that Cur once escorted her to check on him, but Pop shooed her out.

"Get some sleep, child. Can't do nothing now but wait."

Sleep came sometime in the early morning hours, and when Erin awoke to find the first rays of dawn on the horizon, she cursed herself for finding even a short time of peace.

She was alone in the room. Fighting panic, she hurried onto the porch. Cur stood in the yard, and when he saw her, he slowly shook his head. No words were necessary. The soldiers had not returned.

She turned and ran back inside, tucking in the oversized Army shirt as she went. Cole's touch seemed woven in its fibers and she'd be damned if she would give it up. Grabbing up her water-stained Stetson, she joined Cur in the yard. Resting against her breast was the Comanche amulet; on her finger was her wedding ring.

Already Cur had their mounts saddled, and Erin wondered if this search for her husband wasn't the real reason fate had led her to the strawberry roan. Funny

216

thing, fate. She'd never thought about its existence before she traveled east. There were times now when she thought of little else.

When she hurried out onto the front porch, Pop came scurrying from the bunkhouse. "You're not chasing them Indians, Miss Erin. Nor them soldiers. Not just you and Cur."

Erin twisted her long hair atop her head and shoved the Stetson firmly in place. "I'm going, Pop. I don't have any choice. You and Cur are welcome to ride along."

"I gotta stay with Herman. He's bad off."

"What kind of arrow was it, Pop?" asked Cur.

"Comanche. Probably off Fort Sill."

"Something's wrong here. Horse Back's kept them pretty tame several years now."

"Can't never tell about them red devils," said Pop.

Erin wanted to scream out at the old man's words and obliterate the thought that her husband might be dead at the hands of her own people. She wondered if she could kill a Comanche even to save Cole, then called herself crazed. Of course she could. These Indians were renegades, outlaws, and as deserving of just retribution as any white robber. Being red didn't automatically make them pure any more than being white guaranteed uprightness.

She ran into the yard and mounted the roan, checking the rifle scabbard. "I'm riding west to check it out. Cur?"

He nodded and swung onto his huge Appaloosa. Grimly they began crossing the trackless countryside. Both could read the signs as clearly as if arrows had been drawn. A herd of cattle had recently passed this way. They rode hard and fast, easily following the tracks.

The landscape altered quickly, from green to brown; with the winter rains not yet come, the hard-packed ground was cracked and dry. The sun was halfway across the cloudless sky when they came upon a shallow creek and stopped to water and rest their horses. To their left rose a high, rugged bluff.

Cur dismounted and, leaving his horse by the creek, walked into the brush just before the gunshots rang out. Erin didn't wait for his return but spurred her horse up a narrow, twisting path that led to the top of the escarpment. Gunshots usually meant trouble, and she was grateful she carried a little trouble of her own, a new Winchester fifteen-shot repeating rifle. Thanks to Cur's instructions, she knew how to use it.

Erin never got the chance. Just as she topped the bluff, she was knocked from the back of her horse by an unseen weight that seemed to fly through the air—the second such occurrence in twenty-four hours, only this time her fall wasn't cushioned by a pool of water. Wincing in pain, she landed with her right shoulder against the hard ground, then gave way to fright at the sight of a half-naked, sweat-streaked body that pinned her down. In panic she struck out and kicked to free herself, but her frantic efforts were in vain. Dust swirled around the grappling pair; when it settled, she looked up into the dark, unsmiling face of a Comanche brave.

Words. What could she tell him that would let him know she meant him no harm? No harm, that is, if her husband was all right. Her mind froze. Grunting unintelligibly, the Indian gripped her long hair and jerked her to her feet. He bound her hands behind her with a rawhide thong, then looked in wordless appreciation at the roan stallion. At least, she thought, he hadn't looked at her in the same way he'd eyed her mount. Not yet.

He gripped the reins of the horse and, pulling the animal after him, shoved Erin deeper into the thickening brush. Behind him her Stetson hat lay abandoned in the dirt, mute testimony to the struggle that had taken place. Terrified that she misunderstood the buck's interest in her, she stumbled ahead. They reached a clearing where stood some half-dozen braves.

These were her people, screamed her mind. Surely she could make them understand she was one of them. A commotion to her right drew her attention, a flash of blue. Before she turned her head, she knew what she would see. Beneath the unrelenting noonday sun, the nightmare of the lonely night had come true. Bound hand and foot together on the ground were four soldiers of the United States Army. Nearby, his arms tied behind him around a tree, his eyes staring at her in disbelief and horror, was her husband Cole.

Chapter Thirteen

"Hevi!"

Woman! The brave's lone word rent the air like a war cry. Answering whoops filled Erin's head. Blurred images of brown bodies and black braids swam in front of her— chilling sensations only, none of them distinct save the awful look in her husband's eyes. Unthinking, she headed for him where he sat, legs extended and arms bound behind a hackberry tree.

"Cole—" The leather thong bit into her wrists as she was jerked backward; pain shot through her arms and shoulders. Under the blow of an iron hand, she sprawled onto the hard ground, dust filling her nose and mouth. It had the taste of despair.

Cole watched in helpless rage as his wife was dragged across the sun-baked earth and bound to a tree eight feet away. Vainly he fought against the strips of buffalo hide that restrained him from reaching her across the scant space. What in hell was Erin doing here? The answer was clear—she had followed him. Damn her foolish, impetuous nature, the wild way she had of plunging into things without thought for the consequences. It was one of the traits that had made her dear to him beyond all other things in life, but he trembled at the realization that it might bring about her death.

Flashes of another woman crossed his mind, of a lifeless body limp and oddly twisted, of blood-stained, pale hair spilling across a barn floor. At least the Comanches had killed Rachel quickly without violating her body. Erin might not fare as well.

Her arms bound awkwardly behind her, around an oak tree, Erin watched the agony on Cole's face, then looked away. He was so near and yet a world away—too far for her to feel the consolation of his touch, too close for her to escape the heat of his rage and fear. Fear. It was a word she'd never thought to apply to her husband. But it was there, unmistakable and frightening, in the depths of his eyes, in the tight set of his lips. And, God forgive her, she had put it there.

Had he been injured in the capture? Erin knew he would not have been taken without a struggle. Anxiously her eyes trailed across his lean face and broad shoulders, then down to the long legs stretched out across the cracked earth. The blue of his jacket was hidden beneath a thick coating of brown dust, but the buttons and braid showing rank were intact. One sleeve was torn, and there was a rent in his trousers leg below the left knee. No blood, no twisted limbs.

Relief flooded her. The formidable Captain Barrett, usually so crisp, so sharp, had never looked better than here in his dirty but blessedly whole state; she tried to tell him so with her eyes and half-smiling lips. For a moment he responded, the grim lines of his face softening to send a quick flash of understanding arcing between them. Then the look was gone, replaced by absolute fury—at his own helplessness, Erin knew, as much as at her capture. She felt the same anger.

The sun hung overhead like a burning coal, hot as only Texas could be hot in October. Rivulets of sweat ran down her throat and pooled in the valley between her breasts. Night would bring cool breezes out of the mountains across the Red River, if any of the captives were alive by then. Erin shook the thought from her mind. Such thinking would guarantee their doom. What they needed was a plan, but nothing she had seen offered hope for escape. Directly across the clearing was the small, scattered band of braves. At her left were their tethered horses; behind Cole, to her right, the four soldiers who had accompanied him lay bound together on the ground.

The one hope that burned in her mind was Cur. Somewhere in the brush her giant friend watched. She was sure of it. If only there was some way she could let Cole know, but when she opened her mouth to speak, he warned her with a look to be quiet. She glanced at the Indians. The whiplike glare in the eyes of a watching brave was enough to render her mute. Perhaps Cole already realized she had not raced foolishly after him alone, even though her past performances could hardly reassure him.

As the sun began its descent in the western sky, she prayed she would have time to explain to Cole why she had followed him. He consumed her heart and mind; it was far better to die with him than spend a future without him.

Sprawled awkwardly as she was on the hard ground at the base of the tree, she wondered what she must look like to him. Thick curls of hair tumbled wildly about her head and shoulders. The leather amulet hung heavily from around her neck. Cole's damp cotton shirt lay heavily against her body, and the buckskin trousers that hugged her skin were in little better condition than her husband's uniform. Hardly the garb for a ladylike wife of an Army captain—a ridiculous thought at such a time, but all she could do was think.

Erin's eyes shifted to the half-dozen braves who were,

at least for the time being, contented with talk and gestures, their interest more on Erin's strawberry roan than on their prisoners, and she almost laughed at the absurdity of the situation. Almost. The realization of the danger facing them chilled any dispassionate view that might flit through her mind.

Cold, helpless rage gripped her. Safe in the white man's world, she had argued the Indians' cause to her husband; with him tied beside her in the wilderness, only his survival mattered. If by some stroke of impossible good fortune she could get her hands on the Winchester tucked inside her saddle, she would gladly turn it on her Comanche captors, men that until today she had called brother.

No matter what happened to her, she must tell Cole how she felt. But his eyes were riveted on the Indians and she let her gaze follow his. This time she let herself really look at them. Beneath their fierce scowls they were little more than children, some of them not above sixteen. Had Erin been allowed to stand, they would have been little taller than her five-foot-five, but clad only in breech clouts, they were muscular and straight as arrows, their bodies gleaming like copper under the bright sun. A single black braid of hair hung down each broad back. Across each high-ridged cheekbone ran a streak of crimson paint.

A renegade band of young bucks was what they were, she figured, runaways from the reservation at Fort Sill, which was not far across the state line in the area which had been designated Indian Territory. Cur had told her how boredom and the need for food to augment government rations oftentimes sent the Indians scurrying for a brief taste of the freedom they had once known in Texas. Soldiers had even taken to riding along as escort on hunting trips to make sure they didn't raid any of the scattered ranches in the Panhandle—or slaughter any of

223

the settlers—but it was obvious this band was not accompanied by any United States cavalry. Having barely outgrown their childhood, these Indians were playing a desperate game. The sympathy she might have felt for them died beneath the knowledge that they might slay her husband.

She watched as they circled the roan, stroking him as they moved. The Comanches were the best horsemen in the West and Erin could tell by the reverent way they spoke and touched the roan that they recognized his superiority. At least, she thought with scant satisfaction, he would be saved from slaughter and from being roasted on the nearby coals, a fate which horses of lesser quality often faced. Comanches liked the taste of horseflesh as much as beef.

The sound of hoofs against the hard earth broke into her thoughts and for one wild minute she hoped it might be the seven-foot Cur riding to their rescue. But she looked in vain for the magnificent Appaloosa. Instead, a spotted Indian pony broke through the brush into the circle of the camp. Astride the horse rode another buck, this one slightly older than the others. An eagle feather, the mark of bravery, was caught in his braid and hung behind his left ear. Tall and straight he sat, and he had an arrogant air. Cockily he dropped to the ground and tossed the spoils of his hunt at the feet of his comrades—a scrawny-looking turkey that flapped its wings helplessly against the dusty earth.

"Food." Erin recognized the Comanche word he muttered.

One of the young braves began to stir the coals, tossing on a few sticks of wood for a higher flame. As if realizing his imminent doom, the turkey squawked loudly and frantically beat his wings against the ground. A Comanche knife slicing across the tom's neck ended the high-pitched protest, but the bird continued to flap helplessly in a widening circle. Blood flowed into the dirt. At last it lay still.

Erin stared, mesmerized, at the crimson knife as it was tucked inside its leather sheath, which hung from a breechclout, and then at the stained ground around the dead bird. Even when one of the braves carelessly grabbed up the carcass and tossed it into the rising flames, she couldn't look away. Smoke from the fire thickened, and the smell of burning feathers filled the still air. The stench was nauseating and Erin swallowed the bile that rose in her throat. She forced her gaze away from the fire—and looked directly into the black eyes of the newly arrived brave, who stared at her from a dozen feet away.

"*Hevi,*" he said softly. Woman.

His appraisal was unreadable at first, and then a grin split his broad face. The smile died; in its place appeared a flat, savage leer. Narrowing the gap between them, he knelt on the ground, his face level with hers. She could smell his breath, which was strangely sweet, a contrast to the harsh, painted visage which moved closer. A low growl came from her right.

"Touch her and you're dead." Cole's voice cut through the air like a lance, lethal and unswerving. To her amazement he repeated his threat in the assonant language of the Comanche.

For a second the brave's eyes darkened, and Erin thought she read surprise and fear in their depths. But only for a second. The Indian looked at the bonds that held the white chief securely to the tree and his old cockiness returned. Standing upright, he pulled a knife from the sheath that lay against his muscled thigh and sent it streaking through the air. Erin stifled a scream as the knife plunged into the bark of the hackberry, not two inches from Cole's head.

Her husband's eyes remained steady and unblinking,

his gaze never leaving the Indian's face. His lips broke into a smile, as if daring his captor to attack. Deliberately he was calling attention to himself—and away from her. Erin's heart pounded with pride and terror at his foolhardy bravery.

"The Comanche grows weak," Cole taunted in the words of the Indian. "Attacks small bands of men and a lone woman." He jerked a nod at his men on the ground behind him. "But can he win in a fair fight?" His lips curled in a sneer. "Untie my hands and prove you are a man."

The air was still, rent only by the sound of the crackling fire and the odor of the roasting bird, mellowed now that the feathers had been consumed by the flames. The brave's back was to Erin and she could only guess at his reaction to Cole's challenge. She held her breath, then let out a quiet sigh as he turned. Her relief was short-lived.

"Is good they still live," he said, raising his fist in the direction of the captives. His moccasined feet struck the ground noiselessly as he walked to the hackberry tree and pulled out the knife. He sheathed the weapon and, joining his companions, looked back at Cole. "We hold death ceremony when sun goes on its dark journey," he said triumphantly.

A babble of voices responded in a ragged chorus, and Erin, fighting panic, made out that the Indians didn't really know what to do with their prisoners. Some seemed to have second thoughts about slaying them, and her hopes rose. Across the hard ground, Cole stared impassively at the scene.

The newcomer stilled the braves with a motion of his hand. "I, Little Hawk, say they die. The woman lives." His dark eyes flicked back at Erin. "Until we have no use of her."

"And I say again you are a coward." Cole's voice was

filled with scorn. "Little Hawk, you are well named. A hawk preys on the helpless and the lame. A little hawk needs others to do his dirty work."

"And I say"—Little Hawk pounded his chest—"that we are Antelope Eaters. We do not go around like frightened women." His gesture took in the gathering band of Comanches, which Erin now saw numbered close to twenty.

Pressing herself against the rough bark of the tree, she watched helplessly as Little Hawk strode to where she sat and, reaching down, yanked at her shirt. The cloth ripped open, leaving much of her breasts bared to the view of the savages around her. Without thinking, she looked to Cole for help. White-lipped, he stared at Little Hawk, his whole body straining at the rawhide bonds that kept him from her side.

The band of Indians gathered closer as Little Hawk reached down once more. His fingers trailed down her throat and Erin poised herself to kick him as hard as she could, her target the breechclout between his legs. The attack was never delivered. Instead of touching her breasts, Little Hawk gripped the leather amulet that had lain hidden under her shirt and jerked it free.

Studying for a moment the sun painted in cinnabar upon its surface, he held it up for all to see. The sun was a Comanche design; Erin knew the amulet was patterned like a war shield. She held her breath, knowing the Indians would recognize it and praying the discovery would somehow keep them all alive.

"It is of our people," one buck said, and the others murmured their assent.

For the first time since her capture, Erin spoke. "It belonged to my mother, Prairie Dew," she said in halting Comanche. Their dark eyes looked in curiosity at her, and she spoke slowly as best she could, cursing all the while that she had practiced listening to the language more than speaking it. "My mother's white father painted it for his Indian bride. It is proof that I am one of you. Comanche blood flows through my veins."

Little Hawk's eyes narrowed. Kneeling close by her side, he studied her face and with his blunt fingers stroked the long red curls that fell across her bare breast. Erin's heart pounded. Doubt was all she could read in his eyes.

"Where is this mother you speak of?" he asked.

Erin fought to keep a tremor from her voice. "She was killed many moons ago when I was a small child." No need, she thought, to tell him white soldiers had been her slayers. "She called me Dawn Flower and told me many stories of my grandmother, Dawn Breeze. With the aid of these soldiers, I seek to find her and my grandfather. I do not know what he is called."

Her eyes followed Little Hawk as he stood and joined the other braves. She looked to Cole for assurance. That he was helping her find her Indian family was far from the truth, but under the circumstances he wouldn't mind the lie. His gray eyes resting on her showed dark worry and the love that he had so recently proclaimed.

The Indians talked briefly among themselves, then Little Hawk said, "We do not know of this Dawn Breeze. And many white men take a squaw."

This time Erin spoke with authority. "I speak the truth. The amulet does not lie."

Murmurings of discontent spread through the group and when Little Hawk attempted to calm them, he was ignored. Erin could see he did not have a tight hold on his position of leadership. Something was making his erstwhile followers fear more than just the opinion and posturings of their loud-voiced brother.

One of the younger braves spoke up. "When he hears of this, Horse Back will not like it. We do not war on our own kind. Even a woman with hair like the rising sun.

228

Her words may be the lies of the white man, but she has a true amulet."

"And who will tell our chief?" Little Hawk asked.

"Horse Back is free to roam the countryside. He knows all," the brave replied proudly. He swaggered over to the fire and, using a half-burned stick, raked the charred carcass of the turkey from the hot coals. With a knife he pulled back the stumps that had once been feathers and split open the skin. Even from a distance, Erin could see the tender cooked meat; for just a moment she felt pride in the effective simplicity of the Comanche ways.

As he passed around the afternoon repast, the other Indians talked of Horse Back, telling of his legendary deeds. For this little while they seemed more like children than fierce warriors and Erin glanced over at Cole to see if he noticed. Her husband sat unmoving, taking in the loud talk about Horse Back as though it were some life-giving potion. It seemed a chilling kind of nourishment. A faint smile curved his lips but no warmth of expression reached his steely eyes.

She was reminded once more of Thaddeus Lymond's admonition that his nephew forget the past and his desire for revenge against the red man. This Indian called Horse Back was a part of that past. Erin was sure of it and for a moment stark panic gripped her. She was not part of Cole's past. She knew in his mind he was in another time and another place where she didn't exist.

Their captors were still talking animatedly, and she took the chance to call him back to her.

"Cole," she whispered. He continued to stare at the Indians. "Cole," she repeated more fervently and was rewarded when he turned to her. "Are you all right?" she asked.

Gradually he focused on her and, with a side look at the Indians, nodded. "No damage yet. Did you have a backup?"

"Cur rode with me. He's out there somewhere. I heard a shot and took off alone while he was off his horse." She glanced past him through the trees and on to the low-lying bushes that dotted the arid land. "He's watching. I'm sure of it."

"You took off alone? That's a bad habit, love."

She ignored him. "What was the shot?"

"One of our friends there"—he indicated the braves who were now sprawled in the shade across from them—"decided to compare my Army rifle with one he used to capture my men." A puzzled look crossed his face. Something about the guns, Erin thought, had disturbed him. Suddenly his eyes were filled with warning, and slumping against the tree, he dropped his head as if in sleep.

Erin glanced at the Indians. Little Hawk was staring at her and then at Cole. She stifled a yawn and followed her husband's example in feigning sleep. The next time they had a chance to talk, she vowed, it would not be wasted on foolish questions. Somehow they must plan their escape.

Cole pretended sleep, even snored a bit and tugged surreptitiously at his bonds until sleep actually overtook him for a short time. When he awoke, a look at the sun dipping halfway toward the horizon told him he hadn't been out long. Silently he berated himself for the stupidity that had led to his capture. He'd been too intent on following the trail of cattle and had carelessly failed to allow for the rear guard the Indians left behind to ambush his small detachment. Too late he realized he'd been too long in the East.

He glanced around the camp; only a few of the Indians were visible, lying desultorily around the clearing in wait, no doubt, for the return of a hunting party.

The soldiers, bound awkwardly together, slumped

wearily on the ground. An air of defeat hung over them, but the corporal caught Cole's eye and gave him a slow wink. If given a chance to fight, the men would be ready in a second. It was a chance they might get. Somewhere in the brush, Cole felt certain, the giant Cur was waiting and watching for the right moment to attack. He wouldn't come this far only to abandon a friend.

Erin stirred restlessly in a fitful sleep, her slender body scratched and bruised from the rough treatment she had received. An old, familiar warmth stirred Cole's loins. Better not to think too much about his wife's body or he'd never have a chance to explore it again.

He forced his mind to the immediate problem at hand. If and when Cur did attack, Cole wanted to be ready to give aid. Slowly he again began to work at the narrow strips of uncured leather binding him. His wrists were slippery with sweat, and he used the moisture to his advantage, stretching the thongs and edging them down to the narrowest part of his arm. He felt a slight give, but the stretch wasn't enough to slip the bonds over his hands.

A shadow fell across him, and he looked up to see Little Hawk standing over him. Neither man spoke as the Indian bent and checked the loops around his wrists. Little Hawk tugged at the bonds, grunted, then contemptuously scuffed dirt over Cole as he left.

Cole watched until Little Hawk had joined the resting braves before he dropped his hands as low as he could and slowly felt around the ground for a sharp rock, ideally a flint but he would settle for anything. No luck. He glanced at Little Hawk, but for the moment the Indian showed no concern for his captive. He inched his body down the trunk of the tree. Almost wrenching his shoulders from their sockets, he explored a wider circle. Smooth pebbles and a few scattered small rocks were his reward.

At last his fingers gripped a large, rough-edged stone sunk in the hard ground—not a flint, but, if he were given the time, it would do. After five minutes he had pried it loose and inched back up the tree until he sat upright. With the stone placed between his wrists he began to rub the leather thong against its sharp surface.

In his awkward position, the work was difficult; after thirty minutes he was able to detect only a discouraging amount of progress. But he didn't stop when he heard the sound of approaching horses. He judged it wouldn't be Cur making that much noise to herald his appearance so he decided to keep on working in order to meet whatever new threat might face him.

Cole was right. Topping the rise was an old Indian on horseback. A strap-held blanket his saddle, he sat tall, loosely holding a rope halter fashioned around the horse's nose. Under his breechclout he wore an Army trooper's blue pants with the seat comfortably removed. Over his red calico shirt was a sleeveless Army coat. A single eagle feather was tied to his long braid. There was a regal weariness about his lined face and weathered body; as he rode around the camp, Cole could imagine he still wore the elaborate war bonnet it had been his right to wear.

Cole knew who he was. He'd last seen him nine years ago in a brief, inconclusive gun battle farther east, and Horse Back had once been pointed out to Cole during a posting to Fort Sill. But Cole had a more important reason to remember him. He had long known it was the nephew of Horse Back who had raided the Cox farm and subsequently been killed by Cole.

Their meeting now had an inevitability about it, but the rage and bitterness Cole had expected to feel were curiously absent. Horse Back, war chief of the Comanches, had years before been defeated by the white man. Despite the dignity he wore like a cloak, the evidence of his downfall was there in the deep grooves of his face and in the haunted look of his eyes. Once he had roamed the land as a great chief, but no more. The buffalo were being systematically decimated and his people had been herded onto the reservation in the Oklahoma territory.

His assessing eyes drifted to the woman who rode into the camp behind Horse Back. Her age, as with most squaws, was hard to determine, but she seemed years younger than her chief. She wore a fringed shirt covered by a long doeskin apron. Her leggings were held in place with wide, beaded garters, and her hair was parted in the middle and hung down in two long braids, as Erin's had the night she'd run away. But these braids were so black they reflected iridescent blue and green light. Trailing in the dust behind her horse was a travois piled high with supplies. From the murmuring braves he caught her name. Tao-nar-sie. She was Horse Back's daughter.

With slight movements Cole continued to rub the thong across the rough stone. His eyes flicked to his wife, who was sitting upright and watching the newcomers. Other braves were drifting into the clearing. They looked almost ashamed as their chief surveyed them. Under the old Indian's glare, even Little Hawk had lost his bravado.

Slowly the old chief began to berate his young braves for their foolishness. "Do you not know," he said in Comanche, "enough to stay on the reservation where the white man has put you? They are strong. We grow weaker each moon."

Little Hawk spoke up. "We have guns, Horse Back. We kill the white man who tries to stop us."

He held up one of the rifles that had been used against the soldiers. Cole studied it carefully. Until his capture, he'd never seen one like it either in the Army or out of it; as an expert in frontier warfare, he should have. Where had the Indians got hold of it?

Horse Back addressed his brave with scorn. "For every

233

white man you kill, many braves die. Where lies the victory in this?"

Little Hawk pounded his chest. "I give up my life with great happiness. Five of the hated soldiers I will kill. The white woman I keep."

Before Cole could berate the brave once more with taunts of cowardice, Erin spoke up.

"Horse Back," she said in Comanche, "I am a mere woman but I have heard much of great chief. I would speak with him." As the war chief turned to look at Erin, the look in his eyes was unreadable but he gravely nodded.

"Horse Back," she repeated, "I am not white. My mother was called Prairie Dew, and she named me Dawn Flower. I have much pride in my Comanche blood. But Little Hawk"—she struggled for the words—"fills me with shame."

"Do you know of this woman's claim?" Horse Back asked the loud-mouthed brave, and reluctantly Little Hawk produced the amulet and handed it to his chief. Little Hawk examined it closely.

"My mother was killed at a place called Sand Creek," Erin said. Then she lapsed into English. "I was just a little girl, but I remember the blood and the screams of the women as the soldiers rode among them."

Horse Back dropped to the ground and knelt before her. He spoke in the white man's language. "I have heard the story told in the Indian camps. It was in the land you call Colorado, in the camp of Black Kettle. The chief was a friend of the white man. The white soldiers came at dawn. Black Kettle raised the flag that had been given him by your President Lincoln. Under it was the white flag of surrender. It was not enough to save the lives of his people."

Little Hawk broke the sad silence. "We do not

understand the white man's words," he said in Comanche.

Horse Back stood and faced his young warrior. "Then you must learn them, young brave," he said. "I speak of old times. Bad times for our people."

Cole could be silent no longer. "The soldiers were not regular Army," he said in English. "Ninety-day wonders, they were called, recruited in a time of need. They were the worst of the Colorado saloons and gold fields, and the Army became ashamed of their actions against the Indians. Did you know such shame when you killed white women and children?"

Horse Back turned his sad, dark eyes on Cole. "Much reason for hatred lies between us. But the time is past when the Indian can war against the white man and win. My braves are young and have not learned this lesson."

For a moment Cole saw on the old man's face the pain and wisdom that had come with the years of travail. He trusted Horse Back. He had no choice.

"If the braves are ignorant, it is up to their chief to lead them."

"I do not know that they will do as I say and turn you free. The white man has taken from them their manhood. For that they will do much that is foolish."

"And I will do much to save the white woman and my men."

"You are brave. But I wonder if you are brave enough? We shall see. My daughter Tao-nar-sie will free the woman who calls herself Dawn Flower and will stand guard over her. You must help yourself. Listen carefully to what I say."

In brusque gestures he motioned the Indian girl to Erin's side. As she cut the bonds that held Erin, Horse Back turned to the young braves lined up behind him. He spoke in the sonorous words of his native tongue, berating them as cowardly makers of war on women. Worse, by their deeds he said they proved themselves as cowardly as the white man and therefore unworthy to align themselves with the Dog Soldiers of long ago.

"They weren't afraid to die," growled Little Hawk. "They didn't behave as old women."

A buzz of agreement came from some of the braves. Cole studied Horse Back intently.

"It is the old women who gave you life, who keep you warm and fed, who have wept much. But all their weeping can't save the Indian. Nor will the acts of a warrior."

"But we have need of brave deeds. What chance have we to prove we are men?"

"Bah. *You* whine as old women now. I challenge you to prove your bravery. If that is what you wish. Are you brave enough to accept a chief's challenge? I say I can beat you in the games of our people. Still can I ride more swiftly than the wind, bend and strike more quickly than the snake. I will hold in my hands more sticks than any two of the weakling children who stand before me."

The braves facing the old chief stirred nervously. "Why should we meet you in combat, even a game, Horse Back?" one of them asked. "You are not our enemy."

But I am, thought Cole. At last he saw the purpose in the chief's taunts and he felt an admiration for the way Horse Back had dealt with the young men. A last, firm stroke against the rock on the ground behind him and Cole felt the sinews of his bonds give way, yet he held his position. Choosing the language of the Indian so that all could understand, he directed his words to the chief. "Your brave speaks true. *I* am their enemy, at least today. And I don't allow old men to fight my battles. I will challenge these"—he paused and sneered openly— "boys. Such children as they can be beaten even by a white man." Ignoring the pain that shot through his arms and back, he held up his hands to show he had managed to liberate himself.

The Indians moved forward threateningly as Cole rose to his feet. His legs almost gave out from under him, but refusing to show any sign of weakness, he stood tall and unwavering.

"I challenge the young men to these games of skill and combat, to a small but bloodless battle, played only for the cattle you have stolen. Whatever happens, the woman and my men go free."

Muttering loud oaths and threats of death to the white man, the braves moved closer but Horse Back motioned them away.

"And if you lose?" the chief asked.

"I don't intend to lose. But if I do, my men will not report your foolish marauding to the Army."

"Our people hunger, even on the reservation. We can take the cattle and still the weeping of our women. Meat will fill their empty bellies and those of their children."

A hint of a smile crossed the old man's face and settled in his dark eyes. Cole knew his challenge of the young braves was as Horse Back wished.

"Horse Back." Little Hawk stepped before his chief. "I say the white man speaks with the tongue of the snake. He wants all and gives only what we have claimed as ours. The woman who calls herself Dawn Flower says she is of our people. I say she stays with us."

The other braves gathered behind him. The air grew still.

Horse Back looked at the Indians, one by one, then turned back to Cole. "My warriors speak to me with silent tongues and I must listen. The games will be played as you suggest. But only your men go free. If you lose, the woman stays with us."

"These are not the words of a great chief," Cole said. "Do your braves tell you what will be?"

The war chief's eyes looked sad. "I have spoken."

Cole fought back the fear that gripped his heart. Erin's life was at risk. The challenge must be met. "And what games do you choose?" he asked solemnly.

"As it grows late, I choose two games on horses. One of riding skill. The second the arrow game."

"Picking them from the ground?" Cole asked, then added when Horse Back nodded, "I've seen it done."

"No!"

Erin pulled free from the chief's daughter and threw herself between the two men. "It is I who can defeat the braves at their games of skill. The white soldier is weak and ignorant. He doesn't know the game."

Cole felt an almost irresistible urge to turn his wife over his knee and apply his hand soundly to the seat of her buckskin trousers. The knowledge that the braves might demand their turn kept him from it. He trained his eyes on Horse Back.

"Does the Indian play his games against women?"

The chief shook his head solemnly. "The Indian accepts only the challenge of the white soldier."

Erin opened her mouth to protest, but a dark, forbidding look in the chief's eyes stilled her words. To the Indians, women—especially young women—were not worthy opponents. To face a woman in a game of skill would be a disgrace. But she couldn't let her husband risk his life without making one more try to stop the games.

"Horse Back," she said, her head high, "at least let me wish the white man well." When the chief gave his assent, she turned to Cole and, putting her hands in his, drew him aside. Her voice was low, and she spoke in English. "Stall. Cur must be near."

"It's too late for waiting, Erin. Our captors are growing restless."

Panic seized her. "But you ask the impossible of yourself! You could be crippled. Or even—" She couldn't go on.

238

Cole lifted her hand to his lips and kissed her fingers. "Thanks for the vote of confidence, love."

Erin jerked away, filled with rage and fear for him. "What you propose is insane. Try to get him to do the lance and ring game. It's not so dangerous—just trying to put a spear through a tiny ring as you ride by."

"The games are set, Erin. I have accepted the challenge." He grinned warmly at her. "Don't be so sure I will lose."

"Would you go to your death smiling?"

"For you, Mrs. Barrett, yes, if necessary. But I don't think it's quite come to that. I ride well enough for the first game, and as for the second, I saw a demonstration of it only yesterday. You made it look easy." He took her hand once more. "I assume you don't mind if I borrow your horse. That's one advantage I'll have that the young warriors haven't counted on."

Words of endearment mixed with imprecations caught in her throat. Surely Cur would come riding in, perhaps even with help, before Cole was forced to throw himself close to the swiftly beating hoofs of the roan.

A rustling in the brush behind them forestalled her retort. Two braves galloped recklessly through the grove of trees. With disbelieving eyes she looked at the horse they towed into view. It was the Appaloosa; riding it, his hands tied behind his back, was Cur.

The giant smiled down at Erin and gave her a slow wink. She stared back at her red-bearded friend in utter amazement. He looked far too contented to suit her. For some reason she couldn't imagine, he had apparently let himself be captured. And with his coming went her last hope that her husband would be saved from the impossible task that lay before him.

Chapter Fourteen

The triumphant braves halted their wild ride in front of the Indian chief.

"Horse Back," one of them said, "you honor us with your presence. We bring you gift." His dark eyes turned arrogantly to his prisoner. "A white man strong as the charging buffalo. A captive of us—the Antelope Eaters." The dark planes of the buck's face were sharpened with a warrior's pride that once more, if only for a limited time and space, the Comanche ruled Texas.

Hands tied behind him, Cur swung one leg over the pommel of his saddle and dropped effortlessly to the ground. With whoops and cries the Indians crowded in on him. Cur stood unmoving, his leathery face impassive, but in his blue eyes, peering out from under a wild thatch of red hair and bushy eyebrows, Cole recognized the hint of a smile flicker and then disappear. Even with arms bound, the bearded giant appeared menacing as he looked down at Horse Back.

The Comanche war chief matched his stare. "We meet again, Tall Tree," he said in the language of his people.

Cur nodded. "You claim to have friends as great in number as the fallen leaves. But not if you treat them wrongly. Has the great warrior Horse Back forgotten our sworn friendship? Are we no longer blood brothers? If I am captive then it must be we are not."

"I friend," the chief said, then continued in English. "But I also leader of my people and must see they keep dignity—not shame them. Braves young, like fight. Don't know they hold Tall Tree because he does not choose to fight. They think they scare you into surrender to their ferocity."

Horse Back grinned hugely with white even teeth before once more assuming a stern expression and facing the brave who had presented his captive so proudly. "Cut Tall Tree loose," he said. The brave protested loudly but was stilled with a forbidding glance from his chief.

Through the foliage of his great red beard, Cur's lips broke into a grin. "Horse Back is wise. I come to help the white chief in the games, not to lie about in the grass and dream of spilling blood."

Cole grinned and said in rapid English, "You were out there listening. What would have happened if they'd decided to skin us alive and leave our carcasses for buzzard feed?"

"I'd have thought of something. The way Hud and I always have. If all else failed, I'd have shot as many of them as I could." He stared, unblinking, at Cole. "Beginning with Erin."

How much of the conversation Horse Back caught was unclear, but he nodded approvingly, then illustrated his command of English. "Tall Tree very brave. But you could not kill all. Young braves deprived of woman could not then be held, even by the great Horse Back. They would perform death dance."

Horse Back paused to give his audience time to think on his words, then added, "But your tests of courage at their hands would assure an afterlife greatly respected by the gods who share it."

"I can't tell you what a comfort that thought is," Cur

241

said, turning his bound hands toward the complaining brave, who cut him loose with one slash of a buffalo skinning knife. Rubbing his wrists, Cur said, "It really wasn't my intention to die at the stake or hang upside down stripped of my skin."

Cole reached out and gripped his hand. The two had never met, yet no words were necessary. Both knew any blood shed that day could be that of them all, including— Cole's stomach knotted—that of Erin, his wife with whom he had shared so much and yet so little. She had woven her way into the fabric of his life, only to leave him with sleepless, lonely nights during which his mind whirled alternately with hatred of her leaving him and loving memories of their sweet times together.

He looked at her, warning her, willing her to silence, but Erin showed no compulsion to obey him. For a second he thought of all the pale, biddable girls with downcast eyes he could have taken to wife. A safe but dull lot they would have been beside his wife.

"You choose wrong, Tall Tree," Erin said to Cur, "to come riding in here all cock-a-hoop." She spit out the words. "You are as foolish as the white chief, our captain. Few white men ride as the Indian does. The braves will win."

"Dawn Flower." Cole spoke sharply across the narrow space that separated him from his wife. "You must have faith in your captain. The white chief does not plan to lose."

Erin's amber eyes flared in golden anger and her words dripped acidly between them. "You may be a white 'chief' to these braves and possess the courage of a thousand, but the white chief is not always wise."

Cur stood looking with interest upon the sparks flying between Erin and the captain he'd just met. Maybe the girl he'd watched grow to rowdy womanhood had finally met her match. Here was no man she could wrap around her finger. Even in their precarious position he was tempted to laugh aloud.

"Well, Erin," said Cole, "it's damned sure I'm not wise or I would never have ridden foolishly into this trap after the men I'm supposed to be leading. But neither would a smart woman have ended up here, unless she trusted the man she was riding after just a little."

From behind Cole came the gruff voice of Corporal MacClanahan. "That's right, Cap'n. We beat twenty-to-one odds plenty of times. Little lady, you got to trust 'im."

Several expressions flitted one by one across Erin's dirt-streaked face; the men, both Indian and white, seemed to be holding their breath, waiting for her decision and forgetting she was a mere woman. At last she looked at Cole, her eyes glowing with a mixture of love, pride, and challenge. Moving closer to him, she gripped his collar and pulled his face toward her.

"I do trust you. As well as love you." She kissed him softly, and he felt pride that in the midst of such danger Erin could exhibit calm courage. She was thinking of him. Watching her step back beside Tao-nar-sie, her head held high and her eyes golden warm and unblinking, he knew that for no other reason than her unselfish bravery, he would love her forever.

"The white soldier and his woman speak brave words," Horse Back said. "It is time to prove them. The sun draws near where the sky meets the earth. We have time for the two riding games." He turned to his young warriors. "Call upon the gods to make you fly like the arrow."

The warriors started away to apply war paint and call upon their gods, but Cole raised his hand to stop them. "Has Horse Back so quickly forgotten his promise? My men must go free."

"It is as you say," Horse Back said in agreement, then added, "They go without their guns."

"Then you might as well shoot them now. They travel far to their home. Many dangers are there."

Again the corporal spoke up. "Cap'n, we're not going anywhere 'til we know you're all right, no matter what agreement you made. Why, if they'll just cut these dadblasted ties and let us stand, that's all we ask." A sly expression crossed his face and he winked. "Or I guess we could go now. Don't want you to go back on your word."

Cole understood the man's hints and weighed his options. If the men left before the games started, they'd be out there to help in case of loss. But there wouldn't be much they could do if they had no guns. The young warriors could trail them easily and they'd end up dead, no matter how Horse Back tried.

Even if the soldiers evaded recapture, without weapons they could hunt no food and would have a nearly impossible job of getting through other roving renegades, both red and white, to the nearest safety.

At last, and with seeming reluctance, he agreed. "My men stay," he said, "but untied and with food and drink. They have suffered enough through the night and this day."

"No guns," said Horse Back. Everybody glanced at the pile of guns thrown under a huge hackberry tree. The war chief motioned to a nearby brave to stand guard over them, and Cole did the same to one of his privates, now free and gnawing voraciously on a leftover turkey wing.

"Nobody will have weapons. These are games to test strength and skill," said Cole.

Little Hawk took charge of the preparations for the contest, directing his fellow braves to lay out a narrow track that extended out of the grove of trees for about one hundred and fifty yards. Arrows were placed lengthwise at staggered intervals of twenty-five yards.

Cole and Cur, each fully aware of the rules, paced

along the track to judge its readiness and the length between the arrows, then returned to the beginning to stand together. Cole looked thoughtfully down the narrow track. Comanches rarely left an arrow on the ground, but he'd never seen a white man pick up more than one or two. Until today, he told himself.

"You planning on trying for the arrows?" Cur asked.

Cole nodded. "You're big for trick riding, but even bigger for their arrow game. The Indian who dreamed that one up was small, lean and stringy."

"I'll be all right," Cur said. "I know a trick or two that might take them by surprise."

Both men looked down the track. "I want you to know," Cole said, "that I appreciate your help. You don't have to do it. Some of my men—"

"Erin's as much my responsibility as yours. Besides, I consider it an honor to ride with the man who can handle her."

Their words were drowned out by Indian ululations that might have been uttered by souls in hellish torment. They looked up to see the Indian brave Swift Wind thundering past, the hooves of his spotted pony flinging divots of sandy cakes behind him. He reached the end of the track and turned.

On the return trip with his legs loosely hooked in the surcingle, he slipped beneath the horse. For a long moment he hung suspended under the horse's belly, the pounding front hoofs almost striking his head and shoulders, and then came up on the other side to lie on his stomach, back arched and shoulders and feet in the air. The other braves whooped at his skill.

Cur nodded his appreciation, then stripped off his shirt and mounted the Appaloosa. Astride the huge horse, his shadow falling across the upturned faces of the watching Indians, he appeared a formidable and confident opponent.

Slowly Cur turned to wink at Erin, who gave him a smile of encouragement before stepping closer to Cole and taking his hand.

"He knows what he's doing, Erin," Cole said.

"How can he? The most he's ever done is ride down a runaway steer and wrestle him to the ground. He'll never fit between that horse's belly and the ground."

Holding the reins loosely in his hands, Cur used his body to urge the horse into motion. Down the track they flew, then turned to head back. Erin watched in astonishment as Cur leaned forward, his hands hooked around the pommel of the saddle, and raised his body from its resting place. A long leg the size of a tree trunk was flung behind him, and he dropped both feet to the ground, bounded upward and swung across the saddle to land for an instant on the other side of the galloping horse. Again with tremendous effort, the muscles of his chest and shoulders corded from the strain, he lifted his bulk upward and sat astride the horse as it crossed the line making the end of the track.

As if trained to trick riding, the horse slowed to a halt in front of an open-mouthed Erin and her grinning husband. Around them the Indians nodded in admiration. It was the four soldiers' turn to whoop their pleasure.

When Cur dropped to the ground, Erin found her voice. "How did you manage that? I've never seen you do anything like it before."

The big man smiled sheepishly. "I never let you see me or else you'd have been trying it."

Horse Back stepped forward. "Tall Tree and Swift Wind ride as equals. The game is even."

His pronouncement stilled the astonishment on Erin's face at her old friend's beautiful ride. Cole's turn was drawing near. A chill breeze brought a hint of autumn as it wafted across the clearing, and Erin shivered. Cole slipped his arm around her and held her tightly against his side. His body felt hard and strong. And invincible, Erin assured herself against all reason. The time for doubting him was past. If . . . if something did go wrong, it wouldn't be because she hadn't shown complete faith in him.

Little Hawk swaggered over to his black pony and mounted. He looked down at Cole, his broad face arrogant and sure. "Now we ride," he said. "We see who is better man."

He whirled around; with little urging the pony streaked down the narrow track and pivoted sharply for the return ride. For one brief second Little Hawk sat tall on the horse's back, his bronze body strong against the pink rays of the late sun. Then with a whoop he leaned forward, thrust his knees under the front surcingle, and headed back, slipping from one side of the animal and then the other, picking up arrows as he rode. When he pulled up quickly at the end of the track, one arrow remained behind him, representing a slim chance for Cole.

He dropped to the ground in front of Cole and held out his hard-won booty. "Your turn, white chief. If you lose, the woman is mine."

"In a pig's eye," Erin muttered in English. In Comanche she said, "The white chief will not lose." She turned to Cole and smiled up at him. "Isn't that right?" she asked, then added softly, "love."

His arms hugged her close. "Right," he whispered into her ear. "Thank God for one overconfident Comanche. Now we have a chance." His lips pressed against her cheek. "Erin . . ." There was so much he wanted to say to her. Yesterday at the creek he'd only begun. But he'd had other things on his mind then, and forswearing words, he'd used his body to claim her as his own.

Erin felt his hold on her tighten. Then he let go and

stepped away. Her eyes followed his hands as he removed the torn Army jacket and tossed it aside. She gazed at the ropes of taut muscles rippling in his arms and across his back as he leaned over to remove his boots. His movements were sure and unhurried, as though this day were no different from any other, and she was filled with pride at his strength and courage.

He stood, lean and eager, and Erin looked with amazement at the sparkle in his eyes. He'd said he would go to his death smiling, if it was for her. Bravely she matched his smile.

In one fluid motion he mounted the roan, who stirred restlessly under the unfamiliar rider. A few gentle words from Cole, and the horse seemed to settle down. *You'd think the horse was a mare the way Cole's charm worked on him,* Erin thought.

As Cole looked down at his wife, he remembered the way she had ridden yesterday. The anger he'd felt had been born of fear; now he concentrated only on matching her skill. His mind quickly darted from Erin to Little Hawk. How had each succeeded? He tucked his knees beneath the front surcingle as he guided the roan to the track and leaned low over his neck. A single nudge with his bare heel sent the horse leaping into motion.

The dash down the length of the track blurred, and he kneed the horse around to pound back toward the crowd of onlookers, some cheering, some jeering. He heard none of it. His full concentration was on the first arrow. He shifted his weight to the right, dropped toward the ground to reach for it—and missed. Not far enough, damn it. And while he cursed himself, one more arrow slipped past him. No matter. The rules did not permit picking up more than one arrow on a side before heaving one's aching body to the other side.

He thought of his cause and abandoned all caution. He heaved upright, freeing his right leg, and leaned dangerously to the left, clinging to the roan's mane, his right foot hooked by a mere heel to the horse's neck. Head inches from the pounding hoofs, he tasted dirt as he reached out. The arrow seemed to fly into his grasp, but both his grip on the mane and his heel were loosening and he could not rise to try for the other side. He took up the remaining arrows on the left, but they would not count.

He managed to pull himself upright, not gracefully he was sure, as the roan roared across the end of the track. Slipping back onto the blanket, he raised the arrows. His heart was heavy that he did not hold them all.

When he dropped to the ground, Erin flung herself against him. Her heart pounded with fear that he had risked himself so foolishly, and with love that he had been so brave. To her, all the arrows in the world were grasped in his hand.

Cole pulled away. "Sorry, love—"

She stilled his words with her lips, in a hard, brief kiss that spoke of her pride and of her overwhelming feelings of tenderness. Together, they turned to face the assembled Comanches.

To Erin's amazement the braves were looking with admiration at Cole. Only Little Hawk scowled. Accepting the offered arrows from his opponent, he said, "The white chief does not match the Comanche. The white chief loses."

A chorus of protests rose around him, from both the red men and the soldiers. Swift Wind spoke.

"The white chief rides as a brave. He does not lose this day."

Horse Back stepped into the circle and looked solemnly at Swift Wind. "My young brave is wise beyond his years. I say the white chief has met the challenge." He looked around at the other braves, who nodded in agreement at his decision. Only Little Hawk responded with eyes darkly disapproving, but under Horse Back's unwavering scrutiny he said nothing.

The old chief turned to Cole. "But no man is the winner. You and your men go free. When you travel over the hill, Swift Wind will ride out and give you your weapons. The cattle remain with my braves. There is much need for them on the reservation." He looked at Erin. "Dawn Flower, you choose to go with the white chief?"

"Yes." Hope flared in her heart.

"Then we must have another game."

The hope died. "No!" she cried out.

Horse Back ignored her protest. "This time we play a white man's game of chance." He turned to Little Hawk. "Do you have the dice of wood?"

A smile broke the brave's solemn countenance. With a quick nod, he went to get them, and Horse Back spoke to Cole. "Long before the white man came to our land, the Comanche took great pleasure in games of chance. Unlike the white man, the Comanche willingly gives up what he has lost. If you should win, white chief, you will find I speak truth." He looked at Erin and then back at Cole. "If you should lose, white chief, you must do the same."

"You ain't gonna lose, Captain," his corporal shouted from behind him.

With a quick nod Cole accepted and smiled at Erin. He pulled her into the shadows of the trees around the gathering. "Is this more to your liking?" he asked in English. "I seem to be gambling once again for the pleasure of your company."

Erin flung her head up impatiently. "But not against a willing loser."

"Is this a confession, Mrs. Barrett?"

Erin thought back to the Washington hotel room. Under Cole's insistent touch, she'd given up the game very easily. But that didn't mean she had lost. Not at all.

"I—" The nearness of her husband overwhelmed her. All she could think of was what had happened when they had abandoned the cards. "I suppose I lost willingly enough."

His eyes warmed to charcoal. "I hope you're as cooperative this time when I win."

Erin dropped her gaze. His chest, damp from the exertion of the ride, glistened like burnished brass in the evening sun. She caught her breath, then looked up at him and smiled. Her fingers traced light, electric paths along the taut, sinewy trail of his upper arm. "Win the game and find out."

Cole's voice was husky. "I plan to remind you of your words. Later, when I have you alone." And he would have her alone, Cole knew that as well as he knew the thrill of having her body next to his. Tonight luck would be on his side.

He made swift work of the game. Squatting across from Little Hawk in the midst of circling braves and soldiers, he weighed the dice in his hands. Small wooden squares they were, stained on each side with a different dye. The bet was on which color would turn up when they were thrown. Again, Little Hawk went first.

"Red," the Indian said and picked up one of the squares, tossing it onto the uneven ground. It teetered on one side, then tipped over to expose a dark brown stain.

Cole studied the remaining dice, then picked up the square that Little Hawk had used. Its weight was uneven, as Little Hawk had no doubt known; its landing could be calculated, as a probability if not a certainty. The square would do.

Carefully he smoothed out the surface of the ground, clearing it of a small mound of dirt, tossing aside a sharp, half-buried rock. When he was satisfied, he glanced at his wife and at the richly colored hair that framed her face.

"Red." He tossed the square. Red turned up, and, with

Little Hawk at last conceding defeat, he was declared the winner.

Cole stood facing Horse Back and extended his hand. "The white man has much he could learn from your people. You gave your word we could all go free. I know you will honor your promise."

Horse Back shook his hand. "We are friends," he said, then turned to order that one of the cows confiscated by the braves should be slaughtered for an evening feast. Logs were tossed on the fire and long sticks sharpened to hold the chunks of meat that would be held in the rising flames.

Cole watched the proceedings. How easily he had slipped into understanding the red man. The years he had carried hatred in his heart seemed wasted years. Horse Back's nephew and his men had ridden in on the helpless Cox family and slain them. That fact would never be erased from his mind. But through the years the Comanches had suffered greatly; they looked at all white men and women as their enemies. Perhaps the greatest crime against them was the willful slaughter of the buffalo, the prime purpose of which had been to starve the red man. Each side had shown dishonor. It was long past time for tolerance, not retribution.

Behind Cole stood his wife and Horse Back's daughter Tao-nar-sie deep in conversation. He looked back. Erin glanced at him—a sly, quick look—and Cole knew instantly she was up to something. She grinned and sidled up to him.

"White chief," she said in Comanche, "you have proven your bravery and your skill on this day. There is only one thing left to do. All white men smell bad to the Comanche. You are no different." Liar, she told herself. "Tao-nar-sie and I prepare the vapor baths while the braves prepare the food. Await our call."

She turned on her moccasined heel and headed for the

darkening brush. Swiftly she and the Indian squaw gathered eight long switches of fallen oak and hackberry, none of the preferred dogwood or willow being readily available in the country where they were camped. At the edge of a secluded grove of trees where the grasses grew thick and soft, they stuck the switches in the ground, two on each side to form a rectangle, their tops twisted overhead to form an arch. Blankets were thrown atop the structure to hang almost to the ground. There was barely room inside for a man to sit.

At one side of the rectangle they built a small fire. On top of the flames they placed a half-dozen flat rocks. Using water from a shallow gourd, Erin flicked a few drops of the liquid onto the hot rocks. Steam hissed into the air. The vapor bath was ready, and she pulled the lower edge of the blanket over the smoldering fire so that the steam could go into the enclosure.

Tao-nar-sie directed Cole to his waiting wife, who stood in front of the structure.

Through the waning light he looked at her with taunting gray eyes—an expression in them she had seen often when he'd thought she had done something impetuous or, she told herself, something provocative.

"Be careful, Dawn Flower, not to get downwind of me. I wouldn't want to offend your sensitive Comanche nose."

"I'll be careful, white chief. Please take off your trousers."

"I thought you'd never ask."

The man certainly had a way about him that made thinking difficult. Erin carefully modulated her voice. "The white chief has a surprise awaiting him."

"The white chief can hardly wait." Deftly Cole slipped the trousers from his long, lean body. Erin had to keep her eyes trained on the first stars of evening; otherwise the vapor bath would go untested.

253

She knelt beside the blanket and, lifting one edge, gestured for him to enter. "You'll have to crawl. There's not room enough to stand. When you get inside, you can either sit or lie down. Whichever you prefer."

He knelt beside her and lightly touched her face. "Oh, I think lying down. Don't you, love?"

"It is the choice of the white chief." This time Erin was unable to keep the tremor from her voice.

As soon as he had disappeared inside, she dropped the blanket. Better to keep him from her view. Picking up the gourd, she hurried to the side where the fire was smoldering under the heated rocks. It took only a few flicks of water to send clouds of water vapor into the close air inside.

"Damn!"

Erin spoke into the bath. "You're supposed to be enjoying this. The Comanches are known for their vapor baths."

"Right," Cole muttered. "In the training manual on the tribe, it's listed under 'Atrocities.'"

Erin flicked on more water. Silence greeted the inrush of steam. After Cole's initial displeasure over her surprise, she had expected him to come out cursing. She waited, increased the vapor, then waited again. The cool night air brushed against her skin. She peeked inside and barely made out her husband's long frame stretched out on the ground.

"Are you all right?"

"Come in and find out."

"Later," she whispered. "Trust me."

He raised his body and leaned on one elbow to face her, his skin glistening in the warm glow from the coals. "You trusted me today, Erin. For that I thank you."

Erin's heart quickened in a rush of love. Maybe going in for just a minute wouldn't hurt the surprise she had planned for later. She started forward, but the sound of footsteps in the brush pulled her back. It was Tao-nar-sie bringing the items necessary for the next part of their plan—a breechclout and leggings for Cole to wear at the evening meal. She took them and placed them inside the enclosure.

"Here. While your uniform is mended and cleaned. Wear these."

She didn't give him a chance to answer but backed away and waited for him to appear, praying all the while that he would accept the Indian garb—a final test that he accepted her and her Comanche blood.

Cole didn't disappoint her. In a few moments the blanket lifted and he emerged to stand in the autumn air. A narrow strip of rawhide encircled his hips; suspended from it a skirt of buffalo hide brushed against his thighs. The leggings fit tight against the calves of his legs. Erin smiled. He even wore moccasins; the rising moon glinted on their beads.

"The white chief looks . . . very handsome."

"Your turn, Dawn Flower."

Erin forced her attention from the magnificent picture he presented. "What do you mean?"

"Take off your trousers—and of course your shirt—and crawl inside. I'll supply the steam."

"But—"

"Trust me."

She glanced over her shoulder. No one was in sight, and moving deeper into the shadows surrounding the vapor bath, she did as she was bid. Under a silver moon she walked to where her husband stood. His eyes burned against her bare skin. There was definite movement beneath that breechclout. She was sure of it.

It took all her strength to kneel and hurry inside the bath. "Please, Cole," she whispered through the blanket wall, "wait. My surprise is not done."

She heard his breathing, and then movement. Steam

billowed into the enclosure. At first the clouds of moisture seemed suffocating, but for only a minute. As perspiration beaded her skin, she felt the weariness of the long day depart and she understood why the Comanches prized their vapor baths. Stretching out on the soft grass, she let the warm vapors envelop her—and thought of later that night. No, she was not through with her surprise. Cole had done as she had asked him and had waited for their night of love; she vowed he wouldn't be sorry.

She listened for the sound of his breathing and realized it had been some minutes since the last billows of vapor had surrounded her. Had he grown weary of waiting for her to emerge?

"Erin." Cole's voice drifted in and she relaxed against her bed of grass. "I have your clothes." One edge of the blanket lifted and he deposited a leather bundle beside her. "A gift from Tao-nar-sie," he said. "Her travois was well stocked."

Erin sat up and pulled the bundle to her. Fringed buckskin and beads were all she could make out of the skirt and blouse. As best she could in the narrow confines, she pulled them on and went out to face her husband. She smoothed her garments. Fringe outlined the sleeves and hem, which dipped to her calves. The front of the blouse was decorated with an intricate beaded design. The garment, made for the shorter Indian squaw, clung to her body. Curls of golden red hair, damp from her bath, fell across her shoulders, and the moon caught the flecks of gold in her amber eyes.

"Dawn Flower is very beautiful." Cole extended his arm. "Shall we dine?" A smile played at his lips.

"Of course," she said, as regally as she'd ever addressed Marcia Smythe-Williams, and they marched toward the camp. It was a curious mixture of whites and Indians which greeted them. If the peace between them seemed unnatural, Erin didn't choose to notice. She smiled at Cur, who sat in their midst, his hand wrapped around a thick stick of wood. On the end of the stick hung a chunk of meat.

Cole was taken over by the four soldiers, who congratulated him on the day; Erin was placed beside Horse Back and handed a stick similar to Cur's. The outside of the meat was seared black from the flames; when she bit into it, she found the inside still dripped blood. Encouraged by hunger and a wish not to insult her host, she forced down several small bites. She looked across the circle of diners; Cole didn't seem to be having any difficulty in eating the raw meat. As the light from the fire flickered on his skin, Erin let her thoughts wander down the enticing path to just how the evening would end.

"Dawn Flower," Horse Back said, interrupting her warm, sweet musings, "tell me more about your mother Prairie Dew."

Erin pulled her eyes away from her husband. Carefully she detailed in Comanche the little she knew—that Prairie Dew had been the daughter of the Comanche Dawn Breeze and an Irishman whose name she had never heard. All she knew was that the Irishman had chosen to live with his wife's people. Together they had roamed across the plains of Texas. Whether they were dead or not, she had no idea, but she hoped one day to find out.

Horse Back remained silent for a few minutes. "Dawn Flower," he said, carefully picking his words, "your quest is near an end. I know their story. Your grandfather is called Lonely Coyote."

Erin allowed her hopes to rise. "Does that mean they're both still alive?"

"Dawn Breeze went to the Happy Hunting Ground long ago. Lonely Coyote still lives."

"I see," she said softly, trying to take pleasure in

knowing that one of her grandparents had not died. "Where can I find Lonely Coyote?"

"He journeyed with his adopted people to the reservation." Horse Back held Erin's hand. "There is much sickness there. You should not go."

Erin merely nodded. Of course she would go. She had no choice. She couldn't dwell on the long-ago death of Dawn Breeze. The part of her that was Indian would not let her grieve long. Instead, she thought of her grandfather. At last she had a name for him and her heart gladdened at the thought that she would meet him soon.

Silently she looked across the clearing at her husband, who sat watching her and Horse Back in solemn conversation. The power of his hold over her took her breath away. In the hurried moments she had spent with Tao-nar-sie, she prepared the way she would show Cole her gratitude and love. Now it was time to get on with the evening.

She signaled to Tao-nar-sie, who stood and motioned one of the braves away from the others. In a few moments the harmonious notes from a Comanche flute drifted on the night air.

"Ah," Horse Back said, "the Love Song." He looked at Erin and then across the way at Cole. "Tao-nar-sie tells me you plan the Love Dance."

"Yes," she said, her breath shallow. The steps to the dance were simple, but still she prayed she would not take a misstep. She wanted to move as smoothly as Cole had in his ride on the strawberry roan.

A tom-tom added a sensual beat to the high-pitched flute. In opulence it couldn't rival the West Point orchestra that Erin had last danced to, but for the purpose she had in mind it was perfect. Its measures matched the erotic rhythms of love.

As Erin prepared to dance, Horse Back explained to the white soldiers the movements in the ceremony they were about to watch. It was up to the woman to select her partner; if she offered for him twice, he could not refuse.

The music grew louder and Erin stepped into the inner circle. Slowly she began to glide to her left the way Tao-nar-sie had shown her, rising heel to toe in cadence with the music, each rise of her foot bringing her before another man. So concentrated were her thoughts on each step that she almost passed Cole by, but his hands resting on his bare legs caught her eye. She stopped in front of him and extended her arms downward for his embrace.

Cole stood to face her and with a solemnity that matched her own followed her guidance. Without missing a stroke of the tom-tom, they placed their hands on each other's shoulders and, at arm's length, began to glide lightly to Erin's left. Round and round they went, the beat quickening, their eyes locked. Under her fingers she felt the coiled strength of her husband, a power she yearned to unleash. Doubts from the past melted under the onrush of desire. The time was ripe.

She stopped their movement in front of Horse Back and turned to face him, her arms at her sides. "Horse Back, I wish to take the white chief as my husband." She felt Cole's eyes on her. Carefully she looked down at the chief.

Horse Back rose. "Does the white chief wish to take Dawn Flower as his Indian squaw?"

"The white chief is ready."

Erin held back a smile. She just bet he was.

"So it shall be," Horse Back said. "Tao-nar-sie prepares the tipi. The white chief must get past his woman's family and lie down with her to make her his wife. Such is the ceremony of the Comanche." He turned to Erin. "But Dawn Flower has no family to defend her."

"Tall Tree is my family," she said, "and you, Horse Back, if you so choose, can take the place of Lonely Coyote."

He looked down at her in surprise, and then the harsh lines of his face were softened by a smile. "You do me much honor." She was sure his dark eyes were moistened with tears. "I will serve as your grandfather."

Without looking back at Cole, she followed Tao-nar-sie through the brush and entered a small tipi that had been erected in a grassy clearing. A small fire glowed in the center and sent its thin plume of smoke into the opening at the top. The soft skin of a buffalo, its fur against the grass, covered half of the ground. Silently Tao-nar-sie departed, being careful to leave the flap of the tipi pulled aside in invitation to whoever might want to enter.

Erin lay down to wait, her long hair spreading almost to the edges of the buffalo hide. Knowing her husband, she didn't figure the wait would be long. She heard movement outside and low voices, and then silence. She held her breath. The fire's muted light played against the walls of the tipi.

She closed her eyes for a second—and then she was not alone. He had entered quietly and dropped the flap across the opening of the tipi. He stood over her, the top of his head brushing against the enclosure's highest point. Erin extended her arms to him.

"Welcome, white chief," she whispered. "Your Dawn Flower awaits."

Chapter Fifteen

Cole stood still and straight, long legs apart, eyes hotly bearing down on Erin as she offered herself to him. His presence filled the small tipi; the strength of his tall, half-naked body blocked out the world. Unruly black hair and the coating of coarse bristles across the planes of his cheeks gave his face a feral look. Flickering shadows danced along the taut sinews of his chest and arms and down to the skin-toned breechclout that hugged his hips and brushed against his hard thighs.

Erin's eyes lingered on the narrow strip of buckskin that covered him. Her body grew warm with desire.

Cole knelt beside her on the buffalo hide and, taking her upheld hands in his, fondled her wedding ring. "My bride surprises me with 'white chief.' Now that we are alone."

Erin's thick lashes lowered provocatively, then rose to reveal a pair of secretive topaz eyes. "It is the way of the savage," she said softly.

"Savage?" His voice was deep and dark. He lifted her fingers to his lips, then kissed the inside of his wrists and her palms. "The word holds much promise for the night."

His charcoal eyes burned down at her in the dim light.

The long hours of tribulation had left his features hard and lean—and uncompromising. Tonight, Erin knew, she could deny him nothing.

"The white chief will not be disappointed," she promised, her voice now strong and sure.

In the firelight she could see a smile of pleasure play across his face, then settle into a searing look of expectation. Suddenly feeling a wild rush of desire, she wanted Cole to push her back upon their crude bed and pound his flesh into hers. Quick and hard, taking her as his.

But he held back, instead tormenting her with soft words and tender caresses. "Then you must do as your chief commands." He slipped his hands down to her shoulders and pulled her up beside him. His lips brushed against hers. "The white chief grows weary of his clothes. Undress me."

Erin caught her breath. The raw, coiled strength of his passion fractured the urge for quick release that had swept over her. Their night of love would unfold as he bid; his first command for her was to strip him naked.

Again his lips touched hers and his tongue teased its way inside her mouth for one sweet second. His thumbs trailed along the throbbing pulse points of her throat, and then he released his hold on her. A soft cry of frustration escaped her lips.

Ignoring the cry, he unwound his lean, powerful frame to stand over her. As she knelt before him, Erin felt an untamable compulsion to tease him as he had teased her. In tiny circles she massaged his chest, each arc lower than its predecessor until at last her fingers reached the band of leather attached to the thong around his narrow hips. The breechclout covered only his manhood, leaving the sides of his thighs bare and offering tantalizingly muscled paths for her fingers to wander.

She inserted a forefinger under the thong and slid it to

the front, then back to the side, abandoning it to run her hands down the length of his legs, lingering only to slip under the apron for one quick brush of her fingers against his inner thighs. She felt a satisfying tremor under her touch and curbed her own impatience. This must be a deliciously prolonged agony of desire.

She removed his moccasins, then unlaced the leggings that encased the calves of his legs. Carelessly tossing them aside, she let her fingers travel upward once more until they rested against his hips. Cole's skin was tight and smooth, his body hard. Still she knelt, her face raised beseechingly, awaiting the sight of his manhood.

She pulled at the end of the thong around his waist. The tie loosened and the breechclout dropped to the floor. Her eyes fastened on the thickening of dark hair across his abdomen, then dropped to fix on the evidence of his passion. He spread his legs and stood, proudly demanding.

Her breath was hot against him. With a low moan Cole dropped beside her on the ground and crushed her against him. His lips claimed hers; his tongue forced its way into the moist interior of her mouth, demanding that she further acquiesce to his will. Willingly she opened up and gave him what he wanted—the plundering of her body.

In her desperate desire, she clutched at his back and pulled him over her, his weight cleaving them breast to breast. Hot bursts of passion shot through her. Forcefully she pulled her lips away from his, then moved back again to thrust her tongue inside his mouth. Sweet goodness greeted her.

Cole savored the intrusion, glorying in Erin's gentleness and savageness, matching his needs and arousing him as she had never done. She grasped his buttocks, squeezing tightly, and he was on fire. Her kiss was primal, her demands absolute. She shredded thought and pushed him to the edge of ecstasy.

He pulled away and, balancing on the balls of his feet, gathered her up and laid her on the buffalo hide. The long copper curls of her hair spread out beneath her, and like the banked fire beside the bed, her eyes smoldered with a heat that threatened to explode.

Old urgings, no less overwhelming because they were familiar, drove him to tug impatiently at the Indian blouse that separated her body from his. Damned lacings! How had she managed to unfasten his leggings with such apparent ease?

Her quivering fingers rested on his hands, guiding them to loosen the bonds that held her buckskin blouse. He slipped it from her body. In the firelight her honeyed skin was smoothly alluring, her breasts full and dark-tipped. His lips moved to where his eyes had rested. He kissed each breast and fondled her with his tongue. She trembled at his touch.

Her pleasure urged him on. He needed no help to loosen the fringed skirt. Slowly he pulled it down her rounded hips. As his hands caressed her, she lifted her hips closer to them. His thumbs massaged the golden thatch of hair between her thighs. Lower he pulled the skirt, slipping it down the length of her slender legs until she lay naked before him.

While he trailed hot kisses across her abdomen, his hands traced erotic patterns up to her breasts and down again. Then he parted her legs and his lips moved in a fiery path to the inside of her thighs.

At last his hand touched the dark, moist valley of her desire, his fingers parting the folds. His kisses were gentle, and her hands pressed into his shoulders, urging him closer. Forgotten was the shy young woman who had lain beneath him the first time they made love. Erin was bold and passionate, unashamed of her need. As he kissed her, she writhed beneath his lips. Her ecstasy was his.

When the trembling of her body slowed, Cole shifted himself upward to embrace her—and found a wildly willful lover in his arms. Her lips pressed against his throat and her tongue teased the sensitive web of nerve endings under his skin. In his lessons of love, Cole had taught her well. Eager to show him she knew how to give pleasure, she took control.

Relentlessly she pushed him back against the ground and rubbed her swollen breasts across his chest, her hands moving down the sides of his body to caress his thighs.

"Love," he whispered.

In silent, sensuous answer she moved lower, her soft breasts trailing against his hard body, her lips following the same path with light kisses of fire. She wanted to melt her body into his, to be one with him forever. Her spirit soared with ecstatic abandon.

Firm fingers stroked her shoulders, urging her downward. She felt his manhood pressing against her breasts, hard and hot and ready. Still she taunted him, guided only by her woman's instincts and her love. Holding him in her hands, she rubbed her nipples against the pulsating shaft and then cradled him between her breasts. Her head bent, cascades of golden-red hair blocking out the world, she kissed him. Again, and then again. Sweet intimate touches that unfolded new glories of devotion and desire.

Strong hands gripped her arms and pulled her up until she lay beside her husband, his eyes burning into hers.

"You drive me wild," he whispered, then briefly pressed his mouth to hers. "Wild," he said once more, this time into her parting lips. She shivered deeper into his embrace and their lips and tongues met, their new-found knowledge of each other binding them as one.

Erin welcomed his body on top of hers and held him tightly with encircling legs and arms. As the rhythmic motions of passion began, Cole's magic enveloped her more thrillingly than it had ever done. Her world was here in his arms; she used sweet savage thrusts to tell him so. Spirit and body she gave to him, and he took them with an unrestrained voracity that drove her mad.

Entwined by love and need, their bodies came together, harder, faster, their passion ascending in a tightly binding spiral until each was shaken by the wild tremors of ecstasy. With heartfelt sighs, they slipped the bonds of earth and drifted onto the glorious plane where only lovers dwell.

For a long while they lay still, each afraid to break the spell that held them in thrall, man and woman, husband and wife. Equal passion met with equal pleasure. Theirs was a true mingling of spirit and will, the inequities of their lives outside the tipi dissolved in their sated desire. Beside them, the fire settled into white-ashed coals that warmed their world.

Cole was the first to move. Pressing his lips to hers for one sweet second, he gazed down at her. His gray eyes glowed with satisfaction.

"Erin—"

"Dawn Flower. Remember?" She smiled up at him.

His fingers trailed through her hair. "Of course. How could I forget? I'm your white chief." He kissed her lightly. "Although, my hot-blooded Indian, you were in control tonight."

"Insubordination I think it's called."

"I'd call it something sweeter than that. Remind me, Dawn Flower, to put you in charge of surprises for our little tribe."

"I take it you weren't disappointed in what I planned for the evening." Suddenly a hot blush colored her cheeks. "Not that everything was planned."

"Dawn Flower, sometimes you have to let your savage nature take over. It can lead to very pleasurable results."

How right he was. Erin nestled in his arms and let dreamy thoughts drift through her mind, memories of what those pleasurable results had been. The tipi was cozily warm and private, and as stillness settled on them, she was soon serenaded by the sound of her husband's rhythmic breathing. Contentment relaxed her; exhaustion from the restless night before and the momentous day just ended pushed her to follow Cole deep into the gentle abyss of sleep.

She awoke to hear the stirrings that came with breaking camp. The fire was dead; through the tipi opening overhead she saw the pale light of early morning. Images of the night before rushed through her mind and she looked at her husband sleeping beside her. Despite the hours of sleep, he still had lines of weariness in his face. Perhaps it was just the thickening beard that made him look tired. But no, there were the telltale shadows under his eyes to bear witness to his ordeal.

She bent her head to kiss his eyes, and, with the tip of a long curl of hair, tickled his mouth and nose. Still he didn't stir and her alarm grew. Could he be ill? One last test, she thought, touching her lips to his. One quick movement and she found herself pressed against the bed of buffalo hide, her husband gazing down in warm amusement.

"I thought you'd never get around to waking me properly," he said.

Erin looked into his warm gray eyes and realized anew the depth of her love for him. "You responded too soon," she purred. "You'll never know what I had planned to do next."

"You can show me on the trail tomorrow morning." He looked at the tipi that encircled them, then smiled down at her. "You don't suppose Horse Back would let us take this on the journey to Fort Concho, do you? As sort of a souvenir? I think we could put it to good use."

Erin avoided his gaze. "Cole."

"Yes, love?" His fingers traced the fine lines of her face. Still she kept her eyes averted—an early warning sign that Erin had something to say he wouldn't like. His voice turned sharp. "What's wrong?"

Her eyes darted to his. "Why do you think something is wrong?"

He shifted his body off of hers and sat up. "Because between us nothing is all right for very long."

"That sounds a little cynical."

"It sounds more than a little accurate."

A small sigh escaped her lips. Cole had the most unnerving habit of bluntly speaking the truth. As he saw it, of course. He wasn't always right.

Carefully she avoided the sight of his naked body. "Well," she said, "get dressed and we'll talk. Our clothes should be outside."

As Erin had said, Cole found his uniform neatly folded on the ground within reaching distance from the opening to the tipi; beside it were the shirt and buckskin trousers that Erin had worn. They were clean, and his uniform had been neatly mended. The trousers would need replacing, but they would do until he got back to the fort.

"How did you manage this?" he asked as he laid the clothes on the buffalo hide.

"Tao-nar-sie. She learned a few things at Fort Sill from the white women." Erin turned her back and slipped into her clothes.

Facing her husband once more, she took a deep breath. There were questions that must be asked, unpleasant facts that Cole must be told. Thank heavens he, too, was dressed. It made conversation so much easier.

"You surprised me yesterday, Cole, with your knowledge of the Indian's ways and language."

"One of the first tenets of warfare is to know your enemy."

Erin shuddered at the word. "Do you still hate the red man so much, Cole? The Indians have suffered just as much as the whites."

His eyes rested on her. "I don't hate the Indians, Erin. At least not in the way I once did." He looked away. "But I've seen atrocities I cannot forget."

Unthinking, she asked the question that had plagued her since she'd overheard Uncle Thad talking to Cole in Washington. "What atrocities, Cole?"

He turned to face her, and she saw in the depths of his eyes the embers of an old pain.

"The slaughter of innocent men and women." He gestured impatiently toward the opening of the tipi. "Do you really want to hear the details now in a Comanche camp? I'll tell you if you want to know. But not until I have you safely back at Concho."

Erin couldn't let the subject go. "But yesterday you risked your life to avoid bloodshed, and your men went along without causing trouble."

"Get one thing straight, Erin. I risked my life for you. I also would have killed for the same reason—had it been necessary and had I had the means."

Erin didn't argue the right or wrong of what he said. She couldn't. During much of yesterday she would have turned a gun on their Comanche captors if she'd been able.

"Erin." Cole took her hand. "The past hasn't left me completely without reason. The Indians kept their word. We both owe them thanks. They have every reason to hate us, yet they didn't take our scalps when they had the chance."

Disquiet left her. Despite whatever ugly memories haunted him, Cole had managed to set aside his hatred and, beyond that, had reached an understanding of the red man's plight. He would no doubt understand what she had to tell him next.

"I can't go with you today, Cole." Simple. Straight.

"Why not, love?" His voice was a thin wire that whipped out at her.

He wasn't going to understand, after all. Anguish gripped her, but she couldn't back down now.

"Because I have to go to Fort Sill with Horse Back and the other Indians. My grandfather is there."

"Your grandfather?"

"Yes. I know now that my grandmother Dawn Breeze is dead, but Horse Back told me last night that my grandfather is at the reservation." A picture of an old man without family flashed across her mind. "I don't even know his Irish name. The Indians call him Lonely Coyote," she added, thinking it no doubt a sadly fitting name.

He pulled her into his arms. "Do you know what you're risking, Erin? That reservation is riddled with disease. I heard talk of a malaria epidemic sweeping through it right now."

"I have to, Cole. I don't have any choice." She lifted her eyes to his. "Please understand."

Cole looked down at her for a long minute, then tightened his embrace. "Understanding and approving are not always companions, love. But I'll not force you to head out south. Not just yet."

She wrapped her arms around him. "Thank you, Cole."

"Don't thank me too soon." His lips pressed against her hair. "I'm coming with you."

Erin pulled away. "What about your Army orders?"

"I'll send a wire from Fort Sill to headquarters at Fort Concho that we had to escort a band of renegades back into Indian Territory." He smiled. "Unfortunately, I'll have to report that the Indians ate the cattle."

"You'd blame poor Horse Back?"

"I won't mention him by name, but by the time I get

back to Concho, the commandant will think we five soldiers single-handedly put down a bloody uprising."

"Maybe you did. One of the cowhands was shot."

"I doubt, love, we'll ever find out who did it. Whoever it was, he's not my main concern. Horse Back has his braves under control now. It's the renegades and outlaws that roam this land who present the real threat. My men and I will have to provide escort for you back to the reservation."

"I suppose I have no choice," Erin said, her eyes downcast.

"None."

Her heavy lashes lifted to reveal a pair of sparkling eyes. In a rush of happiness she proceeded to show him her pleasure with an ardent kiss.

"Careful, wife. We haven't tried out a tipi in the light of day. Besides," he said, looking down and stroking her face, "my beard is scratching you. I need to shave."

The rough bristles had felt very erotic against her skin last night, she started to tell him, but she had no chance. A quick kiss, and he was gone. Erin braided her hair, folded the Indian garb they had enticed each other with the night before, and stepped out into a cool, clear morning. Walking through the brush, she was surprised to see their tipi had been set up only a short distance from the camp. Last night she had felt they were nestled among the stars.

Entering the large clearing that had served as a campground for the braves, she blushed to see that both soldiers and Comanches were packed and prepared to leave.

She sought out Tao-nar-sie. "Thank you," she said, placing the buckskin clothing in her arms. "For everything. The white chief's name is Coleman Barrett. He and I and the other soldiers will be going with you to the reservation." Alarm flashed across the Indian's face

271

and Erin hurried to explain. "We seek my grandfather Lonely Coyote. The soldiers will do you no harm."

Tao-nar-sie smiled her pleasure and left to pack the tipi she had erected the night before for the white chief and his squaw. Erin walked toward the area of camp where the horses were tethered. Cur was standing beside her roan stallion, which was saddled and ready.

"Good morning, Mrs. Barrett," he said.

Erin grinned sheepishly and looked around for her husband. He was nowhere in sight.

"He's talking to the corporal," Cur said, pointing toward the grove of trees behind her.

How transparent was her purpose where Cole was concerned, Erin thought, and with a smile of thanks she headed out to look for him. Her moccasined feet brushed soundlessly against the ground as she came upon him and the corporal, backs turned to her, heads bent in conversation.

"We're going with Mrs. Barrett on to Fort Sill," said Cole and Erin flushed with pleasure. Mrs. Barrett. This morning the name had a sweet and wonderful sound. She listened while her husband gave orders to have his men ride on ahead.

"The trip shouldn't take more than a couple of days and then we'll head on back to Concho," he said in dismissal and, turning to face Erin, handed her a thin slice of pemmican and a bunch of wild grapes.

"Breakfast, love," he said. "The soldiers are heading out now and most of the Comanches have gone on ahead with the cattle." He looked up at the red-bearded giant who awaited them. "What about you, Cur?"

"I need to be getting back to the Rocking J and let everyone know Erin is all right. And in very capable hands." His grizzled face became somber. "Besides, we left behind an injured man. I want to check on him."

"Of course you must return," she said. "Wish

Herman well for me, and please understand why I can't go with you. Grandfather—"

"I know," Cur said, his large, shaggy head nodding slowly. "Horse Back explained. If I had a family somewhere, I'd be looking for them, too."

Standing on tiptoe, Erin pulled his head down to plant a kiss on his hairy cheek. "You've got a family, Cur. Hud and Julie and me. And Cole. Thank you for being here when we needed you." She touched his hand. "I'll let you know later"—she felt Cole's eyes on her—"what my plans are."

Erin silently watched Cur mount and ride away.

"Your plans are to go to Fort Concho with your husband," Cole said as Cur disappeared down the hill.

His words warmed her. He wanted her with him. "It's the timing that I wasn't sure of," she said. "We don't know what we'll find across the Red River." Behind Cole she spied Tao-nar-sie and her father waiting on horseback to begin the journey. "It's time to go," she said, cutting off his reply.

She gave a last glance around the camp. All was clear. Except for the signs of a recent fire, the Indians had left the land as it was found.

Within minutes four riders headed out across the plains in the wake of the small band of soldiers whose dust was faintly visible on the rise of the next hill. In front were Erin and Tao-nar-sie; behind them rode Horse Back and Cole. The men's voices drifted across the still land. Munching at her meal, Erin listened to them talk.

Cole's concern was about the rifles that the braves had used to capture his men. "I've not seen any like them before. A long barrel and a snubbed stock. *Stevenson* was carved into the handle. It's a brand I've not heard of."

"My braves are foolish," Horse Back replied. "They find the weapons half-buried on the reservation. The white man's guns give them power to leave." His voice saddened. "I fear they will suffer for their foolishness when they return. The cattle will not be enough to set things right."

Their talk turned to conditions on the reservation. "My people live in tipis now," Horse Back said. "At first the white man says they must put the old ways behind them and live in houses made of wood. But the Comanches grow weak with the white man's illness. When they cough, they spit blood upon the ground."

"Tuberculosis?" Cole asked.

Horse Back nodded. "And more diseases come. Now the fever kills my people. And still they must remain upon the reservation."

"I'd heard about the spread of malaria. Aren't they getting care?" Cole laughed despairingly. "Don't answer that. The Army doesn't always care for its own soldiers."

Throughout the morning Horse Back's voice droned on with tales of horror about Fort Sill—of men and women forced into a life of agriculture for which they were ill prepared, of clothing shabbily made, of rations withheld at the slightest provocation.

"Ration day is a time of celebration and of shame," he said. "Each family receives a card that must be shown. The day is held each two weeks by the white man's calendar. The women line up to receive the food that must last them until the next ration day dawns. Sometimes the food is bad. Sometimes it is less than had been promised. And sometimes it is withheld."

"And where are the men?" Cole asked.

"They make sport of the day. Cattle are put in a pen. The braves ride them down as they once did the buffalo. The women and children wait to skin and cut them up. Many fights break out."

"I see the shame you spoke of," Cole said, "but where is the celebration?"

"My people feast and gamble. They race their horses.

Sometimes they are foolish and lose what they have been given. They go home with their hands and bellies empty and their hearts heavy. Like Little Hawk and the other braves, they try to run away."

"What is the Indian agent doing all this time?"

"If he is a good man, he tries to keep peace among the people."

"And is he a good man?"

Horse Back shrugged. "You see for yourself," he said, then settled back in silence.

Erin glanced back at the two men—one sitting tall and straight in his blue Army uniform, his broad-brimmed hat pulled low over his eyes; the other aged but still proud in his red calico shirt and sleeveless Army coat, his lined face held up to the overhead sun. Cole smiled in greeting and Erin's heart quickened. Saddened by the war chief's tale, she still reacted with a rush of warmth to her husband's smile. Riding so near and yet so far, with his long, black-booted legs resting against his mount, he was at once a torture and a comfort.

By noon they had forded the Red River and headed north toward the Wichita Mountains and Fort Sill; when night fell, they joined up with the soldiers to make a rough camp beside a clear stream and sleep under the stars, the women together and the men flanking them on either side. Huddled alone in the bedroll that Cole had insisted she use, Erin missed her husband very much.

Late afternoon of their second day of travel they arrived at Fort Sill. A Comanche patrol, part of a newly formed Indian police force, met them at the entrance to the fort, its leader a brave wearing sergeant's stripes on his Army jacket. His eyes flitted across the strange band of travelers before settling on his chief.

"Horse Back, it is good that you return. Our people grow hungry."

"The ration day should have come and gone," Horse

Back said.

"The agent's clerk delays the ration day until the bucks return to the reservation."

"Sergeant." Cole's voice was sharp and commanding. "The braves should have been back already. They were ahead of us on the trail."

The Indian turned a dark, angry face to Cole. "They have returned."

Cole studied him for a moment, then turned to Horse Back. "Perhaps I should go with the sergeant to see what is wrong. Is there some place my wife can stay?"

Horse Back nodded. "Lonely Coyote does not live far. Tao-nar-sie and I will take her there."

Cole nodded in approval, then turned to MacClanahan. "Corporal," he said, "you four go on to Sill and report that I'll be in later. Get some grub and take care of the horses."

"Yes sir, Cap'n."

Cole pulled his horse beside Erin's roan. "Take care, love," he said, resting his hand on hers. "I don't know how long I'll be. Send Tao-nar-sie if you need me."

"I'll be all right," she assured him, all the while dreading the moment they would part. She had wanted him with her when she met her grandfather. The reason was simple—she was proud of Cole and very much in love. And she needed him very much indeed.

As he rode away with the Comanche patrol, she turned her attention to Horse Back and his daughter, following them around the edge of the Army fort and out across the dry, rolling terrain of the reservation. The grass was sparse and dry.

She looked around in puzzlement. "I thought this area of the Oklahoma territory was green and fertile."

Tao-nar-sie spoke up. "It used to be, Dawn Flower. But the white man was given the right to drive his cattle across the reservation. For the fee of one dollar each day.

276

When the land is green, the white man takes his time. There is little left for the Indian's pony."

Erin shook her head sadly. Ever since they'd broken camp yesterday morning she had heard nothing but sad tales about the Indians' plight. She saw no evidence that the stories had been lies.

The three rode on in silence for half an hour longer. At last they saw a weathered cabin on the rise of a hill, barren except for a huge sycamore. They splashed across a shallow, rocky creek and approached warily.

Nearby was a shed with a bony cow mooing forlornly. A few chickens scratched at the gravelly soil. A buggy with a lanky horse still in the traces was tied to a post at the front of the cabin. When Erin dismounted, a dark-suited man, small bag in hand, walked out to stand beside the buggy.

The man glanced at Horse Back. "Glad you're back. The old fellow can't make it for much longer."

"Oh, no!" Erin cried in distress.

The man scratched his scraggly gray beard. "And who might you be?"

"I'm his granddaughter," she said. The words felt good on her lips.

His watery eyes widened in surprise. "Didn't know he had one. And I'll be willing to bet neither does he. You might be able to do him a might more good than any medicine I can come up with. All I could do was build up the fire a bit."

Erin glanced at the thin ribbon of smoke rising from the chimney at one end of the cabin. "You're a doctor?" she asked.

"Yep." He extended his hand. "Doc Yarbrough."

Erin shook his hand warmly. "Can I see him now?"

"Pardon my bluntness, miss, but you'd best not tarry. That blasted tuberculosis has a tight hold on his lungs. He'll not live to see the night through."

Before he had finished speaking, Erin was in the open doorway. Gradually her eyes adjusted to the dim light and she saw the cabin consisted of just one room. Against the wall in front of her a narrow bed sat close to the floor. A blanket was thrown across a figure lying on the bed. A child, she told herself. The small rise beneath the blanket could not possibly be the body of a man.

She stepped quietly into the cabin and tiptoed across the room to kneel on the dirt floor beside the bed. Long white hair, thin and lank, spread across the pillow. Turned toward the faint glow shining through an oiled paper window was a face as old as time. Lonely Coyote. Her grandfather.

Tears pooled in Erin's amber eyes; she reached out and stroked the silver hair. "Grandfather," she whispered. There was no response and softly she said his name. Lonely Coyote's eyelids fluttered. She was sure of it.

She drew closer to him. "Lonely Coyote, it is your granddaughter Dawn Flower. Daughter of Prairie Dew. Granddaughter of Dawn Breeze. I have come to take care of you." She swallowed the catch in her voice. "To make you well."

Beneath the heavy wool blanket the frail body stirred. He heard her and what's more, he understood. For a long while he lay still while Erin talked to him, carrying him with her through the years of her life, telling him of the good times she'd seen with her father Shaun Donovan, of her pride in her Comanche heritage, of Hud and Julie, and, last, of her husband who would see that the Indians were not abused.

When she had finished, she leaned closer to place a kiss upon his cheek and found that it was damp. She brushed her fingers against Lonely Coyote's face and realized that sometime during her discourse he had shed a few tears.

Resting her head against his chest, she listened to his

278

raspy breathing. When it stopped, Erin didn't realize it at first, thinking instead that he was having less difficulty drawing in air. The truth, that he was dead, came hard, and she bent her head to let the tears of sorrow flow.

After a while she looked up to see Horse Back standing beside her. He took her arm and helped her to her feet. "The Antelope Eaters mourn with you, Dawn Flower." His weathered hand pointed toward the open door.

Erin looked out to see a half-dozen Indian braves walking slowly toward them. Behind them the setting sun spread splashes of purple across the horizon.

"Others still come," Horse Back said.

"How did they know?"

"They know. Lonely Coyote was an honored man. Already they prepare his grave. Come. Tao-nar-sie and the other women will prepare him."

Erin went out into the dying light of day. Behind the cabin a narrow, deep hole had been dug into the hillside. Soon the buckskin-clad body of her grandfather was carried out. With careful hands his knees were bent against his chest and, turned to face tomorrow's rising sun, he was lowered into the ground.

As a lone brave shoveled the dark earth over him, a plaintive, tuneless song carried over the land. The Death Song, Horse Back explained. The singer was Tao-nar-sie.

How great his people were,
How great a patriot he was,
How he loved his country and his people,
How he fought with them, with no thought of the
*   Happy Hunting Ground until his people thought of*
*   it for him.*

Dry-eyed, Erin listened, then watched as a medicine pole was thrust into the ground beside the grave. From the tall shaft were hung a beaded buckskin suit, a lance, and a bow with one arrow caught in its tight string.

Her fingers rested on the leather amulet that hung around her neck. A shield against trouble. She knew what she must do. Moving slowly to her grandfather's grave, she removed the amulet and hung it on the pole alongside the buckskin suit. It was her last tangible link with the half-breed Prairie Dew who had given her life, but gladly she passed it on, knowing that Lonely Coyote could now kill the ample buffalo and other game that waited for him in a better land.

Chapter Sixteen

Cole knew the truth as soon as Erin entered the outer office of the Indian agency near Fort Sill. In the few hours since they'd arrived at the fort, a weariness had settled on her shoulders—a condition, he sensed, that was born of grief rather than the hectic events of the past two days. Sadness was in her eyes and in the grave set of her lips. Her grandfather was dead.

He stilled the harsh words that had been on his lips, angry words he would have directed toward the pasty little man behind the room's lone, uncluttered desk.

"I'm sorry, love," he said, moving toward his wife.

"He was an old man," Erin said simply. "At least I was able to talk to him before . . ." Her words trailed off into the stale air of the small room.

"Captain Barrett."

Cole ignored the high-pitched voice of the man seated behind him. "Is there something that needs taking care of?" he asked, taking Erin's hands in his. "Something I can do?"

She shook her head. "The Comanches have already conducted the death ceremony. They take care of their own. And that's how they looked at Lonely Coyote, as a Comanche." A look of anguish crossed her face. "Oh,

Cole, as I was riding back here I saw such signs of misery. The Indians were so thin and lost. Even the children. And their clothes looked like the leavings of a poor white family."

"Captain Barrett." The voice was an impatient whine.

For the first time since she'd entered, Erin realized she and Cole were not alone. She looked at the whiner behind his desk and then at her husband.

"On the ride back in," she said, "Horse Back said there had been trouble. Something to do with the braves and the cattle the braves brought back. He's the one who directed me here to the agency."

"How did that old war chief find out? It took me an hour to find the stock penned behind the warehouse next door. When I rode into the fort to find out what was going on there, I was shunted from office to office and finally directed out here again."

Erin remembered the way the Comanches had known about the death of Lonely Coyote without being told. Her lips broke into a gentle smile. "I suppose there are some things we'll never understand about the Indians, Cole. They sense things, as though they can read minds."

"'They?' Sounds as though you didn't inherit the trait. Which I must confess comes as a relief." Cole grinned warmly at her.

A chair scraped roughly across the wooden floor. "Captain!"

Cole turned to face the impatient speaker, who was now standing and drumming his fingers against the desk, his smooth, pale face twisted into a frown. Like a petulant child, Cole thought. In his job as assistant to the Indian agent, the man should, at least, have had a wrinkle or two from the misery he must have witnessed; at some time during his rides about the reservation he should have picked up a little color from the sun. A paper shuffler. The worst kind to deal with.

"Mr. Myers, you seem in a great hurry for my attention. That's a condition you may regret."

Myers reached forward and straightened an already neat stack of papers on his desk. "I have a multiplicity of reports to compose, Captain Barrett. The decision I made earlier today cannot be rescinded."

Erin took one step toward Myers. "What decision?" she asked.

Cole reached out to grasp her arm. "Erin," he said, "Milton Myers is clerk to the Indian agent, who is off the reservation for a few days. It seems that Myers decided the Rocking J cattle should be confiscated from the Indians and turned over to the warehouse."

Erin's eyes flashed angrily at the little man. "Who gave you the right to do that?"

"The government of the United States," Myers answered. "I am responsible to the Bureau of Indian Affairs in Washington. Not to the Army, nor to private citizens. I did what I had to do. Those cattle were obviously stolen."

"That's not true!" Erin's indignant voice filled the room. "Those cattle are from my guardian's ranch. As his representative, I owned them and, with the full cooperation of the United States Army, turned them over to the Indians."

"Something neither you nor the Army had the authority to do without going through the proper authorities," said Myers. "Besides, the removal has already been accomplished."

"Then you'll have to unaccomplish it."

"That, I am not empowered to do."

Helpless rage overcame her and she turned to Cole. "We've got to do something to get those cattle distributed where they can do some good. The Indians I've seen thus far are a miserable lot—except for those braves who managed to get away for a few days. Isn't this man here to help them?"

"Apparently that's not his prime consideration, love," Cole said, then turned to the clerk. Arguing with the officious man was futile, he knew, and they would have to look elsewhere for a solution. There was one way, however, to deal with paper shufflers like Myers. Give them a little more paper.

"Mr. Myers." Cole's voice was brisk and authoritative. "Mrs. Barrett and I recently returned from Washington."

"Mrs. Barrett?" The clerk's eyes widened in surprise as he looked at the pants-clad Erin.

"According to a directive out of the Department of Indian Affairs, private individuals and institutions have the power to settle goods and provisions on those Indians who have been placed on government reservations. Those goods and provisions can include, but are not held exclusively to, fresh produce and packaged food, textiles and other clothing items. And livestock."

Myers opened his mouth to speak, but Cole continued with his barrage of governmental bombast. "Such provisions cannot include money, bonds, or other negotiable documents. And of course no liquor. Officials felt the rotgut whiskey that finds its way to the individual agencies more than served that purpose. I suggest you do your job and see that such goods are distributed properly and not confiscated illegally."

Myers sat down hard in his chair. "I know my job, Captain Barrett. The Indians are not to be encouraged to raid and pillage."

"Or eat," Erin said.

"Rations will be distributed in two days, Mrs. Barrett. The braves can claim their cattle then."

"I've heard how that works," Cole said. "They get what is left after the fort is supplied, and the people working at the agency take their share of the stock. Those cattle are not part of the regular provisions and should be given directly to the braves who brought them in."

"As I told you before, Captain Barrett, they've already been turned over to the warehouse." He shook his head slowly, then muttered, "I just don't know why I didn't know about that directive." He reached for a stack of papers. "Now if you will excuse me . . ."

Erin opened her mouth to reply, but Cole again took her by the arm and this time hustled her out the door. "You can argue with that fool all day long, Erin, but you'll get nowhere," he said as they walked into cool evening air and stood beside the small building. "The Army is filled with his kind and you'll find at least one behind every door in Washington. You don't get anywhere by arguing with them. They have a fanatic's zeal for following the rules—as only they can interpret them."

"That's criminal!"

"I'm afraid that's the one thing it's not. It's hard for you to understand, love." Smiling, he touched her arm. "You don't exactly make a habit of following rules."

His touch softened the edge of her anger and she grinned at him. "That's not entirely true. I do exactly as I'm supposed to in a game of twenty-one."

A night of love in a Washington hotel room flashed through Cole's mind. "You won't hear any complaints from me."

For a moment Erin forgot her distress. Cole Barrett certainly had a sweet way about him, even in the midst of trouble. And there had been little else but trouble since she'd first invaded his quarters back at West Point.

"Cole, what about the directive? Is it too late for Myers to follow it?"

He pushed his hat back on his head and grinned at her. "Don't ask too many questions about that directive, love."

Erin looked at him in astonishment. "Why, Captain Barrett. You lied! There's no such regulation."

"For all you and I know, there could be. At least Myers will be a little more cautious in confiscating goods from the Indians. And I can take great pleasure in picturing him searching the Department's books of regulations for directives that favor the Indians."

Erin looked at him with loving eyes. "You're showing a flair for twisting the truth."

"I knew I'd win your approval."

"So what do we do now?"

"There's not much we can do." He looked around at the buildings which constituted the agency. Night was fast settling in, but he could still make out behind the office the quarters for the workers and their families, and down a narrow path a general store. The large, ramshackle warehouse sat farther up the hill; visible under the rising moon were the surrounding pens for the stock.

"By the time the Indians get here in two days," Cole said, "most of the cattle will be gone. Even Milton in there didn't bother to deny it. Political appointees like him are seldom concerned with the ethics of their actions."

"Can't we just go claim the stock with the Rocking J brand?"

"There will be a manager up there, no doubt, who'll object. Unfortunately, he'll have a book of regulations which he'll claim supports whatever he wants to do."

"So you're giving up?"

"Judging me, love?"

Erin flushed. That was exactly what she was doing. "Let me rephrase that. What do we do next?"

"There's a small settlement between here and Fort Sill. We'll check into the hotel for a good night's rest." He stroked his wife's arm. "You've had a rough day. You

286

deserve it."

"And tomorrow?"

"I'll go into Fort Sill. Major Carter, one of the commanding officers here, is an acquaintance of mine, a West Point man. I talked to him earlier this afternoon and he was entirely sympathetic to our cause. Maybe he can help."

"And what do I do?"

"You rest up for the journey to Fort Concho. We need to start out as soon as possible. I've already sent a telegram to headquarters about my whereabouts."

Erin protested what she viewed as being shuffled to the side of the action; she continued to do so as they mounted their horses and rode toward the small settlement a mile away. Cole was adamant.

Erin's mind raced. Surely there was something she could do at the Indian agency while Cole was twisting a few military arms at the fort. If only there were some way she could get at her money in Dallas quickly and simply, she could get the attention of that clerk Myers and, what was probably more important, of the manager of the warehouse where the cattle had been placed. But a telegram would take time, and besides Cole would frown on out-and-out bribery. An honorable man could sometimes be a real burden.

Cole was obviously of the opinion that she couldn't help him. An idea formed in the back of her mind, a simple way to prove him wrong. All she needed was a little cash. Docilely she agreed to go to the hotel.

From under a broad-brimmed hat pulled low on his forehead, Cole trained skeptical eyes on her. "Are you up to something, Erin?" he asked bluntly.

"Judging me, love?" She smiled her sweetest smile.

He laughed and raised his hands in surrender. "Good point," he said, and they rode the rest of the way in silence.

287

Erin wanted and needed Cole to believe in her, but she felt a twinge of unease that in this instance he had trusted her so quickly. She didn't want him to get out of the habit before he had completely acquired it. If her plan worked, he might never trust again, but then, she thought with a kind of twisted optimism, if it didn't, he might never know what she had done.

The hotel was small but clean, and when Erin entered their room on the second floor, her strength seemed to dissolve. Too much had happened in the past few days. Physically she was exhausted; emotionally she was drained.

Cole sensed her feelings and arranged a hot bath for her in the room. With gentle strokes he washed her body; then his arms enfolded her as they slept throughout the night.

The day dawned crisp and clear, sunlight streaming through the open window as Cole opened his eyes to the stained wallpaper of the hotel room, then shifted his gaze to the woman beside him. A tangle of red hair spilled across her pillow, and the thin bedcovers did little to disguise the contours of her naked body. In repose she looked delicate and vulnerable—and more desirable than any woman he had never known. Involuntary urges stirred him; only the faint shadows of fatigue under her closed eyes kept him from awakening her with insistent lips and hands, kissing and stroking until her desire matched his own.

With regret he forced himself out of the comfort of the bed, all the while telling himself he would have years to awaken her in the delightful manner he had been contemplating. For now Erin needed him in ways that went beyond the physical. After all, he was more than her lover; he was her husband. Her arrival in Indian Territory had been marked with nothing but problems, from the sad loss of her grandfather to the small-mindedness of the agency clerk. Realizing that Lonely Coyote was old and ill, she'd taken the death with sad stoicism. The clerk's mishandling of the Rocking J cattle was another matter because it had been avoidable.

As he dressed, Cole remembered the way Erin had come to him at West Point in her time of trouble with Colonel Turpin; the memory of his failure to get her money back still rankled. Well, he thought as he pulled on his boots, he'd see that the Indians received that cattle if he had to rope each and every steer and deliver it personally. Not, of course, that this situation would ever come to that. There were other, more subtle, ways of coercing bureaucrats.

Erin began to stir, and Cole sat beside her on the bed, smiling down at the lovely lines of her face. His gaze settled on her lower lip, pink and provocative. Lightly he kissed her.

Her arms stole upward to wrap around his neck and hold him tight. The kiss deepened. Then her eyes flew open and she pushed him away.

"You're dressed," she said.

Cole's eyes traced the golden red curls that framed her face, the slender neck, the soft rise of her breasts above the edge of the bedcovers. "I figured one of us had better be or we'd not get out of this room today."

"You're a hard man, Captain Barrett."

"As a matter of fact . . ."

Erin's lips twitched into a smile. "That's not what I meant." She glanced around the room; as the memories of yesterday washed over her, the smile died. "Are you still planning to go see this Major Carter at Fort Sill?"

Cole nodded. "He's a good man. We'll work something out."

"Of course you will." Erin looked away, hoping her husband couldn't see the worry in her eyes. Yesterday the clerk Myers had been unwilling to listen to suggestions about the cattle. Would today be any different? The idea that had occurred to her yesterday came back, but she still hadn't figured out a way to solve her initial problem—a little cash.

"Erin, I need to ride on to the fort. There's no telling how long I'll be there, and I want to get provisions for our journey and I must alert Corporal MacClanahan about leaving for Concho." He stroked her arm. "As much as I'd like to prolong our stay here in this room, I really do need to report back to Colonel Grierson." He grinned. "I might even be able to forestall a court-martial for being absent without leave."

Erin started guiltily. "Oh, Cole, could there be any problem about your bringing your men with me into Indian Territory?"

Cole shook his head. "Grierson's a good man. But you married a soldier, Erin. My commission carries with it certain obligations I can't ignore. We'll leave as soon as possible."

He stood and pulled a small roll of bills from the inside pocket of his coat. "Here's some money for breakfast." Glancing at the buckskin trousers thrown across a nearby chair, he said, "And you might also want to buy a few things for yourself."

Erin nodded, knowing full well he took the movement as an agreement to do as he suggested and at the same time telling herself that she hadn't actually committed herself to anything that could later be translated as a lie. She had other uses for that money besides food and clothing.

After a lingering kiss and a promise to return as soon as he could, Cole left. The door closed behind him and Erin got to work. Pulling on her buckskins, she decided not to braid her hair. She needed to look as feminine as possible; in her travels with her father she had found men invariably assumed they were smarter than what they mistakenly viewed as the gentler sex. It was an assumption more than one gambler had lived to regret.

After a long while in battle with an inadequate comb, she almost changed her mind about the braids, but at last the golden red locks fell softly against her shoulders. Tiptoeing down the stairs, she almost made it out the door of the hotel before being discovered.

"Ah, Mrs. Barrett." A questioning voice drifted across the small lobby and pinned her in place. "Can I help you in some way?" the desk clerk asked.

"Yes. Where are the horses stabled?"

"Behind the hotel."

Erin nodded in dismissal and stepped into the cool October air. She needed to work fast. With any luck, Cole would be held up by the old Army buddy he had mentioned, as he had been by that other officer months ago in Charleston. Only this time she wouldn't seek him out.

At the stable she ordered the roan saddled and was soon heading out on the return trip to the Indian agency. When she arrived, she by-passed the office and headed for the warehouse on the hill. The door was open and she stepped into the musty interior. Gradually her eyes adjusted. The building appeared to be one large room, a long counter separating the front from the stacks of supplies at the rear. The place looked deserted.

"You want something, girlie?"

Erin whirled around. From the corner of the room a shaggy-haired man seated behind a small table stared at her. With his feet propped up on the table and his chair tilted back, he didn't bother to rise. By his feet stood a bottle half-filled with whiskey and a greasy empty glass.

Girding herself with the justice of her cause, Erin smiled. "Are you the gentleman in charge?"

"You might call me that. Whatcha need, girlie?"

Sunlight filtering through a window high overhead

cast irregular light across the man's face. His close-set eyes looked like bullets, and a white, puckered scar angled across one cheek. His face was lined and hard, but curiously his lips were full and pink, like a woman's. Or the underbelly of a snake. An altogether unpleasant man to deal with, Erin decided.

"I need the cattle you received yesterday," she said. "The ones with the Rocking J brand."

He snorted an unpleasant laugh. "Don't we all! But that's prime stock, girlie. What makes you think they're for sale?"

Erin met his stare. "I've traveled all over the southwest, mister. I've noticed most *everything* is for sale." Walking toward the table, she passed through the sun's rays slanting down from overhead and her bright hair seemed to light up the dingy room.

The man dropped his feet to the floor and sat up. "Who sent you? That agent checking up on me again?"

"No one sent me. I'm acting on my own." Erin lowered her lashes and, without seeming to, studied him carefully. She had hoped to challenge him to a straightforward game of cards, but the man was just low-bellied enough to want a pot sweeter than money. Giving him a winsome smile, she looked deep into his narrow eyes. "But I didn't say I wanted to buy the cattle. I had something more interesting in mind."

Even in the dim light she could see his glance raking over her pants-clad body. "Keep talking, girlie."

Erin forced a smile. "Well, Mr.—"

"Taggart. Bull Taggart. You can call me Bull."

The name seems to insult the animal, Erin thought. "Well, Bull, surely we can think of something. You'll be the loser if we don't."

Bull grabbed up the bottle of whiskey and, filling his glass, swallowed most of the dark liquid. He set the glass back on the table and gave a low snicker. One of his front teeth was missing, and when Erin inhaled she decided he was in dire need of a vapor bath.

"I'm not saying, girlie, we can't. I can always say some of them pesky redskins run off the cows. If I have a good enough reason."

Erin knew the answer, but she asked the question anyway. "What reason would you accept?"

His soft lips smirked obscenely, and Erin found her eyes riveted to the gap in his teeth.

"Gets kinda lonely around here. Ain't had me a woman since I caught one of them squaws tryin' to steal a chicken."

Anger overwhelmed her, not for her own honor but for that of the woman he had raped. Fighting an urge to crack the bottle of whiskey over his ugly head, she concentrated on the more subtle way she planned to hurt him. Bull Taggart was no different from most of the arrogant men who had opposed her across a poker table. Just a little cruder. Her face settled into a smile.

"You're awfully hard to resist, Bull."

"I am if you want the cattle."

"I do, Bull, I do. But let's make it interesting."

"Girlie, I'm already so interested I can hardly sit still."

"Won't someone be coming in?"

"Not expectin' nobody 'til this afternoon. Besides, we can always lock the door. How 'bout it?"

"Don't rush me, Bull. A girl likes to take things slower. Got another glass? I worked up a thirst riding out here."

He disappeared into the dark behind the counter and returned with another tumbler, filled it, then set it down hard in front of Erin. "Drink up, girlie."

Erin lifted her glass and, as Bull tossed down his whiskey and refilled the tumbler, only barely managed to keep from pitching her drink in his face. Images of gaunt Comanche faces flashed across her mind. She set her glass aside. "Got any cards around here, Bull?"

His full lips pouted. "Why you want cards?"

"It's been my experience a man gets more enjoyment out of something he's worked for."

An ugly grin rent Bull's scarred face, and he had to work to focus his eyes. The liquor was taking effect.

"You tryin' to set up a poker game?"

"That or twenty-one. Whichever you prefer."

"Hot damn! I gotcha, girlie. Never did know a woman with a head for numbers. Twenty-one it is. I'll go get the cards."

"And get a pencil and paper while you're at it. Just so everything is understood before we begin."

Muttering to himself, he disappeared once more into the dark and returned with a well-worn deck of cards, a pencil stub, and a wrinkled piece of paper.

"Okay, Bull, now write out an agreement that the cattle belong to the bearer of the note."

"What the hell you tryin' to pull, girlie? Them cattle ain't yours yet."

Erin forced herself to have patience. "I'll have to win the paper from you, Bull."

He eyed her warily. "And if'n you don't?"

"Why, then I guess you're the winner." She refused to put into words what he would win. From the leer on his face, she knew there was no reason after all to pull the small roll of bills from her pocket. Taggart was interested in more physical stakes.

He wet the end of the pencil with his tongue and laboriously worked over the piece of paper. Erin could only trust he wrote down what she wanted him to. Silently she renewed her vow to learn to read as soon as possible.

Bull set the paper aside and picked up the cards.

Erin batted her eyes at him. "I know that twenty-one is a man's game, Bull. But don't you and I each have to turn up a card to see who gets to hand them out?"

Bull chuckled. "Hand 'em out! Sounds jus' like a woman. It's called dealin', girlie."

"Whatever you say, Bull." The smile on Erin's face turned to solemn concentration as she reached for the cards. "Let's cut for the deal."

A mile away two uniformed officers rode toward the settlement hotel from the direction of Fort Sill.

"Sorry I can't do more to help you, Cole. I know watching over ration day tomorrow must not sound like much, but sometimes it's enough." Major Sam Carter shook his head. "The trouble is there's not enough people around here—officers included—who care enough to see the government stands by its word."

Cole grimaced. "So I've been finding out, Sam. I'll appreciate anything you can do."

"The problem here is the agency has a right to those cattle even if they weren't stolen, as long as no one has papers to prove ownership. I take it your wife doesn't have a bill of sale?"

"Unfortunately, no. She left her ranch in somewhat of a hurry."

"Then the cattle may be distributed any way the officials choose."

"I understand," said Cole. "Regulations. Were you able to find out anything concerning those rifles I asked you about yesterday? The ones the braves were using?"

"Not much. You say they were marked 'Stevenson'?"

"Right. The Indians said they found them half-buried near a cabin on the reservation. Horse Back said something about making them turn them in."

"As far as I can find out, the Army here has never ordered any rifles labeled Stevenson. The closest company I could come up with is one we buy supplies from. W. R. Stevenson out of Chicago."

Cole nodded. "I'd forgotten about that company. Didn't it go into the munitions business a year or so ago?"

"They tried," Carter explained, "but the guns they were offering didn't meet government specifications. Besides, the Army wasn't in the market, seeing as how there wasn't a war going on. Shouldn't be any of those Stevenson guns around here. Of course sometimes some of the men at the Indian agency pull a deal or two we're not aware of, and certainly wouldn't condone. The manager of the warehouse, for one. Bull Taggart. He's mean and slippery, and almost always drunk."

They pulled up in front of the hotel. "You'll let me know if you find out anything, won't you? You can write me at Fort Concho. I have a bad feeling about those guns, Sam. For the time being, let's just keep this between me and you."

"Of course." He glanced at the heavy saddlebags behind Cole's saddle. "You get outfitted all right?"

Cole nodded. "Enough to see us down to Fort Griffin. We'll stock up some more there before heading on down to Concho."

"That's a long ride, Cole. You got some men to ride along?"

"Corporal MacClanahan and three others rode up from Concho with me. I'm sure they'll be glad to get back to the simple life of tracking down Apaches. They'll be joining up with us shortly. Come on in so I can introduce you to my wife."

Sam shook his head. "I still can't believe you finally took the big step."

"When you meet her, you'll understand."

"Blond and like a fragile doll, I'll bet. That's the kind you always seemed to take to."

For a moment Cole gave a fleeting thought to Rachel Cox, and then the image disappeared, replaced by the vibrant face of Erin. "Fragile?" Cole said as the men dismounted and headed for the door. "You may be in for a surprise."

The clerk met them in the small lobby. "Captain Barrett, your, uh, wife stepped out sometime ago."

"What are you talking about?"

"Yessir. Asked where the horses were stabled. I seen her heading lickety-split in the direction of the agency."

"When?"

Under Cole's sharp stare, the clerk shifted nervously. "Right after you rode out. Must 'a been at least an hour ago."

"Problems?" Sam Carter asked.

Cole nodded. "I wish I could say I was surprised," he said, heading for the door. "Those cattle belonged to Erin's guardian. She's probably trying to repossess them."

Carter grinned. "Now I *know* I want to meet your wife. Mind some company?"

"Not at all."

Conversation stopped as the men galloped along the well-marked trail leading to the agency. There were a few people milling about the area, most of them in the vicinity of the general store. Cole glanced up at the warehouse. The door was closed, and outside a lone horse was tethered. A strawberry roan.

Mean and slippery. That's how Sam Johnson had described the warehouse manager. And Erin was inside with him. Cole spurred his horse up the hill and, jumping to the ground, kicked his way through the locked door.

"Cole!"

He followed the sound of Erin's voice. In the corner of the room behind the door, two figures seemed to be grappling. One clear image struck him—a man's huge hand caught in the tangles of his wife's red hair.

In one stride he reached her and pulled her free. Her

297

assailant swayed, and Cole's fist landed hard against his jaw. Without a word the man fell back against the table, then crumpled into an unconscious heap on the floor.

Cole whirled around and pulled Erin against him. "Are you all right?"

Suddenly overcome with the realization that perhaps she had acted hastily in riding out to confront Bull Taggart by herself, Erin swallowed guiltily and pushed away. "Of course I'm all right," she said, trying to sound righteously indignant.

"He didn't—"

"He didn't do anything. Not even win at twenty-one. For one thing he was too drunk, and for another he was too stupid."

Cole's eyes were leaden. "You rode out here to play cards?"

Erin shifted nervously and tried to remind herself how brilliant her idea had been. A cough from the doorway kept her from replying.

"Cole." Sam Carter stayed outside. "Everything all right?"

All right? Cole looked at his wife and couldn't decide if he should kiss her or turn her over his knee. Both actions would give him satisfaction. Directing his words to the open door, he grinned down at her. "If not all right, at least normal. Come on in and meet Erin."

"Perhaps your wife would prefer to wait until later."

Erin prayed she would slip through the cracks in the warehouse floor. Why had Cole ridden out with his officer friend? He wouldn't approve of her behavior any more than Cole did. And what was worse, he'd think Cole was married to a fool. If Cole had any sense at all, he would be embarrassed for both her and himself.

"Erin?"

Pride stiffened her will. "I'd be pleased to meet your friend."

The officer entered the warehouse and the introduction was swift. "Major Carter," she said in acknowledgment. On the floor the warehouse manager groaned.

"Mrs. Barrett, I'm most pleased to make your acquaintance."

Erin decided against holding out her hand for him to kiss. Somehow it didn't seem appropriate.

The major turned to Cole. "I will be riding on. Unless you would like company going back to the hotel." He glanced down at Bull Taggart. "If he gives you any trouble, call on me as a witness. It's a shame he passed out from all that liquor. And Mrs. Barrett," he said, his eyes glinting with warm appraisal, "if you'll stay over another day, I would be honored if both you and your husband could join me for dinner at the fort tonight."

Unconsciously Erin glanced down at her buckskin trousers. Was there time to go by that general merchandise store and find a suitable gown?

"Thanks, Sam," Cole said, "but we're going to have to head out for Texas as soon as possible."

Carter nodded and said his good-byes. As he walked outside, Erin remembered the tattered piece of paper she had thrust in her pocket. "Cole, stop him. I've got a document signing over the cattle to whoever has this paper. Maybe Major Carter can make certain all of the stock gets turned over to the Indians."

Cole took the paper and read it. "Well, it says what you must have dictated. I'll be right back." Outside, he called to Carter to halt and handed the paper to him. "Will this help you out any, Sam? Erin wants the cattle distributed to the Indians and no one else."

The major read the crude document and looked up at Cole with a grin. "It's not exactly a bill of sale, but it will do. Under my supervision soldiers will be distributing those cattle tomorrow and not Taggart and that mealy-mouthed little clerk Myers. Give my congratulations to your wife for getting Bull Taggart to sign it. He's a slippery bastard."

"Not in a game of twenty-one. Especially against Erin."

"I'll have to remember that. Don't worry. I'll have some men out here early tomorrow to see that the distribution goes smoothly. Might even keep some of the Indians from gambling away their food supply."

He paused a moment. "That's a beautiful woman you've got in there. And an unusual one. Not at all what I expected. You must be very proud."

"I am."

"All I can say is, life at Fort Concho is going to be interesting for the next few months. I hope your wife doesn't adjust too much to military life."

"For her own safety, she'd better."

"You've a point there. Can't have her riding about the countryside unaccompanied. Too many Lipan Apaches still on the warpath down Southwest."

It was a sobering thought as Cole reentered the warehouse. Erin caught the stern look on his face as he bent over the still body of Bull Taggart.

"Smells like a still. More likely the liquor than my fist that's keeping him out."

"I'm sorry Cole for embarrassing you."

He straightened, and she was shaken by the anger in his eyes. "By God, Erin, you better be sorry for more than that. You could have gotten hurt. Or worse."

"From Taggart?" She had to make Cole understand. "He was almost passed out when you came in. He couldn't believe I'd beaten him, but when he tried to stand he pitched forward and fell against me. I guess it looked like something else to you."

Cole shook his head. "Erin, if I weren't so angry, I'd laugh. We seem to be always riding to each other's rescue

300

and complicating matters."

"So why be angry?"

"Because that was a damned dangerous thing you did. I told you I would try to take care of the problem."

"I was only trying to help. Which I did. The only thing I regret is that your friend saw me like this." She looked down at the disheveled clothes.

"Major Carter thinks you're quite an unusual woman."

Erin blushed. *An unusual woman.* Somehow the phrase didn't seem appropriate for an officer's wife. She'd made a fool of herself in front of Cole's friend. She knew enough about decorum to realize that. Why hadn't she thought things through before she'd ridden wildly out toward the Indian agency? Why didn't she *ever* think things through?

She had a long time to ponder the questions as she rode back with Cole to settle the hotel bill before meeting up with MacClanahan and the other soldiers and heading south. Somehow she would have to become the wife Cole wanted and deserved. She loved him more than she loved life itself. Remembering all too well how the freedom she'd run to in Texas had become an open-air prison, she vowed to conform to the strictures of her position as an officer's wife, no matter how difficult they proved to be.

Chapter Seventeen

When the small party set out on its journey southward toward the Red River, the pattern was set—Corporal MacClanahan and one of the privates riding ahead, the other two bringing up the rear behind Erin and Cole. They made good time on the well-traveled road, but two hours before sundown gathering storm clouds forced a halt to their travel.

Riding through the oppressive air had sapped Cole of his eagerness to cover the miles as quickly as possible, and, with a word to Erin that she should wait with two of the soldiers, he took the other men and left the trail in search of campsites. Protection was what he was after— from the elements that threatened them and from any renegades who might come across their camp.

For Erin and himself, he found a suitably secluded site fifty yards from the trail, an outcropping of rock overhead forming a natural roof against the impending rain. When MacClanahan reported he'd found a similar place farther upstream, he sent the corporal back with the news.

Within minutes Erin rode through the thick brush that protected the campsite on two sides. Behind her was MacClanahan.

"You planning on leaving early, Cap'n?" the corporal asked.

"Be here by sunup," said Cole. "We've still a long way to go before Fort Griffin."

"Yes, sir." Within seconds MacClanahan had disappeared into the brush.

Alone with her husband, Erin stood beneath one of the huge hackberry trees that lined the creek and looked around. Even in the gathering gloom, her eyes glinted. "Brush on two sides, a rock wall and creek on the other two," she said, then glanced across the slow-moving water to the sharp bluff that rose on the other side like a protective wall. "You've done well, Cole. We'll be as snug as we were in the hotel."

He answered her smile. "Now that you mention it, we will." The air was heavy with the threat of electricity. His own body crackled with the same forceful spark.

Their eyes held for a moment, then Erin watched unblinking as he moved about the clearing to gather wood for a fire. Her amber eyes blazed with an emotion not unlike his own. She'd never looked more desirable. Loose curls of golden-red hair fell across her breasts, and her legs, astride a gnarled root of the hackberry, were long, their shapeliness outlined by the well-worn buckskins molded to them.

Cole took his time and savored the warmth of her gaze. With careful deliberation he circled her to unsaddle the horses, then watered and fed them before securely tethering them under a thick bower of trees. Together he and Erin unpacked their provisions for the night, their hands occasionally touching, and after Cole had built a small fire beneath the protection of the overhead rock, he placed a bedroll and an extra blanket on the ground close to the low flames.

When Erin saw the sleeping arrangements for the night, she walked over to kneel beside him and spread out

303

the rubber cloth and blanket that composed the bedroll. From one of the saddlebags Cole removed his mess kit which contained a small slab of beef. Using several thin branches, he fashioned a spit over the lowering flames of the fire and, spearing the meat, set it to cooking. Potatoes and onions were set in the mess kit at the edge of the heat—enough food for the next few days should game and fish prove scarce. Satisfied on one front, he turned to his wife.

His eyes on her, he slowly unbuttoned the jacket of his Army uniform and tossed it on the ground. His fingers rubbed against the mat of hair across his bare chest.

"How about a bath?" he asked.

Erin glanced past him at the stream. The air around them was heavy and still. "We'll have to be quick about it. A storm's on the way."

"It most certainly is."

Erin smiled into his eyes. Cole wasn't talking about the weather. As she rose to her feet, Cole moved very close, his eyes warm as charcoal, his bare chest glistening with sweat. With gentle, insistent strokes his hands moved down her hips and pressed against her buttocks, burning his thighs into hers, making her feel the hard, demanding evidence of his need.

Her own desire flared to match his as hot hands tugged the buckskins down the length of her legs and tossed them aside. The Army shirt that she'd borrowed days ago brushed the top of her naked thighs. Stepping back, she slowly unfastened the buttons of the shirt and pulled it open to reveal breasts swollen and dark-tipped. Soon the shirt joined her buckskins on the ground. She moistened her lips and turned to stroll slowly toward the creek, expecting at any moment that her husband's hard body would crash against hers.

When it didn't, she paused at the water's edge before gingerly stepping into the slow-moving current. The water was not nearly so cold as she had feared. Glancing over her shoulder to advise her husband of that fact, she stared in wonder at him. He had paused to strip his trousers from his body, and he stood on the bank, legs apart, naked and magnificent in his arousal. Wide-eyed, she looked up and saw a storm of hot anticipation on his face. His eyes were as dark as the clouds behind him. He had read the look of arousal on her face. He would not be denied.

Suddenly she recalled her words to Bull Taggart earlier in the day. A man enjoyed what he had to work for. She would let Cole work a little, for what he knew was his for the taking. In a deliciously inept attempt to get away from her tempter, she splashed toward the opposite shore, but her efforts were as futile as she knew they would be. Diving headfirst into the deepest part of the creek, Cole streaked underwater toward her, grabbed her ankle, and pulled her down into his arms.

They broke the surface of the water and his lips ground fiercely against hers, teeth and tongue demanding submission. Wrapped up in her love-game, she fought, her fists striking his chest, her legs pushing against the current of the water. She succeeded only in rubbing her body erotically against his. A victim of her own struggles, she was gripped by an ungovernable urge to wrap her legs around him and beg for the deep thrusts of his manhood.

Cole lifted her arms and pulled himself hard into her embrace, her hands reaching over his shoulders to press along the corded muscles of his back. Overhead, rolling clouds blocked out the purple rays from the setting sun; the creek water lapped unheeded about their waists. Erin's head fell back to welcome smoldering lips across her neck and throat. Her bare breasts were full and hard tipped against his chest. Stormy sensations raged through her, tumultuous cravings that were almost pain. A bolt of lightning rent the sky, its brief splash of harsh radiance illuminating her full, parted lips and amber eyes darkened with turbulent desire.

She breathed his name hoarsely and, with promised ecstasy eddying around their tightly pressed bodies, wrapped her legs around him and took him down, down into the swirling vortex of her welcoming warmth.

Cole's own frenzied tempest matched hers. His feet planted on the rocky bed of the enveloping stream, he entered her body to thrust deep and hard inside her. Waves of passion pounded against his every thought save that of *Erin, Erin*. Like an erotic song, her name resounded in his head, and his body moved faster and faster to the rhythm it evoked.

A frenzy of unpent desire raged on, and the fury of their lovemaking roiled the slow-moving currents of the stream. Wildly pleasurable paroxysms burst within them, each tremor coming harder and faster than the last until the inky darkness of ecstasy enveloped them. Like storm-tossed lovers they clung together for security in their weltering world.

As the storm clouds pressed their threatening weight against the heavy air, fat splats of rain hit unnoticed against the surface of the water. Still Cole held her tightly, as though a loosening of his embrace would send her floating away from him forever. He'd spent hours building up his desire and he couldn't let it go so quickly, no matter how complete had been his satisfaction. Arms and legs wrapped securely around him, Erin clung with equal fervor, and only when the single drops of precipitation melded to form a sheet of driving rain did their bodies part.

Lifting his wife in his arms, Cole strode to the water's edge, then hurried up the bank and across the now-muddied clearing to the security of their rock-roofed camp. With gentle hands he set her down on the bedroll beside the still-burning fire, then, stepping out once more into the wall of rain, gathered up their clothes.

Tossing them into a crumpled heap beneath the small shelter, he dropped his long, lean body down beside her and, head bent, lifted her hands to kiss them.

"These bring me much pleasure, love," he whispered, then looked up at her. "Everything about you does." Erin trembled at his touch and at his words.

Thunder rolled in the distance as Cole enfolded her in his embrace. "Cold?"

"Not now."

He ignored her disclaimer and pulled one of the Army blankets around them, holding her close, his lips teasing her ear. With one hand he brushed the damp tendrils of hair away from her face. "I love you, Mrs. Barrett."

"And I love you, Captain Barrett."

For a long while they sat wrapped in each other's arms and stared into the rain. Such contentment filled Cole that he was startled to feel Erin shudder once again. He moved back to look into her eyes. "Is something wrong?"

"Not with you, Cole. Not ever with you. It's just that when you called me Mrs. Barrett a few minutes ago, it made me think about our destination." Staring past him into the falling rain, she snuggled closer.

"It won't be long now until we're home," he said. "Fort Griffin and then on down to Fort Concho. At least Concho is the place we'll both call home until I get orders to go elsewhere."

Home. It had a warm sound that should have been settling. Somehow it wasn't. Erin pulled her head from where it had been tucked under his chin. She knew she had to force from her mind the memory of her husband's lovemaking and the comfort of his presence, and allow their little Eden to be invaded by serious doubts about the months that faced them.

But she'd do a damned better job of voicing her doubts if she weren't wrapped in the same blanket with his naked body next to hers. Pulling herself farther away from the comforting warmth that he offered, she draped the extra blanket around her body and sat closer to the fire. Cole made no move to stop her.

"Cole, remember how I left you in Mobile?"

Thunder rolled in the distance as Cole's eyes, dark and stormy like the night that surrounded them, bore into her. "It's not something I'm likely to forget."

"I didn't leave you on a sudden whim or fit of temper. At least not entirely," she said, looking blindly into the falling rain. "Although it must have seemed it."

His voice took on the grating edge of disbelief. "Are you saying you had a reason to leave? One that any rational person could accept?"

Her eyes darted to him for one moment. "I think so. In Mobile I saw myself as ill suited to be your wife. For a few minutes today I feared it was a certainty."

He dropped the blanket around his waist and shifted closer to kiss the edges of her lips. "You call what we just did ill suited?"

Erin sighed and for a moment closed her eyes. "I'm trying not to think about what we just did." She forced herself to look at him. "Please don't change the subject."

"I didn't know I was. Weren't we discussing our suitability as husband and wife?"

"Which involves more than just . . ." Her voice trailed off for a moment. "You're making this very hard for me."

"Good. It's what I intended to do."

Her eyes blurred with unshed tears as she looked at him. "If I don't tell you how I feel, Cole, there will be a barrier between us. Is that what you also intend?"

Cole had to fight down his anger. "For God's sake, Erin, of course not."

This was going badly, she knew. She was only driving him further away from understanding.

Her eyes locked with his. "Back at the agency, Cole, I wanted to help you secure title to the cattle. And I did. But that wasn't the only thing I accomplished. I angered you and embarrassed you in front of your fellow officer. Major Carter must have thought I was a fool."

"Did you hear him say anything to that effect?"

"Of course not. Officers are trained better than to speak what's on their mind."

"Am I included in that statement? After all, I'm an officer."

"I—" She looked away. "I'm not talking about you right now."

"Let's assume then, love, that you consider I tell the truth. Major Carter was quite besotted with you. Said he could imagine a lively time at Concho after you arrive."

"And you thought that was a compliment?"

"Erin, you don't know how stale life at a frontier fort can be. You'll be a breath of fresh air."

"Entertainment, you mean. I'll entertain the troops with my escapades." She hurried on, cutting off his rejoinder. "Don't placate me, Cole. I may be unschooled and illiterate, but I'm not stupid. At Fort Concho or anywhere else you might be stationed, I would be the butt of jokes. Can't you see me with my McGuffey readers sitting in a classroom with six-year-olds? Perhaps the commandant's wife could help me with my lessons."

"Alice Grierson is a wonderful woman. She would do it and not think any less of you. I rather imagine she would admire your courage. And so would anyone else whose opinion I would value."

"You're an ambitious man, Cole. You've admitted as much, and I admire you for it. In many ways you remind me of Hud. I can't see you'll have much of an Army career with me at your side."

Cole settled into the darkness away from the fire. "And you're willing to give up without a struggle? That

309

somehow doesn't seem like you, love. True, I didn't know much about you when I married you—including how much I love you. But from the beginning I knew you were a fighter. No one less than that would have escaped a graduation ball and tracked me down at West Point. Or stood up to that misguided sheriff when he maligned my character."

"You're right, Cole. I'm not a quitter, but I'm also not a fool. My father was a dreamer who always sought an elusive poker hand or bottle of whiskey that would bring him happiness. Of course he never found it. His main accomplishment, although he never realized it, was in teaching me to be a realist. To see the world as it really is."

"And sometimes, love"—his voice was softly caressing—"to gamble that you can change it. There's another thing I haven't forgotten—the way you let your heart overrule your good sense in dealing with Hilmer Turpin. You were willing to take a chance that he could help you with a cause you cared very much about. Aren't you willing to give me the same consideration?"

Thoughts tumbled through Erin's mind. Somehow he was taking her words and deeds and turning them back on her. A clever man, her husband, as well as an accomplished lover, and she allowed a glimmer of hope that he might also be right. For a long moment she stared out into the falling rain, watching the torrent slowly lessen, then turn into a light sprinkle and at last a gentle mist. Through the distant clouds she could see the silvered moonlight begin to break through.

Beside her Cole sat quietly and waited for her to realize the import of his argument. Not that she wouldn't go with him, regardless of what she decided. He just preferred to introduce his mate in life to his fellow officers without having to resort to something drastic, like tying her hands and throwing her across his mount.

At last she spoke. "Of course I'm going with you. You won't have to hogtie me and drag me down the road." Cole smiled, wondering if his wife *could* read his thoughts. Such a trait could prove unhandy.

"I'm serious, Cole. You must understand the problems we may face." She looked out to the creek. "How many officers' wives would have bounded into the water the way I did and cavorted so shamelessly?"

"Are you sorry you made love to me with such abandon?"

"Of course not. I'm rather . . . pleased that things went so well. But that doesn't answer my question."

"Erin, I really haven't researched the lovemaking practices of my fellow officers and their wives, although I can name more than one that would probably be willing to forfeit a month's salary for what we just enjoyed so freely."

"The men, maybe, but not the wives." Erin leaned closer to him, and moonlight fell across her rounded breasts above the edge of the blanket. "I'm only asking you to think about what I'm saying. I tried to tell you back at the Rocking J that we needed time to get used to one another. Outside of bed. You seem very sure that you want me at your side throughout your career. I suppose I want you to prove it."

"I thought I just did."

"I'm talking about the long weeks and months ahead. We can't always be making love."

"We could try."

Erin wrinkled her nose. "And have you grown tired of me too soon? I think not. All I want you to do is be patient and help me when I do something foolish." She raised a hand. "Not that I'm planning on it, but sometimes things work out differently from the way I picture them."

311

"Like visiting Bull Taggart?"

"Actually, that went just about the way I figured it would."

"Erin, you can't always depend on luck falling on your side. You want my patience and my help. Did you think I would offer you anything less? But if you ever subject yourself to such danger again, you'll find my patience at an end and my help not quite what you had in mind. Unless you are planning on being regularly whipped."

For the first time since they'd taken refuge under the crude shelter, Erin allowed herself to smile into his eyes, to see with clarity the lean, tanned lines of his face and the dark curls of hair that she loved to fondle.

"A whipping, you say? We might try that sometime." She glanced at the glowing fire. "Is the food done yet?"

"It could probably cook a little longer. Why?"

She dropped the protective covering of the bedroll and leaned forward, her breasts brushing against his arm. "Because I need more reminding of just what it is you're offering me, husband dear. Don't forget we've got a hard road ahead of us and we might not be able to find such seclusion every night."

Now that was a thought to chill a man's soul. Cole's finger traced around her lips and down her throat to linger on the hardening tips of her breasts. His voice grew husky. "You're a practical woman, Erin Barrett. You make the best use of your time." He pulled her tight against him. "But you've selected a poor way indeed to convince me you'll be a failure as my wife."

Five days later a weary Erin and Cole, followed by the equally weary band of soldiers traveling with them, rode past the sentries that stood outside Fort Griffin, Texas, and headed for the post command. The days had been spent in hard riding on the well-marked trail, Cole as

carefully watchful as his men. On the few nights he and
Erin had been able to find privacy, they'd made love with
a frantic urgency that surprised them both, as though
each feared what faced them in their new home.
Constantly Cole assured her all would be well, and Erin
believed him.

As they rode past the barracks and around the parade
ground, Erin felt curious eyes following her progress and
she almost regretted that she had not used the money
Cole left her at the hotel to buy more suitable attire. She
had enough things going against her without adding to
them her scandalous pants and Army shirt.

"I'll wait out here with Corporal MacClanahan," she
said to Cole as they dismounted in front of the
commander's office.

"I'd rather you didn't, Erin. The corporal needs to get
the men on to the barracks and there are some lonely men
around here eyeing you. I just need to check with the
adjutant about where we can stay for the night. That and
see when the next stagecoach is leaving for Fort Concho.
Traveling that way will be a great deal more comfortable
for you than riding horseback."

"Only if you're with me. I'm not traveling alone."

"The men and I will be near by. Now let's go inside and
make the arrangements."

Erin sighed in acquiescence. Much as she preferred to
avoid the scrutiny of the officer Cole would be talking to,
there was no need to start an argument now. Besides, she
would be less open to view inside the building than she
was standing beside the roan and jawing with a
formidable-looking captain. She wrinkled her nose in
disgust. How in the devil, after days on the road in the
same Army uniform, did he manage to look so dignified?
The most she'd been able to do was work out the tangles
in her hair.

Leading the way into the stone building, she ignored

313

the surprised look of appraisal she got from the young lieutenant who sat behind the desk, and stepped to one side to stand in what she hoped was unobtrusive quiet. Cole took charge, addressing with authority the young officer.

"Is your commanding officer in?"

The lieutenant snapped his attention in Cole's direction. "No, sir. Won't be back at the post until day after tomorrow. Can I help you, sir?"

Cole outlined their needs, and Erin didn't miss the raised eyebrows of the lieutenant when she was referred to as Mrs. Barrett.

But the young officer made no other sign that anything was less than usual in their arrival, and she pushed her worries from her mind.

"The next stage won't be leaving for Fort Concho for a couple of days, Captain Barrett," the lieutenant said. "But I may be able to help you in another way. There's a supply wagon going down there early tomorrow. Some special orders or something that just came in from Fort Sill. You and your party can ride along with the sergeant who'll be driving. That's sometimes more comfortable than the stage. If there're not too many supplies aboard, you can make a bed in the back and stretch out. Sometimes relieves the tension of the journey and the ladies find it restful." He smiled at Erin.

"What'll it take, about four days to get to Concho?" asked Cole.

The lieutenant shrugged. "About that usually. Shouldn't expect much trouble until you get near Concho. Lipan Apaches still kinda active down there, I hear. Not that the sergeant will appreciate it. He claimed he was all right traveling alone, but he'll be better off with you and your men serving as escort."

"See what you can set up. In the meantime, where can we freshen up? And we'll need a place for the night. I

314

wouldn't want my wife staying outside the fort down in The Flat, even overnight. I take it the settlement is still as wild as it used to be."

The lieutenant grinned. "Wilder. At least that's what I hear. One of the officers' quarters is empty until the end of the week. There's no problem with your staying there."

Following the young officer's instructions, Cole walked with Erin to the two-story quarters which was to be their home for the night. From the open doorway she could see the furnishings were sparse but adequate.

Cole declined to come inside. "I need to see to my men, Erin, and check on that supply wagon. I'll arrange to have someone draw you a bath." He stroked her hand. "Enjoy your solitude, love. I'll join you as soon as I can."

She stared at his departing figure. On a military post Cole was definitely in command. Far from being irritating, the thought was comforting. Later, when a servant girl appeared and announced she had been sent by the family next door to help for the evening, Erin also appreciated Cole's efficiency. While Erin soaked in a tub of warm water, a package was delivered from the sutler's store.

The servant, a young girl named Cora, opened the package at Erin's bidding. Inside were a few toiletries, one simple woolen dress, a petticoat, and a cotton shirt. After donning the dress and twisting her red hair into a mass of curls atop her head, Erin studied her slim figure in the mirror. Green and trimmed with lace around the low-scooped neck, the gown fit her perfectly. And it was long enough to cover her moccasined feet.

They dined in the neighboring home of Captain and Mrs. Patrick Dean. Following the lead of her hostess, Erin was glad to let the men carry the conversation, which turned at last from Army news of campaigns and promotions to the arrangements Cole had made for the following day.

"We'll head out early with a wagonload of supplies going down to Concho," Cole said, "although I must say the sergeant who's in charge was not too happy to have us along. Osborne, I think his name is. You ever met the man, Captain Dean?"

Dean shook his head. "I don't think he's assigned to Griffin."

"As best I could tell, he's working out of Sill. Isn't it unusual for supplies to follow this inland route down into Texas?"

"Unusual, but not unheard of. Most shipments to the interior come by boat across the Gulf to Indianola and are hauled up to San Antonio and on to the frontier forts."

Cole nodded. "Well, I wouldn't think anything about the shipment except that Sergeant Osborne seemed determined to discourage us from riding down with him. Didn't seem to want a military escort." He glanced at Erin. "Not that I care one way or the other. Erin can rest occasionally in the wagon."

Dean grinned. "I can understand your concern, Captain Barrett. Your bride is a treasure worth guarding."

Mrs. Dean patted Erin's hand. "Where is your home, my dear?"

Erin stirred nervously. "Texas. Outside of Fort Worth."

"And is that where you met your husband?"

"Close by," she said, trying to stick to the truth. There wasn't much about their history together that could be related in after-dinner polite conversation, especially not the way he'd challenged her to a poker game in a Dallas stable when she was only sixteen. It *was* the way they had met; unfortunately, it would prove as inappropriate as it was interesting to relate. Before she was trapped by

316

similar questions, she would have to come up with a story to satisfy even the most curious of the soldiers' wives.

Cole read the plea in her eyes. "We really must be going, Mrs. Dean. Sergeant Osborne threatened to leave without us if we're not at the wagon an hour before dawn. I think the man would do it."

Good-byes and thanks were hastily exchanged and Cole and Erin spent a final night of passion before heading out on the long road across central Texas. Mounted and ready by five the next morning, they joined the wagon and their small band of troopers at the entrance to the fort.

"Erin," Cole said, pointing to the driver of the heavily loaded wagon, "this is Sergeant Osborne."

She barely made out a frowning face peering out from under an Army cap. "Good morning," she said.

The sergeant grunted an unintelligible reply, then turned to Cole. "She be able to keep up? We ain't stoppin' 'til the horses let us know it's time."

"She'll keep up," Cole said tersely, then glanced into the back of the wagon at the boxes of supplies. "What are we hauling?"

"Medical supplies."

"Looks like a lot of bandages. Some kind of campaign planned?"

"I didn't ask no questions, Cap'n. Jus' do what I'm told."

Cole circled the wagon and reached down to open one of the wooden boxes. It was nailed shut. In the dim light he could barely make out the crate's lone identifying mark—a scrolled letter S.

Osborne's gruff voice split the predawn quiet. "I'm headin' out, Cap'n. You and the woman can do what you want."

317

With a silent promise to inspect the boxes when they reached Fort Concho, Cole motioned Erin to ride beside him. The two fell in beside the wagon to begin the long journey across central Texas to what promised to be their new home.

The days passed as slowly as Erin had feared. Stops were brief—at stations or close-by watering holes—and then only when the horses needed a rest. For practicality she began braiding her hair again. Not once did she complain of the hardships or accede to Cole's suggestion that she ride in the wagon, preferring to ride as far away from the unpleasant sergeant as possible. Whether she could survive a life in which civilized behavior was the rule remained to be tested, but by damn she could prove herself on the trail. Even though Sergeant Osborne failed to acknowledge her toughness, she knew she had won the admiration of Cole's men.

A day's journey outside of Fort Concho the small band rode down a long, sweeping hill toward a wooded valley where the Concho River crossed their trail. From overhead an autumn sun beamed its welcoming warmth. The air was still. In the distance a hawk circled lazily in the azure sky. All in all, a peaceful day, Cole thought, and wondered at the prickling of his spine.

He glanced at Erin. "Are you all right, love?"

Erin sat tall in the saddle, stretching her body as much as she could. "Except for some permanent bends I don't think I will ever straighten out, I'm fine."

"Do me a favor, will you? While we ride through the valley, stay here between the wagon and me."

She looked sharply at him. "Any particular reason?"

"No. I just don't want you to lose your way this close to home."

She relaxed. "Home. The word definitely has a nice sound to it. I don't know how I could have thought otherwise. Does Concho look much like Fort Griffin?"

"I really wasn't there very long. My orders sent me down to San Antonio and by the time I got back I knew where to look for you."

"But you must have spent some time there. In the bachelor officers' quarters, I suppose."

"Actually, I had arranged to rent a room from one of the married officers. A man I knew years ago when I was stationed at Fort Belknap. He helped me through a difficult time. Until we can arrange something else, I'm sure we can stay there."

A difficult time. Erin waited for him to explain, but when he didn't she asked him to describe the fort.

"Even in the little while I was there, Concho struck me as more permanent-looking than most outposts. Most of them, like Griffin, were erected hastily by the soldiers who'd live there. The men at Concho made a hash of the local stone and pecan wood they were forced to use in construction and got the craftsmen from one of the German settlements—Fredericksburg, I think it was—to come in to assist."

Erin grinned. "Fascinating, Captain Barrett. But what I really want to know about is a store where I might buy a dress or two. And are there by any chance some gambling saloons nearby?"

"There are some across the river in Saint Angela. Not, of course, that you'll be riding across to visit them."

"Why, of course not."

Cole found his thoughts wandering to the stillness that surrounded them. As they rode into the deepening woods, he felt a return of the uneasiness he'd felt a short while ago. The troop sensed it, too. He could tell by the way they spread out from the wagon and rode quietly, their eyes darting about them. But the forward guard sent no warning and he tried to relax.

As the trail dipped down to the narrow crossing where

319

they would ford the river, Osborne pulled his team to a halt.

"What's wrong, Sergeant?" Cole asked.

"Just giving the horses a rest. And a little water." Unmindful of his fellow travelers, he dropped to the ground and unhitched the team, then led them down to the river's edge.

Cole watched him carefully. There was nothing wrong with caring for the animals. So why had Osborne sounded so defensive, as though he dared Cole to challenge his words?

A movement of leaves to his right caught his eye. Corporal MacClanahan, riding beside him, saw it, too, and turned his mount to investigate, slowly pulling his rifle from its scabbard and cocking it. The noise echoed in the stillness. From the depths of the woods there was a blur of brown movement, and a cry of "Apache!" issued from the corporal's throat. It was the last sound he made. A gunshot rang out and he slumped lifeless in the saddle.

"Under the wagon," Cole barked, and Erin did as she was told, dropping to the ground and crawling on her stomach to the relative safety her husband had indicated. Stunned by MacClanahan's death, she was barely aware of what she could hear and see from her vantage point— the pounding of horses' hooves, a flurry of leaves and dust.

Sudden sounds jolted her to the present—the high-pitched war cries of the Apaches, followed by deafening gunshots that seemed to come from everywhere. Somewhere out in that maelstrom was her husband. A uniformed body hit the ground not twenty feet from where she lay. Scrambling from her position, she saw it was one of the privates. Without thinking of her own safety, she crawled to his side but one glance at his twisted body told her he was beyond her help. She paused only to close his sightless eyes, then returned to the space

320

beneath the wagon to rail at the helplessness of the living when surrounded by death.

Then more horses joined the melee and she realized the wild ululations of the Indians were fading into the woods. Once more she scurried from her hiding place in time to see an unfamiliar band of mounted bluecoats disappear into the woods after the retreating Apaches.

Her eye fell on the two dead soldiers who had accompanied her and Cole on their long journey into the Indian Territory and then back into Texas. She knew she must postpone her grief. Behind an ancient red oak, she saw the body of a dead Apache. Two more lay mortally wounded deeper in the woods.

Panic seized her. "Cole!" Her cry bounced off the surrounding trees. Afraid to stay behind but more terrified of losing herself in the dense thicket in front of her and of not being where Cole could find her when he returned, she hurried back to the wagon. Unconcerned by the fiery battle, the roan was cropping grass close to the river's edge. A blue-suited figure moved from behind him.

"Sergeant Osborne!" The sergeant looked across the way at her but before she could question him, she heard the sound of approaching horses. The cavalry that had ridden to their rescue, no doubt, she thought. Along with Cole. He would most definitely be with them.

The first figure she made out circling through the trees toward her was an officer, not Cole and yet somehow familiar. He was almost upon her before she realized who he was—Gerald Nathan, Hilmer Turpin's nephew who had taught with Cole back at West Point.

If she was surprised to see him, he was astounded when he recognized her. And no wonder. He'd never seen her in her Western garb.

"Miss Donovan!" He pulled his horse to a halt.

Erin looked past him, her eyes riveted on the familiar

321

Army mount he had in tow. Across the saddle lay the uniformed body of an officer.

"Cole?" Her voice was at once a whisper and a cry.

Nathan dropped to the ground. "Miss Donovan," he said, "if it's Captain Barrett you're looking for, I'm afraid I have bad news for you. The captain has been shot."

Chapter Eighteen

Gerald Nathan's words shocked Erin into action and she took command.

"Spread some blankets in the grass," she ordered one of the corporals, "and let's get him off that horse." She turned to Nathan. "How bad is he?"

"A shoulder wound, Miss Donovan. I'm afraid he's lost a lot of blood."

"Mrs. Barrett," she corrected, ignoring the stunned look in Nathan's eyes. She knelt beside her unconscious husband and with hands that trembled despite her resolve to remain calm, she ripped at his bloodied jacket and shirt. His wasn't the first bullet wound she had ever seen and she thought it wasn't serious. But the loss of blood could turn a simple wound into something far worse.

She glanced at the wagon. "Anything of help in those crates? They're marked as medical supplies."

Sergeant Osborne spoke up. "Box is marked emetics and antacids. Far's I know they ain't useful for gunshots."

Erin looked at him in disgust. "That's ridiculous. Have one of the soldiers open them and see if there's something I can use."

Nathan spoke up. "Now, now, Sergeant. Help Mrs. Barrett by opening the crates yourself. Surely there are at least some bandages in one of the boxes."

Nathan gave Erin another appraising look and then went to stand by Osborne who, with his back to Erin, was prying open one of the top crates. He pulled out a roll of cotton bandage, thrust it at Nathan, and quickly nailed down the lid. The backs of both men effectively hid the remaining contents of the crate from Erin, who was standing impatiently beside the prostrate body of Cole.

Finally, with material at hand, she dampened one end with water from her canteen and cleaned the wound as best she could, pausing only when Cole moaned. Then she wrapped his shoulder tightly with the remaining material to stop the flow of blood that had started up once again. Throughout the tortuous procedure his eyes remained closed, and she listened for a moment to the sound of his shallow breathing.

When she was satisfied that little more could be done until a doctor examined him, she stood. "Let's pitch out some of those boxes and make a bed in the wagon." A sharp look passed between Sergeant Osborne and Nathan. "Is something wrong?" she asked.

"Nothing," Nathan said. "It's just that we can't leave them behind. Army regulations, you realize."

Erin's eyes flashed in golden anger. "What do the regulations say about getting shot?"

"Now, now, Mrs. Barrett. I think we can make a satisfactory pallet for him if we shift a couple of crates up beside the driver."

When Erin saw he would not concede the necessity of leaving some of the crates behind, she gave in. In minutes she was uncomfortably ensconced in a corner of the wagon, Cole cradled in her arms.

"I'll ride on ahead," Nathan said. "The doctor will be ready for you when you arrive."

For the first time since his arrival, Erin really looked at Gerald Nathan. He seemed to her just as unpleasant as he had been when she'd last seen him at West Point, despite the additional insignia on his collar.

Cole had indicated several times that Army top brass was buried in tradition and refused to modernize its procedures. In fact, he had left West Point partially to escape what he had told Uncle Thad during their dinners in Washington was hidebound stupidity. The advancement of a man as small-minded as Gerald Nathan seemed proof he was right.

"Major Nathan," she said scathingly, "isn't it your place to escort a wounded officer back to the post? In case there's another attack?"

Nathan pulled himself tall in the saddle. "With Colonel Grierson off the post, I'm second in command. My duty lies there."

Behind them one of the soldiers coughed and Nathan hastily conceded, "But I can leave half my command to help. And of course to take care of those not so lucky as Cole. The ones who died."

His words sounded more sarcastic than sympathetic.

"Then be gone and let the fort know we're coming," said Erin, "if that's what you think is right." Turning her attention once more to Cole, she brushed a matted lock of hair from his forehead.

"Oh, I intend to do that, Mrs. Barrett, but I am curious about one thing."

Erin looked up at him. "And what is that, Major?"

"The reaction at Fort Concho when a subordinate I sent out—no, allowed to go out—to secure cattle to feed soldiers and their families ends up coming back late with no beef. Instead, he brings a wife nobody knew he had."

Erin started to speak, but he held up an admonitory hand. "Army posts are rather close-knit, you'll find. There'll be talk."

Nestling her husband more deeply in her arms, she looked up at Nathan defiantly. "Cole wired about the cattle and what held him up. He had a command at the mercy of renegade Indians. He had to deal with the situation in the best way he could." She looked past Nathan at the blanket-covered body of Corporal MacClanahan, now draped across one of the horses. "Cole saved that man's life. It wasn't until he neared Fort Concho that he lost him."

She looked back to the soldiers who had made it unscathed through the Apache attack and spied one of the privates under Cole's command. "Isn't that right, soldier?" she asked, beckoning him nearer to the wagon.

The private nodded and ducked his head as he mumbled a reply.

"Speak up," Erin urged. "Didn't Captain Barrett save your life?"

"Sure did, ma'am," the private said, looking her in the eye and then down at the ground once more. "Beggin' your pardon, Major, but without Cap'n Barrett, we'd probably all be dead and scalped."

Nathan looked at the soldier, then shrugged. "Very well, Mrs. Barrett. I'll see you at the fort." He motioned to five men and rode off in a great jangling of spurs and canteens.

Erin bent her head and pressed her lips against Cole's warm brow. There was certainly no reason for Gerald Nathan to question her marriage. It had been fully cleared by Thaddeus Lymond before they ever left Washington. Cole's uncle had wanted him happy enough to forget his thirst for vengeance against the Indians. He also hadn't objected to his nephew's coming back West where the investment opportunities were ample for both of them.

And as for why Cole had never announced the marriage, she thought as the wagon began to pull out

326

onto the trail, that was a private matter, just between the two of them.

The small contingent arrived at the post before dawn, and a stiff and sore Erin watched intently as Cole, still unconscious, was lifted from the wagon by two tired soldiers and carried inside the hospital. The Army surgeon, a short, balding man, led the entourage into a side room which contained only six beds, all of them empty. Erin held her breath as he quickly unbandaged Cole's shoulder.

"Who tended him?"

"I did," Erin said from her position on the opposite side of the bed.

"Good job." He smiled at her. "The name's Scott. And who might you be?"

"Erin Barrett. I'm the captain's wife." Her voice contained a tremor. "How is he, Dr. Scott? Will he—"

"Don't think there's any danger of his dying. But I'll let you know as soon as I've examined him closer."

Erin nodded and leaned against the bed behind her to watch the proceedings. A man's voice from behind caught her attention.

"Mrs. Barrett, could I speak with you for a moment?"

She turned to look at a young lieutenant standing in the doorway. "I'm busy," she said in a loud whisper.

"Major Nathan sent me, ma'am."

Deciding the lieutenant wouldn't leave until she had dismissed him more firmly, she reluctantly left her husband's bedside and led the young officer to the hospital entrance where their conversation wouldn't disturb the doctor.

Early morning light cast a soft illumination on the surrounding buildings visible from the doorway, but Erin had too much on her mind to be curious about her new home.

"What does Major Nathan want?" she asked the

young officer brusquely.

"The name's Lieutenant Williams, Mrs. Barrett. The major sent me to escort you to your quarters."

"That won't be necessary, Lieutenant. I'm staying." Erin's eyes flashed golden daggers at the young man.

"Mrs. Barrett—"

"Lieutenant Williams," Erin said, quelling his protests with a set look. "My husband has been traveling all night in an uncomfortable wagon. When he regains consciousness, I don't want the first thing he sees to be a stranger hovering over him, or what's worse, no one paying him any mind."

Williams cleared his throat. "But my orders from Major Nathan were to escort you to your quarters, Mrs. Barrett."

Erin tempered the sharper words that were on her lips. "I realize you're simply following orders, but I'm not in the Army. Please tell Major Nathan I'm staying."

"But, Ma'am—"

"Lieutenant," Erin said, "are you prepared to sling me over your shoulder and take me to wherever the major thinks appropriate?"

Erin saw a fleeting smile twitch at the young officer's lips, as though he might welcome the idea of carrying her off. For a moment each stood his ground until, with a shrug of resignation, the lieutenant retreated into the early morning light.

Turning her back on the fresh air, she hurried through the hospital's central ward and into the smaller side room to take her place once again across the bed from Dr. Scott. Cole lay still, his eyes closed, as the doctor swabbed the open wound on his shoulder.

Erin gripped her husband's hand which lay limply on the sheet. "How is he, Dr. Scott?" she asked.

"Bullet went clean through. No broken bones. Not much tissue damage." He paused a moment to look up at

328

Erin. "He'll be all right in a week or two, Mrs. Barrett. Just needs rest and care."

"He'll get it."

The doctor allowed a smile on his solemn face. "I'm sure he will."

Taking a vial of clear liquid from the bedside table, Dr. Scott soaked a large wad of cotton. "Get a good hold on that hand," he said. "Carbolic acid. Might smart a little but it'll keep the wound from getting infected. Nothing uglier than a festering bullet wound. It'll have to be cleaned regularly."

Even unconscious, Cole stirred restlessly under the doctor's painful ministrations. Erin shuddered. Her husband's strong shoulder shattered by a bullet. Despite the doctor's assurances to the contrary, *shattered* didn't seem too strong a word, not when the injury drained him of his vitality. He'd always seemed so strong and invincible. Even when she'd feared what might happen to him in the riding games against the Comanches, he'd been in control.

With smooth efficiency Dr. Scott bandaged the wound and Erin noticed that for such a short and squat man, the doctor had hands that were amazingly long and slender. And gentle. That was the important thing.

Finished for the time being with his patient, Dr. Scott looked across the bed. "Mrs. Barrett, the captain may be out for most of the day. Why don't you go get some rest?"

Erin shook her head. "I want to be here when he wakes up."

"Thought as much. That's why I put him in one of the smaller rooms. Just you and the captain will be in here. Actually, it will be better for you to stay. I'm sure our Major Nathan wasted no time spreading the news of Cole's marriage. The whole place is probably abuzz with speculation, so pull up a chair and make yourself as

329

comfortable as possible. I'll be in the main ward if you need me."

In the silence following the doctor's departure, Erin sat beside her husband's bed and let her thoughts wander, not to any possible gossip about the two of them, but to yesterday's attack. She and Cole had spent part of their long journey from Fort Sill discussing the Lipan Apaches who still raided in Texas from their main camps across the Mexican border. According to Cole, the Apaches used bows and arrows in their raids. She wondered if Gerald Nathan knew anything about the guns the Indians had been carrying yesterday.

No longer the subordinate instructor of artillery she had met at West Point, Nathan was now very much Concho's second in command. Obviously he enjoyed the part. She had seen his kind before. Give him a little power and he puffed up like a toad. A few winning hands and he was an expert at cards.

As far as she was concerned, his place had been beside the wagon making sure it arrived safely back at the fort, but he'd chosen instead to take a different, faster route. Perhaps even Cole himself would not expect anyone in such a lofty position to serve as guard for a lower ranking officer, but she could—and a great deal more than that, when the injured officer was her husband and he had been shot by a gun that shouldn't have been used in the battle.

During the long ride after the attack, Erin had found that while most of her attention had been centered around Cole's condition, she'd had long stretches of time to consider the bitter irony of her position.

She was caught between Cole's job to drive the Indians from the ever-widening frontier and her intense sympathy for them. Sometime in the early hours as the wagon creaked monotonously under her she had truly admitted for the first time that the freedom of the nomadic Plains Indian was clearly doomed, and her husband must do his part to drive them onto reservations. Good access to guns only gave the Indians the means to prolong their own agony, and the inevitable end would come much later. The longer the conflict, the more lives of settlers, Indians, and soldiers would be lost. Cole's life could be one of those and for a moment, in the quiet isolation of the small ward, she gave in to anguish.

But such thoughts were fruitless, and she turned her mind to more helpful speculation. Perhaps his injury might end his Army career. As she looked down at him, she was ashamed for thinking of herself. How pale he appeared against the white sheets of the hospital bed, as white as the bandages that were swathed around his shoulder. Funny the way his hair looked even darker than usual as it curled across his forehead. How was it possible, she wondered, to love a man's hair so much? And wasn't it strange she'd never tired of looking at his lashes or thick eyebrows?

Cole, she wanted to cry out, *Cole, I love you.* Knowing his wound wasn't serious and trusting the doctor, Erin still would have given a large part of her fortune sequestered back in her Dallas bank just to see a response to her silent cry—to see Cole's gray eyes open and look up at her and his slack lips curve into a smile.

The minutes slipped by slowly and despite her best intentions, Erin felt her eyelids grow heavy and she slept, her head tilted sideways at an uncomfortable angle. The doctor's hand on her shoulder startled her to wakefulness, and she rose stiffly, rubbing her neck.

"Is something wrong?" she asked, forcing herself to look into the doctor's eyes. "Has Cole—"

"Captain Barrett has slipped into a much-needed deep sleep. It's you I'm concerned about. You look exhausted."

His hand steadied her and Erin rested her hand on his

for a moment. "I'm tough, Dr. Scott." She turned to bend over Cole. "He is sleeping more peacefully. I can't thank you enough for your kindness but I'd really prefer to stay here. Gerald Nathan left orders for me to be stuck away with some friends of Cole, but they're strangers to me."

"That would be Captain Pierce, I imagine."

"I think that was the name." Erin remembered the little Cole had said about the Pierce family. They'd somehow helped him through a difficult time out at Fort Belknap. She wished more than ever that he'd told her more.

"Captain Jonathan Pierce." A female voice purred the name from the doorway and Erin, startled from her thoughts, looked up to see a woman at least five years older than she staring at her in open disapproval. She was a white-blond, pale-skinned woman with pouty lips and a rounded face, a type that might be considered a beauty by men. But her eyes were pale blue and cold as winter's ice.

"Captain Pierce," the woman continued, "is my father."

"Why, Miss Pierce, what a surprise to see you here," Dr. Scott said as he moved away from the bed. "Calling on the sick and wounded isn't usually part of your daily rounds." Before she could respond, he turned to Erin. "Mrs. Barrett, may I present Maranda Pierce."

Erin followed the doctor away from her sleeping husband. Before she could respond to his introduction, the woman spoke up. "Of course you could have knocked me over with a feather when Gerald—Major Nathan— told me about Coleman bringing a wife to grace our drab post. Why, the whole place is positively starved for the sight of you." Maranda Pierce spoke with the sort of phony southern accent Erin associated with women pining to be considered ladies.

The women eyed each other. Maranda Pierce was

332

wearing a red woolen dress which carefully outlined a pair of large breasts and hips that matched them in size. Between these attributes was a small waist; Erin decided it was the result of a most uncomfortable corset. Maybe the corset gave the blond her rather sneering look. It is hard to smile when in pain.

Ignoring the cold look of appraisal cast on her own disheveled appearance, Erin frowned. She had promised Cole to do her best to adjust to frontier Army life, but he hadn't described the likes of Maranda Pierce. And there was no way he hadn't ever noticed her.

Erin spoke in a carefully modulated voice that would have pleased Marcia Smythe-Williams. "I'm pleased to meet you, Miss Pierce. Cole told me he and your father are old acquaintances."

"Yes. Cole served under my father when he was only an enlisted man. Before he went back to West Point and got his commission." Her full lips parted in a smile that bespoke events best left undescribed to Cole's wife. "I was just a child myself, but I have fond memories of the hours he spent with my family." *And with me.* Erin could hear the unspoken words in her voice.

"Funny that Cole never mentioned you, Miss Pierce." Erin smiled sweetly, but all the while her mind raced. Could big-hipped Maranda be a part of a past her husband thought best not to bring up? And then she blushed in shame that she could think such angry thoughts about Cole when he lay wounded and unable to defend himself against the insinuations of his visitor. Asking him about Maranda was something to put on the list of things to do as soon as he was well.

"Miss Pierce," she said, "it's my understanding I'm to stay with your family until Cole is well enough to make other arrangements for us."

"That's right. Cole had been staying in the upstairs bedroom next to mine before he left. It was my understanding," she said, her voice filled with innuendo, "that he left on patrol to purchase cattle."

Her eyes drifted once more to Erin's buckskin attire and up to the bright hair straggling out of braids hastily pinned up. Her prim mouth clearly told Erin that Maranda thought Cole would have been better off bringing back even a small herd rather than this little creature who claimed to be his wife.

Behind Erin, Cole stirred restlessly.

"I'm sorry, Miss Pierce—" she began.

"Maranda, please."

"Maranda. Cole needs quiet and rest right now. In a day or two when I feel comfortable about leaving him alone, I'll be happy to take advantage of your offer of hospitality. I'm sure Cole would want me to, and of course his wishes are my primary concern." Well, usually they are, she thought, except when he is being particularly unreasonable.

Maranda murmured appropriate words of sympathy about Cole's injury and, with a curt nod to Dr. Scott, took her spectacular body from the doorway. As Erin grimaced at the young woman's departing back, from the corner of her eye she caught the surgeon grinning at her.

"I think you handled that very well, Mrs. Barrett. Maranda can be a bit overwhelming."

Erin shook her head. "Dr. Scott, in the past two weeks I've been attacked by both Comanche and Apache war parties, I've traveled across half of Texas on horseback, and I've held my injured husband in my arms during a frightening nighttime trip to safety. Maranda Pierce is no more overwhelming to me than a flea to a buffalo."

The doctor's smile broadened. "Mrs. Barrett, you have a way with words and aren't afraid to speak up. With the Indian raids slowing down, things have been a little quiet around here, but it's my firm opinion that life at Fort Concho is going to pick up its pace considerably. Your

334

husband is to be congratulated on his charming bride.''

Somehow the good doctor's words were not comforting. Erin looked down at her dusty buckskins and then at her sleeping husband's face. "I rather hoped to fit right in without causing much of a stir after the first big surprise. At least I promised Captain Barrett I would try. Perhaps the flea to a buffalo comparison was a bit hasty."

"I take it you don't know much about military life."

"Not exactly."

"Then you're in for some interesting lessons in the coming days. Army life is tightly regulated, I'm afraid. Rank is everything. An enlisted man can spend his entire career without once addressing a commissioned officer, and of course their wives seldom mix socially. Not that your husband always follows the expected norms. From the little I know of him, Coleman Barrett is a somewhat unusual man. Even in the short time he has been here, he's managed to check in on the men who've been ill or injured. Something, I might add, Major Gerald Nathan has yet to do."

Erin's eyes gleamed with satisfaction. So Cole didn't always do what was expected of him, did he? His lecturing words following her little adventure with Bull Taggart came to mind. Cole could hardly expect her to be a model of perfection when he raised a few eyebrows himself. She would certainly bring up the doctor's comments when it seemed appropriate and when Cole was on his feet again.

And as for Gerald Nathan, Erin bit back the rather caustic comment she had been about to make concerning the fort's second in command. She didn't trust him, although she certainly had nothing to base her opinion on but a general impression. He certainly didn't deserve to outrank Cole. That he did so could only speak ill of the Army, an institution she had never held in much esteem.

Not that she could let her opinion of the Army influence her now. Cole was a career officer and she would have to cope.

"Mrs. Barrett, at the risk of repeating myself, your husband is liable to be out for several more hours. His body is telling him to sleep, and there's little he can do about it. Why don't you wash some of the dust off and get some rest yourself? You can use one of the beds in here, at least for tonight." His broad face broke into a smile. "That way you can put off getting further acquainted with the Pierces."

Erin looked down at her buckskins and cotton shirt. She could imagine what her face and hair must look like. This was hardly the way she had planned to make her initial appearance at her husband's post. After a quick stop by a stream to bathe and, in the seclusion of some thick brush, a change into the green dress Cole had bought her and a quick twisting of her hair atop her head, she would have been ready to meet Colonel Grierson himself, as well as the voluptuous Maranda Pierce.

But there had been no time for dallying after the ambush by the Apaches. She looked at Cole. Of course he would want his wife to look presentable.

For the first time in hours she managed a smile. "You talked me into it, Doctor. Where can I find a tub of water?"

"I'll have the corporal fetch one in here for you." His smooth face broke into a grin. "Wish I could talk the troops into bathing as easily. Tried to tell 'em once a week would do wonders for their good health. You'd have thought I told them to flail their bodies with a horsewhip just as often. The least they can do is keep from tracking in manure to the barracks." He shook his head in disgust. "Cavalry's the worst. But don't get me started, Mrs. Barrett, on how things ought to be around here. You'll never get your bath."

"Dr. Scott, there was a package in the wagon that

brought Cole in. You know, the one with the medical supplies."

"I know the wagon, but I wasn't told about any medical supplies being delivered. Of course, with the Army I'm never surprised when I'm kept in ignorance about things that should be my concern."

Erin frowned. "That's what Sergeant Osborne said they were. Some kind of medication." She thought a minute. "I remember. Emetics and antacids."

"Good God!"

"That's what I thought. At any rate, the package has some personal belongings of mine. Do you think it could be brought here along with that tub of water?"

"Certainly," said Dr. Scott, and within the hour Erin was lathering her body in a tub of warm water that had been placed near the foot of her husband's bed. For privacy's sake the good doctor had ordered a sheet hung across the doorway leading to the central ward. In other circumstances Erin would have thought the cozy scene almost domestic. If only Cole could get up and scrub her back . . . She'd have to lecture him on his remiss husbandly ways as soon as he woke up. Right after she kissed him and told him how much she loved him.

By the time she noticed Cole's eyelids beginning to flutter, Erin was dressed in the green gown he'd bought her at Fort Griffin, and her hair, hanging loosely about her shoulders, was almost dry. When she looked down at him, she was pleased to see a weak smile.

"Hello, love." His voice was barely a whisper.

Erin restrained herself from falling on top of him and covering his face with kisses. Instead, she leaned over to brush her lips against his, being very careful not to touch his injured shoulder.

"Welcome to Fort Concho, Captain," she said softly. "Let me be the first to say we're most happy to have you back with us."

Cole's smile strengthened. "Show me."

Erin knew just what he meant, and she kissed him again, this time with a little more fervor. "It's been almost a week since we've done more than kiss good morning and good night, husband dear," she whispered in his ear. "I had in mind a little more than sweet kisses to celebrate our arrival home." She lifted her head and smiled warmly down at him.

"Home? Did I hear my wife say home?"

"Yes, you did. And now you're not going to hear another thing except orders to eat and sleep. Dr. Scott came in a few minutes ago with some chicken soup the commander's wife sent over." She nodded at the bowl on the bedside table. "Guess who is going to spoon it down your throat?"

He shifted his weight in the bed and groaned a low "Damn."

"Take it easy," Erin said. "You're not to move or else you might open up that wound. Doctor's orders. If you don't obey, he will soak you good with carbolic acid again. And of course I'll tell him if you've been naughty."

Lifting his head slightly, she placed a spoon of clear broth against his lips and waited for him to swallow.

"Good boy," she said.

Cole's gray eyes flicked up at her. "Boy? It *has* been a long time, wife."

"More reason to eat the soup," she said, again placing the spoon against his lips. "You'll get your strength back faster and can prove me wrong."

It was a slow process, but gradually Cole managed to eat most of the soup, urged on, Erin was sure, by her description of what he would need to do to prove his manhood once he was well. And he would not, she assured him, have any choice in the matter. She was delighted to see some color return to his face.

"By damn, Erin, I seem to have taken to my bed and board a first sergeant." He lifted his good arm to stroke her hair and his eyes drifted over her face and down to her breasts. "A very lovely one, as a matter of fact. Washington could put you in charge of recruiting."

"I'm very clean, that's for sure. Dr. Scott has a positive hatred of good old Texas dirt and grime."

Cole's face sobered. "Have you seen Gerald Nathan yet?"

"He brought you back to the wagon when you were wounded." Erin grimaced. "Not that he stayed around long to be sure you were all right."

"Gerald Nathan was out on the trail?"

Erin nodded. "With a few other soldiers."

"Doesn't sound like Gerald—excuse me—Major Nathan."

"How did someone like him jump in rank above you?"

"I'm not sure, but I intend to find out. I've got an idea, though." Cole closed his eyes for a moment.

"Don't talk any more, Cole. The man could be a general for all I care. You need to rest."

He opened his eyes and grimaced. "Damned inconvenience is what this is. I planned to welcome you grandly to your new home once I was able to make arrangements for it."

"Until you get your strength back, my home is in the bed beside yours, Captain Barrett." Her eyes blurred with tears. "And when you awoke you gave me the grandest welcome I could have wished."

Cole squeezed her hand. "Have you been to the Pierce quarters yet?"

"I haven't left your side, Cole." Erin looked at him carefully. "I have, however, met Maranda. She paid you a visit while you were still asleep."

Cole grinned. "A bit much, isn't she?"

"That's one way of phrasing it. I suppose we'll be staying with her for a while?"

"Until I can get us quarters of our own. There's something in our room that belongs to you."

Erin settled closer to him on the bed. "What have you got?" she said.

"A trunk of clothes." He watched her carefully. "You might remember them. There's a white dress among other things—"

She broke off his description with a kiss. "Oh, Cole," she said breathlessly, "my trousseau. From the train. How on earth did it get here?"

"Well, I had the thing carted across the South and over half of Texas."

"You were very sure I'd be joining you here."

"I never doubted it for a minute. Besides, until you got here, it was all I had of you."

With a tremor Erin got up off the bed and moved away from Cole. "You're better off with me across the room. I'm liable to lose control and break open your wound. There are some things we simply must postpone."

"At least don't move out of sight. You look awfully good to me."

"Well, I hope I look presentable to anyone who might drop by to visit. Dr. Scott had a tub of water and my clothes delivered to the hospital. I bathed and changed in here."

"Then it wasn't a dream. I could have sworn I woke up some time ago and heard the sweetest sound. Like an angel singing. Or like my wife humming softly while she bathed. And then this—this vision arose at the foot of my bed. A naked woman, of all things, here in the hospital."

Erin tingled with pleasure at the thought Cole had been watching her. "How nice for you," she said warmly.

"Most definitely. And what a woman. Damp hair as red as sunrise and a face to haunt a man forever. Breasts full and ripe and ready to be stroked. As well as the gentle curves of her hips and the long legs. And between those legs—"

Erin turned her back to him. "If you keep talking like that, Cole, you're going to find that naked woman beneath the covers of your bed and you'll never heal. Dr. Scott will keep us here forever."

"Is that supposed to be a threat, love?"

Erin whirled to face him once again, her eyes darkly warmed. "A rather poor one, isn't it? Rather, let me make you a promise. As soon as you can manage, I have some things I'd like to try out on you. Things I thought of while you were asleep." Leaning against the bed, she stroked her fingers through his hair. "Take a long nap this afternoon, Captain Barrett, and if you're strong enough after supper, I'll tell you what a few of them are."

At the same time Erin was tucking her husband in for an afternoon of rest, Maranda Pierce sat across from her mother in the parlor of their assigned quarters and sipped at a cup of tea. *Wouldn't you be surprised, Mother dear,* Maranda thought, *if you knew what I am thinking about. Cole Barrett's naked body lying in that hospital bed.*

She'd been thinking about that body for most of her life—ever since a darkly handsome private Cole had worked about the yard of their quarters at Fort Belknap. As a captain, Daddy had discouraged her having anything to do with the enlisted troops. As though officers were always gentlemen. How little Daddy knew!

Even at twelve, Maranda had possessed a lustful imagination. Cole might not have paid her much attention, but she'd spent hours watching him from behind the curtains in an upstairs bedroom. In the Texas heat the seventeen-year-old soldier had sometimes removed his shirt when he was alone on yard detail. His bronze skin had glistened in the sunlight. Maranda could see it yet.

Not that he'd ever paid any attention to her. She knew full well he'd had some silly ideas about the daughter of one of the ranchers in the area. She'd noticed how he carried with him a packet of papers, and sometimes sneaked them out to read. Obviously they meant a lot to him, but when she finally had had a chance to steal them, what a disappointment they were—nothing but girlish letters from someone named Rachel Cox. The rancher's daughter, she was sure.

With them had been a tiny daguerreotype. Mousy little thing, Maranda had thought. She'd started to return the letters and had then decided that would be foolish. It was time Cole Barrett thought about someone else.

The trouble was, even after Rachel Cox was slain by Indians, he had never looked her way and she'd had to satisfy herself in other ways. Cole might have ignored her but no one else did. Already, at twelve, she'd possessed the body of a woman.

When Cole had returned to her life a few months ago, she'd known immediately he would be a perfect mate—both in and out of bed. Not intending to spend his career as a captain the way her father was doing, he showed signs of going far—maybe even becoming a general assigned to Washington.

But he would never make it to such a post married to that dirty little upstart she'd seen in the hospital. He'd made a terrible mistake, one Maranda would have to correct. The marriage couldn't be very old, for he'd made no mention of it in the short while he'd been at the fort. Even Gerald Nathan apparently hadn't known about it. Maranda had certainly brought up the subject of Cole when she was alone with the major, and he'd never said anything about a Mrs. Barrett. Not that he liked to talk about Cole. Not at all.

342

Maranda's full lips broke into a smile. Nathan would help her out—she was sure of it. He'd do anything to hurt a man he apparently detested. With the major it was probably nothing more than jealousy, even though he had managed to outrank Cole. Maranda's motives in trying to separate the couple were not any more honorable. She wanted Cole in her bed, and on more than just a temporary basis.

As she listened to her mother prattle on, she decided to pay Major Gerald Nathan a visit. With Colonel Grierson so often out on patrol, the major often commanded the fort, a situation that had proven mutually beneficial.

She placed her cup of tea on the parlor table. "Mother, didn't Daddy say he wanted to read that latest volume out of Washington on shipping regulations?"

Agnes Pierce looked at her in surprise. "I haven't the vaguest idea, Maranda. Your father doesn't talk to me about his military affairs. You would be much more likely to know."

"I'm just sure he was talking about that particular book last night at supper. You know how he is about keeping his shipping orders correct. If you can spare me for a while, I think I'll go over to the post library and see if I can get it for him."

"That will be nice, dear."

Seeing her mother already slipping away from the present and into the daydreams which occupied much of her time, Maranda fluffed her blond hair and made a hasty departure. After a brisk walk across the parade grounds, she entered the headquarters building and informed the lieutenant who served as adjutant for Fort Concho that she would be using the library for a while.

Turning toward the library which was housed in a room behind the unoccupied office of Colonel Grierson, she paused a moment. "Oh, by the way, is Major Nathan available?"

"He stepped out a few minutes ago, Miss Pierce. I'll report you were asking for him when he returns."

She didn't have long to wait in the small, cluttered room for Nathan.

"Miss Pierce," he said on entering the library and shutting the door firmly behind him, "what an unexpected pleasure this is. How can I be of service?"

Maranda looked at him in frank appraisal. Major Nathan was of medium height, brown-eyed, and sharp-faced. Even pale and stretched out on a hospital bed, Cole Barrett had been more appealing, dark hair tumbling across his forehead, lips still and waiting to be kissed into wakefulness. She'd felt a strong urge to slip under the covering sheet, but unfortunately another woman had stood between her and the prostrate body she wanted. Gerald Nathan was here and willing, two traits that gave him a certain amount of charm.

"I'm sure we can both think of a way you can help me, Major. But first I have a question."

A look of impatience crossed Nathan's face. "What is it, Maranda?"

At least with Gerald, Maranda thought, one could get right down to business. "This morning you told me there was a Mrs. Coleman Barrett. What do you know about her?"

Nathan snorted in disgust. "Not a lot. Her home is here in Texas but he knew her back at West Point. I didn't know they were serious about each other until I saw her yesterday at the site of the ambush. He must have gathered her up on the trip I authorized to get cattle. Too bad the soldiers detailed to him are either dead or mighty loyal. The story they're telling is that Indians stole the whole herd."

Maranda heaved an impatient sigh. The last thing she was interested in was a few stupid cows. "So they haven't been married long?" she asked.

"Couldn't be more than a few months, if that."

"Newlyweds." Her blue eyes narrowed. "I've heard tell separation puts a strain on such a young marriage. And he couldn't be too proud of her since he never mentioned having a wife."

Nathan watched her carefully. "What are you proposing, Maranda?"

"Couldn't you find a way to keep Cole away from Fort Concho? Maybe for weeks at a time?"

"If I had sufficient reason. Lucky for me Colonel Grierson usually likes going on patrols himself, and he likes Cole. What would you be up to while he's away?"

"Why, what an evil mind you have, Major."

"Just realistic, Miss Pierce."

"All I would want to do is make Mrs. Barrett feel at home here. As much as I could. Of course it might be an impossible task. The poor thing got such a miserable start."

Nathan nodded. "Don't try to convince me you're being unselfish, Maranda. You seem to get what you want, no matter the odds." He loosened the top buttons of his jacket. "And so do I."

Maranda moistened her parted lips with a pink, catlike tongue. "Why, Major Nathan, what do you mean?"

"You know damned well. You're good at doing favors for me, Maranda."

"Anything."

"How fortunate that your father lets you rummage about his office. You'll have to be on the lookout for some more procurement orders for me."

"Of course, Gerald. Although that wasn't exactly the request I thought you were going to make."

"But it's also not the *only* thing I want, Maranda."

"I should have known it wouldn't be. As friends, we should always help each other out whenever we can."

"I couldn't have put it better myself." Nathan reached

345

over and slammed shut the bolt on the lone door into the room. "And now for that second thing."

Maranda's hands cupped her full breasts. "Whatever you say, Major Nathan. After all, you're in command."

His thin body pushed against her bounteous form; his hands roughly pulled up her red woolen skirt. Maranda sat at the edge of the table and parted her legs. Deftly she worked at the buttons of his jacket and then on down to those of his trousers, which fell to the floor around his ankles.

Nathan's thin lips pressed against hers briefly and his hands fondled her hips and thighs. "As usual, Maranda, I find you're not wearing anything under your dress."

"It makes things so much simpler, don't you think?" As she wrapped her legs around him and pulled him into her body, she thought how much she liked it this way. Quick and pleasurable, a hard table as a bed.

There was only one thing she would change. In place of Gerald Nathan wrapped in her arms and legs, she thought of the hard, strong body of Captain Coleman Barrett thrusting its way to satisfaction. It was an old fantasy but one, she vowed, that would soon be fulfilled.

Chapter Nineteen

Erin's world quickly settled into a routine which revolved around helping her husband through the slow process of healing, and she learned little about daily life at the fort. For the next two days she followed Dr. Scott's orders, cleaning and bandaging the wound and barring visitors that might disturb Cole's rest. After two nights in the bed near him, she met Jonathan and Agnes Pierce and then moved into Cole's old quarters in their extra bedroom for what became a longer stay than she'd intended.

On the fourth day, just as Erin was hoping Cole could leave the hospital, his wound festered slightly, settling a fever on him that hung on for almost a week; when she wasn't decrying the way his body had so quickly been endangered once again, she was blaming herself for his setback. By staying long hours at the hospital, Erin avoided seeing or talking to Maranda Pierce. She did not want a repetition of their first conversation.

After a mild October, November blew in wet and cold, promising a harsh winter in a land that was already bleak and hard. Bundled up in her warm cloak, Erin hurried to the hospital on Cole's ninth day there. Surely the stout stone walls built by the German immigrants would hold out a Texas blue norther and someone would have a fire going, she assured herself, but as she entered the small ward she fully expected to see Cole huddled beneath a stack of heavy blankets, his teeth chattering, his brow once more hot with fever.

Instead he was standing beside a crackling fire, fully dressed and grinning warmly at her.

"About time you got here," he said, holding out his good arm.

She asked the first thing that popped into her mind. "How did you manage to get your arm in that coat sleeve?"

"Is that any greeting for a husband?"

She looked at the dark curls that fell across his forehead, at the lips which twitched with the beginning of a smile, at the lean, strong lines of his body the blue uniform could not disguise. Love filled her heart.

Her eyes locked with his. "Answer the question. We'll discuss a proper greeting later."

"That we will, love." He narrowed the gap between them until her cloak brushed against his trousers. "As for the jacket, I have no idea why I struggled so long to get it on. Your help would have been most welcome."

"Do you have much use of your left arm?"

"Enough for this," he said, both arms pulling her close, but she noticed he hugged her closer on his uninjured side. Then his lips touched hers and she forgot everything except how good he felt.

He lifted his head to look down at her. "I have a surprise for you," he said, a glint in his eye.

"You always do."

"Not like this one."

Intrigued, Erin pulled away. "What is it?"

"I'd rather show you."

Erin nodded and without another question she walked beside him through the main ward of the hospital and out into the damp, cold air of the November morning. For a man who had so recently been flat on his back, he had a stride that was decidedly brisk, she thought.

As they walked alongside the parade grounds, Cole's strong right arm around her, they passed many of his fellow officers and she quickly found out how popular her husband was with them. All stopped to express their pleasure that he was on his feet again, some looking curiously at her but most welcoming her warmly. Cole seemed at home in the Army, more contented than he had been back in Virginia. Once more she thought that, as his wife, she must find her place beside him in the setting he had chosen. So far, it had gone well. If everyone was as easy to get along with as Dr. Scott, she would have no problems.

At first she thought he was taking her to the officers' quarters occupied by the Pierce family, but instead he stopped in front of the two-story stone building next door to that dwelling.

"Welcome home, Erin."

She knew immediately what he meant, and her eyes blurred with unexpected tears. Home. Somehow from his hospital bed Cole had been able to arrange this and, what was even more surprising, to do it without her finding out. The man was indeed full of surprises and all of them pleasant.

"It's not a tipi, of course," he said, his voice solemn, "but I think it will do against the winter weather."

Erin looked at the shallow covered porch that stretched across the front of the structure, at the curtained windows, and on up to the ribbon of smoke curling out the chimney.

"It will do," she said softly. A sudden blast of wintry wind reminded her of a matter far more important than the nesting instinct she'd discovered in herself. She held Cole tightly. "Let's go inside. You need to be by a roaring fire."

They opened the door on a respectable-looking servant girl in a gray dress. She was putting a large log atop a carefully built fire.

"You're Mrs. Grierson's Verlene, aren't you?" Cole asked.

The girl poked at the log before answering. "Yessir, I am, Captain Barrett."

"How kind of you to come," said Erin. "Mrs. Grierson was at the hospital one day and was most gracious."

"Yessum, she is. She hopes to get more help over here real soon."

Erin and Cole, arm in arm, made their slow way through their first home, Erin delighted to see the complete furnishings and Cole delighted to see her ecstatic response to everything.

The main room was sparsely furnished with a mixed collection that seemed to go together—an oak coat tree, bookcase, and small desk; a Chippendale sofa and two Windsor chairs. A bright Mexican rug reflected the meager light from two small windows.

The dining room was graced by an oval table and four dining chairs with the graceful flowing lines of Queen Anne styling. Along one wall stood a side chest with a mirror over it. On the table were boxes of what she took to be dishes and utensils. One glance into the kitchen next to the dining room showed Erin all she wanted to know. It had a stove. They could eat comfortably—and well, if Mrs. Grierson loaned them a cook.

Upstairs, she discovered a huge bed with a canopy that almost scraped the ceiling, a walnut dresser with attached candle stands, and a huge matching wardrobe.

Erin threw her arms around Cole and kissed him exuberantly. "How did you ever manage all this?" she asked.

"I had it sent from San Antonio a long time ago," said

Cole. "It's been in storage."

Erin kissed him again. "I love it all," she said. "Always thinking ahead and so sure of yourself, aren't you, darling? Just like lugging my trunk around."

They knelt together by the trunk sent from next door and now resting by the bed, and opened it. Erin removed the white dress and held it up in front of her, the gold band on her finger gleaming in the wintry light coming through a narrow window.

"With this dress I thee wed," she whispered.

Cole reached for the counterpane and whipped it from the bed so that it landed heavily on the Dresden dresser set and sent it clattering to the floor. The sound rang over the noise made by Verlene as she unpacked the dishes below.

Erin looked longingly at the soft quilts covering the bed, imagining herself there with Cole, but a crash from downstairs convinced her the completion of their homecoming would have to wait.

"As tempting as you are, Captain Barrett," she said, her eyes smiling into his, "we'll have to postpone a few things."

"Maybe after lunch we can send Verlene on an errand."

"After lunch you're going to rest. The Pierces are expecting us this evening and I want us to have a long time together without interruption."

Cole moved closer. "Damn the Pierces."

"Why, Coleman Barrett," Erin said, then gave in to a long, satisfactory kiss. Another crash from below forced her to pull away reluctantly. "I'm afraid I'm needed downstairs, but you lie down and rest for tonight. If things work out the way I hope when we return, you're going to need all the strength you can muster."

To Erin's satisfaction, Cole did as he was instructed for the rest of the day. In the evening he escorted her next door for the four-course dinner prepared by Agnes Pierce in honor of his dismissal from the hospital, and Erin had to fight an impatience to have him home again to herself. Dessert, brandy, coffee, cigars—the list of temptations presented by the Pierce family to keep the couple from leaving seemed endless.

And how could two men find so many absolutely nonsensical things to talk about? Guns, of all things, and the methods for procuring supplies. When she realized from their talk that Captain Pierce was in charge of procurement, she remembered the peculiar guns both the Comanches and Apaches had used and she knew what Cole was after—information about how the Indians might have gotten them. She'd have to be patient.

Her patience didn't last long. Sitting beside the two women and trying to listen to the men, she shortly became irritated by the chatter of Maranda, who was persistently and coyly interrupting, even flirting with Cole as she talked about their younger days at Fort Belknap. In desperation, Erin tried to think of something she had in common with Agnes Pierce, who was bent over a piece of embroidery, but the woman could talk of nothing but recipes for cooking.

If, as Erin was beginning to fear, Agnes Pierce was a typical Army wife, Erin would have a hard time indeed fitting in, a fact she knew would please Maranda. She'd bet dollars to doughnuts Maranda had marked Cole as her own and still had him in her sights, married though he was.

Erin's agitation grew and finally she interrupted the men. "Cole," she said with wifely concern, "aren't you getting tired? It's been a long day."

He looked across the parlor at her, one corner of his mouth twitching into a half-smile. "It certainly has." He turned to Pierce. "Maybe we can talk again tomorrow, Jonathan."

"Certainly. Just glad to find someone interested in the work I do." He smiled at his daughter. "Maranda is usually the only one who lets me bend her ear."

With insincere apologies for departing so early, Erin accompanied Cole to their own quarters and hustled him upstairs.

"You're right, love," he said as he closed the bedroom door behind him and stifled a yawn. "It's been a long day. You must be exhausted."

Erin tossed her cloak aside and lifted her arms to take the pins from her hair. A mass of red curls fell about her shoulders. "With the right provocation I could probably summon up a little energy."

Cole moved closer to entwine his fingers in her hair. "You'll have to be more specific, love. I figured I'd be asleep before my head hits the pillow."

"You are and you're likely to lose that head."

Cole grinned at her. "Something wrong, Mrs. Barrett?"

"I—" Erin paused. There certainly was something wrong, but she refused to tell him of her need for reassurance that she would make a suitable Army wife. That was a problem she would have to work out for herself. Tossing her head back, she covered her troubled thoughts with bold words. "You rat. After all my loving care, I deserve better than to be teased."

"I know exactly what you deserve," he said, his smile settling into a hot look of need that melted her bones. "And believe me, Erin, you're going to get it."

"Is that a promise?" she asked as she began to unbutton his jacket. "Let me help you keep it." When she had slipped the coat and undershirt from his body, she looked at the small, livid scar left by the Apache bullet. "You will, of course, be careful."

"Of course. I plan to take a great deal of care."

Slowly they finished undressing each other, their

hands exploring with an eagerness born of long denial, their lips and tongues touching until they burned with desire. As they slipped beneath the bedcovers, their probing strokes became more insistent, each scorching the other with hot, erotic demands, but when Cole shifted to lay his body on top of hers, she felt him wince involuntarily. Instantly she took control, pushing him back down onto the mattress.

"I'm in command now, Captain," she said, her lips hovering inches over his, her hair brushing against his lean face. "You're under orders to follow my lead."

"Pulling rank?" he asked.

Her fingers trailed down his chest to linger on his abdomen. "If that's what you want pulled." Her hand moved lower to discover a waiting hardness that made her forget everything else. Lovingly she caressed him, her lips burning against his throat and chest, before she shifted to wrap him in her arms. As she lay stretched out atop him, her legs spread wide to welcome him in.

With a low moan Cole responded with an eruption of energy that frightened and thrilled her. In vain she tried to restrain her passion, but as strong arms held her and eager lips sought hers, she gladly gave in to his demands. He gave no sign of pain or holding back, and each time he thrust deep inside her, sharp thrills of ecstasy coursed through her body.

As if each had stored up a desperate need for the other, they came together with silver-quick movements, faster and faster until the world splintered into a million pieces around them. When their tremors of fulfillment slowed, still they clung to one another. Avowals of love were whispered and returned. In his arms Erin felt completely at home, but for one brief second she shuddered from fear that such happiness could not last.

Snuggling in his arms, she tried to give voice to her thoughts, but he silenced her words with a kiss.

"Later," he said, his voice trailing off into a whisper, and in a moment his steady breathing told her he had fallen asleep.

The next morning he dressed and was gone early, leaving her to settle into her new home. Several of the officers' wives called saying they had come to welcome her into their midst, but she soon saw that it was curiosity that had brought them, and under their assessing eyes she was often sorely tried by the effort to maintain her role as gracious hostess.

One day stretched into another with little variety. Each morning Cole left to sit behind a desk somewhere on the post; each evening after dinner he sat beside her in the parlor for a while. Usually he had a book in his hand, but he never offered to teach her to read, for which she was grateful. A new school was scheduled to open up after the first of the year and she hoped perhaps to arrange for private lessons.

In the meantime she tried to content herself with embroidery, but despite Agnes Pierce's guidance, she found that for someone who could shuffle a deck of cards and deal them out using only one hand, she turned decidedly inept whenever she picked up a needle and thread.

Sometimes when she felt Cole's gray eyes studying her, she sensed he was trying to figure out if she was content. She expected him to ask her outright whether she found life on a military post distasteful. Only to herself would she admit that maintaining conformity to the demands of Army life was onerous, particularly after the heartbreaking scenes she'd witnessed on the Indian reservation around Fort Sill. Her daily life seemed trivial, and she felt more hemmed in than she had expected.

Even with the approaching winter the days were long, and she had no opportunity to explore the landscape astride her strawberry roan. Longingly she thought of the

355

fancy riding habit Mrs. Carlson Craven-Hix had wanted her to purchase for her trousseau back in Washington. Perhaps if she had been able to pull that little ensemble out of her trunk Cole might have agreed to a short ride. But no, she had outsmarted herself, being so sure that buckskins were all she would ever need. When would she ever learn to think ahead?

Just when she had decided she might never ride again, Cole surprised her. Admitting he was tired of his forced inactivity, he borrowed a sidesaddle for her, and with Erin uncomfortably garbed in a full-skirted gown, they rode sedately out the gate and circled the fort grounds. For Erin, the quiet ride proved totally unsatisfactory, and the roan balked several times to show his displeasure at the skirt trailing down his belly.

For Cole, the outing brought a return to duty, for the next morning he received orders to go out on a patrol that would take several days. Erin was convinced the orders came much too soon after his injury, but a quelling look from her husband kept her from uttering more than a mild protest. He was gone for three days, and when he returned she tried to show him how much she had missed him. Unfortunately Cole seemed too exhausted to appreciate her efforts as much as she had hoped.

After two days of rest, he was off again and the pattern was set. No sooner was he rested up from one patrol than he was sent out on another. He was even called out on the eve of their first Thanksgiving together, and Erin thought it ironic that he was patrolling for hostile Indians the day before the families at the fort were to celebrate Thanksgiving, a feast originated by the red and white man together.

But she had to live with the patrols that called him away. This was why he had wanted to come back to Texas—to fight the Indians. It had taken attacks by both Comanches and Apaches for her to accept his position, but accept it she had. That was one argument between them she had settled and she didn't want to say anything which would make him think otherwise.

Nevertheless she found it hard to accept the reality that he would be gone on their first real holiday together. It gave her little consolation that Colonel Grierson would also be away. The Apache Victorio had been reported in the area and he must be captured or forced back across the Rio Grande.

The absence of her husband and some of the men didn't deter Mrs. Grierson from planning a party in honor of the holiday. Wild turkeys had been killed in the brush across the Concho River and each of the officers' wives would be bringing a special dish to add to the feast.

The evening of the party was cool and crisp and Erin donned a particularly attractive frock, an ecru lace-trimmed green velvet which Mrs. Craven-Hix back in Washington had assured her brought out the loveliness of her tawny skin and red hair. She'd wanted to wear it for Cole; since he couldn't be here, she would at least make a decent appearance in his name.

She had dressed early and then had begun to pace the floor, an activity she was engaging in with increasing regularity, when a knock at the door brought Cole's situation and his problems with Indians back to her. The visitor was Maranda Pierce.

She was tempted to tell Maranda she had much to do to get ready for the evening's festivities and didn't have time to talk. Instead, she took the forthright course and let her visitor in. When she took Maranda's coat, she was startled by the purple satin gown that swathed the young woman's ample figure. Then her attention was caught by a small packet of papers which the blonde held pressed against her bosom.

"We need to talk, Erin," she said. "Where we won't be disturbed."

Gesturing toward the parlor, Erin regarded the blonde with the care she'd give to a poker opponent. Maranda was up to something and she had best be on her guard. Erin could only hope that whatever that something was, it wasn't dependent on her reading anything that was in the small packet.

"I have something to give you," Maranda said as she settled into the chair that had become Cole's favorite. Lifting the packet, she looked up at Erin. "These belong to Cole and my conscience wouldn't let me keep them any longer."

Instinctively, Erin's guard went up. "Why are you returning them to me? Shouldn't you be handing them to my husband?"

"Probably. But I thought you'd find them much more interesting. They're letters from Rachel Cox. She was Cole's dearest *amour* when I first met him. Of course he was very young, but I don't think anyone ever gets over his first love, do you?"

Settling on the sofa, Erin looked Maranda in the eye. "I'm more concerned with his last love. Maranda. Me."

Maranda smiled sweetly. "Then perhaps you will just pass these on to Cole. There's a picture of Rachel in amongst the letters. A small daguerreotype taken before she was mutilated by a band of Comanches."

Maranda's words hit Erin hard, just as the blonde had known they would, but Erin hadn't spent years at a poker table without learning to keep all expression from her face. She smiled incuriously even as her mind raced. So here was the special past that Uncle Thad warned Cole to forget. His first love slain by the Comanches. No wonder he had carried such hate in his heart.

But the bigness of that same heart had allowed him to see the problems of reservation Indians and to help her find her grandfather Lonely Coyote. Surely Cole's understanding extended to the death of Rachel. But why hadn't he told her about it? Back in the Comanche camp he'd promised to talk about his past once they'd arrived at Fort Concho, but as they had settled in to their routine, the subject had never come up. Could he be harboring more pain than he wanted to admit? Didn't he trust her to understand?

A new heaviness of spirit and regret assailed her, but her voice was steady as she said, "How did you get possession of the packet, Maranda?"

"The attack happened when Cole was stationed at Fort Belknap, along with my father. He stayed with us afterward and I guess the letters just got mislaid."

"And you didn't return them?"

"Take a look at them. You might be glad I didn't."

"I'm not going to read those letters, Maranda," Erin said honestly, omitting the real reason why. "They were written a long time ago, and to somebody else."

Maranda pulled a handkerchief from the folds of her satin gown and dabbed at her eyes. "It was all so sad. We thought for a while Cole would die of grief."

"But he didn't," Erin said over the pounding of her heart, and then she added the lie, "I know he's over the past from the way he told me about it."

Maranda's lip twitched. "I see. Well, at least I've got this off my conscience. I must be going. It's almost time for the party to begin." When Erin walked her to the door, she paused a moment. "You will see that Cole gets those letters, won't you?"

"Don't worry," said Erin, a smile on her face, "I'll take care of them." When she was alone, the smile died. She could imagine the scene when she gave them to Cole. "Here," she would say, "Maranda thought you might want these back. And by the way, would you like to tell me about Rachel Cox?"

No, that would never do. She thrust the packet under the finery in her tumbled lingerie drawer, but the image

359

of Rachel Cox stayed in her mind. Even in the faded daguerreotype, she looked soft and beautiful—and blond. Erin had learned from Fiona Barrett a long time ago that Cole preferred blondes. If only Cole had told her about the young girl he'd held in his heart for so long . . .

The thought of going to a party and being among people she had little in common with was unbearable. In her current frame of mine, she wouldn't have a good time. But Alice Grierson had extended her a personal invitation to attend, and as a dutiful officer's wife, Erin couldn't refuse.

When she entered the Grierson home, she scarcely noticed the appreciative looks cast her way by the young officers. Maranda, looking a little pinched around the lips, walked over to greet her.

"I'm glad you made it. I thought you might change your mind."

"Of course I'm here, Maranda."

Maranda smiled. "You'll add so much to the festivities."

Erin's eyes narrowed. "In what way?"

"You never know what opportunities might arise. Now if you'll excuse me, I do believe one of the gentlemen is summoning me to dance."

When Gerald Nathan came over to kiss her hand, Erin caught the blonde looking at them with a harsh, critical eye, and she wondered why it would matter to Maranda that Nathan paid attention to another woman. Erin certainly didn't plan to encourage him. She'd never forgotten the cool reception he'd given back at West Point to her story about his uncle's perfidy. Any decent man would, at least, have been filled with embarrassment because a member of his family had behaved so badly.

One room of the commander's quarters had been cleared for dancing, and Erin allowed herself the pleasure of a whirl or two around the floor, away from the presence of Major Nathan. Silently she thanked Marcia Smythe-Williams for the dour dancing instructor she had hired. At least in one area Erin was as accomplished as the other women. But she found herself unable to relax and, declining another request for a dance, stood quietly for a moment at the side of the room. Without thinking she took a cup of punch that Nathan brought her and sipped at it. If it tasted unusually strong, she attributed that to the recipe that had been used. Maybe some illiterate cook had misinterpreted it.

After the third cup, she didn't even notice the taste. But for some reason the room had grown strangely warm.

"Would you like a breath of fresh air?" Nathan suggested when she indelicately mopped her brow with the lace edge of her sleeve. She never *could* remember to tuck a handkerchief somewhere about her person.

Nodding in gratitude, she followed him into the starry night. Indeed the air was bracing, and when he excused himself to take care of an undisclosed piece of business, she thought little of it. She was, after all, not six feet from the door, and the lights from the commander's quarters filtered out to provide ample illumination for her to see her own way back.

Left alone, she found herself listening to the conversation of a nearby group of young officers who had apparently come outdoors to smoke cigars. She didn't plan to eavesdrop but once she realized the topic of their conversation she didn't pull away either.

"This Barrett," one of them was saying, "got himself in a little trouble back in Virginia."

"Doesn't sound like the Captain Barrett who's assigned to Concho. You're new here. You must have made a mistake."

"No mistake. Coleman Barrett from Richmond. Taught at West Point last year. Yes, it's the same one. Got involved in a murder."

Erin gasped and then, with the hated words burning into her mind, slipped into the shadows to hear more. Whatever effects the punch had had on her were negated by the mention of the scandal back in Richmond.

"Tom McEnery, now I know you're mistaken," one of the men said. "Either that or lying. Captain Barrett is as fine an officer as you could hope to serve with."

"I tell you I'm not wrong. And I'm not lying either. There was a woman involved, too. Along with stolen money. Now there's two motivations which have led many a man astray. Even this captain you're so proud of."

"The captain has a beautiful wife. The kind anyone would want to take to bed with him every night. You got the wrong man."

Erin blushed. But she didn't move away. Now was no time for silly modesty. In saloons and out on the range she'd heard enough man talk to take it in stride. This Tom McEnery was a bastard, pure and simple. He must be to tell such half-truths about her beloved Cole. And where had he picked up the story? He was new on the post, fresh from back east no doubt. There must be rumors circulating back there even now, thanks to that ignoramus of a sheriff in Virginia.

If there was one thing Erin had learned since coming to Concho, it was that Army people, both men and women, loved to gossip just as Cole had once told her. Now he was the object of it. Considering that he had an illiterate, part Indian wife, Erin felt he already had enough to contend with in his pursuit of a career.

First Maranda with her story of Cole's first love, and now a fuzzy-faced lieutenant with scandalous lies. Erin decided she'd been passive too long, and without bothering to question the wisdom of her actions, she advanced on the group of officers.

362

"Lieutenant McEnery, may I speak to you for a moment?"

Soft light from a nearby open window flickered onto her face and she was certain the loud-mouthed young officer could see she would not be denied.

One of the men stepped up to greet her. "Mrs. Barrett, good evening."

From the corner of her eye she saw a startled look flash across McEnery's face. "Good evening, Lieutenant Williams," she said to the young man who had spoken, then returned her gaze to the object of her anger.

"Lieutenant McEnery, I believe you have some misinformation about my husband which needs clearing up."

McEnery was now staring openly at her. Good, she thought. He wasn't used to a direct attack. Whispering behind someone's back was more his style, and he would certainly never expect a woman to face him down.

"Mrs. Barrett—"

"Mrs. Coleman Barrett, Lieutenant. My husband is the one you accused of murder and theft."

"Now Mrs. Barrett, I was only repeating what I had heard. I never expected the captain's wife would overhear."

"And I, Lieutenant McEnery, never expected to hear lies about my husband bandied about among a group of officers and supposed gentlemen."

McEnery stared at her in astonishment, but unaware that her voice had drifted inside the Grierson home through the open window or that a crowd had gathered behind her, Erin gave him no chance to speak.

"My husband was completely cleared of any suspicions against his good name, Lieutenant. He only got involved in the case back in Virginia because he was asked to investigate a theft."

"But wasn't there some woman involved?" McEnery asked in a weak attempt at bluster.

"There most certainly was. Me. I was the victim of a swindle, and as he knew the thief personally, Cole tried to return my money. The man was dead by the time he caught up with him."

"But I was told—"

"Forget what you were told. It's the truth you should be more concerned with." Remembering the Army hierarchy, Erin decided to put it to good use. "If you can forget your tale of misinformation, Lieutenant, I will be more than happy to forego reporting it to your superior officer."

McEnery spluttered a weak protest but at last he agreed to her suggestion and Erin whirled to face the other officers.

"Is there anyone else who questions my husband's good name?"

Lieutenant Williams grinned at her. "Mrs. Barrett, I doubt if any of us would be so foolish." He offered her his arm. "Allow me to escort you inside for a little refreshment."

Still flushed with anger, Erin nodded and turned to face an unexpected bevy of interested onlookers, most of them women who looked decidedly displeased that she had faced down a group of men by herself.

Erin lost patience with them. Several would refrain from gossip, but the majority would be busy speculating about what had really happened in Virginia.

Then she lost patience with herself. Once again she'd acted without thinking. She could have handled the situation more delicately and not called attention to the accusations against Cole. McEnery was a fool, and anyone with a lick of sense would have realized his story connecting Cole with anything dishonorable couldn't be true.

Gripping Lieutenant Williams's arm, she walked inside and, assuring him she would be all right, stood unobtrusively to one side. She looked around the crowded room. There was no one in sight she could call friend. Not that she felt sorry for herself. She just knew that she didn't belong.

On this holiday evening the fates seemed to conspire against her as she found herself surrounded by talk about the first Thanksgiving.

"You know, back in Massachusetts I found it easy to accept that the Pilgrims actually sat down with the Indians to celebrate the harvest," one woman said. "If they'd landed in Texas, I doubt they'd have survived the meal, much less have lived to repeat the celebration the following year." She laughed sharply, and Erin's ears burned. "Can you see us sitting down with a band of Comanches?"

"Not if we wanted to keep our scalps," another said amidst the sound of laughter.

All right, Erin thought. She was supposed to fit in with these women. This was one conversation she knew something about.

"Excuse me," she said with polite reserve as she turned to the woman who had been speaking. "I couldn't help overhearing what you were saying about the Comanches. You must realize that in their war against the white man, they've suffered, too."

"I beg your pardon?" one of the women said as a hush descended on the men and women within earshot. "Are you actually defending the savages?"

"I'm not defending them. It's just that there are two sides to consider. The Indian is the one who lost his rights to the land."

"And what about the scalps the white men lost, not to mention women and children? You're speaking about something you know nothing about."

365

Erin tried to will herself to be quiet, not to answer the woman. But her gaze fell on the long table covered with platters of food. Roast bird and potatoes, corn, mince pie, hot breads and crocks of butter. Across her mind's eye flashed a picture of gaunt brown faces and wide, dark eyes empty of hope. She had seen for herself the impoverished conditions forced upon her people by the white man. The contrast was too much.

She looked at the small crowd that had gathered around her. They seemed to be waiting for her to speak. The weight of their stares, coming after Maranda's visit and the encounter outside, was too much and she spoke loudly. "You'd best be careful if you're afraid of Comanches. There's one here tonight."

"What on earth are you talking about, Mrs. Barrett?" one woman asked. "An Indian? Here?"

Erin's smile was brittle. "Not far from where you sit. I would think you would find it singularly appropriate for the holiday. Apparently you don't."

Major Nathan appeared at her elbow. "Is this an attempt at humor, Mrs. Barrett?"

"Of course not, Major Nathan. I never make light of Indians, and the reason is simple." She looked him squarely in the eye. "I am one of them."

The room became deadly quiet.

"What the devil are you talking about?" Nathan asked.

"I'm talking about my ancestry. My grandmother was a full-blooded Comanche. My mother fell victim to a massacre by the white man. A band of rowdy soldiers, to be specific." She looked around the room. "It is I who should be afraid, surrounded as I am by my mother's enemy. You see I am not. Nor am I ashamed."

"Erin."

She turned at the sound of a woman's voice and saw Alice Grierson standing beside her.

"Erin," the woman repeated, "perhaps you would like to sit down for a while and let me fetch you a cup of punch."

"No, thank you, Mrs. Grierson." For the first time all evening Erin was able to smile sincerely. "You are most kind, but I've suddenly lost my appetite for both food and drink." She turned to Nathan. "If you will excuse me, Major, I think I'll stroll back to my quarters. I've a sudden need for a breath of fresh air."

With a nod to her hostess, Erin walked past the murmuring onlookers and out into the night. Alone with her thoughts, she felt her heart thundering and her knees shaking. True, she had been upset and provoked. True, she had only spoken the truth. But as she hurried through the cold night toward her lonely quarters, she could only think that if she ever hoped to fit into the life Cole had picked out for them, she had done something terribly wrong.

The foolishness of her impulsive actions hit her during the next few days. In all her time on the post she had done little, despite all her fine talk on the subject, to achieve Cole's desire that their life together would really work. She hadn't lived up to the promises she'd made herself on the way down from Fort Sill when they'd discussed the problems they might have.

She hadn't really tried to be the kind of wife he needed, but how quickly he had accepted her flighty thoughtlessness. He'd grown to understand the Indian's fight against the white man and had accepted unselfishly all her faults: she was Indian; she was illiterate; she was less than truthful; she possessed few ladylike ways. She was not at all the sort she imagined Rachel Cox to have been.

To add to her dark thoughts, it was becoming clear that someone, most likely Lieutenant McEnery, was still spreading rumors about their marriage and the murder back east. She thought of the strong punch Gerald Nathan had given her. She'd like to blame her actions on the drink, and thus on Nathan, but she couldn't. That was the coward's way out.

Why had Gerald given her the punch? To see if she'd do something ridiculous? Or did he want to embarrass Cole? The idea seemed preposterous, but there was no doubt she was providing an entertaining scandal for the whole fort. Several of the bachelor officers gave her sly winks on the occasions when she ventured to cross the parade ground, but she hardly took them as signs of friendship. Apparently they figured that anyone who was part Indian would most likely welcome the amorous attentions of any white man.

The women didn't treat her any better. Whenever she went for a stroll or a shopping trip to the sutler's store, she was greeted with whispers and curious stares. The problem was, she decided, the women had too little to do except wait to pack up and move on to another post. They were forced to lead such restricted lives. No wonder they gossiped for diversion. Except for occasional stagecoach trips down to San Antonio, they were really not much better than prisoners of their environment, but that realization did little to ease her mind.

As the days passed, she began to stay inside and deal endless games of poker, betting with herself to keep from thinking. She longed to see Cole, then dreaded telling him of her disgrace. Mostly, she dreaded the hurt that would be in his eyes.

One evening, a week after Thanksgiving, unable to face the close walls of her lonely bedroom, she lingered on the front porch for a breath of fresh air and noticed a figure walking across the parade grounds toward her. A broad-brimmed hat was pulled low on his face to ward off the brisk north wind, but his long, steady stride and the sure movement of his body made her catch her breath. Cole had returned.

"Good evening, Cole." The voice came from the porch of the Pierce home, and Erin stepped into the shadows to watch as Cole stopped to greet Maranda. On the still night air their voices were distinct.

"Hello, Maranda. Do you know if my wife is at home?"

"Oh, she's at home, all right." Erin could imagine Maranda's cold blue eyes undressing Cole. "It's a good thing you've come home. We can have a celebration. Nothing, of course, so exciting as the one last week at Thanksgiving. It's not every day we have such entertainment as was offered then."

Under no circumstances did Erin plan to cower in the dark and listen to that sly voice describe her disgrace. She stepped into the moonlight and called her husband's name.

With a brief nod to Maranda, Cole moved quickly up to the porch, pulled her inside to the privacy of the front hall, and kissed her soundly. Desperate for his love and approval, Erin held him tight against her breast and reveled in the sweet reminder of just how good he felt in her embrace. He tasted of wind and weather and the dirt of the open road, his face was darkened with thick black bristles, his uniform was soiled and in need of mending; but he drove her wild with desire. Even so, for the space of one heartbeat she gave thanks he had not yet been turned against her.

Cole pulled away and whispered into her hair. "I'll be on you here on the hallway floor, Mrs. Barrett, if you aren't careful. And I planned such a slow seduction. The thoughts of it kept me going on many a long, cold day."

Erin shivered against him. "You're going to take your time?"

He looked down at her and smiled. "I'm going to try."

"I wish you luck," she said, drawing closer to outline

369

his parted lips with her tongue.

With a low, feral growl, he picked her up in his arms and headed up the stairs.

Clinging to him in desperate longing, Erin burned hot kisses across the nape of his neck. When he laid her on their bed, her arms would not let go of him. Cole was her life. Her being melted into his.

"Erin," he whispered hoarsely into her ear, "you drive me mad."

The sound of her name on his lips filled her mind and heart. Eager hands clutched at his coat, rubbed down his chest and on to the hard bulge between his legs. In movements as roughly demanding as her own, Cole ripped open the bodice of her muslin gown to reveal breasts swollen in anticipation of his kiss.

Tearing off her clothes with an urgency that matched hers, Cole explored her body with teeth and tongue and lips. A passion unlike anything Erin had ever known gripped her, and she writhed beneath him, pulling in frustration at the uniform covering his hard, hot flesh.

Cole responded to her need, leaving her embrace only long enough to discard his clothing, tossing it into a tumbled pile on the floor and then returning in one smooth motion to her encircling arms and legs. He entered quickly and they became one, electrifying pulsations obliterating thought as they clung together past the final explosive moment of ecstasy and into the gentle downward movement toward contentment.

Cole tried to speak, but Erin kissed his words away unheard. Tomorrow was soon enough to talk, tomorrow when the cruel day would cast its harsh light onto their nest of love. Tomorrow the world would intrude.

But not tonight. Under the gentle blanket of darkness, she would not think past the moment that presented itself. Cole had wanted their lovemaking to be slow, but she had been too frantic and afraid to let him take his time. Cuddled in his arms, she was able to convince herself that her fears of losing him had been foolish.

Raising her head, she pressed her lips to his and was pleased to feel the warmth of his response.

"Cole," she said softly.

He held her tight. "What's on your mind, love?"

She looked at him and smiled demurely. "If you don't mind my being so bold, I think I'm ready to be seduced."

Chapter Twenty

Bright sunlight drifted through the canopy over the bed, and Erin opened her eyes with a start. She felt the covers beside her. Cole was gone.

How could she have overslept this morning and missed breakfast with him! Her confession to him about Thanksgiving must be made now, before the outside world intruded. Scrambling from the bed, Erin pulled on a pink gingham day dress, brushed half the tangles from her hair, and hurried down the steep stairs and into the dining room. Cole, sharply dressed in the clean captain's uniform she'd had waiting for him, turned from the narrow window that framed a view of the mesquite-covered terrain surrounding Fort Concho.

"Good morning, Erin," he said, a glint of appreciation in his gray eyes. "I trust you're rested this morning."

Cole's quiet strength and warm smile filled the room, a cold and lonely place when he was away. For a brief, luxurious moment Erin allowed herself to remember the fulfilled passions of last night and, despite the agitation that had driven her downstairs in such a flurry, smiled with abandon. Kissing him quickly on the ear, she whirled away to the table.

He pulled a chair out for her with a gallant flourish,

then sat close beside her in a similar chair, leaving the wide expanse of gleaming table largely bare. He reached for her hand, but she evaded him gently once more and shoved a cooling cup of coffee toward him.

"I am rested," she said, "all things considered, but perhaps you need sustenance. You're up rather early."

"Duty, unfortunately." His eyes dropped to her curving lips. "I'd much rather have lingered upstairs until you woke up."

Duty. The word hit her like a cold wind. It killed the happiness of their morning reunion, and for once Erin was able to ignore the provocative innuendo in Cole's voice. She kept her eyes on the Blue Willow coffee cup he held and absently admired his long sensitive fingers. "What kind of duty do you mean?" she asked.

"I had a message earlier. Colonel Grierson wants to see me."

"Do you have any idea why?" she asked, fighting to keep her voice steady. If the colonel's business with Cole concerned her, she must speak now. Here was the opening she needed to broach a discussion of Mrs. Grierson's Thanksgiving. She was still groping for the right words when Cole sidetracked her.

"I don't know why," he said, "but I did raise the question about the procurement of the medical supplies we were wondering about. He promised to send queries to find out if our goods got detoured to one of the other frontier forts. Maybe McKavett or Davis."

"Did you ever talk to the sergeant who was bringing them down? He certainly didn't want me to get a look at them when I was demanding something for your injury."

"Osborne? He's been transferred to the new San Antonio post. Maybe he took them with him," said Cole. "Either way Pierce could be in trouble. Remember, he's in charge of procurement."

If Captain Pierce were in trouble, Erin thought, he

certainly wasn't the only one. Her mind went back to the problem that had brought her downstairs, and her amber eyes grew dark with a worry that Cole misunderstood.

Cole watched her carefully. "You seem upset, love. I doubt that Colonel Grierson wants to send me off the post again so soon. I rather think my name has come up too often for patrol duty as it is."

Erin had thought of the possibility that he might leave again, his absence providing a postponement of any distasteful discussion, but she'd quickly pushed it from her mind. No matter how upset Cole became when he heard her story, he belonged with her. In any event, the odds were that if she failed to apprise him of her impulsive outburst at the Thanksgiving festivities, someone else would.

"I hope you're right," she said, her solemn voice bearing evidence of her heavy heart, "although after you've stayed around here for a while you may decide being out on patrol is more peaceful. Whether or not you run into Apaches."

"I know Army life is hell on women and horses." Cole's gray eyes rested warmly on her, and lifting her hand, he brushed his lips against her wrist. "I didn't marry you for peace and quiet, love. Any man who wants only that would be better off getting a mongrel pup."

The touch of his lips lingered against the pulse point of her wrist and her heart raced. She studied the lean, tanned lines of his face and the endearingly defiant curl of black hair that fell across his forehead. With his steady gaze and the half-smile that played at his lips, he looked so sure of their love. Wrapped up as she was in the problems that lay between them, she was certain Colonel Grierson wanted only one thing—to discuss her indiscretions—and she couldn't let Cole leave without warning him of what to expect. Desperate Indians with repeating guns were a big enough problem for any soldier on the frontier without adding surprises about more wifely indiscretions. She must be the one to tell him.

"Cole, you don't understand."

His eyes held hers. "What's wrong, love?"

Erin freed her hand from his distracting hold. She needed to concentrate on what she said, to tell him the complete truth. She hesitated. He would certainly understand, but what of the future? Would she always fall short of acceptance in post society? Would he always have to defend her? In time regrets would come . . . and he would remember the placid life he could have had with Rachel.

She opened her mouth to confess all, but her words were stilled by the sound of Verlene bustling through the door, a cup of coffee in her hand.

"Morning, Miz Barrett. Here's some coffee to get you started and I'll have breakfast out in just a moment. Sorry I didn't hear you come down."

"I'm not really very hungry, Verlene," Erin said, more impatiently than she'd intended. "The coffee will be enough."

"Yessum," said the servant, her eyes downcast. Placing the cup of steaming liquid on the table, she backed from the dining room without once looking up.

Ever since Thanksgiving the woman had refused to look her in the eye. No doubt she'd heard idle chatter about Erin. She might even have contributed to it. As a servant in the Barrett home, she was in a prime position to gather tidbits for a willing audience. Or maybe she just feared the Comanche in Erin would someday go berserk and start wielding a tomahawk. Erin smiled at the absurdity of the idea.

The last thing Erin needed was to alienate Alice Grierson's servant and possibly Mrs. Grierson herself. The commander's wife was still friendly in passing; she was the only real lady on the post in Erin's estimation.

Mrs. Grierson had even paused one day when they'd met beside the parade ground, to tell Erin that Verlene planned marriage to a certain Corporal Botkins and might as well stay with the Barretts until the happy event. The gesture had been a kindness to Erin and had also allowed Mrs. Grierson to begin training another servant. The only one who hadn't been satisfied with the arrangement was Verlene.

Cole caught his wife's distress and with a glance toward the kitchen turned back to his wife. "Erin, what's troubling you? Is it just a servant problem?"

From the kitchen came the sound of a cabinet door closing with a slam.

"*Just* a servant problem?" Erin said. "That's like saying *just* a war."

"Good point," Cole said, grinning. Perhaps her worries were nothing more than domestic ones after all. She'd never claimed to be a housekeeper.

He stood, pulling her up against him. "I'm late for my meeting now, love, or I'd stay to hear you out. If you can wait, we'll talk as soon as I get back." His fingers brushed through the long red curls that tumbled about her face and his lips met hers in a lingering kiss.

"Perhaps," he whispered into her hair, "we won't talk immediately."

Oh, yes we will, Erin thought. *For all my resolutions this morning it will be Colonel Grierson who will burn your ears, and you'll want to do little else but talk.*

For a moment she leaned against the hard wall of his chest, her head nestled in the crook of his shoulder, and took strength from him. Then she pulled away from his embrace, her head held high. She refused to cling to him like some vaporish female. If only there were time for them to talk.

A quick kiss and he was gone, leaving Erin to fill in the time until he returned. Clearing his breakfast dishes from the table and giving a few encouraging words to a silent Verlene, she went upstairs to spread the covers on the bed and gather up the clothing they'd left strewn about the floor. For a long time she hugged against her breast the uniform jacket he'd worn on patrol. Funny how she'd once hated that uniform without any regard for the man who wore it.

An hour after he had taken his leave, Cole returned, far more sober and thoughtful than he had been at breakfast. Grierson had learned only that in the past month no medical supplies such as Cole described had arrived at Fort McKavett or any of the other frontier forts. Pierce, who had searched once more in vain for procurement papers, was as puzzled as anyone. The only possible person who might be able to shed light on the situation was Sergeant Osborne, the surly wagon driver now gone to San Antonio.

Cole had made an appointment to talk further with Pierce in an hour, but right now missing medical supplies were the least of his problems, and he sought out his wife in the parlor of their home. She was seated on the sofa and staring blindly into space, so lost in thought that she had not heard him enter. His strong-willed, beautiful Erin, with her rich red hair and finely boned face. In the pink muslin gown that fell softly against her high, full breasts and narrow waist, she looked fragile, as though the cold, cruel world could crush her in an instant.

He stood in the doorway, waiting for her to see him, and finally said, "Hello, love. I'm home."

Startled from her reverie, she rose to greet him with a light kiss, then returned to her place on the sofa. Her gaze became riveted on the bright, bold patterns of the Mexican rug at her feet.

"How did you meeting go?" she asked.

"Erin, we need to talk."

She looked up at him. "I suppose the meeting was

377

about Thanksgiving and my contribution to the party."

He sat in the Windsor chair to her right and pulled it closer. "No, it wasn't, Erin, but your name was mentioned."

She picked up a green velvet pillow and began to smooth the fringe around it. Her face burned with shame that he should have been subjected to official criticism because of his wife. Especially galling was the knowledge that the criticism had come from a man Cole admired.

"I'm sorry you had to hear about my disgrace from someone other than me." She turned the pillow and smoothed another edging of gold fringe.

"Disgrace? You're too hard on yourself, Erin. Colonel Grierson didn't refer to Thanksgiving in such a harsh way." Lifting the pillow, he tossed it aside, then took her hand and tried to tease her from her worry. "As I recall, 'uproar' was the word he used."

A smile twitched at Cole's lips, but Erin was too agitated to notice. "I don't think the word 'uproar' is a big improvement. I spoke out loud and clear so that everyone could hear me. Without thinking first, of course. I didn't say anything I wasn't feeling. I just let two things pile up on me."

"Two? What else happened?"

Erin heaved a deep breath. At least Cole wasn't acting as though he despised her—not yet.

"Some new officer started spreading talk among a few of the men about you being mixed up in Hilmer Turpin's death, and about a mystery woman being involved. I tried to set them straight and got all upset over nothing. Unfortunately the argument got a little loud and—"

"And you were overheard."

Erin nodded, deliberately omitting any mention of the resulting gossip and the sense that she had been ostracized. She'd find a way to keep it from extending to Cole.

378

Cole tightened his hold on her hand. "I told you about the gossip on an Army post. Rumors of Turpin's death and my involvement were sure to find their way here. I'm surprised they didn't come sooner."

"Then Colonel Grierson didn't mention that?"

"No. Nothing about that."

No, Erin thought, Grierson must have been too busy talking about officers and their Comanche wives. Her heart quickened. Even if Cole would never admit it, any disgrace that fell on her would carry over to him.

She'd heard the other wives talk about how the Army really didn't want families on the posts and discouraged their presence. Grierson must have taken Cole to task for bringing in a troublemaker as his wife. Had the colonel perhaps suggested Cole place her elsewhere, at least for a while? Had he threatened Cole with an official reprimand if he failed to comply? She'd heard enough gossip over afternoon tea to know such things were done.

She looked Cole directly in the eye. He'd not be able to lie; it wasn't in his character.

"So what exactly did Colonel Grierson say?"

"Just that there had been some ancestral discussion over Thanksgiving dinner."

"Only on my part. None of the other women bothered to volunteer information about their pasts. Not, of course, that it would have been as colorful as mine." She stood and began to pace the length of the Mexican rug. "How did the colonel find out? Didn't he return last night with you?"

"He heard some idle gossip, that's all."

"But surely he told you more." She studied him carefully. Cole was holding something back. She could read it in his eyes.

"I told you it didn't matter," he said, standing and pulling her into his arms. "I don't care what anyone outside this room thinks or says—as long as it doesn't

379

hurt you. Things can't have been pleasant here for you."

Erin forced her lips into a smile. Somehow in his arms no problem seemed quite as bad as it did when he was away. For his sake she would soothe her troubled heart and try to let the matter die.

"No," she said in complete candor, "things around here haven't been pleasant. Mostly thanks to myself. At least no one knows I'm a gambler born and bred. There's that to be thankful for." Her amber eyes softened as she looked at the lines of fatigue on his face. "But I don't imagine you had an easy time out on the trail. Let's say we both managed."

The next few minutes were spent in mutual consolation, and Erin almost convinced herself everything would be all right. So what if no one spoke to her except her husband? He was the only one at Fort Concho who said anything she wanted to hear. And while he was away on patrol she could concentrate on one of the goals she'd set for herself upon agreeing to be his wife. She'd learn to read.

With dismay she heard him say he had another appointment, this one with Jonathan Pierce.

"And it has nothing to do with you, love. Army business. Will you be all right?"

"Of course." She gave him a quick, wifely kiss and accompanied him to the door, handing him his hat. "Verlene and I have a great deal of work to do. I'll be just fine."

As she closed the door, she wondered just why she had told that particular lie. There was absolutely nothing she could help the servant with, especially considering Verlene's discomfort when they were in the same room. Well, Cole wouldn't be as apt to worry about her if he thought she had something to occupy her time.

She flung a shawl about her shoulders and went out the back door. She could at least take some air among the mesquite growth behind their quarters, but she had no sooner settled on the path she had already worn during Cole's long absences when Verlene called her back with a message, delivered she said by someone from headquarters.

"They said it was right important, ma'am." Verlene handed the message over, eyes averted. "It's from Major Nathan, they said, and that he'd be in his office till dinnertime."

"Thank you, Verlene." The girl turned and went into the house, casting a curious look behind her. Erin sighed. At least she didn't have to worry about what the note said. Verlene had made it clear that Nathan wanted to see her. The question was whether or not to answer his summons.

She debated for a moment, finally deciding it might help Cole if she found out what Nathan had on his mind. Thinking that the wolves seemed to be circling, Erin headed around her home and across the parade grounds. The major was waiting for her when she arrived at his office. As sharp-faced as ever, she thought, despite his warm greeting.

Motioning her to a visitor's chair, he smiled at her, then sat down behind his desk. "I've always felt a little guilty about the way my uncle swindled you, Erin, and I'd like to make it up to you now with some friendly advice."

Erin eyed him carefully. Beware of unasked-for advice, especially the "friendly" kind, her father had always warned her. About some things Shaun Donovan had been right on target.

"I'll listen to what you have to say."

"I hope so. It's rather disturbing news, I'm afraid. About your husband."

Erin forgot her caution. "What about Cole? Has something happened to him?"

"No, no. At least not yet."

"Then what are you talking about?"

"I like a direct woman, Erin. You get right to the point. I'm talking about the promotion that should have been coming Cole's way. You're a smart woman, Erin. Unfortunately, you're also rather outspoken. I'm afraid your behavior last Thanksgiving may have hurt your husband's chances for advancement."

"You're not telling me anything I haven't already figured out. Besides, I can't take back the words I said."

Nathan's smile was unpleasant. "How true. But you can remove the daily reminder of them."

Erin stifled a cry. As hurtful as the words were, she realized they hadn't been completely unexpected. The idea had been hovering over her like a black cloud all week.

"Meaning me," she said softly.

"A harsh solution, I'm sure. Perhaps too great a sacrifice to make, but when I saw the papers sitting on Colonel Grierson's desk, I felt I owed it to you to speak up."

"The papers about Cole's promotion?"

"That's right. It's my understanding the colonel doesn't intend to sign them."

So that was why Cole had been summoned to Grierson's office early this morning. A promotion had been denied him. How like her husband to have kept his disappointment to himself.

But he should have shared his news with her. She was, after all, his wife who had sworn to stand by him through the good times and bad. She wasn't much help to him if he didn't let her know when those bad times came along. But of course his behavior made sense if she were the cause of them.

Erin stood abruptly. No need to linger here any longer.

Gerald Nathan had wreaked all the havoc he could in her life and she wouldn't hang around for him to gloat or do what would be infinitely worse, offer sham sympathy. She had some serious thinking to do and she could only do it in private.

After a quick good-bye, she hurried back to the sanctuary of her home. For once she was glad Cole wasn't there to greet her. Hurrying upstairs, she found the small stack of letters from Cole's past and studied the faded picture with them. When she'd taken it from Maranda's hands, she'd only glanced at it long enough to tell the girl was beautiful. Now she gave the daguerreotype a more studied look.

Gazing back at Erin was a young girl, her hair pale and softly curled around a delicate, smiling face. She had the look of an angel, one who would grow into a genteel lady, and tears sprang to Erin's eyes. Here was the woman Cole should have married. Rachel Cox would never have disgraced him and ruined his career.

Unfolding one of the fragile letters, Erin stared at the unreadable words and imagined they told of a young girl's undying affection for a gallant and handsome young soldier.

And what about Cole's affection for his wife? He loved her. Passionately. But would he love her forever? When he gazed once again at the picture of his lost love, would he regret that she could not write him such words?

Honorable Cole. He would never speak of his disappointment in her, but she would read it in his eyes. As the years passed, she would feel it in the distance that would inevitably separate them. Because of her, he would be trapped in a mediocre career. Trapped in a mediocre marriage. It was a fate he didn't deserve.

So she'd been right after all when she'd run out on him in Mobile. Instinct had told her they didn't suit. She'd tried to tell him that when he'd found her at the Rocking J. But pressed down into the grass by his hot, demanding body, she'd let herself believe things could work out. He'd been so sure. He'd been so wrong.

She had to make him see the foolishness of struggling through the years together, the futility of coming after her again. Methodically she refolded the letter from Rachel Cox and put it back in the packet, along with the picture. She'd tuck it away where he would find it someday after she was gone. If he found it too soon, he would only think she'd been foolishly jealous.

The conclusion she'd been skirting around settled heavily in her mind. She had to make Cole think she wanted a divorce. After last night such a thing wouldn't be easy.

But that was last night. Even with Cole on the post, sometimes the days passed slowly. Unable to work up enthusiasm for Army life, she had never asked him to share the office work he did when he was on the post.

An idea now formed in the back of her mind, a crazy idea that would, for a time, heap more shame on her husband's head. But it would create a temporary scandal, one that would go away after he had permanently divested himself of his wife. Quickly she undressed and searched through the trunk for her buckskin trousers. She concentrated on her actions—slipping on the trousers and shirt, pulling on a pair of boots she'd bought at the sutler's store, much to the salesman's surprise for officer's wives didn't wear such garb, and twisting her hair into a knot atop her head.

While Verlene was outside doing laundry, Erin left the small bedroom that had been a nest of love. She didn't glance back. The pain would have been too great, perhaps strong enough to make her change her mind. And that she mustn't do. She wasn't acting impetuously but with

384

careful consideration. No matter how much her actions would appear to the contrary, she was thinking only of Cole.

When Cole returned shortly before noon, he was surprised to find Erin gone and settled down to wait for his wife. An hour later when she still hadn't returned for lunch he began to worry. Was she visiting someone without leaving word? It didn't sound like her. Was she shopping? Even the most prolonged trip to the sutler's store shouldn't take this long.

At the back of his mind was the nagging thought that she had done something both of them would regret. He hadn't told her everything Grierson had said in their meeting—about the ugly talk concerning Erin's Comanche heritage—and Erin had realized it. He had seen it in her eyes. Sometimes she was too smart for her own good.

He walked out to the porch and looked around. From his vantage point he could see almost every building on the small post. The air was brisk, and a cold breeze blew in from the north. Several soldiers paraded across the grounds, but there were few civilians in sight. Certainly not a red-headed one with a proud step and sparkling amber eyes.

His uneasiness grew. Bounding off the porch, he almost ran to the stables to find his fears were not unfounded. Two hours ago Erin had ordered the strawberry roan saddled and, the hostler reported in shocked tones, had sat astride the horse as she rode it out.

"She was wearin' men's clothes, Captain Barrett. Said somethin' about Saint Angela. Tried to tell her you wouldn't like it, but she wouldn't listen."

In minutes Cole was riding toward the west. Crossing the Concho River, he guided his horse into the small

385

settlement of Saint Angela. Other than a scattering of homes and stores, the town was composed of saloons and gambling halls where, despite repeated warnings from superior officers, the soldiers could lose their pay. What in hell had brought Erin into the town? She had been dressed in men's clothes, the hostler had said. Cole previewed various activities performed by Erin in buckskins. The vision that stayed with him was one of Erin gambling.

Just as Cole had foreseen, the roan was tied to a post in front of the Lucky Lady Saloon. When Cole entered the shabby building, he found Erin seated at a back table, a deck of cards in her hand. She faced a dark-suited, bearded man with the pale complexion of one seldom away from the tables. Standing around the seated pair were a half-dozen men whose grizzled demeanor suited the dismal room. With her red hair piled atop her head his wife looked like a precious jewel in a tawdry setting.

When he walked up, all of the men scattered. Except for the dark-suited gambler.

"Let's go, Erin," Cole said.

She looked up. Her eyes were wide and bright. Too bright, Cole thought.

"I'm not through." She ruffled through a stack of coins in front of her. "I'm on a winning streak."

"That's not what I would call it. Let's go."

The gambler opened his coat and rested his hands at the edge of the table. The men who had been standing around the table backed away and Cole could see that Erin's opponent was wearing a gun tied low.

"The lady said she wasn't through," the man said. "I want a chance to get my money back."

Cole rested a hand briefly on his holster, then allowed both hands to hang loosely at his sides ready to upend the table to shield Erin. Wearing a flapped Army holster, he knew there was no way he could outdraw the man.

386

In the quiet that descended on the room, he looked unflinchingly at the gambler. "The game's over," he said.

The man's red-rimmed eyes flared with an anger overlaid with fright. He made no move toward the gun, settling instead for bluster. "Listen, here, no little chit is going to—"

Cole reached down and, grabbing the lapels of the gambler's coat, jerked the man to his feet. "Is going to what?" he asked, pushing the man away from the table.

The gambler's right eye began to twitch. The seconds stretched out. At long last he shrugged. "Nothing," he said. "I've no quarrel with you, Army man. As you say, the game's over."

Cole watched as the bearded man hurried through the swinging doors that led to the street; then he looked at Erin, who sat white-lipped and still. Gradually the noise of the saloon filled the air around them. "Let's go," he said.

Erin couldn't answer right away. A scene of long ago burned in her mind, a saloon in New Mexico where her father had met his death over a card game. The saloon hadn't been much different from the one she was in now. The one where Cole . . . The image was too painful to complete.

"I didn't think—" she began.

"You seldom do, Erin," Cole said, his anger returning now that the moment of danger was past.

Her amber eyes focused on him. She had to finish what she had begun. No matter how close he had come to danger. No matter how tempting it was to do whatever he asked.

To cover her anguish, she pretended to be overcome by an anger as strong as his and stood to face him. "There was no danger. Until you came barging in here to rescue me."

His eyes were the color of steel. "Are you saying I shouldn't have come after you?"

"I'm saying it wasn't necessary."

Cole reached out and touched her arms. "Erin, what in the hell is going on? Why are you even here?"

She stepped out of his reach. The next few minutes were very important to them both, and she had to think straight. She had reasoned everything out carefully. She couldn't change her mind just because he had touched her.

"I got restless after you left. I didn't know what people would be liable to tell you while you were out."

"And you didn't trust me to judge what they said?"

"*Judge?* There seems to be a great deal of judging going on. Lately I've been restless a lot, and I guess I'm just tired of it."

The fragile world they'd constructed fell apart and crashed into the three feet of space separating them. And just as Erin had intended, the gulf widened and was filled with all the fears that had followed them from Virginia to this untamed land.

The hurt in his voice tore at her heart, but she stood stoically when Cole finally answered. "Tired of others . . . or of me? What about last night?"

"You know how last night was. But, Cole, we can't always stay in bed. I told you back at the Rocking J I didn't belong on an Army post. Surely you can see I don't." *Ride away with me,* she wanted to cry, but the words died unspoken. All that would achieve was a quick end to the Army world he had chosen long before he'd met her, a loss he would live to regret.

"So what are you suggesting? That you spend your days in Saint Angela and your nights with me? It won't work, love. You're an Army wife. Your place is beside me."

She forced the words from her lips. "I guess that will

have to be changed. You're right, of course." She looked around the dingy saloon at the sullen enlisted men who glanced away quickly when she caught their eyes. They were afraid of Cole, no doubt. They'd been willing enough to greet her when she'd first come in and demanded a game of twenty-one.

She looked back at Cole. "Saint Angela will hardly do. But I have friends in San Antonio. I can go down there."

"This is madness," Cole said. "I love you. You love me. But I guess that love is not strong enough to overcome the tedium of the life I've asked you to live."

His voice cut through the still air. "I'll not come after you, Erin. Not this time. The choice is yours."

So there they were. He'd spoken the words she had provoked him to say. How selfish and shallow he must think her. If it would keep his love strong, she would scrub floors and take in washing for the rest of her life, but he needed a lady who could take her place beside him as he rose through the Army ranks. And that she would make a mess of.

"I'm not asking you to come after me, Cole. Actually, it's better if you don't. As much as I hate to say it, I imagine you ought to consider a divorce. Is it unheard of in the Army?"

"No. Just unusual." A tinny piano behind them played a popular song of the day and Erin almost gave way to tears as she thought of the title. "I'm Only a Bird in a Gilded Cage." Even as she stepped back to avoid running into the safety of Cole's arms, she thought the song appropriate.

He seemed to listen with her to the music, then said, "I can't fence in a free spirit. Even if I kissed you into submission, it would only last until the next time you got bored. I can't fight that, love."

"I don't imagine your career will be ruined. After all, I'm deserting you, not the other way around."

They stared at each other for several moments, but there seemed nothing else to say. Gathering up the coins from the table, she walked out with him, and they rode in silence back across the river and on to the fort.

As they left the stables, Erin marveled that it was still daylight. The longest day of her life had not yet come to an end. Cole said he would escort her back home—his voice hardened at the word—and if she preferred he would then spend the night in the bachelor officers' quarters. Erin could merely nod in agreement, knowing that if she spoke she would recant everything she had led him to believe in the saloon.

Cole wasn't so hesitant. Stepping onto the covered porch of their quarters, he looked down at her with leaden eyes. "Can't you say it, Erin? Can't you say you don't want me to sleep with you one more time? You'll be lying of course, but you can at least tell me to go away."

Erin drew on her last ounce of courage and met his gaze. "You know I can't, but that doesn't mean it would be right. Or make tomorrow any easier."

"I certainly wouldn't want to make things hard for you, love. It wouldn't be the honorable thing to do."

Erin started. The bitterness in his voice wrenched her heart and without another word she turned and ran inside, closing the door behind her, waiting to see if he would follow. As the seconds stretched out into agonizing minutes, she realized they had said good-bye and she forced herself to go upstairs for a sleepless night.

Early the next morning Erin, her trunk packed with the belongings Cole had brought for her from Mobile, caught the stagecoach to San Antonio. Carefully, she had packed everything, not wanting to leave the smallest article behind that would remind him of her. The money that Cole had given her before he'd left on his last patrol she had placed on the bed. Her gambling winnings would buy her ticket, and once in San Antonio, she could wire

Dallas for money. She'd never had a chance to tell Cole that finances were the least of her concerns.

The packet of letters she tucked away in the bottom of the wardrobe, where he could find it later and turn his thoughts to what should have been.

When she climbed onto the stage, there was no one to bid her good-bye. For that she was grateful. If anyone had shown her the least sympathy she would have found it impossible to hold back the unshed tears that brightened her eyes.

Just as the stage jerked into motion, she saw a blue uniform in the shadows cast by the headquarters building. Someone tall and lean was standing quietly by, watching the stage depart. With eyes beginning to blur, she stared at the unmoving figure until it was out of sight.

Chapter Twenty-One

A cold morning wind struck with foul impotence against the stone walls of San Antonio's Ursuline Academy, rattling the windows in their wooden frames. Inside the small Catholic school for girls, Erin pulled her gaze from the bleak February scene outside and studied the open book in her lap.

The words "Sir Galahad" were scrawled in a fancy script across the top of the page. She'd first heard the name an eternity ago—could it have been only last summer?—when Cole had mentioned himself deprecatingly in comparison to the knight of old. She had sworn that as soon as she had the skill she would read about the inhumanly strong man he had referred to. She would not shirk from that vow.

> *My good blade carves the casques of men,*
> *My tough lance thrusteth sure*

A smile played for a second on Erin's lips, allaying the pain in her heart. The poet Tennyson must have had someone like Cole in mind when he had penned this particular verse. *"My tough lance."* Cole had certainly possessed that, right along with patience, understanding, and a tenderness she'd never know again. The light that had flashed briefly in her amber eyes died. Better not think such thoughts.

"Is there something wrong?" a young voice asked, and Erin looked up at the golden-haired girl beside her.

"No, Gabrielle," she said. "The words just took me back to something I'd rather not remember."

"Then put them aside," the fifteen-year-old said in the blunt manner that Erin had come to appreciate. "There is much pain in this world without seeking more."

"You'll get no argument from me there, but I promised myself a long time ago that when I learned to read I would find out about this Sir Galahad. It's just that circumstances were different then."

How simply put, Erin thought. Circumstances had indeed been different on that brief honeymoon following her hurried-up wedding. Again she looked at the printed page.

> *My strength is as the strength of ten,*
> *Because my heart is pure.*

For one sweet moment she was transported from her austere classroom to the Victorian splendor of a private railroad car, and her darkly handsome husband was once again close by her side. Her gaze shifted to the wedding ring she'd been unwilling to remove from her finger and she thought of Cole. When he had said he wanted to be like Sir Galahad in order to love her more, she had scoffed. She hadn't doubted his strength nor his heart. With the feel of his hands still on her body, she had wondered how he could possibly love her more.

Erin shook off the mood as quickly as it had come. She'd rejected that love and she had no regrets. She'd had no choice. Yet how could she have guessed how lonely a winter could be without him? No matter how busy she kept herself, there was always within her a heaviness she could not dispel. Most likely Cole had already taken the first steps that would lead to the dissolution of their marriage. She would need more than the strength of ten to discard that gold band when the legal documents were at last delivered into her hands.

Erin read the words again, then rested the book of poetry on her lap to gaze once more out the window. Down a slight incline the meandering San Antonio River, stirred by the brisk winter wind, lapped at the dead grass along its banks. In selecting the site for their convent and school on the northern edge of town, the Ursuline nuns had chosen well, Erin decided. Once this interminable winter was past, the grounds would be lovely in spring.

The original building, one of the sisters had told her in broken English, had been constructed by a fellow Frenchman for his intended bride, but the young woman had refused to leave her homeland. Rather appropriate, Erin thought, that she should spend much of her time in a place founded on broken dreams.

A long-ago promise to Cole had brought her to the academy soon after her arrival in San Antonio almost three months ago. She had told him she would learn to read, and while he would never know she had done so, she wanted to keep her word. The Ursuline nuns had not questioned her request for instruction, and she'd been moved to make several charitable donations to the sisters for their private school.

Reading had come surprisingly easy to her, and she wondered why she had fought it for so long. Really, it wasn't much more difficult than the mathematical problems she'd handled at such an early age.

To someone who didn't know Erin very well, her move to San Antonio had seemed smooth. Soon after arriving, she'd met an old friend of Julie's, Christine Bridgewater, who was telling fortunes in a cantina on the town's west side. Recently separated from her lover Big John Grissom who'd gone back to his old home somewhere in the south, Chris had been quick to see Erin's pain.

"Something's bothering you. A man. Nothing else could make you look so poor-spirited," she had said when Erin had called upon her at her apartment.

"You were a friend to Julie when she and Hud were having troubles," Erin responded. "I guess you can be the same for me."

"Keep busy. That's the secret. It keeps you from thinking. As I recall, you can deal a tough hand of twenty-one. How about working with me at the cantina? It's about as respectable a place as you're likely to find in this town—outside of some of the private clubs. A woman with your looks is bound to pull in a fortune."

"I already have a fortune, Chris, not that it's ever done me much good."

"Then buy the place. It's up for sale."

Erin looked at Chris incredulously and then smiled. Erin Barrett, proprietor. It had a certain respectability to it, and running a business would occupy her time.

Within weeks the place, renamed the Hidden Nugget in honor of the Australian gold discovery which had made Erin wealthy, had become the most popular gambling hall in town, and not just among the usual habitués. Often members of the town's elite could be seen there after a late night at the opera or theater, seeking a little diversion at one of the tables.

The Nugget's success was due to judicious management, Erin told herself, but business certainly hadn't been hurt when she'd hired a half-dozen female dealers who always conducted themselves as ladies and who were counted among the most beautiful women in town.

The ironical thing was that she herself had never been tempted to sit in at one of the games. There was far too much to keep her busy, seeing that the bar was well stocked and keeping the customers happy, especially when they failed to walk away from the tables as winners. In her position as owner and manager, she found herself dressing the part. High-necked, heavy clothing hung loosely on her thinning body, and her red hair was wound tightly in a severe bun at the nape of her neck. Since arriving in town, she'd never been tempted to wear her buckskin trousers. Too well she remembered the looks she'd received at the saloon in Saint Angela; the last thing she wanted now was to attract a man.

Not that her new life was devoid of consolation. Just when she'd given up on finding respectability, she'd made many friends among the society set that visited the Nugget and had even accepted invitations to several of their parties. Once, remembering the charity balls she'd planned for New York, she'd held a benefit dance for the Comanche cause, and after some initial resistance from the few who remembered too well the Indian wars, she'd managed to raise a tidy sum to send to Major Carter at Fort Sill.

But other than Christine, there was only one person in San Antonio that she felt comfortable around—Gabrielle Deschamps, the orphaned girl she'd met at the convent. With her delicate features and fair beauty, Gabrielle looked like an angel, and yet there was a forthrightness about her that Erin found refreshing. More and more, without any talk about what brought each of them to the academy, they had drifted into each other's company.

On this cold February day as she sat in the drafty room at the convent, Erin, warmed by the presence of her new friend, smiled at her. She was answered by a frown.

"M'amie," said Gabrielle, "the smile on your lips does not travel to your golden eyes. You seem as sad as the first day we met."

Erin shifted her gaze out the window. "It's just the

396

weather. Who can be happy on such a gloomy day?"

"I think you would not be happy if the land were bright with sunshine. Inside"—Gabrielle touched the rounded breast above her heart—"where it matters would not be spring."

Erin felt herself softening toward tears so she sat stiffly in her chair. "You don't know what you're talking about," she said more sharply than she'd intended. "In a few weeks the flowers will start to bloom and you'll find me positively silly."

"I think not. And while you do not say so, you think I am too young to know about the *affaires* of the heart. But I am not. Such things were, after all, my mother's business."

Erin immediately regretted her harsh words. "Gabrielle, please forget I said anything. Sometimes I speak before I think. It's been a problem to me."

"But not for me, Erin. I have long wanted to tell you my story. Perhaps it is time you knew."

"About your mother? One of the nuns said she was a widow."

"This is true. My father was killed in a great battle in the war with the North. Before I was born."

"And your mother owned some kind of business?"

"My mother was indeed a woman of business. She was a courtesan. You are surprised, no?"

For once Erin was at a loss for words and she felt a little like the women must have felt at Thanksgiving when she'd told them she was an Indian. By the time she had summoned up enough presence of mind to assure the young girl that it certainly didn't make any difference what her mother had been, Gabrielle was hurrying on.

"Do not think I am ashamed of Colette Deschamps. She was a kind and loving mother." Her blue eyes twinkled. "And very successful. She numbered among

397

her friends the wealthiest men in San Antonio. They helped her invest her money. I am not an impoverished orphan."

"And what about your father? Was his name Deschamps?"

The light in Gabrielle's eyes died. "No. My father was called Cordero. He came from farther south. Around Laredo." She paused a moment. "I can see the question you are too polite to ask. Why am I not Gabrielle Cordero? My father's family did not recognize my mother. And in turn, when she found a way to support her infant daughter, she did not recognize them."

"How long have you been here with the nuns?"

"Four years. It is almost time for me to make my own way in the world. The sisters have taught me all they can."

"Alone, Gabrielle? You always have me."

"My mother has arranged for my study in the East at a college for respectable young women. Far away from Texas. I will respect her wishes. I fear it is you, Erin, who will be alone, in spite of the parties you attend."

"Like your mother, I have my business."

"But you are not like my mother. She was a woman who set aside the pain of her loss and learned to enjoy life. You still ache for what you fear is gone."

"For what I *know* is gone."

In reply Gabrielle merely shrugged as if in acceptance of whatever Erin chose to tell her. No probing questions or even curious looks that might cause pain. Wise beyond her years, Erin's young companion was indeed a friend.

Erin could hardly wait to introduce her to Hud and Julie, who had at last returned to Texas from an extensive European tour. Any day now she expected them to be in town, ready she was sure to give her sympathy for her failed marriage. As soon as she had felt confident in her writing, she'd sent them a letter briefly explaining that she was separated from her husband. No details. Just the basic fact. There was no need to tell either Julie or Hud that her world was torn apart. She knew they'd be able to read between the lines.

Well, she certainly didn't plan to play the distraught divorcee when she faced them. Such a role, no matter how real, would only lead to tears and self-pity. Instead, carefully keeping the armor of her active life in place, she would show them the gambling establishment she had nurtured to success, and in a show of nonchalance, she would display the pages of reports that had been written by her own hand.

Reports. The thought reminded her that she had business to attend to in town. Not that she minded. She liked to fill her days with activity so that at night when she finally tumbled into bed in her apartment above the Nugget she was exhausted enough to sleep. With a quick look outside to make sure the day had not given way to one of the sudden storms that had beset San Antonio in the past weeks, she turned to Gabrielle.

"How would you like to have lunch in town? At the Menger Hotel." Actually it was the adjacent Menger Brewery that Erin needed to visit, but she could also treat her young friend to a meal at the fanciest hotel in town.

Gabrielle smiled brightly. "The Menger? It is such a lovely place." She glanced down at the drab woolen dress that was the school's uniform. "But I am not dressed for such a restaurant."

"Nonsense. You look fine," said Erin. "I used to worry about such things, and worse, which fork to use. I was always afraid I would make a fool of myself, which I usually did."

"You?" Gabrielle's blue eyes widened in amazement. "But you have a dignity about you that invites only respect."

"There are a number of people in New York and Texas who would be surprised to hear it," Erin said.

Within minutes the two were wrapped in somber cloaks and, a heavy wool blanket across their laps, were riding in Erin's buggy across the San Antonio River toward the Alamo and the nearby Menger Hotel. With Erin's expert gloved hand on the reins the high-stepping gray which pulled them shied only once, when a mule-drawn streetcar thundered past them on its tracks heading to the western edge of the town.

Erin secured the horse on a street that ran beside the hotel.

"Wait for me in the courtyard," she said to Gabrielle. "I'll be in the brewery for only a minute. Just long enough to place an order for some kegs of ale."

"This brewery is good?"

"It's supposed to have the best beer in the country. That makes it good enough for the Hidden Nugget."

Erin's business was quickly attended to in the adjacent brewery, and she joined Gabrielle in the flagged courtyard of the hotel.

"Now for lunch," she said, glancing around the enclosed garden. Even after a hard winter the landscaping along the perimeter was lush and green. With the harsh wind blocked away from her, Erin loosened the brown hood of her cloak and motioned for Gabrielle to walk on into the hotel restaurant ahead of her.

Chancing to look in the reflecting glass of a nearby window, Erin almost smiled. Wisps of red hair had worked loose from the bun at her neck, softening the tight lines that had settled on her face in the past weeks, and the cold air had given a ruddy cast to her cheeks. All in all she looked healthier and happier than she had in a long time. No matter that the look was a complete lie. She cared little for the picture she presented the world.

How quickly she changed her mind. From behind her

400

came the high-pitched laughter she'd not heard since she'd left Fort Concho, the sound of Maranda Pierce flirting with a man. Erin wasn't sure how she knew with such certainty; perhaps it was the laughter coupled with the heavy patchouli perfume the woman always wore. The air of the courtyard was filled with the sound and scent of the voluptuous blonde.

Well, there is no avoiding her, Erin decided, and, grateful that she looked presentable, she whirled around to get the inevitable confrontation over with. Not six feet away was Maranda, bigger and blonder than Erin had remembered, hanging onto the uniformed arm of a tall, lean Army officer.

It was the man who held her gaze. Beneath the narrow brim of an Army cap, dark hair spilled across a broad forehead. The face was more weathered than Erin remembered and the gray eyes more deep set, but there was no mistaking the fact that the man escorting Maranda Pierce into San Antonio's finest hotel was Erin's husband Cole.

For a long, awkward moment no one spoke. The only movement was Maranda pulling herself closer against Cole so that a full breast rested in the crook of his arm. A gesture of possession meant for her to see, Erin knew, but it drove her to break the brittle silence.

"Hello, Cole," she said, amazed at the steadiness of her voice. If she were to maintain her control she couldn't keep looking into his steely eyes. She was, after all, only human. "Hello, Maranda," she said, dropping her gaze so it settled on a palm leaf just behind the woman's shoulder.

"Erin." Cole's voice stroked her with the sound of her name. She'd thought never to hear it from his lips again and the heart that she'd hoped was beginning to mend shattered into irreparable pieces.

But he must not know it. He had found consolation

and he must think she had done the same. But with Maranda! The thought burned a fine edge of anger onto her pain. She had been betrayed. Resolutely squaring her shoulders, she looked directly at Cole, her amber eyes wide.

"What a surprise to see you. Are you here on leave?"

His gaze bore down on her. "I've been transferred to the Army post here, Erin. I'll be living in San Antonio."

"Have you been in town long?" she asked, at the same time cursing her need to know.

"We arrived only a short while ago."

We! Enough, she thought. The next thing he would say was that he would be sharing quarters with the woman on his arm. Well, by God, she wouldn't give him the chance.

"I'm sure you will enjoy your assignment," she said, her voice holding the impatient tone of dismissal.

He pulled away from Maranda. "You don't find San Antonio boring?"

"Not at all," she said, her head held high. Cole had rightfully accused her of being bored at Fort Concho. They both knew he was recalling those words. She couldn't resist glancing at Maranda. "At least no more than you will."

Maranda opened her full lips to speak, but Erin gave her no opportunity. "I have a previous engagement or I would offer to buy the two of you a drink in welcome. There's someone waiting for me inside." She lowered her lashes. She could think of absolutely no reason to inform either of them that the "someone" was a fifteen-year-old girl.

"No matter," Maranda said in her throaty voice. "We need to move on to the lobby and get a room."

Grateful that her leather glove concealed the wedding band she still wore, Erin intended to extend her hand and make the parting civil and complete. But she couldn't do it. Her eyes were watering dangerously as it was, and the anger that she'd held onto was fast dissipating into despair. Let them think what they would, she could only nod a quick goodbye. Then, with a whirl of her long brown cloak, she hurried through the portal that led to the hotel restaurant.

Gabrielle was nowhere in sight, and the headwaiter informed her that the girl had exited only moments before through a side door that led onto the street. Erin followed in her footsteps and found Gabrielle standing beside the buggy.

"I listened, *m'amie*," she said, "and thought you would like to exit quickly."

"You thought right," Erin said. Wonderfully smart Gabby. Cole should have been so sensitive. It was an unfair thought, but in her abject state she didn't care. Accurate or not, any thought was all right if it would help her get through the next few minutes without breaking down. Then a few more minutes and a few more.

In the buggy she concentrated on the busy afternoon streets. Maranda and Cole! The names penetrated her thoughts. As she pulled the carriage to a halt in front of the academy, Gabrielle sat quietly for a moment, then reached out to touch Erin's hand.

"I am truly sorry, *m'amie*."

Her gentle sympathy wore away Erin's stoical silence. "He's my husband. Or at least I suppose he is. I've heard nothing yet about a divorce." Erin shuddered. "That's such an ugly word. Does it shock you, Gabrielle?"

"I am only shocked by the woman he was with."

A picture of the overripe Maranda leaning against Cole flashed through Erin's mind. "I can agree with you there. At least I found out something about Cole I never knew before," she said with more spirit than she'd exhibited all day. "While at times he shows incredibly good judgment, at others he shows abominable taste."

But, having seen that Gabrielle was safely inside the academy, Erin couldn't retain her anger during the cold ride home. At the Hidden Nugget, only half-full on this weekday afternoon, she came face to face with Chris.

"What's wrong, Erin?" she asked.

Unable to accept Chris's sympathy and at the same time retain control, Erin dismissed her with a shrug and turned to her favorite worker at the Nugget, a six-foot, blond bartender who went by the single name of Hilda. There wasn't a man in town, drunk or sober, who tried to cause trouble in the Nugget when Hilda was around. She simply wouldn't allow it.

"I placed our order at the brewery," Erin informed the stoutly built woman. "Let me know if we need any liquor. But later, please. I'm afraid I have a headache." Without looking at either Chris or Hilda, both of whom were studying her carefully, she spoke into the smoky air. "I'm going upstairs. I'd appreciate it if I'm not disturbed."

"Erin—"

"Please, Chris," she said in a broken whisper, "not now."

Chris stepped to the bar and picked up a bottle of brandy. She thrust it into Erin's hand. "Here," she said. "This might help with the headache. It's worth a try."

Erin managed a smile. Chris's offer was a gift of love, and although Erin probably wouldn't take so much as one sip, she accepted it with gratitude.

Clutching the bottle in her hands, she hurried up the winding staircase to the sanctity of her small apartment. As she closed the door behind her, Erin tried to tell herself she hated Coleman Barrett for making her suffer, for offering to marry her in the first place, and for replacing her with Maranda Pierce. But she was too honest to succeed. In Fort Concho he had asked her to remain with him and she had refused. Even if she had been right in that refusal, she knew that in failing to set aside her love for him, she had only herself to blame.

Cole stood in the afternoon shadows of the squat building that faced the Hidden Nugget and stared up at a window that he figured was part of his wife's current abode. Thanks to some friends at the San Antonio Army post, there wasn't much he hadn' heard about her business success, although he still didn't know where she'd gotten the money to buy the cantina and refurbish it.

Not that it was any of his concern. His responsibility had ended when she'd walked out on him for the second time. Erin had chosen the life she wanted to lead. He was damned better off without her.

Seeing her again had been a shock, though he'd known he would, but not on his first day in town and not with Maranda on his arm. Erin certainly had misunderstood the situation, if the fire in her eyes had been any indication. Well, let her think what she would. Did she really expect him to live the rest of his life as a celibate?

Whenever he felt he was ready for the companionship of another woman, however, that woman certainly wouldn't be Maranda. When she'd asked to accompany him on his journey to his new post, he'd sworn it was the final act of gratitude he would perform for Jonathan Pierce. Maranda had claimed to want only a shopping trip into the city, but the journey alone had taken more than a week, the weather had been abominable, and it had been obvious that in coming to San Antonio, Maranda was after more than a few new dresses. She must have thought him no more sensible than the lonely men she

405

usually gathered about her.

Maranda had been furious when her mother had insisted on going along as a chaperon, but Cole had welcomed Mrs. Pierce's presence. Too bad Erin hadn't seen Agnes waiting in the hotel lobby, he thought. Then again, maybe it was better she hadn't. Let her think what she would.

He remembered the darkened skin beneath her eyes as she'd looked from him to Maranda. For a moment when she'd first recognized him those amber eyes had been filled with a glow he remembered only too well. Despite his resolve, he'd felt an inclination to grab her and plant on her lips a kiss that would rekindle the fire of their passion.

It was best he hadn't. No doubt those shadows under her eyes were caused by late nights at the Hidden Nugget. At last she'd gotten what she wanted—a place to gamble to her heart's content.

Well, he had business to take care of, too. Army business. It was a last endeavor for the institution he had once thought would be the center of his life, but it had a particular savor for him—the arrest of Major Gerald Nathan.

Nathan had recently been reassigned to San Antonio, a change he had asked for himself after much of his authority had been subtly, and steadily, usurped by Colonel Grierson. He obviously didn't know Cole had plans for incarcerating him in the post stockade.

Reluctantly, Cole left the shadows across from the Hidden Nugget and directed his step toward the footpath that ran alongside the shallow waterway known as San Pedro Creek. The net he'd carefully fashioned, with Colonel Grierson, to capture Nathan was almost ready to be pulled in. Nathan was a gun smuggler—both Cole and Grierson were sure of it—but they needed proof. In the next twenty-four hours, Cole hoped to get it.

Cole already was convinced Nathan had murdered his uncle Hilmer Turpin. A letter from Uncle Thad in Washington had contained the information that Nathan had purchased his sudden rise in rank. For the sum of four thousand dollars, the exact amount Turpin had swindled from Erin. There was no way that Nathan could legitimately have raised such a sum. Not that his guilt could ever be proved. There were no witnesses to the murder so Cole hadn't mentioned his suspicions to anyone else.

But the guns were another matter. Here Nathan wasn't acting alone. His partner in crime was the surly Sergeant Osborne, who'd been so reluctant to accept an escort out of Fort Griffin. According to a special agent Cole had set to watching Osborne in San Antonio, the sergeant soon was to keep an appointment with a known smuggler from Mexico, someone who might be very interested in buying contraband guns. The meeting was to take place in a clearing beside the creek a block west of Military Plaza. The information had been easy to come by, the agent had said; he'd simply gotten the sergeant drunk.

Even in wintertime, growth along the creek was thick, and Cole had little trouble in finding a hiding place that would give him an unobstructed view of the meeting site a half-dozen yards away. He didn't have long to wait. Osborne was the first to arrive. Clad in civilian coat and trousers, a dark bundle tucked under one arm, he looked smaller than he had in his sergeant's uniform. Smaller and meaner. Weak rays of sunlight fell on his grizzled face. His eyes were wide and wary beneath an overset forehead, and he paced nervously along the narrow pathway, like an animal ready to flee at the least sign of danger. Cole would have to be careful that the opportunity which presented itself was not lost.

The Mexican arrived shortly. Señor Juan Ramirez, according to the information passed on to Cole. Ramirez was purported to be an importer and businessman on both sides of the border. In the carefully tailored suit that fit his short, spare body well, he looked the part of a businessman, and a prosperous one at that.

Unfortunately the Mexican was cautious. Even from a short distance away Cole could not hear Ramirez's whispered words, and he had to watch helplessly as the two men huddled together. From the expression on Osborne's face, he gathered the negotiations were not going well. Talk ceased as a man and woman, arms around each other's waist, strolled past. Lovers sharing their warmth on a cold winter afternoon.

As they passed out of sight, Cole watched Osborne thrust the bundle at Ramirez. The Mexican accepted it and the two men shook hands. Cole smiled. The deal had been struck. After a quick glance around the clearing, the sergeant turned his back and headed down the path. He was soon out of sight. Ramirez waited a moment, then turned away from the departing Osborne and began to stroll leisurely along the creek. His small, dark eyes seemed to look right into the thick bushes where Cole had secreted himself, but their unmistakable gleam gave no indication of alarm.

"Señor Ramirez." Cole stepped into the Mexican's path.

Ramirez pulled to a halt and let his dark eyes slowly trail up to the face of his accoster. The worry that flitted across his face was brief and almost undetectable.

"You have the advantage, Señor," Ramirez said in silken tones. "Or rather, Captain," he corrected himself, his eyes on Cole's uniform and then on his holstered gun.

"My name is of little importance," said Cole. "It is what I know that should concern you."

"Then I suggest we make the business appointment for tomorrow, Captain, and I will listen to all you have to say."

"Unfortunately, what I have to say can't wait until tomorrow. By then, you will most likely be on the far side of Laredo. It is to your advantage to listen now."

Ramirez stared into Cole's unflinching eyes for a long moment. "Very well, Captain. If you insist."

Cole's attack was direct. "I know about your deal with Osborne," he said.

Beneath his pencil-thin mustache, Ramirez's mouth twitched but he gave no other sign of unease. "Is this Osborne a man I should know?"

"I would say so. You've spent the last few minutes talking with him."

Cole could almost hear the man's mind whirring in thought.

"Is it possible," he said at last, "that the sergeant has not been discreet?"

"It is more than possible. The sergeant has a weakness for a particular kind of drink that is made from cactus. It comes from your country."

Ramirez nodded slowly. "He is not the first man to fall under the spell. He asks me to supply him with more. That is all, Captain. Tell me what is the harm in that?"

"Nice try, Señor, but there is no need to smuggle liquor into San Antonio. Guns are different, though." Cole gestured to the bundle. "Like the one under your arm."

His shot hit the mark. Ramirez's dark face broke into a nervous grin. "Ah, Captain. Perhaps it is you I should be meeting instead of the thirsty sergeant." His dark eyes assessed Cole. "You and I are both sensible men. There is no reason we cannot reach a solution that would be profitable to us both."

"None at all. But there is only one deal that I will consider. Tell me what I need to know and I will let you return to Mexico without pressing charges."

"Ah," Ramirez said scornfully, "an honorable man."

His eyes beaded. "You take me for a fool." His voice was strong, but the twitch in his lips intensified.

"That is the one thing I don't take you for."

"You have no proof that I buy the sergeant's guns."

Cole ignored his bluster. "I don't need much to bring charges. The investigation will take care of the rest."

A sly smile crept onto the Mexican's face. "Then, Captain, why not do so? Why let me go free?"

"Because you have knowledge I need. The name of the man who is behind Osborne. I want proof of his guilt."

"But this I do not know. I deal only with the sergeant."

Cole held back the argument that sprang to his lips. For once, he decided, Ramirez was telling the truth. The Mexican almost sounded hurt that he could not reveal more. Well, Cole decided, I will give him the chance.

"When are the guns to be delivered?" Cole watched carefully as the Mexican calculated his response. Would the American captain do as he had threatened and have him arrested? Beads of sweat formed on the man's brow.

At last Ramirez shrugged. "Do I have your word, Captain, that I will be allowed to leave your lovely town?"

"You do."

"*Así es la vida*. A man in my business must make the best deal that presents itself. The guns arrive at the end of the week."

"How?"

"They come into the Gulf of Mexico by boat and then are brought by rail from Indianola. I am to be informed tomorrow morning as to the site for the final transaction."

"But why such an arrangement? To get the crates into Mexico, wouldn't you have to send them back the same way? Couldn't the deal have been struck down on the coast?"

"Ah, but the captain assumes all my business is south

the Rio Grande. There are many in Texas who pay *mucho dinero* for such weapons."

"Including outlaws and Apaches, I suppose."

"As I said before, Captain, a man in my business must take the best deal he can."

And sometimes so must an Army captain intent on uncovering wrongdoing, Cole thought. He would have much preferred to throw the wily Mexican into the stockade and to conduct his questioning there. But then Nathan might get away. Besides, Ramirez was a greedy man, without principle. Watched carefully enough, he would make a mistake down the line and eventually get the punishment he deserved.

The problem was Cole still had no proof the recipient of money was to be Gerald Nathan. For that, he needed a spy, someone other than the special agent he had already used. Since the agent had gotten Osborne drunk, the sergeant had stayed clear of him, as though he suspected something was wrong. And there was no one else on the post Cole trusted. What he needed was a civilian.

With a few blunt words about what he would do to Ramirez if he caught him in town again, he concluded his negotiations with the Mexican. The slick calm of the smuggler gave way to a nervous tic as he thrust the bundle into Cole's hands and scurried into the late afternoon gloom. Cole pulled the paper open and stared down at the unassembled rifle. On each stock was the letter *S*. These were from the same source as the rifles found by the Comanches at Fort Sill.

Cole wasn't surprised. Somehow Nathan had set up a network of gun smugglers using Army personnel. In the hands of desperate men, either white or red, the weapons were a threat to peace in the West. The smuggling had to be stopped.

As he left the pathway, he found himself walking in the direction of the Nugget. The closer he got, the more his

thoughts turned to his wife. Despite his strong resolve t
let her go her own way, he wanted to walk into the plac
sweep her into his arms, take the kiss he'd denied himse
at the Menger, and then excuse himself to see to Arm
business. There was a strong possibility that she would b
furious. The thought made him smile.

His mind turned to the conversation with Ramire
The guns were coming in by rail from Indianol
Something unrecalled about the railroad line worried
the back of his mind. When he was only a half-block awa
from the gas light that illuminated the entrance to th
gambling hall, his eyes fell on the answer to the questio
that had been bothering him about the railroad, as well a
the answer to his quest for a spy. Standing on th
sidewalk not twenty feet in front of him was the sever
foot Cur. Cur worked for Erin's former guardian Hu
Adams. It was Adams who owned the railroad.

He paused a moment to think. Cur was trustworthy
he'd certainly proven that in the Comanche camp. And a
an employee of Adams, he could easily have learned o
the special shipment coming in by rail. He might eve
know what was to be in the crates. At least he coul
probably convince Osborne that such was the case.

As Cole drew closer, he saw that Cur was not alone.
man and a woman stood at his side. The woman was
dark-haired beauty in a sweeping green velvet cloak,
feathered hat set at an angle atop her head. The man, n
much taller than she, was nevertheless distinctiv
because of the power that emanated from his dark, stror
frame. Hud and Julie. Cole would bet on it. His first da
in San Antonio was, indeed, proving to be an interestir
one.

Hud glanced around, his dark eyes watchful as Co
drew near.

"Mr. Adams," Cole said, extending his hand, "I'
Coleman Barrett."

412

Hud nodded. "Captain Barrett." As Cole had suspected, the man's grip was strong and sure. "May I present my wife Julie?" Hud added.

"Good evening, Mrs. Adams," Cole said; then he turned to Cur. "It's good to see you again, Cur." The giant smiled in greeting.

"Captain Barrett," said Julie, "I've been looking forward to meeting you for a long time."

"As have I," said Hud. "Cur speaks very highly of you. And I can assure you that's a rarity."

Julie grinned. "Anyone who can tame Erin deserves admiration."

"Mrs. Adams—"

"Call me Julie, please."

"Well, Julie," Cole said, casting a glance at the Hidden Nugget across the street, "hold up on your praise."

Hud stepped closer. "You mean because you two are not together right now? I was hoping that was only temporary."

Cole studied him for a minute. "And why is that?"

"Because you're the one man who can keep her from being her own worst enemy. Cur told me as much, and now that I've met you, I've got a hunch he's right. Erin may have a lot of money, but she's a little short on common sense sometimes."

Cole's eyes narrowed. "Money?"

Hud nodded. "From gold on her land in Australia. You didn't know?"

"Erin has a habit of withholding facts when it suits her," said Cole.

"You mean she lies."

"I see you know her well."

Hud's mouth broke into a half-smile. "Sure do. I don't suppose she's changed."

"I'm afraid not."

"She just needs a strong hand," Hud said.

"It won't be mine."

A cold wind swept around the corner of the building and fluttered the feather in Julie's hat. She stepped between the two men and rested her hand on Hud's arm. Her soft, dark eyes remained on Cole.

"I'm sorry to hear you say that, Cole," she said. "It took me a long time to figure out what a good man I had in Hud. I almost let him get away. If Erin does the same with you, she'll regret it the rest of her life."

Chapter Twenty-Two

Cole stood in the stream of afternoon sunlight filtering into the small room behind the Hidden Nugget's main salon, his eyes trained on the giant Cur, and asked the question that had been hovering in his mind throughout the hour he had been waiting for the man to arrive.

"Did Sergeant Osborne take the bait?"

Cur shrugged his massive shoulders. "Seemed to. Couldn't get him to say this Gerald Nathan's name, but he's to send word here if his boss will see me. I got a feeling the answer will be yes." Beneath the full red beard that covered Cur's lower face, a pair of lips twitched into a smile. "Didn't give him much choice."

Cole's sigh of relief was audible. Much depended on the success of the plan he, Cur, and Hud Adams had worked out the evening before. When Adams had heard of Cole's problem, he had offered his help. After all, he'd said, it was his railroad line between San Antonio and Indianola that was being used to ship the contraband guns.

When Cur had suggested setting up their clandestine meeting at the Nugget, Cole had almost declined. But he'd decided he wouldn't seek out Erin, and though her presence seemed to fill the saloon, he had not caught so much as a glimpse of her. Her assistant Chris Bridgewater had eyed him suspiciously when he'd entered at noon and had asked about a back room. However, his mention that Cur would be meeting him there had seemed to soften her resistance, and under the watchful eye of the bartender Hilda, who matched Cole in height and girth, he had been sequestered in one of the Nugget's private gambling rooms.

The past hour had gone by slowly, and fighting an impatience to get on with the business at hand, Cole waved toward a whiskey bottle and the glasses that sat on the poker table between him and Cur. "Let's have a drink, and you can tell me how it went."

Cur nodded and settled his huge frame into a chair, his back to the wall. "Won't argue with you there. I'd kind of like to get the taste of Osborne out of my mouth." He took the glass of whiskey offered by Cole and swallowed its contents in one gulp. Tiny droplets clung to the red bush around his mouth until he wiped them off with the sleeve of his buckskin coat.

"Was he suspicious at all when you showed up on the post?"

"Surprised, maybe, but when I mentioned the name of Juan Ramirez he was too nervous to do anything but listen. I told him just what we planned last night," said Cur. "Said Ramirez came snooping around the railroad office early this morning to find out when a certain shipment would be coming in. Osborne was quick to believe the lie and figure out that the Mexican was trying to double-cross him. No surprise to me he did. It's the kind of dirty trick he would most likely pull himself."

"You seem to have judged the sergeant quickly and accurately."

"I've seen his type from London to Australia. Both in and out of the penal colony. There's more than a few of that kind right here in Texas."

Cole nodded in agreement. "And in the Army. How did you let him know you were aware of what was in the shipment?"

"Said Ramirez offered me a cut from the sale of the guns if I would tell him what he wanted to know." The giant's dark eyes twinkled in his grizzled face. "Here I added a little embellishment. Told him Ramirez was thinking of maybe holding up the train and letting Osborne think someone else got hold of the guns, but he needed inside help. That's why he approached me. I told the sergeant the Mexican had cheated me before, and anyway, I figured there was more profit to be made if I dealt directly with the source of the guns. Namely Osborne's boss."

"And where does he think Ramirez is now?"

"He'd been trying to deliver a message to him all morning. After talking with me, he somehow got the idea Ramirez wasn't around any longer as either a customer for the guns or a threat who might steal them."

"He thinks Ramirez is dead by your hand?"

"That's the impression he got."

Cole settled back in his chair and twirled the untouched whiskey in his glass. "Ever thought of going into spying for the Army full-time?"

"I've no use for authority. Except the kind that comes with friendship attached."

"I'm beginning to know the feeling. What did Osborne say when you told him you wanted to deal with his boss?"

"Refused at first. Then I hinted there might be a delay in the shipment. The only way delivery could be assured was if I could talk to the man in charge of the deal. I kinda had him by the short hairs."

He did indeed, and Cole fought back a growing sense that the end of his quest was in sight. He mustn't be carelessly overconfident and mess up the deal, not when the end of the investigation was so close. After the inconclusive business with the medical supplies, both he and Grierson had been watching Nathan. There had been no reason for him to be out in the woods the day of the Apache attack except to meet with Osborne and sell the guns.

After Cole had been deposited at the Fort Concho hospital, Osborne and the wagon had disappeared for a while; shortly afterward guns with the curious S brand had started appearing in odd places, mostly in the hands of captured outlaws and Apaches.

And as best Cole could tell from watching Nathan and Maranda, the major had made damned sure he was informed of all shipments into the fort. When Nathan had sent Osborne down to San Antonio and two months later had arranged to follow him, both Cole and Grierson had become convinced he was doing more than just removing himself from under Grierson's watchful eye. More than likely he'd been setting up his biggest sale thus far. Yesterday's conversation with Ramirez had proven they were right.

But proof of Nathan's culpability was thus far nonexistent. Cole wanted the business concluded. As soon as he could put it behind him, he had a much more important matter to take care of—the dissolution of a contract that he'd once viewed with pride.

He looked thoughtfully at Cur. "You said earlier Osborne is to send word here. Are you sure that's wise? He might connect you with Erin and then to me."

"Not the way I put it. Told him I had something going with the big blonde that tends bar."

Cole grinned. "Another lie?"

Cur shrugged his massive shoulders, but his reply was lost when the door of the room was flung open and the two men looked up to see an angry Erin glaring down at them.

"Chris told me you two were back here." Her eyes

418

flicked past Cur and settled on Cole. "What's going on?"

Cole didn't reply at first. For a moment he remembered the way Erin had looked those months ago when he'd opened the door of his West Point quarters and found her flashing eyes staring up at him. In her yellow satin gown and with a mass of red curls piled elaborately on top her head, she'd looked sweetly provocative and, despite his misconception about why she was there, innocently vulnerable.

Not now. Less than a year later, she had lost the maiden's blush from her cheeks and shadows underlined her expressive eyes. He could almost feel sorry for her if he hadn't been so angry at the decision she had reached. She was a woman now, not a girl, and women lived with their commitments and decisions, just as men did. Whether they brought them happiness or not.

He rose to his feet. "Just trying out some of your whiskey, Erin," he said, then turned to Cur who was still seated. "Let me know when you get word about that matter we were discussing. I'll be in my room at the hotel."

Moving past Erin, he picked up the Army hat that hung from a hook beside the door and pulled it low on his forehead. For one brief moment his eyes rested on Erin, and then, with a quick nod, he was gone.

The room was quiet, save for Erin's sharp intake of breath. How could Cole leave without even a good-bye! Surely he owed her more than just a nod. But even in her hurt and anger, Erin knew it was a thought she couldn't hold for long. She'd done far worse to him. Twice. Under the circumstances he would have been justified in turning her over his knee.

And just where had he been in such a hurry to go—his hotel room? Was it possible Maranda Pierce was waiting for him there? A chair scraped across the wooden floor, and she realized with a start that she wasn't in the room alone.

Cur pulled himself to his feet. "Erin, I'm going out to the bar. Should be a message delivered here for me before long."

Erin only half heard. "A message?" she asked.

"Seems to me," Cur said as he moved toward the door, "you're thinking of something else besides what I'm saying."

"I'm thinking, Cur, that maybe I'm not very bright."

"You used to be. I've seen you take a table of gamblers for whatever they were foolish enough to wager."

She shrugged. "Poker's simple compared to my problems now. There aren't any rules to go by. No odds to figure. I never thought I'd let Cole walk out on me like that. And to another woman."

"So why did you?"

"I didn't have any right to stop him."

"Since when did having rights ever stop you? You want to talk to the man, go after him."

"And interrupt his love tryst? I'm not sure he would be in his room alone."

"He's still your husband, Erin. You have the right to go see him." He paused in the doorway. "And if you think he's sharing a room, you're wrong. The Army has a room at the hotel for officers. Least that's what Cole told me."

Erin stared at the door that closed behind Cur. The man made good sense. Of course she had the right to talk to Cole. They couldn't keep running into each other as they had the past two days and continue to maintain a façade of strained civility. Not after what they'd shared. A complete break, that was what was needed. If he was going to be in San Antonio for long, she would simply have to leave town.

As soon as the decision was made, Erin stopped looking for reasons to justify her seeing Cole. Unable to keep her

420

heart from pounding at the thought of seeing him again, she looked down at her drab brown dress. But not like this.

With a quickness to her step that had been absent for a long time, she hurried out to the bar. Along with Cur, Hilda and Chris awaited her.

"I have to go out for a while."

"You haven't eaten lunch, Erin," said Chris.

"I'm not hungry."

"Men don't like a skinny woman," said Hilda, glancing up at Cur who leaned across the bar beside her. Erin looked at Hilda in surprise. In the few months she'd known her, the bartender had never shown the slightest interest in what men wanted, except to drink.

"I'm not trying to attract a man," she said over her shoulder as she headed up the stairs to her apartment. To face Cole for what would probably be the last time, she wanted to wear something definitely more feminine than the dowdy dress that had become her uniform. She'd just said she didn't want to attract a man, but that wasn't entirely true. Not if the man in question were Cole.

Perhaps she would wear the sapphire gown and matching cloak Hud had sent her for Christmas. She'd never worn it, but this afternoon seemed as good a time as any to put it on.

In half an hour she was hurrying back down the stairs, a swirl of blue wool enveloping her. Golden red curls, freed from their imprisonment, framed her face and floated against her shoulders, and fire lightened her eyes. With a nod to the two open-mouthed women by the bar, she pulled on a pair of gloves and strode outside to her carriage.

As she guided the buggy down the busy San Antonio street toward the Menger, she concentrated on the traffic. After a long, hard winter, there was a hint of spring in the crisp, clear air, and Erin felt her spirits lift.

Whatever she had to say to Cole would come naturally; after all, she was simply letting him know in a civilized manner that they couldn't stay in the same town.

At the Menger desk she asked for the suite that had been reserved by the Army for its officers. "I believe a Captain Barrett is currently staying there." When the clerk's eyebrows rose, she couldn't help adding, "I'm Mrs. Barrett."

"Of course, Mrs. Barrett. Room 360."

In minutes Erin was knocking on the door.

"Hello, Cole," she said as soon as he appeared. "May I come in?"

He stepped aside. "Certainly, Erin," he said as he closed the door and followed her into the small sitting room that was part of the suite. "May I take your cloak?"

"I don't intend to stay long. It's just that you left so suddenly from the Nugget we didn't have a chance to get some things cleared up."

Erin's heart was pounding. To her own ears she sounded stiff and uncomfortable. Why was it so difficult to talk to him? She'd never had trouble before.

"What did you want to talk about?"

"Some"—she paused to sort out her jumbled thoughts—"some unfinished business. Do you plan to be in San Antonio long?"

It wasn't a good start, but he did keep staring at her and she couldn't keep from staring back. Tumbled across his forehead were black curls that definitely needed pushing back, and his lean, solemn face needed something—a kiss?—to lighten its somber look.

"Why are you asking, Erin?"

Well, he certainly wasn't going to make this easy for her. But now was not the time to lie.

"Because I want to know if we are going to keep meeting the way we did yesterday and today."

His eyes glittered darkly. "And if we are?"

She looked away. The chasm between them stretched to infinity. "Then I'm going to have to learn how to handle the situation. I'm not as coolly in control as you are."

His answer was a long time coming. "I see. Or at least I think I do. My being here disturbs you, I take it."

Disturbs? What an inadequate word! Her whole being cried out for her to throw herself in his arms and beg him to take her back. She'd try very hard to be a good Army wife if only he would hold her once again.

At last she found her voice. "Have you done anything about the divorce?"

"Not yet."

The words cut through her composure like slivered glass. *Not yet.* No doubt he'd get around to it when he had the time. "Perhaps," she said, "you can work it into your Army schedule now that you're in town."

"A man finds time for what he really wants to do." His voice softened. "You look tired, Erin. Not been sleeping well?"

"I've been sleeping just fine. After all, I grew used to sleeping alone back at Fort Concho."

He ignored her barb. "Then I guess the Nugget is proving too much for you to handle."

"Not at all. I want it to be the best. I'll accept nothing less."

"Smart woman. Neither will I."

"Does that include Maranda Pierce?" Erin could hardly believe the words had slipped out. But damn Cole, he looked so sure of himself. She wanted to make him as uncomfortable as she was.

"Surely you didn't plan for me to be a celibate, love. Maranda has her uses."

Words of anger caught in Erin's throat. If she had planned to make Cole uncomfortable, she had certainly failed. But she wasn't through.

"I'm sure she does," said Erin with a calm she was far from feeling. "Like giving me a packet of old love letters that belonged to you."

Cole nodded slowly. "I found them when I was packing to come down here and figured something like that had happened. Did you really mind seeing them? You should have known me better than that, Erin. If you let them upset you—"

"I just wish you had been the one to tell me about Rachel Cox. And about her death."

"Perhaps I should have. But what good would it have done to bring up those old hurts? I've buried them. They're part of a past that has no affect on us."

"Rachel was very beautiful, Cole. She would have made a suitable Army wife."

"She was a child. When I knew her, we were both children." Cole moved closer and his manly presence enveloped her. "That pale, flat likeness of Rachel would never suit for a lifetime, Erin. A man wants a real woman."

"Surely Maranda will fill that order. She gives every appearance of being just that."

"Appearances can be deceiving," he said, moving still closer, his trousers brushing against her skirt. "For instance, I assumed you were dependent on Hud Adams for your money. You should have told me you were rich."

Erin's eyes focused on the scarf at his neck. "I don't see what difference it could have made. Besides, you ought to be relieved that you won't be financially responsible for me."

"And if I had to accept such a burden?" His voice was laced with sarcasm and his hands reached out to grip her shoulders. "Don't you think I could manage to keep a roof over your stubborn head? I told you long ago I had a few investments in Texas. Most of them are in San

424

Antonio. You'd not go hungry."

Erin looked up to speak and was startled by the anger in his eyes. Then his lips covered hers, smothering her protests. It was a hard kiss which gradually softened into dark moistness. It had been so long since she'd tasted such goodness. Her hands pressed against his chest, then stole up to encircle his neck and hold him close.

Hungry lips and tongues probed in an explosion of desire as Cole's hands stroked her back and cupped her buttocks, pulling her tight against his demanding manhood. She trembled with a shudder that reached into her soul. Mindless of time and place, she knew only that at last she was complete again. Cole was in her arms the way he'd been in her thoughts since she'd left Fort Concho, and his passion was as thrilling as she had dreamed. He lifted his lips, then pressed them into her hair, and she was lost in the wonder of him.

A sharp knock at the door shattered the spell; then Cur's terse words filtered into the hotel room.

"Cole. It's come. Everything is set."

After a moment, Cole found his voice. "Go on down to the lobby. I'll be with you in a minute."

Erin stiffened in his arms. "Unfinished business?"

Cole's breath was hot upon her neck. "For a while."

Erin knew the answer, but she had to ask. "Anything to do with the Army?"

"It doesn't concern you, Erin."

She pulled away. "I'm sure it doesn't."

"Let me walk you downstairs."

"I'd rather stay here for a few minutes and freshen up. If the Army wouldn't object to my being in the room alone."

"Not at all." Too quickly he grabbed his hat and was gone. Erin didn't move for a while. Cole had changed, and yet he hadn't. The man who had made love to her on countless nights was the same man who'd kissed her

425

today. And yet he had talked about Maranda as if he'
shared his kisses with her, too.

Impossible. He must be lying. But there was only on
way to find out. Letting herself out of the room, sh
descended to the hotel lobby to find out the room numbe
of Maranda Pierce.

Chapter Twenty-Three

By the time Erin descended the stairs and approached the desk in the Menger lobby, her thoughts were as confused as they'd been before she'd talked to Cole. And before he'd kissed her. What if he had been telling the truth and he was sleeping with Maranda? What if she'd pushed her husband into the arms of that calculating blonde? Such a move on her part wasn't at all what she had planned.

When she'd left Fort Concho, if she had considered Cole's life without her at all, she'd imagined him with someone ethereally lovely like Rachel Cox, certainly not with earthy Maranda Pierce.

Erin felt the anger inside her grow. Maranda was wrong for Cole, and in the long run she would do his career as much harm as a gambling Comanche would have. Erin had to know the truth.

The hotel clerk took one look at Erin's firm countenance and quickly told her Maranda's room number. "I don't believe she's gone out yet," he said without being asked. "Although her mother is having luncheon in our restaurant. Perhaps you'd like to join her."

Erin stared at the clerk for a moment. "Mrs. Pierce is

427

here also? Sharing a room with her daughter?"

"I believe she is." He glanced down at the registe
"Yes, that's correct."

Now why hadn't Cole mentioned that Agnes Pier
was staying at the Menger with her daughter? Could Er
be right in suspecting he wanted to give her the wro
impression? Honorable Captain Barrett? Perhaps the
was more to Cole's reassignment to San Antonio than h
been apparent at first.

Erin moved swiftly to the second floor and knocked
the door to which she had been directed. It was flu
open.

"It's about ti—" Maranda began in a strident voi
then stopped when she realized who was there. "Wh
the hell do you want?"

Erin grimaced. "Well, that's about as gracious as
expected, Maranda. Do you mind if I come in?" N
waiting for an answer, she stepped inside the spacio
room.

Maranda, her body as resplendent as ever in a for
fitting gown of scarlet, slammed the door.

"If you're looking for Cole, he isn't here right now

Erin whirled to face her. "Maranda, I don't imagi
he's ever been here, unless your mother was present
She smiled. "How is your mother, by the way? Am
keeping you from joining her for lunch?"

Erin watched the expressions flicker across Marand
face: first surprise, then anger, and at last resignatio
The blonde would never make it as a poker player.

"I'll eat later," said Maranda. "I've sent word
Gerald Nathan at the post to see if he will join me."

"Gerald is in San Antonio?"

"He has been for a couple of weeks. That is, of cours
why I'm here."

Erin studied her thoughtfully and felt a curious kind
pity soften the anger she'd brought with her into t

oom. Maranda's clinging to Cole's arm yesterday now eemed pathetic. She'd wanted very much to give the mpression that she and Cole were lovers, probably because she wanted it to be true. Could she be trying to ettle for Gerald Nathan?

"Then you and Gerald are more than just friends," aid Erin.

Maranda shrugged. "He's an Army man. That's what I want."

"That's one of the ways we're different, Maranda. I don't like the Army. I don't understand it. How could a man like Gerald Nathan outrank Cole? Did he buy his promotion?"

Erin had been merely speculating, but the defensive ook on Maranda's face told her she was right.

"And what's wrong with that?" Maranda asked.

A great deal, Erin wanted to say, but she doubted Maranda would understand. Now that she was no longer ealous of this blonde's relationship with Cole, she ealized something. Maranda might be beautiful and wily, but she wasn't very smart.

Gerald Nathan was different, however. From the first time she'd set eyes on him in the West Point ballroom, he hadn't trusted him. She was certain he had purposefully taken her outside at Thanksgiving so that he could overhear the new lieutenant's slanderous emarks about Cole. Well, her loud-mouthed reaction certainly hadn't disappointed him. The only one she had disappointed was Cole.

The last time she had seen Nathan, he had called her nto his office to discuss the denial of Cole's promotion to major. Could that story have been a lie?

Erin's mind raced. She'd spent her too-brief marriage convinced that she was doing her husband harm. Yet the damage to his career had also come from within the ervice to which he had devoted his life. Namely, from

Gerald Nathan.

Nathan had been the one who'd convinced Erin t[o] leave. Like a fool, she'd done just what he'd suggeste[d] She wasn't any smarter than Maranda. Rage filled he[r] heart and mind. Erin had always prided herself on he[r] independence, and yet when Cole had gone on patrol, sh[e] had proven herself easy prey. She had to see Nathan an[d] face him down.

She looked at Maranda. Whatever animosity she ha[d] felt toward the woman was gone. Maranda wanted t[o] marry Nathan; the worst thing that could happen to he[r] was to get her wish.

Besides, Erin had something much more important t[o] contemplate—why Cole had seen fit to misrepresent hi[s] relationship with Maranda. Except for the kiss, that wa[s] the most provocative thing he'd done in their tw[o] meetings.

Erin bid Maranda a hasty good-bye and hurried dow[n] to her carriage. The Army post was located a few mile[s] northeast of town on a rise known as Government Hil[l] The road leading out to it was well traveled, and as Eri[n] sat on the edge of the buggy seat and urged her hors[e] along at a fast clip, she couldn't decide who had her mor[e] disturbed—Cole or Gerald Nathan. She'd see Gerald firs[t] and then Cole. Surely he'd settled the Army business tha[t] had called him away from her.

She thought of Cole's kiss, and the idea that had bee[n] lingering at the back of her mind ever since she'd see[n] him yesterday came to the fore. She and Cole belonge[d] together. No matter what the circumstances. No matte[r] what kind of sacrifices either of them had to make. And [if] the way Cole had kissed her was any indication, he kne[w] it, too.

Her spirit soared at the thought and she becam[e] impatient to conclude her confrontation with Nathar[n] With the post's limestone water tower as a beacon, Eri[n] made fast time on the road and was soon guiding the carriage through the sally port on the south side of the fort. She had no trouble in getting directions to Nathan's office. In fact, several officers offered to direct her there personally, but she declined.

The adjutant who greeted her gave her bad news. "The major rode out of here not more than a half hour ago," he said. "He didn't say when he would return."

"Do you know where he was going?"

"Major Nathan isn't much on telling his business," the lieutenant said flatly. "But I believe he took the road that leads north to Salado Creek."

"And what about Captain Barrett? Is he in his office?"

"I haven't seen him today, ma'am."

Erin nodded her thanks and made a quick departure. She knew the road that led to the creek. Holding her cloak and skirt close to her body, she climbed into the carriage and clucked the horse into a canter. The clear blue sky overhead and the crisp afternoon air added to her exhilaration as she headed in the direction of the creek.

It was Erin's ability to track a horse rather than fate that brought success in finding her party. As the trail branched off, she spied the hoofprints of a horse that needed shoeing heading off on a narrow path toward a distant line of cypress trees and thick brush. She had seen the same tracks as she'd left the fort, and she knew she had her man. The path gave out a hundred yards from the trees and, securing the horse to a sturdy bush, she started out on foot.

Within minutes she was in the shadows cast by a tall cypress and she paused to listen to the shrill call of a mockingbird announcing her arrival. A cool breeze ruffled the leaves of the brush and made the tall, wild grass that lined the creek bank sway. No human sound came to her ears. She proceeded with caution and was

431

suddenly held up by a tug on her skirt. Whirling around
she saw that her hem was caught on the sharp spines of
cactus plant and she knelt to free it. As she started to rise
she saw from the corner of her eye a pair of dusty boot
pointed in her direction. Her gaze trailed up the blu
trousers and jacket of an Army uniform and she looke
into the narrow, scowling face of Gerald Nathan.

"What the hell are you doing here?" he asked.

"Looking for you," she said, rising and brushing th
dust from her cloak. She refused to let Nathan know hi
sudden appearance had unnerved her. This wasn't at al
what she had planned.

Nathan's eyes narrowed. "Who sent you?"

"No one, Gerald," she said with contempt. "I followe
you here on my own. I have something I want to clea
up."

She had wanted to disturb his confidence, but from th
look in his eyes she realized she had done the reverse. I
her eagerness to confront him, she had admitted to bein
alone. Until this moment, she had never considered th
fact that Gerald Nathan might prove to be dangerous.

To cover her disquiet, she went on the attack. "Tell m
the truth, Gerald. Was Cole ever up for promotion?"

"Not likely. Not with the reports that went in on hi
to Washington."

"Then you must have sent them. There's not a bette
officer than Cole anywhere," Erin said with pride
forgetting for the moment how much she hated th
Army. "He would never stoop to buying his rank."

Nathan stepped closer, his bullet eyes peering at he
"What is that supposed to mean?"

"You know very well. Although where you got th
money, I can't imagine." In her anger at the man wh
had fooled her with his lies, she forgot all caution. "Co
once told me your family had lost about everything in th
war. I imagine the most money any of them have seen i

432

years was the four thousand dollars Hilmer Turpin stole from me."

Even as she said the words, she saw the truth. "How much does a major's rank cost these days, Gerald?" she asked. "Something close to the amount your uncle gave up his life for?"

"What do you know about that?"

"I'm not stupid, Nathan, although I may be a little slow. You killed your uncle, didn't you?"

A low growl came from his throat. "You'll have a hell of a time proving it," he said, his hand whipping out like a snake and grabbing her arm to jerk her against him. As quickly as he had attacked, she fought back, striking his face and body with her free hand and kicking out at his booted legs, but she was no match against his strength. Within seconds she was imprisoned in his hold, her arms twisted painfully behind her, her face inches from his. When he spoke, his breath was as foul as his words.

"And you are a stupid woman, Erin. As stupid as Maranda."

Erin shuddered at his contempt and, in silent bitterness, acknowledged that he was right. Back in the carriage was a rifle that she carried for protection. It had never occurred to her to bring it for a confrontation with such a lowlife as Gerald Nathan, and now she knew she would pay for her mistake.

To her horror she saw his close-set eyes darken to a look she recognized, and she was filled with loathing for being regarded in such a way by him.

"You do what you're thinking about, Nathan, and you're a dead man."

"I doubt that." His hold tightened. "Although it might be worth it to find out what Barrett has been enjoying."

Erin spat in his face. "That you will never know."

She stared at him defiantly, goading him into a rage that might make him careless. He twisted her arms higher toward her shoulders and she winced with pain.

"I like a woman to suffer," he rasped, "and to fight. Maranda always gave in too easily. I only wish I could enjoy you right this minute."

Gripping her arms behind her with one hand, Nathan reached into his pocket and pulled out a soiled handkerchief, which he thrust into her mouth. Erin gagged, feigned she was choking, but to no avail. Removing his Army scarf, he tied it around her head, effectively securing the gag in place. Erin kicked and flailed as he jerked her toward a thick copse where his horse was tethered. With one arm wrapped around her waist, he removed a lariat that was suspended from the saddle and bound her hands behind her; then he jerked her deeper into the thicket to tie her securely to the trunk of a tree.

Erin sat very still. Nathan had forgotten her feet. Once he was gone, she could at least thrash about in the brush and perhaps call attention to herself. Her hopes were dashed when he tore a piece of material from the hem of her skirt and, using one end to bind her ankles, tied the other end to a nearby bush. Like a side of beef, she was trussed and helpless.

Legs apart, Nathan stood over her. "You'll have a little while to wait and think about what I'm going to do to you, Erin," he said in a whisper. "If I didn't have someone to meet, you'd be finding out now."

He reached down to stroke her throat and breast. Erin twisted her body away from his hated touch and he jerked her back. "Keep it up, Erin. It excites me. When we're alone, I'll have you fighting me and then begging for more. Too bad we'll have to postpone our little celebration. I got here early to be sure I wasn't going to be ambushed, but not early enough for what I'm planning now."

So they were not to be alone, Erin thought as Nathan

turned and pushed his way through the brush. Whoever was coming would surely see her horse and carriage. Vainly she tugged at her fetters. Bile rose in her throat. She would gladly have given up the Nugget if doing so would have gotten the gag removed from her mouth.

How long it was before she heard any sound she had no idea, but it must have been only minutes. A rustling in the brush to her right caught her attention and she turned to see Nathan driving her carriage through the thick growth, the whip she never used snapping with a sickening sound against the horse's flanks. Silently she cursed the man for being so cruel and for being wily enough to cover her tracks. The brush closed like water behind Nathan and in a minute even she couldn't make out the exact place through which he had driven her rig.

Nathan was expecting a visitor, someone he obviously didn't want anyone to know about. Otherwise he would have met him at the post. Long minutes dragged by. At last the sound of voices drifted through the brush. Men's voices. They drew nearer, and to Erin's astonishment, she made out the deep Australian accents of Cur.

"I tell you I've got buyers for the guns. All you have to do is supply them," Cur said.

"At the price I mentioned?"

"I don't know about that. I'll do the best I can."

Erin's heart pounded. So this was the reason Cur had interrupted her meeting with Cole. To catch Nathan in some nefarious scheme to peddle guns. No doubt the same kind of guns both the Comanches from Fort Sill and the Lipan Apaches had used. Cole had been tracking their source for a long time.

Somewhere in the vicinity Cole was watching and listening. She was sure of it. For the first time since Nathan had grabbed her, her spirit lightened. Cole would never let her come to harm.

But what about him? Nathan was vicious and smart.

435

She'd certainly learned that this afternoon. When he finally came to claim what he wanted of her, she couldn't let her presence deter Cole from making his arrest.

Incredibly, she heard the voices lower as if the men were moving away. She twisted as best she could on the ground, but the resulting sound was drowned out by the wind in the tree above her. The tree. Rearing back, she turned to place her face against the smooth trunk of the cypress. Too bad she wasn't tied to a rough-barked hackberry or oak.

But never mind. With no thought as to whether she might scar her face, she rubbed the edge of Nathan's Army scarf against the tree. She stopped for a moment to listen for men's voices, but she could no longer hear them. Desperate, she rubbed harder, felt a sting each time she cut her skin, and at last met with success. As the scarf edged down from her mouth, she used tongue and teeth to dislodge the hated handkerchief.

"Cur!" Her voice was little more than a croak. "Cur!" she managed louder. And at last, "Cole! Help!"

She hadn't long to wait. The brush in front of her rustled, but it was Nathan, not Cur, who stepped into view, a pistol raised in her direction. By the time Cur came crashing in behind him, his seven-foot frame causing the ground to shake, Nathan was kneeling beside her and the cold barrel of the gun was pressed against her head.

"I don't know who you really are," Nathan said as he looked up at Cur, "or what you're up to, but you step any closer and I pull the trigger."

"That would be a mistake." A deep voice whipped out from behind Nathan, its punctuation the click of a hammer on a gun. "Remain perfectly still, Nathan, and you have a chance to live."

Erin's eyes darted upward. Standing over Nathan, a gun pressed to the back of the mayor's neck, was Cole.

Nathan's sharp face was covered in sweat. "You wouldn't dare," he said.

"What have I got to lose? If I let you take her, she's dead anyway. And I'll track you down. There will be no place you can hide."

Erin had never heard a more deadly voice than Cole's, or a more loving one.

"And if he doesn't get you," Cur growled, "I will."

An eternity of waiting ensued, and then Nathan slowly lowered the gun. Cole jerked him to his feet. "Watch him," he said to Cur, and turned to Erin. With deft, sure motions, he untied her and pulled her into his arms.

Erin crushed herself against his body, letting its strength flow into her. It was foolish to feel so scared now that the danger was past, but she couldn't help it. She needed Cole. She always had. As she lifted her face to brush her lips against his, his eyes glittered down darkly.

"What in hell were you doing here, Erin?" he asked, his fingers brushing her cheek where she had rubbed against the tree. It was a gentle, soothing touch, but the words that accompanied it were hardly the declaration of love she had awaited.

She pulled away. "I . . . I wanted to talk to Nathan," she said, shuddering at the mention of his name. "He lied to me back at Fort Concho. Said you would never get a promotion because of me. It was one of the reasons I left."

"Then I have another reason to despise him."

"We both do, Cole. He's an evil man. I heard him conspire with Cur to sell the guns. If you need me to testify."

"There's no need, love. I was farther back in the brush, listening, too. I had come across the creek to take an unprepared Nathan by surprise. I must admit that when you cried out I was the one taken unawares."

Nathan pulled at his bound hands but stopped when

Cur pressed the gun barrel against his head. "Go ahead and you'll save us a trip back to the post."

"I'll take him back," Cole said. "You make sure Erin gets to town all right." He looked at Erin. "I'll be at the Nugget as soon as I can, but it may be awhile. I've several things to attend to."

Erin looked at him in astonishment. Army business. It always took precedence. And here she had been hoping he would pull her back into his arms and declare undying love.

Now hold up, she told herself. Angry words were no way to convince him she wanted more than anything in the world to be his wife. Cole obviously had a duty to take care of. If she were to try once more to be an Army wife, she'd have to get used to it, but she'd be damned if she would ever enjoy it.

Not that he had actually asked her to come back to him. Perhaps she was reading too much into his kiss. "I'm all right, Cole. You needn't worry about me."

"I *always* worry about you, Erin. You give me little chance to do otherwise."

So he worried, did he? Good. She smiled warmly at Cole, then with Cur at her side directed her attention to tracking down her horse and carriage. When they had maneuvered the rig back onto the slope that led down to the creek, Cole was already mounted. Beside him on his own horse was Nathan, his arms still tightly bound.

Cole looked down at her. "I'll see you as soon as I can, love." His lips broke into a smile.

Erin gave him an answering smile. *Love.* What a wonderful word. But only on Cole's lips. She couldn't wait to tell him how he made her feel.

In the meantime she'd ride quietly back to the Nugget and wait patiently for Cole to return. But as she watched him ride away from her, his long, strong legs gripped

around his horse, she knew it wouldn't be an easy thing
to do.

The sun was just settling behind the building across
the alleyway from the Nugget when Erin, looking out of a
window in her apartment above the saloon, spied Cole
riding down the dusty side street. In the past two hours of
waiting she'd lost her patience and her resolve to accept
without question whatever duty called him to do.

Couldn't Cur have seen to getting Nathan back to the
post? That might not have been strictly according to
regulations, but there were times when rules definitely
had to be suspended—especially if doing so meant
keeping Cole by her side. Whatever paperwork had to be
seen to could have been taken care of later, after she and
Cole had talked.

Apparently Cole hadn't seen things that way. Under
the circumstances, if the honorable Captain Barrett
thought he could just march right up the stairs and claim
his conjugal rights, he had another think coming.

Even Cur had been quick to abandon her, choosing
instead to stay below and talk with Hilda. Why, he'd even
stopped to brush the dust from his clothes before
entering the Nugget. Erin had never seen him behave in
such a fastidious manner.

And, after showing initial concern for Erin, even Chris
was not too eager to talk, caught up as she was in reading
a letter she'd received that day from her lover Big John.

Erin was sorry she had changed into the soft yellow
silk dress that showed her full breasts and narrow waist to
such advantage, sorry she had carefully brushed her hair
until it shone with the brilliance of sunlight. It would
serve Cole right if she were waiting for him in her
buckskins.

439

Too bad the apartment was just one large room, the main piece of furniture being a fourposter bed. She placed herself well away from it when the firm knock came, then bade Cole enter. As soon as he came through the door and closed it behind him, her resentment melted in the warmth of his presence. The Army cap was pulled low on his forehead and his gray eyes glinted with approval at the way she looked. How ruggedly handsome he was with his lean, tanned face, his broad shoulders and narrow hips, and those magnificent long legs encased in blue trousers and calf-high black boots.

"Hello, love," he said softly.

It was a while before she found her voice. "Did you get your business taken care of?"

He tossed his cap onto the dresser and ran his fingers through the shock of black hair that fell across his forehead. "Even got a confession. Both his and Osborne's."

"You know Nathan killed his uncle, I suppose. He as much as admitted it to me."

"He claimed I gave him the idea. Remember when we went to see him at West Point? I said something about a man making his own future. It was the only advice I ever gave him he took to heart. He left right away and rode cross-country all the way to Virginia. Got there before we did and went straight to the cabin on the old Turpin place."

"But his own uncle, Cole. I don't understand."

"He'd learned about some guns the Army had rejected and had already made plans to make some money off them, but he needed to be out west. Then, when you came in with a story about four thousand dollars, he saw a way out of the Point and into a promotion in Texas."

"So why did he hate us so? He should have been grateful."

"He was afraid of being caught. Remember the wagon

440

we accompanied out of Fort Griffin? There were guns beneath those medical supplies. Guns he meant to trade to the Apaches. We got in the way and he spent the next few weeks trying to get rid of them. Most of the shipments came in as post supplies. Maranda was the one who tipped him off about when they would arrive, although I doubt if she knew what she was doing."

"You're not going to arrest her, are you?"

"I don't really have any charges to bring against her. Besides, Maranda is her own worst enemy."

A silence settled over the room, and Erin was sure Cole could hear her heart pounding. "And that brings us to us," she said at last.

She caught her breath as Cole unfastened the top buttons of his jacket. Her eyes settled on the hand working at the neck of his coat. A wonderful, loving hand that could perform such magic on her.

"I have something to show you," he said.

He certainly does, Erin thought, her eyes trained on the column of his neck and throat, but she held back the words for she saw him pull a piece of paper from an inside pocket. A promotion, no doubt. After all, he had stopped the sale of guns that might possibly be used against soldiers and civilians alike. At the very least, he should be a colonel.

She reached out for the paper and, turning her back, took it into the muted light drifting in through the window. Before he could react, she quickly scanned the official document. Cole had a new title all right, but it was one she would never have guessed. Mister.

A smile lit up her face. He had resigned his commission and not told her. The wonderful rat. He had done it for her. The hope that she had allowed into her heart after his kiss was now a reality. Only it was better than she had dared dream. After tonight, he would never have to wear that hated uniform again. Her smile broadened. She knew just the way to get him out of it.

It took all of her poker-playing resolve to turn back to him with a solemn expression on her face.

"This looks very official," she said, waving the paper in the air.

"It is. And final. Would you like me to tell you what it says?"

"That won't be necessary."

Cole's eyes rested on her for a long moment and his lips twitched into a smile. "You can read."

She touched the paper to her cheek. "It's a skill that can come in very handy. I can also write. I've already started a letter campaign to Washington about injustices against the Indians at Fort Sill. After all, we honorable Barretts have to see to our duty." A thought clouded her happiness. "You won't regret what you've done, will you? Leaving the Army, I mean."

"Life at Concho was hell after you left. I tried to throw myself into my work, but everywhere I turned there was something to remind me of you. I knew the Army was no longer for me—with or without you—and I decided to help Grierson finish the gun business and then resign and pick up my life down here."

"With," she asked softly, "or without me?"

Cole's eyes burned into hers. "Do you have to ask?"

"I'll go back with you to Virginia, if you want, Cole. Anywhere you say. My place is beside you."

"You'd have saved us a lot of grief if you'd realized that months ago."

"I only wanted what was best for you. I love you, Cole. I have since I was sixteen and sat across from you at a poker table in Dallas. I may not be the best thing for you, but you'll not get rid of me again. Seeing you yesterday made me realize it. Even the Army—"

"Forget the Army. And the East. Our future is here, love. In Texas. I knew it when I left West Point. I told

442

myself it was because of some old hates and the investments I had made here. But of course that wasn't true. The best thing about Texas was that it was where I could find you."

Cole stepped closer and brushed his lips lightly against hers, then kissed the corners of her mouth. Erin trembled under the feathery touch.

Time was wasting, and she whispered into his mouth, "There's something I've been wanting for a long time, Cole."

His hands stroked her shoulders, but she pulled away. "A rematch," she said, smiling at the look of puzzlement in his face. Tossing the paper onto the dresser, she opened the top drawer and pulled out a deck of cards. "Another game of twenty-one."

"It's not what I had in mind, love."

"Trust me." She reached once more into the drawer and pulled out a leather pouch that jingled with the sound of coins. "Would you mind playing on the bed?"

"Sounds like a good idea. But isn't that what I'm supposed to say?" asked Cole as he moved past her, his arm brushing against her breast.

Warm desire rushed through Erin as she watched him pause beside the quilt-covered bed and reach inside his coat.

"Your money's no good here," she said, walking slowly toward him and tossing a golden coin on the bed. "Although you will need to ante." Her eyes assessed wide shoulders and tapered hips, then slowly moved down long legs whose muscled strength was evident beneath a blue wool uniform and calf-tight boots.

She looked up and smiled into his eyes. "Shall we start with your pants?"

Now you can get more of HEARTFIRE right at home and $ave.

Preview
Four Brand New
ZEBRA
Heartfire
Romance Novels...

FREE for 10 days.

No Obligation and No Strings Attached!

♥

Enjoy all of the passion and fiery romance as you soar back through history, right in the comfort of your own home.

Now that you have read a Zebra **HEARTFIRE** Romance novel, we're sure you'll agree that **HEARTFIRE** sets new standards of excellence for historical romantic fiction. Each Zebra **HEARTFIRE** novel is the ultimate blend of intimate romance and grand adventure and each takes place in the kinds of historical settings you want most...the American Revolution, the Old West, Civil War and more.

<u>FREE</u> Preview Each Month and $ave

Zebra has made arrangements for you to preview 4 brand new HEARTFIRE novels each month...FREE for 10 days. You'll get them as soon as they are published. If you are not delighted with any of them, just return them with no questions asked. But if you decide these are everything we said they are, you'll pay just $3.25 each— a total of $13.00 (a $15.00 value). **That's a $2.00 saving each month off the regular price.** Plus there is NO shipping or handling charge. These are delivered right to your door absolutely free! There is no obligation and there is no minimum number of books to buy.

TO GET YOUR FIRST MONTH'S PREVIEW...
Mail the Coupon Below!